IT CALLS FROM THE DOORS

AN EERIE RIVER PUBLISHING ANTHOLOGY

Dedicated to the guardians of our doors.
Stand strong.
Don't let them in.

IT CALLS FROM THE DOORS

Eerie River Publishing
www.EerieRiverPublishing.com
Hamilton, Ontario Canada

This book is a work of fiction. Names, characters, places, events, organizations and incidents are either part of the author's imagination or are used fictitiously. Any resemblance to actual persons, living or dead, or actual events is purely coincidental.

Paperback ISBN: 978-1-990245-43-5
Hardcover ISBN: 978-1-990245-44-2
Digital ISBN: 978-1-990245-42-8

Edited by Lyndsey Smith
Compiled by Michelle River
Cover Design Michelle River

Special thanks to our Jr. Editors, Tim Mendees, David Green, Callum Pearce, Chris Hewitt, Austin Shirey, Holley Cornetto, Kim Rei and S.O. Green.

Contents

Knock, Knock!
A Foreword
by Dave Jeffery

Doors.

They keep things out, they keep things in. They can be our security, giving us peace of mind when the ills of the world need to be held at bay. They can be our barrier to freedom, suffocating hope and robbing us of time and space.

Doors as a vehicle for inspiring shivers have always been a key feature of horror and supernatural literature. Whether it is Stephen King's infamous Room 237 in *The Shining*, the foreboding basement of Richard Matheson's *Hell House* or Shirley Jackson's *The Haunting of Hill House*, the idea that an innate piece of timber has the ability to fill us with terrible anxiety is always deliciously consistent. So much so that writers and filmmakers continue to return to it.

But one of the most important concepts is that sometimes a door is not a door to a room in houses with dark and haunting pasts. Doors are also portals to dimensions beyond our comprehension, gateways to worlds that exist on the fringes of time and space, or within realms of the sinister and evil. There is no greater example of this than the introductory images of Rod Serling's *The Twilight Zone*, a door thrown wide and allowing us to step though into incredible universes and mysteries, along with that hideous, blinking eye.

This anthology is about what is on either side of the doors, be they open wide when we need them to be shut tight, or slammed shut as our gaoler lumbers away, uncaring of our screams of despair. It is about doors in houses or lurking in the woods, portals to other worlds in the most innocuous and inventive places. It is about people whose lives are touched by the decisions they make when they open those doors, or the consequences if they do not.

Eerie River Publishing has curated some serious talent for this anthology, the authors creating stories that will take you to the very edge of reason; stories that will challenge your ability to lie in bed at night without one eye cast firmly upon the wardrobe, that crack in the wall, or the closed bedroom door, just as you hear the creak on the stair.

But as we all know, doors also keep secrets. Are you ready, dear reader, to pull on the handle and discover the incredible, horrifying truth? You are? Then that is a good thing, and I wish you well on the journey you are about to take.

Before you set out, I offer a word of warning - with some doors, it's not always the best idea to knock first.

Dave Jeffery
September 2021
https://www.davejefferyauthor.com/

KELDER CHURCH
DAMIEN ALLMARK

The aged hulk of Kelder Church sat in near ruin at the summit of the hill.

Richard watched Lauren crouch atop the low stone wall. "Remind me why we're doing this?"

"Because it's fascinating," said Lauren. "Think of all the things we might find. Treasure, relics, holy artefacts."

He finished her sentence with a grin. "Disrepair, mould, and tetanus."

Lauren punched his shoulder. "Come on, please!" she whined.

"I'm not saying I won't go. I'm just asking why. Why are you so keen to get in there?"

She considered his remark for a long moment. "I don't really know. It just pulls at me, draws me in. Always has. I need to see what's in there. Every time I look at it, I get this...I dunno...buzz? Don't you feel it?"

Richard stared at the skeleton of the church. "Nope."

Lauren rolled her eyes and sighed, but a grin tickled the

corners of her mouth. "Bloody hopeless, you are. What did you find out about the church's history?"

"Almost nothing. It's weird. The locals seem uncomfortable whenever I even ask, and no one really wants to talk. A couple of the old dears in the coffee shop said they thought they remembered attending service there, but even they couldn't tell me why it was abandoned."

"Weird. Let's go see." Her face glowed with forbidden excitement. She hopped off the wall and disappeared into the underbrush.

Richard paused and regarded the derelict husk for a moment. Kelder Church lingered on the hillside more than a mile from the nearest settlement, and despite its dilapidation, long lost magnificence radiated from the ruins. One of the two bell towers succumbed to the passage of time long ago, but the other protruded above the shrubbery, tall and proud. The angular tower roof resembled a chess rook and held all the gravitas of any medieval fortress. Through the intricate, arched windows shone the azure blue of the sky behind. Unlike so many other abandoned buildings, no ugly concrete blocks marred the openings, and only the most rudimentary fencing protected the site.

Richard's attention turned to the overgrown chaos of the graveyard. He steeled himself with a deep breath and plunged into the gauntlet of green. Thorns and nettles bit at him as he fought his way through the vegetation.

"Oi, wait up!" Richard called. His foot caught in a knot of brambles. He tripped and landed face-first in a patch of bare earth with a grunt.

Lauren cackled. "Full of grace and poise, Richard, as always!"

He regained his feet and dusted dry soil from his polo shirt. "Shut up. We can't all be dainty. Some of us were born with the dexterity of a comatose yak. Where are you, anyway?"

"Over here! This jungle thins when you get nearer the church."

"Marco!"

"What?"

"Never mind," he said. He sought her voice and pushed his way into the dense thicket.

She roared with laughter when she saw him. "My days, Richard, you're a mess."

"I thought you'd known that for years."

Lauren plucked a foot-long length of weed from Richard's hair. "Traditionally, the lady wears the flower." She pressed it to her ear and posed as if for a photo shoot.

Richard snatched the bramble from her hand and hurled it into the bushes, grimaced, and picked a thorn from his palm.

"Well, that'll never threaten us again," said Lauren.

The ruin loomed above them. Rubble from the collapsed tower lay strewn across the churchyard, and glassless windows gaped like a skull. Dead vines and ivy coiled along worn granite walls. Ancient graves and monuments lay forgotten and desecrated by time.

They picked their way through the last few weeds and approached the colossal archway that once held the main door. Graceful curves of carved stone stretched twelve feet above them and met below the remains of an elaborate rose window. Leaves of tarnished granite morphed into Celtic crosses which sketched the cracked outline of the enormous circular portal. The absence of stained glass revealed the forbidding darkness of the church interior, and the sheer scale of it stopped them in their tracks whilst they stared at the architecture in awe.

Richard broke the silence first. "So, which of your theories do you reckon will prove true?"

"Huh?"

"You had so many ideas and theories of what might be up here. Which one do you reckon we're really going to find?"

Lauren snorted. "I think 'theories' is a bit much, or do you actually expect a tribe of hobgoblins?"

"Nah. It'd be ogres in a building like this, not hobgoblins. I know I was drunk, but how did you talk me into coming up here after all those campfire ghost stories we told?"

"Maybe the stories about loot and buried treasure sunk in as well. I ain't taking the blame for this one."

"If my bones get ground up for anyone's bread, I'll be most displeased. Just saying."

Lauren shrieked with laughter. "You could write an angry letter to *The Times*?" she spluttered.

Orange stains dripped like tears from the battered security door's hinges, and years of exposure rendered the faded prohibition notice illegible.

"Doesn't look all that solid," said Lauren. She nudged the security door, and the lower hinge snapped. The strained metal squealed, the door pivoted on the other hinge, and Lauren dodged backwards. Her hands grasped the bottom edge of the door and stopped its fall. She yelped in pain and recoiled. The door fell with a clang. She bent double and clutched her hand, spouting a spectacular string of profanities.

"What happened?"

Lauren stopped swearing and glared. "What do you think happened?" She showed her bloody palm to Richard, then wiped her hand on her jeans.

Richard pulled a packet of tissues from his pocket. "Here, let me." He pressed a tissue against her ivory skin to soak the blood, then wrapped another around her hand. "Hey, there is an upside to hay fever. Always got some of these."

"Thanks." Lauren gave Richard a simple smile, and his heart soared. "Now, let's try that again, shall we?" She felt gingerly along the underside of the door and lifted it enough for Richard. The hinge creaked in protest. "Go on, get under there."

Richard hesitated, but eager to impress, he dove forward, misjudged the gap, and clouted his head against the door. Stars flickered in and out of his vision, and the red heat of pain spread from his crown throughout his head. The door sang an echo, and he heard Lauren snicker. He rolled onto his back and jammed his feet under the raised door. Lauren ducked through the gap. The door dropped with a clang and settled in a cloud of dust. The hinge groaned once more and then silenced.

Richard clambered to his feet, groaned, rubbed his head, and then patted at his dirt-encrusted top.

"You're just never clean, are you?"

"Hey, next time I'll hold the door, and you can lie in the mud!"

"Nah, you're alright." Lauren winked a topaz eye.

Richard's attention lingered for a moment on Lauren while her eyes scanned their discovery.

Glassless windows glowered at them. In the far corner lay fallen beams from the roof, but an eerie darkness permeated the structure. The interior remained unsullied, apart from the ravages of time. Ranks of pews remained subordinate to the altar, which commanded the room despite the rubble strewn around it.

Profound silence seized Richard, and he became aware of all the minute sounds around him. He heard the rush of blood in his eardrums, heard Lauren gulp quick, excited breaths beside him, and heard the gentle breeze whisper in the eaves of the collapsed roof.

"Wow," gasped Lauren. "I never believed we'd actually do this," she whispered.

Richard watched her gape at their newfound kingdom. "Nor did I." He matched the level of her voice. Despite their isolation, a subtle unease welled within him. A tightness in his chest descended, and he realised his breathing was ragged. He did not want to disturb the darkness. He wanted to flee, to retreat to the sunny safety of the weed-filled churchyard, but his eagerness to impress Lauren kept him resolute.

Her hand snaked into his, and his concerns evaporated

like the morning mist. She guided him into the main hall, and he didn't resist her gentle tug.

Richard sneezed. "Bloody stinks in here."

"It's not so bad. Mouth breathing, that's the key."

They picked their way past the pews. Each breath Richard drew felt thick, tangible, as if he could taste each particle of decay entering his body. Mould festered in the dark corners of the chipped wooden benches, and rotten hymnbooks festooned the shelves.

A harsh glare penetrated the shattered roof and caused Richard to squint when he raised his eyes. Brilliant sunlight glinted from the scattered remnants of the stained glass window. A wisp of cloud drifted past the rafters to violate the otherwise unbroken teal sky.

Lauren released his hand and pressed deeper into the bones of the church. Atop the altar, with its head held high and wings tucked, perched the dirt-encrusted shape of a bird.

"What is it?" Richard asked.

She didn't respond, but instead blew a deep breath across the altar's figurehead. Grime and dirt scattered and exposed the golden relief of a magnificent eagle. The bird's ruby eyes sparkled in the dark.

"Oh my God," Richard hissed. "Why would anyone leave this here?"

"I don't know," Lauren murmured. Her gaze flicked around the bird's intricate features, and she brushed the dust from its head and back. With her sleeve, she smeared a clump of sodden earth from its wing.

Reluctance weighed each step, yet Richard approached the altar anyway. The manner in which the sunlight twinkled in the rubies gave the impression of sentience, as if the eyes stared deep into his soul. He shuddered.

"It's freaky."

"It's spectacular," Lauren whispered.

Her eyes sparkled when they met his and then flicked to the spiral staircase, which climbed the remaining tower. She winked playfully at him, bounded across the dirty floor, and danced around the scattered debris. "Come on," she urged.

"Wait!" Richard scanned his surroundings. His skin fell cold, and a great shiver shook his body. Over the top of the pulpit crested a wave of scarlet blood. It cascaded across the dais and pooled around the base of the altar. Richard blinked, shook his head, and the blood vanished. He rubbed his eyes. "Did you see that?"

"See what? Come on, Richard. Keep up."

He chased after Lauren, feeling as if the eyes of the eagle tracked him all the way into the stairwell. He took the worn stone steps two at a time in an attempt to catch Lauren. Sunlight cascaded from the top of the stairs and burned his eyes. He flinched, missed the top step, stumbled, and almost fell onto the tower balcony. His heart pounded a complaint against the abrupt exertion, but his nerves evaporated in the heat.

Lauren's hands rested on the rough granite balustrade, her back to Richard. Her platinum ponytail danced in the subtle breeze while she stared at the expansive countryside.

Below them, the overgrown graveyard gave way to rolling fields and dry stone walls, copses of trees and distant villages, and far in the distance, the Atlantic coast.

Richard yearned to stand closer to Lauren, to hold her, to wrap his arms around her, to rest his chin on her shoulder. He wanted to hold her like a lover, for them to lose themselves in the beauty of the moment. The radiance of her smile robbed him of any interest in the scenery.

She broke the spell. Her sapphire eyes flickered with child-like wonder. "Have you ever seen anything like it? Look, you can see the coast! That's got to be twenty miles. And over there, that's Cornfield Manor, isn't it? And the moors behind it." Lauren's feet danced around the rough granite stones of the tower, and her wounded hand pointed to distant landmarks. She noticed his attention on her instead of the view and stopped. She wrapped her arms around him and squeezed him tight.

Richard's heart leapt into his throat. For long seconds, he was as frozen as the eagle. He felt the warmth of her body against him. He moved to embrace her, but she spun away from him and laughed. "Sorry," she said.

"For what?"

"I just know you weren't so keen to come in here, but I shouldn't have hugged you." She rubbed her bandaged hand.

"That's okay, really," he stuttered.

"Come on! Let's see what else there is." She vanished into the darkness of the stairwell.

Richard followed, and his eyes fought the blackness. He braced himself against the walls, and he felt moisture, a thick, slick, oily substance between his fingers. He kicked each step he descended until he escaped the claustrophobic stairwell and entered the church nave. Panicked, he stared wide-eyed at his hands, but they were dry and dusty, just like before. He drew in a deep breath, a relieved sigh, but the stink of mould assaulted him. A violent coughing fit racked his body. His watery eyes scanned the room, and his heart skipped.

No Lauren.

"Lauren!" His voice betrayed him. He hacked the phlegm from his throat and tried again but heard no response. Panic enveloped him.

"Lauren!" he bellowed. He ran down the centre aisle when a dull clunk behind him caused him to whirl so fast he almost fell. A door in the far wall creaked, and Lauren emerged, head cocked to one side.

"What?" she said.

Relief enveloped him, but the heat of embarrassment rose in his cheeks.

"Just couldn't see where you went," he grunted.

Lauren beamed and raised her injured hand to beckon. "Come on," she said. "Come see what I've found." Claret stains drenched the ragged tissue, the impromptu bandage, and blood trickled down her arm.

He dragged deep, slow breaths and followed. From the altar, the eagle watched him leave.

The vestry lay beyond the door. Robes and shawls adorned one wall under a row of mahogany cupboards. Piles of Bibles and hymnbooks lay untouched on a cobweb festooned bookcase. The bitter stench of decayed paper and old books gone to ruin threatened to overpower him. Richard covered his face with his hand, gasped for breath, and struggled not to relapse into coughing. His pulse rose with his dread until his heart thrashed in his chest like a caged beast. He fought to control his ragged breathing.

"I've got to get out of here," he whispered.

Lauren raised her eyebrows, and her forehead creased. "Why?"

"This place is grotesque."

She smirked. "It's just an old building, Richard." She saw his pained expression, and her grin vanished. "Are you feeling okay, mate?"

He covered the ground between them in two strides and, startled by his own confidence, gripped her shoulders.

"Look around you." His eyes bored into her, and his voice threatened to catch in his throat. "All the stuff left here. This place wasn't abandoned. It was evacuated!"

Kindness radiated from her eyes, and her full smile brought dimples back on her cheeks. "It's just an old building. Don't let it freak you out. Come on. Stay with me. Let's keep going. Who knows what more we'll find?"

"But, it's so dark," he protested. He became aware of how feeble he sounded.

She smiled and again melted into the shadows. "The fire will guide our way," she said.

"What fire?" He froze.

She stepped into the light with an eyebrow raised. "What what?"

"What did you say about a fire?"

She cocked her head to one side. "I didn't say anything. Come on." The impenetrable dark wrapped around her, consumed her, and left Richard alone with his terror.

Richard found himself trapped, torn between fear of abandonment and fear of the deep, dark recesses of the place. For the first time he could remember, he didn't want to follow Lauren. He felt her recklessness endangered them both, but moreover, he didn't trust her any more either. He was shaken, and he was petrified. He was desperate to decamp, but he couldn't bring himself to abandon Lauren to the peril seemingly invisible to her.

With a massive force of will, he drove himself into motion and penetrated the ebony abyss. His hands scoured the walls while he fought the tears of a terror he didn't understand. His eyes adjusted to the light, and he found Lauren at the start of a long, narrow hallway.

The bust of a golden eagle perched atop its plinth glowed from the murky depths at the far end of the corridor. Its ruby eyes pierced the darkness and bore into Richard.

"The eagle followed us here," he hissed. The moment the sentence left his lips, he realised how preposterous it sounded.

Lauren's laughter pealed like a bell in the darkness. "Well, it's obviously not the same one, muppet." She approached the plinth. "They do look very similar, though, don't they? Such craftsmanship. It's stunning."

"It's terrifying."

Lauren chuckled. "It's just a sculpture."

"Come on, Lauren. Let's go, please."

She reached the base of the altar, lifted a hand, and caressed the cast golden plumage with two fingers.

The eagle's head turned, its beak opened, and a fountain of red spewed across Lauren, but she didn't react.

Richard blinked and the scene reset. "Lauren," he whimpered.

"A minute more, Richard." Her gaze on the eagle didn't shift while the bird's ruby eyes glared at Richard.

"Why are you so obsessed with that thing?" he asked.

"He watches out for us."

Richard's heart leapt into his throat, and he whirled. His rational brain worked to convince him he hallucinated, but ice seized his spine.

"What?"

"He watches out for us. He will send the fire. The fire will guide our way," she intoned.

The fear enfolded him. His voice quavered. Frozen tendrils enveloped him, and a cold sweat spread across his forehead.

"What are you talking about?"

She lowered her head, and her hair cascaded across her face. When she swept it back to look at him, her pupils were vertical slits of muddy yellow in oceans of black.

He fled. His dirty trainers skittered on the stone floor, and he fought for grip and balance. The light behind him promised safe haven, and he fell toward it, fingertips on the ground like the start of a sprint, before he was able to regain traction.

A clatter of footsteps and cackling laughter echoed while she pursued him. Along the length of the corridor, flames danced in torches along the walls, flaring at his approach and dying back when he passed.

"Richard! Come back!"

He didn't spare the breath to reply, but sprinted in a blind panic until he found himself in the nave of the church. He skidded to a stop but barely noticed the pristine, high vaulted roof. From the altar, the eagle glowed untarnished gold. Ruby eyes shone like lasers from the reflected sunlight that filled the airy room.

A breathless Lauren appeared at his side. "What's the matter with you?" she demanded. Her hand touched his shoulder, and her crisp ice blue eyes searched him. "What is going on?"

"You're asking me? What were you talking about? You said someone is watching us? Fires guiding us?"

Lauren's wide eyes searched his face. "What? I don't know what you're on about! What fires?" she squeaked.

"What you just said, in the corridor! You were muttering about fire and someone watching us!"

"Richard, you're scaring me. I don't know what you're talking about."

Richard withdrew from her.

She matched him step for step.

"I need to get out of here." His eyes searched for the exit but didn't recognize the walls around him. Fresh white paint shone from all sides but went almost unnoticed in his exhausted confusion.

Lauren's hand cupped the back of his head, and she drew him into a long, passionate kiss. Her tongue darted around his mouth. For an instant, nothing else mattered.

The eagle watched them from its perch above the altar.

When she drew back, her eyes twinkled, and a smile curled the corners of her lips.

"Do you still want to leave?" she asked.

Richard stared, and his mouth worked like a beached fish.

Lauren unzipped her fleece jacket and discarded it.

"How about now?"

Richard stammered.

"Stay with me here," she murmured. She reached for the back of his head, blinked, and her eyes again became dull yellow slits.

Her hold on him snapped. He ducked her arm and sprinted from the altar, down the gleaming marble chancel. Sunlight from the stained glass window cast a glorious display on the floor before him. He risked a glance over his shoulder.

Lauren strolled up the aisle, and the glow from her orange eyes cast shadows across her sunken, hollow face.

"Don't go," she purred. "It'll be so good for you to stay. I'll make sure of it." Her voice was light and airy, but a deep growl echoed each word and reverberated through the floor.

He scrambled toward the exit. Where the old and broken security gate once stood towered a magnificent, ornate oak door. Richard yelped in terror and saw the church in its true form. Burgundy banners fluttered in a gentle breeze and swung from eaves in the undamaged roof. The flicker of flame from lit torches glittered from the shining, polished pews. Golden sunlight glinted through the spotless windows and cast saffron mites around the room.

Indistinct figures of the congregation, little more than silhouettes at first, filled the pews. Their eyes bore, unblinking, into Richard, and their forms solidified with every pace Lauren strode. Dark, tattered clothing clung to their scrawny frames. Hats and veils didn't obscure their sallow, rotten faces. Grey, flaccid flesh hung from their skulls, and blood dripped from their countless lesions and wounds.

From the pulpit behind them all, the eagle spread its wings and shrieked a scree that echoed around the hall. Less than twenty feet from Richard, flames burst from Lauren's hollow eye sockets, licked up her cheeks, and danced through her hair. Necrotic lines spread from her wounded hand and painted a darkened purple tapestry up her arm.

"Stay with me, Richard," she cooed. "Join me. The fire will guide our way." The echo grew louder until each word resonated through him. Lauren's voice was lost in the din. Black veins crossed her dead, vacant face. Pus dripped from a sore on her chin. Her injured arm withered and shrank into a stump, and blood cascaded across the floor.

He hammered the oak door with his fists, but he felt as if he pounded upon a granite cliff face. He threw his entire body weight against the pristine varnished wood, but the door was resolute. The heat from his back grew ever stronger, and sweat prickled his back. He turned, pressed against the door, and heaved in desperation.

The congregation shambled from their pews in silence, like a wedding recessional, and formed unkempt ranks behind Lauren. In perfect unison, they advanced on Richard and trapped him against the immovable door.

Through tears, he whimpered like a frightened puppy. With flame engulfing her skull, Richard's first, unrequited love smiled a warm, comforting smile, and she reached to kiss him again.

Damien Allmark
About the Author

Damien is a fledgling author from Bristol, England, who has previously featured in Dark Magic, also from Eerie River, as well as 'Sword and Sorcery' and 'Dark Dossier' magazines. When not wrestling with the keyboard he can be found at the wheel of a bus, or at home with his wife and young son.

www.damien-allmark.co.uk
Facebook: Facebook.com/damienallmark

The Waiting Room
Matthew R. Davis

In the cold, unyielding years to come, Avantika Kapoor would often wonder how differently things would have played out had Zac not been so good at his job—if he'd never seen the door that was not a door.

When it happened, they were walking along the central hallway in the fourth and uppermost storey of the old Bentleigh Hotel, watching the denuded floorboards for trip hazards and other dangers. In the two decades since the Bentleigh had closed, its carpets stripped and its furnishings yanked like rotten old teeth, many a soul had made their way inside to crash in empty rooms or spray their tags on the peeling walls. The halls and rooms both were littered with plastic drink bottles, lidless tin cans, and used needles, all caught up in drifts of dirt and dust.

Not the kind of place Tika usually found herself, certainly not in the low heels, pencil skirt, and crimson blouse she was wearing today.

Zac Hutson, however, looked right at home. His

fluorescent green shirt, mud-coloured Yakka work pants, and steel-capped boots were well worn; as a field engineer, he was often on-site during construction, renovation, and demolition. Take away his clothes, though—a thought Tika brushed off with an embarrassed mental shrug—and he might still look at one with such a place. His thick beard and deep eyes made him appear older and wiser than his thirty-odd years, might have sat well on an indigent who'd seen all the pains the world had to offer and was willing to share them with younger bums over a trash fire and a cheap bottle.

He caught her looking and tipped the brim of his hardhat to her. Tika returned a taut smile, hating the way her own helmet sat loose on her head and pulled at her tight, professional bun. Zac slowed to a halt before a stretch of formerly featureless wall and examined the graffiti there.

"That's odd," he said.

"How so?"

Tika had been sent on evaluation outings to derelict buildings before, and nothing about the urban art left on their walls held any interest for her. The piece currently under Zac's inspection was hardly out of the ordinary. Someone had sprayed a two-metre upright rectangle from the floor halfway up the wall and filled it in with blood red, adding dark blue highlights and a neat circle for a handle. A door, forever closed beneath arcing tags like 3SIX9 and RUDDY GORE.

Zac glanced back down the corridor, and Tika followed suit. Each side was studded with matching shallow alcoves that contained recessed doors, their red skins faded to the shade of old blood—six a side, twelve a floor over four floors. Yet only forty-seven in total, according to the floorplan.

"There should be a room here," Zac said.

Tika's tablet showed her an area the same size and shape as the other rooms, only this one was crosshatched to show disuse. "Looks like you're right."

He knocked on the fake door and nodded at the hollow sound. His fingers slid out past the painted edges and found subtle seams where the wall's wood met a lighter, thinner substitute.

"A-*ha*. There's a panel of sheetrock here, blocking off the alcove."

"What's it matter?" Tika shifted her tablet in her arms like it was a restless baby. "We're here to establish whether it would be cheaper to refit or demolish and start over, not look for old renovations."

"But why seal the whole thing off? Why not just remodel it like the rest of the rooms?" Zac tugged his beard, a habit Tika found rather endearing. "From outside, we saw that one window on the top floor wasn't boarded up. I wonder if it's this one. And why."

"Well, it's not number 13, so it's probably not cursed."

"We need to know what's up. The building's okay, structurally speaking, so we could keep the framework and upgrade the property from there—replace the electrics and waterworks, repair and refurnish."

"That's what my report is going to say, yes."

"Right. But we can't sign off on that without a proper

examination. And I want to know why the previous owners felt the need to hide one of the rooms."

He reached to his belt, and his hand came up with a folding utility knife. The blade popped out and Tika flinched, so quickly controlled that Zac didn't notice.

"I'm going to check a bit further up," she said, and turned away as Zac placed the tip of the knife to the wall at the top left corner of the painted door. The blade punching into the drywall, tearing through its soft skin, was enough to drive her into the next room.

This one was as empty as the others, unless you counted the rubbish left behind by temporary squatters: the flattened box of a prepaid mobile, a scattering of cigarette butts, the empty skins of home-brand bread bags. The boards nailed to the opposite wall were there to block off the exterior door. She knew from the outside that each room had a hung balcony, its steel balustrade a metre high—tiny baskets attached to the wall with thick cables firm at forty-five-degree diagonals, except where one or two of them had snapped and left their burdens to tip into a drunken lean.

If she could step out onto this balcony and look down into the Bentleigh's front yard, she knew what she'd see: a detritus-strewn wasteland stretching from the hotel to the fence that guarded it from the city street, once a garden but now an ugly bombsite littered with jagged chunks of concrete and pieces of the Bentleigh that had been too useless to sell or had been tossed outside by trespassers. A few broken-backed chairs poked their bent legs up at the morning sky like middle fingers, and someone had even removed one of the red doors from a room inside and thrown the portal out to lie face-up on the rubble like an entrance to the underworld.

Tika checked her notes until Zac had finished carving up the corridor wall and put his knife away. When she returned to his side, he was pulling the painted door free, neatly extracted like a piece of art he intended to keep.

"Knew it!" he exclaimed.

Another shallow alcove lay behind the drywall, identical to every other—or almost so. The door that waited within remained a rich red, as if its entombment had preserved it, and a padlocked bolt had been screwed to the wood.

"Wonder what's different about this one?" Zac mused, reaching for the bolt. The whole mechanism fell to the floor at his touch as if discarded, rustless but useless. The door showed no sign of having been so secured and swung open beneath his hand in an easy, almost eager manner.

"What the *hell*." Zac's broad back blocked her view of the room. "You better stay out here, Tika. Let me check it first."

Zac trod through the hidden door slowly, as if careful not to dirty the carpet with his dusty boots, and Tika soon realised that was exactly what he was doing. This room had been sealed long before the hotel's abandonment, and its carpet had not been pulled up. Red and green it was, bearing a vaguely Celtic design different to the one she'd seen in old photos of the Bentleigh. The room must have been shunned fast and hard, for it remained fully furnished and ready for use.

Zac stood in the centre and turned on the spot, taking it all in. When he glanced at Tika with a wrought brow and gestured for her to stay back, she ignored his advice and took three steps inside.

The wallpaper was a deep shamrock green, a neat fit with the dark-chocolate wood of the skirting boards and furnishings. The centrepiece of the latter was a tall closet directly across the room from the entrance, its door slightly ajar like a sly grin. To the right of that was another door, this one open to display a slice of the bathroom within—white porcelain, black-and-white checked tiles. Jutting out from the right-hand wall was a double bed, made, crisp white sheets peeking out over a doona two shades darker than the green that dominated the room, two plumped pillows waiting for heads to display. In the corner to her right, a round table was attended by two chairs, and here was a single sign of use, of life: a deck of cards had been arranged into a half-finished game of Patience. To her left, a small kitchenette consisting of a polished counter and a sink, an old bar fridge tucked beneath, a metal kettle standing guard on top; then a TV unit enthroning an early colour set complete with rabbit-ears aerial. To the left of the closet was a cheap but hearty red curtain, which presumably covered a door leading to the balcony.

"I don't get it," said Zac, and turned to see her standing behind him. "Hey, Tika, come on. I told you to stay outside. Let's go."

He brushed past, turning in the doorway to see if she was following. She did, but not before she gave the room one last penetrating pan and noted a couple of details that stuck in her mind, joining a cluster of others that nagged at her awareness but remained undefined for now. Zac closed the door behind them, its number given by brass digits that gleamed as if new.

Room 409.

"Well, I've seen all I need to see," he said, and his tone was jovial, but Tika could see how hard he had to push to get there. "Let's head back to the office."

"Are you okay?" she asked. Zac was usually unflappable, or perhaps the opposite: a cheery flag that flapped and flowed with the wind, bold and supple and free, something to look to for affirmation.

"Yeah," he said, and her expression must have broadcast her disbelief. "But, well…I don't like that room. It's all wrong."

"What do you mean?"

"Didn't you notice?" She wasn't sure what he meant, whether it was the painting or the shoes or something else, but he seemed to take her confusion for ignorance. "Never mind. We've got all we need for the report. We don't need to come here again."

Zac strode off like he'd just remembered an important appointment, and Tika hurried to catch up. Approaching the stairwell—the lift shafts had sat silent for twenty years—she glanced back to where the painted door, cut out so neatly by Zac's knife, stood up against the hallway wall.

When is a door not a door? When it takes you nowhere.

Zac didn't say anything else until they reached the

ground floor and hurried out into the morning light. He looked back at last, up at the face of the old Bentleigh Hotel with its empty hanging-basket balconies, and muttered about reassessing the wiring, the waterworks. Earlier, he'd seemed optimistic that the skeleton of the building could be refleshed, given a new nervous system and a fresh skin; now his brow was heavy with disapproval, and he seemed to be leaning toward a complete rebuild. She couldn't have said why, but Tika understood his reservations.

As they drove back to the office, two details about the room plagued her mind. The first was the painting hung above the double bed. Her eyes had passed right over it at first glance, its colours perfectly in tune with the rest of the room: a standard beach scene, not dissimilar from the blandscapes mounted in hotel rooms the world over. But the water was too green, an ocean of St. Patrick's Day beer, and the sand a deep rot-brown; what looked like palm trees edged into the frame from both sides, but their asymmetrical fronds didn't look like any she'd seen before. The sun that was sinking into or rising out of the horizon was a black as deep as a hole in the canvas.

The second detail, of course, was the shoes. Six pairs were lined up against the wall between the closet and the bathroom door, toes touching the skirting board. She hadn't had time to note them all, but the first pair were a style that hadn't been popular in decades, if ever—black leather dance shoes with a wide white vamp that made her think of spats—and the next two pairs were identical, simple canvas plimsolls she'd often seen on the feet of nurses and cleaners.

The room hadn't even been cleared before it was sealed off and forgotten. That was perhaps the thing that bothered Tika most. Strange enough that 409 had been cordoned so completely...but what dire circumstance could have demanded such urgency?

◇━━◇━◇━━◇

Tika couldn't get started on her report straight away, as she had another assignment to clear up by the end of the day. But while she worked at her desk in the open-plan office, her mind kept veering off and returning to Room 409. A few details, both obvious and less so, kept her staring through her screen and fiddling distractedly with a pen. She only realised she'd been tapping it against a paper pad when she caught Emery Earl staring at her from across the room. She winced an apology, and he sent back a smile that was not reflected in his eyes. He was still watching when she got back to work, but she made sure not to use her pen for further percussive purposes.

That night, back in her apartment—Number 1 in a single-level building, reassuringly nothing like 409—she slipped out of her shoes, stockings, and bra, treated herself to a glass of red wine after dinner, and was wondering whether she was sufficiently reinforced to call her mother when the phone rang in her hand. This was no case of filial telepathy, however.

"Hey, Zac."

He'd never called her before, though they'd exchanged numbers should the need arise. At this hour, feeling relaxed and a little too lonely with the warmth of the wine in her blood, she wondered if he were calling for reasons other than work. The wine had her pleasantly disposed to the possibility.

"Avantika. Hey."

Oddly formal right off the bat. Professional call, then.

"Did you get a chance to file your RUR on the Bentleigh?"

"No, I had another report to draft. You?"

"I'm about to send it now. I figured we should get our opinions in line first."

Tika put down the wineglass and sat up, intrigued. "Okay. But I thought we agreed a refit would be easier and cheaper."

"No. The wiring is shot to hell, and I think there might still be asbestos. I'm going to strongly recommend we pull the fucker down and start from scratch."

She tapped her nails on her table for a moment. "Well, *that's* a load of bullshit, because everything was fine until we found that room. Something about it's put you right off, and to be fair, it doesn't sit well with me, either. So what's really going on here?"

Zac took a deep swallow of something before he spoke. Was he drinking?

"I told you that room was all wrong. Do you understand why?"

"It's the wrong layout," she said, a realisation that had come to her whilst playing red-pen chopsticks to an attentive audience of one. "None of the other rooms looked like that. The furnishings are different, too. I'm guessing the Bentleigh was renovated after the room was sealed off."

She could almost hear his impatient nod. "Yeah, yeah, and?"

"And it's really bothering me that they didn't even clear the room out first. They left the TV, the painting, the shoes, everything."

"Sure, right. What about the bathroom?"

"What about it?"

Zac sighed, then spoke like he was coming to something he'd been wanting to blurt out from the moment she'd answered the phone.

"Since this morning, have you seen anything..." He paused for three seconds, as if carefully considering his question. "Weird?"

"Define *weird*."

"That answer tells me you haven't. You'd know it if you...look, I don't know what else to say. Just don't go there again, Tika, even if...you should file your report tomorrow and insist the Bentleigh is fucking levelled, all right? It's very important you back me up on this. It has to *die*."

Tika clutched at her glass, fingers twirling anxiously around the stem. "Talk to me, Zac. What is all this?"

"I hope you don't find out." A long, weary breath. "You're a good woman, Avantika Kapoor. Never mind what your mum says, I think you're doing great. Good luck to you, mate."

And he was gone.

Tika put down the phone, thoughts racing. He'd ended

the conversation in a very definitive way, and she knew he wouldn't answer if she rang him back. He'd said his piece and was intent on leaving it at that.

What bothered her was that it had sounded very much like a farewell.

◇━◦━━━◦━◇

Tika rose at her usual time the next morning, ready to fight her way through Friday to the weekend. As she watched her twin go through its daily make-up routine in the mirror, her mind returned to Zac's phone call and picked over his mention of the bathroom. Whatever bothered him was something he'd thought almost too obvious to mention. She'd always prided herself on her intelligence, so the idea she'd missed something nagged at her like a disappointed mother. She imagined herself as a guest staying in 409, her own shoes lined up against the wall as she showered in the bathroom, crossing to the crimson curtain to let in the morning light—

She froze halfway through applying her gingerbread nude lipstick, her reflection's eyes wide in sympathetic shock. *That* was the detail that had so bothered Zac, and rightly so. The Bentleigh building was a tall pillar, only the hung balconies breaking the flat grey surface of its face. So how could 409 possibly have a bathroom through its back wall?

The chamber should have jutted out alongside its balcony like a misplaced Lego brick, and she'd seen for herself that no such architectural oddities existed. Not only was the layout of 409 different to every other room she'd observed in the Bentleigh, but it didn't even match the floorplan.

Room 409 was at odds with the very reality around it.

"Impossible," she whispered, shaping the word with half-coloured lips. She rushed her make-up and tried Zac whilst putting on her shoes, but the call rang out. At this hour, he might still be on his drive to work, true...but the lack of an answer sat heavy in her gut.

Resolving to call him again later, Tika stuffed her phone and a salad into her bag and fetched her keys. Running through a mental list—*check, check, check*—she opened her front door.

On the other side, Room 409 was waiting.

Tika froze, hoping for some tell-tale sign that this was an unusually vivid dream. No such relief was forthcoming. The fridge hummed behind her in the kitchen, birds sang outside to the constant stream of passing cars, and her front door opened directly into Room 409.

It seemed to her an age before she was able to move. Not daring to set foot through the door, she clutched hard at the jamb and stared in. Everything was as it had been the day before, back at the Bentleigh where this room belonged, and she knew that if she were to step inside—a motion that felt to her far too much like entering the mouth of a waiting predator—she would be able to hear the muted thump of her steps on the carpet, feel the stiff and impersonal texture of the doona beneath her fingers.

This was no vision. The room was here.

Tika swallowed hard, leaned back, and closed her

apartment door. She held onto the handle for a few seconds, trying to slow her galloping heart, then opened the door again.

Still Room 409 lurked at her threshold. And now she noticed what she should've seen the day before. Even after decades of disuse, the place was entirely free of dust and debris, as if it had just been cleaned in preparation for its next guest.

She almost dropped her bag in fumbling for her phone, her hands shaking as she pulled up Zac's number and tried to call him again. It rang on and on, as she'd known it would, and now she understood why. Zac had been first to set foot inside the room, and last night, he'd found it in his own home. But she waited out each pair of digital rings, clinging to an irrational hope that he would pick up and tell her what was happening, how to escape it. As she did so, she stared into the room and saw that it was not *quite* the same as the day before.

A seventh pair of shoes had joined the queue against the wall between the closet and the bathroom. A pair of battered steel-capped work boots.

Tika dropped the phone into her bag, numb. There would be no answer from Zac, not now or ever again. He'd gone back into the room, out of curiosity or simply because he'd had no other choice, and then...what? There was nothing overtly menacing about 409, and it must have been empty after years of enclosure, yet she couldn't keep from thinking of the place as an open mouth waiting for its unsuspecting prey to walk on in. That unbidden notion drew her eye to the closet directly across from the room's entrance. Its door was cracked open an inch or so, and she remembered her first sight of it, thinking of it as a sly grin.

She slammed her own door shut again, reminding herself that if she didn't get out of there in the next couple of minutes, she'd miss her bus and be late to work. She'd slipped up once before and been warned that any further tardiness would mark her as unsuitable for the higher positions she hoped to attain. She *could not* allow that to happen, impossible rooms be damned. So how was she going to get out?

She opened the door a third time, saw 409 grinning at her through the gap, slammed it and locked it. Her apartment had no other external doors, something that had never bothered her until now. If there happened to be a fire, she thought, she'd just have to jump out the window.

Tika hurried over to the lounge and dragged open the drape until the floor was brightly painted by the morning sun streaming in through a front wall made almost entirely of glass. Her mother had expressed concern at the lack of security provided by this feature, but right now Tika wouldn't have wished it any different, for a pane in the centre of the window pushed out to almost ninety degrees when unlocked, and that would give her just enough room to squeeze out into the block's small, token garden. She shoved the window open, then sighed and shucked off her low heels, tossed them outside along with her bag. Hoping she wouldn't tear her blouse or stockings, she rucked up her pencil skirt enough to free her knees and awkwardly clambered through, landing on her rump with a whuff of bruised dignity mixed with incredulous relief.

After putting herself back together, Tika pushed the window down and hesitated before pressing it closed. It occurred to her that the front door might now open into Room 409 from both directions, in which case she'd need another way to enter her apartment. She left the pane just a touch ajar, enough to squeeze her fingertips in under the jamb, and imagined her mother screaming in disbelief at the sight—but what else was she to do? No one came into the little yard during the day, and if they did, they wouldn't notice the open window unless they were actively looking for a way in. Besides, right now her job security was more important than any other kind. Her bus was perhaps a minute away, and so was the stop she'd have to reach in order to catch it.

Feeling set upon from all sides—a familiar sensation throughout her life as a woman that receded at times only to surge back upon her when least expected or wanted—Tika hurried out of the yard and booked it for the bus stop. She arrived at the same time as the bus itself, counted this as a victory, and hoped it would not be the last on a day already too full of surprises.

❖⚬━━━⚬❖

She thought of nothing but the room all the way to work and carried it into the office with her, mental real estate she would dearly love to offload. Why hadn't Zac warned her about finding 409 behind her own door? Looking around the open-plan work area, at her colleagues bustling by on their day-to-day errands, the answer quickly became clear.

He hadn't told her about the room for the same reason she could tell no one else. After all, who the hell would believe you if you said an old hotel room had followed you home to wait outside your own front door?

She craved a fortifying wine, but that was out of the question for hours yet. In lieu of any other vices to lean on, Tika found herself hitting the coffee harder. By eleven o'clock, she'd downed two cups and felt so full of the stuff her teeth were almost floating. She wondered if she were acting more jittery, if anyone would notice—other than Emery, of course, who seemed to notice everything. When her bladder could be ignored no more, she hurried to the washrooms. No one was around to hear her strong stream and sigh of relief, to ask why she looked so fraught in the bathroom mirror as she rinsed her hands, and Tika appreciated that solitude.

Until she opened the washroom door and found herself looking into Room 409.

"No," she said, her weak left knee giving way for a moment. "No, no, *no*."

She shut the door, exhaled heavily, opened it again. Where the hallway should have been waited 409, as patient as death itself. She closed the door and backed away, shaking.

It hadn't just followed her home, it had trailed her to work, too, and no doubt anywhere else she might think to go. *Fuck*. She was all too familiar with the practice of stalking, had tried to keep certain men at arms' length as if that coolness would help should they develop unwelcome notions, but this was some next-level shit. She was being stalked by a *room*. How exactly did one deal with that? She could hardly appeal to HR or file a police report about a one-bed, one-bath.

Tika heard an odd, ugly sound erupt from her throat and slapped one hand over her mouth. That was the kind of laugh you heard from people either skating on the edge or hopelessly plummeting over it. She wasn't going to be like them. She wouldn't be broken by a mere *hotel room*, even if it *was* uncharacteristically peripatetic.

She was still trying to talk herself down from outright panic when the bathroom door burst open. She realised it was only Andie coming in, the usual cream wall of the office hallway visible behind her, but not before the sudden intrusion wrenched a gasp of shock from her throat. Her colleague cocked a curious eyebrow as she sidled by and headed for a cubicle, and Tika despaired of the gossip her reaction may have engendered. But perhaps Andie, chatty little jobsworth that she was, had brought her hope.

Tika stood at the mirror and pretended to check her make-up until Andie exited the cubicle to wash her hands.

"Are you okay, Tika?"

"I'm fine," she lied. "Just a little jumpy today. Too much coffee, I think."

She followed her workmate to the exit, waiting to see if she was alone in this trap. When Andie opened the door to reveal only the usual hallway, Tika swallowed a yelp of relief and slipped out after her. Another victory snatched from 409's waiting jaws—but how much longer would this odd haunting continue?

She returned to work, bent under the increasing weight of this burden, and there was to be no distraction from it. Her previous project had now been taken off her hands for assessment, and she was faced with the report on the Bentleigh Hotel. Zac's file had been waiting in the office email folder all morning, and now she opened it, hoping he'd imparted some small hint that might help her. But no; he'd written a standard report in his usual businesslike tone, knowing any hint of strangeness would lead to questions he couldn't easily answer.

Ancient wiring & waterworks could be replaced & we could gut the building to remove any asbestos, but in my opinion the structure is shaky & could lead to problems down the line, injury lawsuits, etc. I strongly recommend demolishing the premises & building from scratch. Any further inspections would also put staff at risk & bad enough that Ms. Kapoor was exposed in the first place. The place is dangerous. It should be levelled before ANY further action is taken.

Tika worked on her own report, drawing her conclusions in line with his. *The place is dangerous.* Oh yes, and not in any regard she could feasibly describe. The only way to lay its peril to rest was to destroy the building entire, and 409 with it. She could understand all too well now why the Bentleigh's staff had chosen to bolt the room shut and wall it off, whence the first six pairs of shoes had come. At some point, the room had taken on a new aspect, and anyone who entered—a guest, two cleaners, then others—had fallen prey to its implacable insistence.

She dug out statements she'd accumulated earlier in

the evaluation process, but everyone who'd spoken about the hotel had been circumspect. Then she searched online for any hint of mystery and disaster in the Bentleigh's past, hoping to find an article about haunted hotels that would offer up some backstory. But life was no movie, and things were not to play out so easily. By the end of the workday, she knew no more about Room 409 than she had at its beginning.

She made sure to stick close to her co-workers on the way out of the office, allowing others to precede her in and out of the lift. Down in the lobby, she took comfort from the transparent glass walls that enclosed her, the bustle of colleagues on all sides. When Andie asked if she fancied tagging along to the pub for an end-of-week drink, a ritual she usually avoided in favour of a quiet night in, she agreed with desperate relief.

"Well, someone's coming out of her shell," Andie said, and then her grin slipped as she saw Emery Earl standing alongside them. Her voice took on a shade of formality as she asked, "Are *you* coming, Em?"

"Not yet, but hopefully," he replied with a smirk, and Tika realised he was aiming for cheeky humour. Andie's forced smile told her she wasn't alone in feeling the joke landed closer to creepy and inappropriate.

The two of them walked at the head of the small work group as they streamed down the footpath to the open, doorless maw of the Hadley Hotel, and they made sure to take seats at the opposite end of their table to Emery Earl.

"I know he tries hard to fit in, but he just kind of creeps

me out," Andie confided after half a glass of wine, her voice camouflaged by the pub's genial cacophony. "I'm glad I'm not in *your* shoes."

"Why's that?" Tika asked, and Andie's glance askance went almost unnoticed as she imagined her low heels lined up against the wall of Room 409 next to Zac's abandoned work boots.

The social inadequacy of a co-worker seemed such a tiny concern beside the strangeness that had overtaken her life in the last two days. Emery kept to himself at the end of the table, nursing a beer with a faint smile as he listened to the chatter of his colleagues, occasionally offering a comment that was quickly swept up and washed away by the flood of conversation from the disinterested party. Tika might have been the only one to notice when he slipped out of his chair and walked to the Hadley's open exit, and her eyes were certainly the only ones to meet his for a moment when he looked back. He jerked his gaze away, and then he was lost in the stream of passing pedestrians.

By seven o'clock, most of her co-workers had departed for home, and she decided to stay a little longer when Andie, the last, made to leave.

"Sticking around to meet a man?" Andie asked, flexing a ribald eyebrow, and Tika hefted her second glass of cabernet sauvignon.

"Who needs one? This is the love of my life right here."

"Aw, such a lovely couple." Andie nudged her goodbye with one elbow. "Get a room, you two."

Tika's smile faded as she watched Andie recede through

the crowd. "Already got one, thanks," she muttered.

She stayed until her glass was empty and a man at the bar sent her a knowing smile for the second time. She headed to the Hadley's bathrooms, lingering until another woman could lead the way in and out, and then she was back on the street again. Night had drawn its cloak over the city, huddled around the million lights of cars and buses and clubs and convenience stores, and Tika was reminded of her utter insignificance—just one of a million fireflies in this everyday eve, one who'd scarcely be noticed when she blinked out of existence. Who would miss her if she were to suddenly disappear? Her mother, who would no doubt see it as the last in a long line of disappointments; a few friends she barely saw anyway, whose lives would swerve around the momentary grief to carry as planned. What mark had she made? Why should she be remembered at all?

Ah, these were just maudlin wine-thoughts. She headed to a taxi rank and caught a cab back to her apartment, trying not to contemplate what might await her there. She waved her card over the driver's EFTPOS machine, and then he was off into the night, leaving her to approach her front door in lone trepidation.

The possibility of finding 409 over her own threshold was too daunting. Tika crossed the small yard to her lounge-room window, ready to prise it open and snake up through it, but her fingers found the frame firmly in place. Gravity must have helped it to settle in her absence.

No choice now but to try the door.

Her heartbeat ramped up as she turned the key in the

lock. Seconds passed as she gathered her nerve. Then she twisted the handle and pushed, her gut clenched, only to see—

Her front hallway, resplendent in all its mundane glory.

The tension left her in a rush of breath. She didn't dare believe her ordeal was over, but she'd at least been granted a reprieve.

Tika entered her apartment, locked the door behind her, dropped her bag on the small hallway table. Now what? Her body called out for another glass of wine, but that could wait until she'd settled in for the night. She checked her home and saw that every door was open except the one at the end of the hall, where she hoped only her bathroom awaited. She didn't fancy having to piss in a cup if 409 had annexed her loo.

Crossing her lounge, Tika fingered the frame of the window and found it lodged as neatly as if she'd pushed it closed from the outside. Frowning, she locked it, stretched, and headed to her bedroom to kick off her shoes and slip into some comfy pyjama pants.

She turned on the light and then paused in the doorway, put on her guard for no reason she could immediately identify. Her room was so familiar that it only took her a couple of seconds to realise what was out of place.

The top drawer of her dresser was open an inch or so, kept from closing by the frothy spill of her best underwear.

Beneath the fringed shade of her bedside lamp, the pull-chain was swinging as if disturbed by a gentle breeze.

And the door of her wardrobe was ajar just a crack,

another sly grin from across an empty room.

Tika froze, trying to compute this information. For a moment, her own bedroom was a terrible reflection of 409. Was that what was happening now? Was this the next stage of her inexplicable haunting? She certainly never left her space in such disarray. Which meant—

The loungeroom window, left open all day and now pulled—not pushed—firmly into place.

The scene at once made sickening sense. She knew exactly what had happened. She wasn't even all that surprised—terrified, yes, but not surprised—when the wardrobe door swung slowly open and she saw, there amongst her blouses and jackets and coats and scarves, the lean figure of Emery Earl. His face was impassive and yet lit with some internal glow, the fingers of one hand twisted tight around a fistful of her underwear as if trying to crush this evidence of intimacy out of existence.

They stared at each other for a long moment, the room's atmosphere freighted with imminence. Then Emery took one long stride out of the wardrobe, two metres and two seconds away, and Tika lunged backwards into the hall. Her weak knee trembled, and she stumbled to the left, already knowing that by the time she corrected her balance and fled toward the lounge he would be too close to avoid. And so she ran down to the other end of the hall, where the closed door of the bathroom waited.

She paused there, reluctant to risk this option—the bathroom window was far too small to allow her an escape route, providing it was even that room waiting on the other side. Emery didn't say a word as he approached, didn't try to threaten or explain, and that silence terrified her. He slowed to a treacle-trickle pace halfway down the hall, edging toward her as if she were a trembling animal who might do him harm if he made any sudden moves, fingers flexing around the handful of stolen silk.

Tika knew there was nothing she could say to forestall him. He'd come too far to walk this back, and certain ruin awaited if he faltered and fled. Her throat was locked too tightly to allow words anyway. She stood against the bathroom door and watched him come on slow as cancer, a snake sliding inch by inch toward a trembling mouse, and she knew there was only one course open to her, should she be fast enough to take it...but it might prove even worse than Emery's eager hands upon her.

The tip of his tongue appeared to wet lips gone dry with helpless abandon, and she decided the devil she didn't know was a gamble worth taking. Tika turned, grasped the handle, and closed her eyes as she twisted open the bathroom door, slipped through in a slippery second, and slammed it behind her. She turned the lock on the inside of the knob and leaned her forehead against the back of the door.

She waited for Emery to pound on the barrier, demanding entrance, and with each second that passed without such an assault, she felt dread compounding in her heart. Finally, she took a deep breath, turned around, and opened her eyes.

Room 409 was exactly as she'd been expecting, only now the ceiling light cast a dim glow across the Celtic-patterned carpet, the shamrock-green wallpaper, the dark wood of the furnishings. The bathroom light was barely any brighter despite the white surfaces present to bounce it back. Other than the dim illumination, nothing had changed.

The room was immutable, impossible, inevitable.

Tika let out a quiet moan of terror. She was here at last. And the only way out, should the door open again at her touch—a boon she knew would not be granted—would deliver her into the hands of a fate more known but no less horrible. She trembled and waited for the room's purpose to reveal itself.

After a long and dreadful minute had passed, she was none the wiser as to her impending fate. She may have been trapped, but she was trapped alone, and that put 409 ahead of her apartment for the moment.

Tika dared to walk further into the room, casting about for any hint of her fate. Her heels thumped softly on the carpet, a deadened tread. She glanced over at the footwear lined up against the skirting board of the back wall and wondered how her own was supposed to make its way there. Was she intended to take the shoes off herself, as part of some coming ritual? That might ensure she never left this place, so she decided to stay shod. What else could she do, then? Check the old bar fridge for something to eat or drink and switch on the ancient TV? Climb into the made bed and wait until the lights went out, until the cold sheets were peeled back and something joined her there in the dark?

She wasn't going to just give up and be swallowed by the unknown. There had to be some way back to the rational world, even if that escape meant walking into the clutches of Emery Earl—and after standing here in a room that shouldn't, *couldn't* exist, fighting tooth and nail for her life seemed so ordinary as to be eminently preferable.

Stepping closer to the table, she saw the half-finished game of Patience spread atop it and wondered who had sat here alone playing it, how many years before that had been. Was it the man who'd worn the leather dancing shoes, the first pair in the queue? Or had he found this solitary diversion already in progress when he'd stayed here? Maybe the game had to be finished in order for its player to leave. That made no sense, but what about this place did?

Tika's eyes turned to the painting above the bed. It seemed to represent a place that was not real, or shouldn't be in a sane world. No sea was that certain shade of green, no trees that alien and suggestive. The black hole sun was a puncture in the skin of the world, and her gaze felt drawn into it. No darkness she'd ever known was so complete. Vantablack might have been invented as a feeble attempt to approximate the utter lack of all light represented by that circular rent in the fabric of reason.

Now, finally, she heard a sound. Something so familiar and mundane, yet laden even at the best of times with a vague sense of unease.

The slow creak of unoiled hinges.

She spun around and saw the closet door edging open another inch. An ominous chill washed through her bones, and she knew it emitted from that gap, that sly grin now widening to encompass her. Whatever waited in there was a million times worse than Emery Earl, and at last she would meet it and understand why Room 409 followed and swallowed the unwary.

No. Tika steered clear of the closet, searching for any other destination. The bathroom would only trap her further, and she'd have to pass right by the yawning closet to reach it. Her eyes fell on the crimson curtain in the back to the left, and before she could think, she hurried across the room. The cold increased in intensity as she drew nearer the closet, as the door crept open another inch, but then she was skirting around it and standing at the curtain. She pulled it to one side and saw, with a rush of hope, that it had been hiding a glass door. Outside was only impenetrable darkness, but it was *outside.* Her fingers fell on the handle.

It refused to turn, of course. That would have been too easy an escape for such a dogged pursuit. She moaned and rattled the door in its frame, found there was a little give to it.

Well, there was no *give* to Avantika Kapoor, and certainly no *give up.* She rose on her toes and bore down on the handle with all her weight, pushed with all the desperate strength she could muster. Once, twice, thrice, again.

"Let. Me. *Out!*"

And all at once, the handle gave and turned abruptly vertical beneath her hand. The glass door burst open, and before she could regain her balance, she was falling through it out into the night.

The black bloomed into a lesser darkness around her, a familiar one teeming with welcome detail and glints of distant light. There, the high-rise buildings of the city she called home, and up there, the louring eye of the white moon. Her heels clattered against metal gridding as she stumbled forward and hit a balustrade, and she realised where she was. She stood on a small balcony fixed to the outside of a building, a hanging steel basket four floors up from the shadowy earth.

She was back at the Bentleigh Hotel—*but how?*—and staggering unbalanced on the hung balcony outside Room 409.

She was free! From there she could call for help, scream until passers-by alerted someone to get her down. She was—

Lurching forward in a sudden, uncontrollable movement as one of the steel cables holding the balcony snapped free from the Bentleigh's outer wall. The platform dropped beneath her, tilting to a sickening forty-five-degree angle, and before she could fix her hands on the railing, she was pitched over the edge and out into the night.

Tika barely had breath to scream as she plummeted, the shoes slipping off her feet to follow her down, and in the couple of seconds she had left, she saw the dark ground rushing up to catch her. She saw the chunks of jagged concrete waiting to smash her bones into shards that would punch through the soft bag of her skin; she saw the red hotel room door that someone had tossed out into the yard, lying flat on its back directly below her. She realised she was going to land right on it, and even had a thin sliver of time to appreciate the grim irony.

But just as she was about to strike the red door, it flipped open below her, and instead of hitting the ground, she fell right through an impossible doorway and into dim light.

She was falling back into the waiting mouth of Room 409, plummeting straight across its tilted planes toward the closet, and then that door flung open to accept her as well, and she dropped headlong into a blackness darker than any in the deepest reaches of space. The last thing she heard was the closet door slamming shut behind her, and in the cold, unyielding years to come, Avantika Kapoor had good cause to wish those jagged teeth of broken concrete had been the last thing she ever felt.

Matthew R. Davis
About the Author

Matthew R. Davis is an author and musician based in Adelaide, South Australia, with over sixty short stories published around the world. He was shortlisted for a 2020 Shirley Jackson Award and the WSFA Small Press Award for his novelette "Heritage Hill", won two 2019 Australian Shadows Awards, and has been shortlisted for multiple Shadows and Aurealis Awards. His first collection of horror stories, If Only Tonight We Could Sleep, was released by Things in the Well in 2020; his first novel, Midnight in the Chapel of Love, was published by JournalStone in 2021.

Find out more at matthewrdavisfiction.wordpress.com.

HOMESICK
CHRIS HEWITT

"This one's a bit of a fixer-upper, but I'm sure you'll find the price—" Dirk opened the door a crack, unleashing all hell as a flurry of hissing, flailing demons knocked him aside.

"Girls! Girls!" yelled Janet as the siblings raced up the stairs.

"Stop pushing me."

"I'm getting my own room, and you're not allowed in it."

"Girls?" cried Janet, wasting her breath. She turned to the disheveled estate agent. "I'm so sorry. Are you okay?"

"I...I will be. A couple of spirited little darlings you got there."

"Demons from the ninth circle of hell, more like," muttered Janet.

"Pardon?"

"Sorry, nothing. You were talking about the price."

The estate agent straightened his tie and resumed his sales patter. "Oh, yes. I think you'll find this doer-upper comfortably within your budget."

"What's the catch?"

"I'm sorry?"

"The catch. Let's not beat about the bush. We both know I can't afford a property in this neighborhood. So, what was it? A crack house? Murder house? Ted Bundy's summer home?"

"Ted who?"

A cacophony of bangs and crashes proceeded a torrent of screaming accusations.

"Sarah! Ann! If I have to come up there..."

Ann's head appeared at the top of the stairs. "She's taken the biggest room."

Janet summoned *the stare*, a glance that would send the devil himself skulking to the naughty step. She saw acknowledgment in her daughter's eyes as she slinked off, mumbling something about fairness.

"Which is it?"

Dirk looked sheepish as Janet stepped into the living room and gasped, the massive room easily as big as their one-bedroom bedsit back in the city.

High ceilings made the space feel even larger, and Janet wandered the room dumbstruck, sidestepping the used needles and discarded bottles, used condoms, the decomposing thing that might have been a cat, and the esoteric bloody symbols scratched across the walls.

Janet saw only freedom, an escape from her cramped cell, a chance for the one thing she wanted more than anything.

Privacy.

She loved her daughters, the fact she'd not murdered them a testament to her motherly instincts. But if she had to spend another six months with them under foot...there were limits.

She pulled out her smartphone and snapped photos of the chaos, her thoughts only for the new furniture she'd have space for.

"We'll take it."

The estate agent perked up. "You will?"

"Yes, it's perfect. How many bedrooms?"

"Three. Shall we take a look?"

"Three! Three separate bedrooms. No, no. *Three* bedrooms will be just fine."

Janet glanced into the expansive kitchen, worktops buried under a wiggling mountain of trash, a squadron of buzzing flies circling overhead. But she saw beyond the filth, beyond the grease and broken windows, out into a garden. In her mind's eye, she saw a sunny day, a BBQ, her daughters playing croquet dressed in period costume, impeccable mannered ladies. Janet shook her head, the stench of vomit and piss a heady cocktail.

Back in the living room, she ignored the stickiness underfoot and large hole torn in the wall, the hodgepodge of wooden boards doing little to hide the gaping feature. "A touch of paint is all it needs. It'll be a lovely home. Our home. Where do I sign?"

The estate agent grinned, holding out pen and papers. "That's fantastic. I have some reliable guys who can sort a lot of this out for you."

Janet didn't hear him. Tape measure at the ready, she snapped photos, dancing through a vision of their new home.

◇─◦◦─◦───◦─◦◦─◇

Four months later, Janet turned the key in the lock, swinging open the front door and holding her daughter's hands as they stepped across the threshold. The smell of fresh paint assailed their noses. Sunlight streaming through clean, modern windows revealed pristine painted walls, glossy skirting boards, and polished hardwood floors. It had taken all her savings and all the money from the divorce, but Janet needed it to be *their* home, *their* new beginning. She squeezed her daughter's hands, and they sprinted off upstairs as Janet floated from room to room, savoring every detail.

On the landing, soothing soft hues chased away any remaining suspicion of lingering shadows. Janet closed her eyes and soaked it in.

"It's my room. You wanted the other room. You can't..."

"But I didn't realize it had an en suite, did I? I'm the oldest. I should get first choice. Mum, tell her."

Janet sighed. When she opened her eyes, heaven seemed a little darker, a little colder. Still, it was a far cry from the hell of their tiny bedsit.

Four doorways led from the landing: two bedrooms on the left, one on the right, and a family bathroom at the end of the hallway where a large roll top bath beckoned. She followed the sound of bickering to the nearest room on the left. A sign on the door read "Private Keep Out" with "Ann's

Room" scribbled below.

Janet rolled her eyes and pushed open the door. As advertised, the largest bedroom sported an en suite bathroom and two large sash windows overlooking a tangled garden, which would need attention before croquet would be a viable pastime. Ann had stacked all her belongings in one corner of the room, and in another, Sarah had followed suit, possessions being nine tenths of their tedious ownership dispute. It was the latest battlefield in a war Janet had long grown tired of, and realizing the folly of taking sides, she retreated.

"Mum!"

"I don't care. Sort it out between you. There are three rooms. Last night, you shared a bed. So, I'm sure you'll figure it out."

The door closed with a satisfying click. Janet returned downstairs, weaving through the countless boxes stacked in the front room, on her way to the kitchen to locate the bottle of Chardonnay she'd brought as a housewarming present to herself.

"To new beginnings and peace and quiet," she said, raising a glass to no one in particular.

The wine tasted sweet, going down easy, and before long, she'd all but emptied the bottle. An hour had flown unpacking, and she'd not heard a peep from her daughters. Even in her tipsy state, a dull alarm bell broke the silence.

"Girls?" she called out from the bottom of the stairs.

No answer.

Nothing but a deafening silence.

The silence she'd longed for filled her with a rising dread as she climbed the stairs onto the landing and entered the room on the left to find it empty but for a bed and bedside table. She glanced out the only window upon the garden below.

Something wasn't right.

The other bedroom was the same—a bed, a table, and a single window overlooking the drive. She checked the bathroom and leaned against the bath, head spinning, trying to comprehend how three bedrooms had become two. The kids had been in the largest bedroom, the one with the en suite bathroom, two windows overlooking the garden. Now, no such room existed, and Janet fought down a rising panic.

"Ann! Sarah! Stop messing about. Where are you?"

She ran her hands along the hallway's freshly painted walls. There had been a door there. She was sure of it. The rear bedroom ran the full width of the property. It left nothing for a second room overlooking the garden, let alone the en suite bathroom she'd seen. She checked the other bedroom.

Empty.

Not a sign of her daughters. Not even an unpacked box. They'd all been piled into the disputed room.

The doorbell rang, and she shot downstairs, wrenching open the door.

"Girls, hilarious. What the hell have you been up to?" she yelled at the silhouetted figure.

"Are you okay, my dear?" said her mother, pushing past. She handed Janet a bottle of wine as she made a beeline for the kitchen, a bouquet in her other hand. "I'll find a vase for these."

Janet stared after her and at the bottle of wine before taking a moment to look up and down the street. It was a beautiful summer's day outside, and her new neighbors attended to their lawns and washed their cars. Children played in the street, laughing and squealing in the sun.

None were hers.

Entering the kitchen, she found her mother rearranging flowers into a cracked vase, the only vase they owned.

"It's a lovely house."

Janet wandered over to the worktop. "I don't know how, but I've lost the kids."

"The kids?"

"Yes, your granddaughters..."

Her mother placed the flowers down to scrutinize her daughter. "My what?"

Janet stared at her mother in disbelief, the bottle slipping from her hand to explode on the kitchen floor as her world fell apart. Her mother rushed to steady her.

"Sarah! Ann! Your granddaughters," she pleaded, searching for a flicker of recognition in her mother's eyes.

What she saw was confusion and concern as a rising wave of terror and nausea threatened to overwhelm her. Memories of her daughters screamed out for validation as her mother brushed back a lock of Janet's hair.

"Are you off your meds again, dear?"

"No. I...err...What?"

"Your meds. You know what happens..."

Janet pushed her mother away, slipping on the slick floor. "I'm not on any medication."

"Oh, Janet, not again."

"Again?"

Her mother walked to the sink and picked up a tea towel. "I told you the pressure of the move, the divorce, and the new job would be too much. But you promised you'd stay on your meds and look after yourself."

The old woman mopped up the spilled wine, placing the glass shards to one side. Janet stooped and took her hands.

"I have two daughters. You have two wonderful granddaughters. I don't understand what's going on, but I know that."

"Ouch! You're hurting me."

Janet looked down, recoiling, at the shard of green glass embedded in her mother's hand. "I'm sorry. I..."

Her mother winced as she pulled the shard from her palm, laying the bloody slither with the broken glass on the wine-soaked towel. Tears welled in her mother's eyes as she stood and retreated to the sink, dropping the fragments into the basin with a crash before running her hand under the cold water.

Her mother sighed. "That's always the problem though, isn't it? You say you're sorry, but you keep hurting anyone who tries to help you. It's not fair, Janet. And now this. You know more than anything I wanted a granddaughter. So, what, you punish me with this cruel joke?"

The old woman shook her head, and Janet sobbed.

She'd never hurt her mother, and yet here was the woman she loved, blood dripping from her hand, unable to even look at her. Janet's guilt turned to conflicted anger. Unable to deny the love she felt for her daughters, she would not, could not, accept the reality her mother pushed, fearing if she accepted a life that wasn't hers, she'd lose her daughters forever. What she needed was proof, but the kitchen was bare, none of the usual drawings pinned to the refrigerator. It had been their fresh start.

She stormed out of the kitchen into the living room and rummaged through the unpacked cardboard boxes. One of them would contain a photo, a schoolbook, anything. As she searched box after box, she recalled all the times she'd tripped over their toys. Now, when she needed one, they were tidied away.

Her mother appeared in the doorway, hand bandaged with paper towels. Blood blotted through the sheets, the cut deeper than she'd let on.

"It's here," cried Janet, throwing boxes aside. "Somewhere. I'll show you. There's a photo. You're in it. The one from last summer. The weekend at the beach. They buried you in the sand. Ann got sunburnt. You remember?"

Her mother inched through the living room towards the front door.

"Please, help me. It's here. It's all here."

"You know I love you?" The fear in her mother's voice stopped Janet's fruitless hunt.

"Please, Mother. I'm not making it up."

She saw her phone on the table and snatched it up. Her

mother slid a little nearer the exit.

"Look!" cried Janet, unlocking the phone and swiping through the photos. Shot after shot, her friends, her family, but none contained Sarah or Ann. Janet looked across to her mother, standing at the front door. "They're...they're... gone." Her knees buckled, and she collapsed into a chair. "Please. You have to help me."

The old woman clutched her hand to her chest, a tear rolling down her cheek. "I will. I'll get help. But I need to take care of this first. Okay, dear?"

Through pitiful sobs, Janet nodded.

Her mother opened the door. "I'll be back, honey. Just...don't do anything silly."

She turned to leave, but a man barred the exit.

"Hi there. I hope you don't mind. I was passing and thought I'd pop in and pick up the sales board and, well, make sure everything went well. I'm not happy unless my clients are happy," said Dirk, the estate agent.

"He'll tell you," cried Janet, leaping to her feet and stumbling through boxes. "Tell her. Tell her about my daughters."

Dirk's smile disappeared.

"She's my mother. Tell her. You met them. Several times, remember? Sarah and Ann."

He looked confused, embarrassed. "Daughters?"

"Yes. Sarah is eleven. Ann is nine," said Janet, her outstretched hand showing her daughter's relative heights. "You met them here. Remember, they pushed you out of the way when we viewed the house. Ann threw up in the back of your car. Please, you have to remember."

Dirk looked from Janet to her mother. "I...I'm sorry. I never met them. I never even knew you had children."

Janet launched herself at Dirk, pinning the estate agent. "Why are you lying? Why are you both lying?"

Her mother interceded, pushing her raving daughter back.

"What the hell? I never met anyone but you before today," proclaimed Dirk.

Janet bristled. "Then tell me why this *three*-bedroom house you sold me only has two bedrooms?"

Dirk and her mother exchanged glances, her mother holding up her hands, allowing Dirk to slip away.

"Dear, you need to take your meds, okay? I'm going to leave with this gentleman, and we're going to go get you the help you need."

Dirk was halfway down the drive, but he waited for Janet's mother. "What the hell is going on? I saw no children. What does she mean, three bedrooms? It's a two-bedroom house. Is this a joke? If this is some kind of shakedown—"

"I can explain. But not here," said her mother, following Dirk along the drive.

Janet looked along the street to where dozens of nosy neighbors stared back at her. They whispered to each other, relishing some new gossip, the concern in their eyes limited to the impact their new crazy neighbor might have on property prices. She slammed the door closed, sliding down onto the polished hardwood floor, wrapping her arms around her knees, and burying her face as she cried.

"Janet?"

The voice sounded distant, unfamiliar, and she'd wanted it to go away, to remain lost in her self-induced stupor. But the sound of her name sought her out in the cozy funk, illuminating a path back to consciousness, back to pain. She opened her eyes, groaning at the sunlight and the crashing recollection she'd hidden from, two daggers that stabbed at her heart with every beat. If her daughters had died, then she could have grieved, but to deny that they'd ever existed, that she could not accept.

The blurry half-figure of a man appeared to rise from the floor, and Janet turned away as the apparition climbed the stairs.

"Leave me alone!"

"It's Tom, Tom Taylor. You rang me. I...I let myself in."

"Just go. Get out of my house." Janet blinked, the face resolving into that of an old man, a sad Santa with shorter whiskers.

"Then who'll find your daughters?"

Janet jerked back to life, sending an empty wine bottle spinning down the hall. "Sarah?"

"Yes, and Ann, wasn't it?"

"Have you found them?"

The stranger sighed and sat on the top step. Janet took in the surrounding squalor of the landing. A mess of splintered wood and drywall filled the hallway as if a tornado had touched down. What remained of the walls had red claw marks torn into them, and she stared down at her bloody, splintered fingernails. Mouth parched, she wiped the dry drool from her chin.

"You haven't found them, have you?"

The stranger shook his head. "I'm sorry, no. But I believe you, and I can help, if you'll let me."

"Tom, was it?"

"Yes. You emailed me last week. I responded, but when I didn't hear back from you...Well, I know how hard it can be. So, I thought I'd check in on you."

That was it, Tom Taylor. She'd found him on the internet. He had a website. What was it? "Misplaced?"

Tom chuckled. "Yes, that's it, themisplaced.com. Not lost, you understand."

"Not lost," Janet repeated. Never had she needed two words to be so true.

———

"That's better. I hope you don't mind," said Tom, handing Janet a mug of freshly brewed coffee.

She'd taken a few minutes to clean herself up, wrapping smiley face band-aids around her throbbing fingertips.

"I remember. You lost someone too," she said, blowing on the steaming black brew.

She'd stumbled across Tom's website one hopeless night, searching for people who'd lost family under similar bizarre circumstances, somewhere between her mother organizing a catchup with Dr. Ehrman and a voice message from her ex-shit of a husband who saw the news of their missing daughters as a sick attempt to fleece him for child support. She didn't remember emailing Tom, but then there'd been so many nights of despair in the last fortnight.

Tom nodded. "My wife, Erin. Thirty-odd years now."

"I'm sorry."

Tom tried to smile and failed. "Thank you. I haven't given up hope. Not yet."

Thirty years. Janet choked down the bitter coffee, knowing she lacked that kind of strength. She'd already considered other ways to rejoin her daughters, painless ways that would take minutes.

As if sensing her dark thoughts, Tom gestured to the dining table and sat. "It'll be different for you. The trail's still fresh here."

Janet sank into the seat opposite. "The trail?"

"When they take things..."

"They?"

"I'm sorry. I'm making a muddle of this. Let me start at the beginning." Tom took a deep breath, his gaze drifting off to sometime else. "We were married three years when Erin fell pregnant. We'd tried for so long. Had all but given up hope, and then it just kind of happened. A boy. Erin wanted to call him Lance after her grandfather. We spent months doing up the spare room for Lance's arrival."

The old man stopped, gaze lost in memory.

"Go on."

Tom wiped his trembling lips. "He'd been home a week. I'd left Erin asleep in a rocking chair beside his crib, and that...that was the last time I saw them."

He stared down at the table, older just for the telling. Janet took his hands, and he tried another faltering smile before clearing his throat.

"The next day, Lance's room had vanished, and worse, no one remembered Erin—not our neighbors, her workplace, her friends, or even her own family. All her belongings, everything, gone, like she never existed." Tom tapped his temple with his finger. "But I remember."

Janet gripped the old man's calloused hands. "What did you do?"

Tom chuckled. "Same as you. I took that house apart. Leveled our home before my family intervened and got me some help."

"Help?"

"They meant well. But it was three years before I got out of the psychiatric hospital, before I'd convinced them I'd forgotten about Erin and my son."

Tom's face transformed into a mask, his smile flawless but for the twitch of an eye. "But I still remembered." He winked. "Ever since then, I've dedicated my life to finding my family and helping others like you."

"But why? Why do we remember?"

Tom shrugged. "A glitch, an oversight. *They* steal away people and things all the time, and no one is any the wiser. But just occasionally, well, maybe some things are too precious to be forgotten."

As bizarre as the old man's story sounded, for the first time in weeks, Janet saw a flicker of hope in her shattered world.

"Who are *they*, and what do they want with my daughters?"

The old man smiled as he stood. "One step at a time.

Listening to the regrets of an old man isn't going to get them back. Best you show me where you last saw them."

⸎

Janet picked a broken fingernail out of the ruined wall. "Here. The door was right here, and the room stretched the full width."

She strolled into the remaining room at the back of the house. "Why didn't I realize? The room they were in was wider than this. It even had an en suite bathroom. It's impossible. Why didn't I notice?"

"Don't beat yourself up. You'd be amazed how little we really see. Much of what we think we *see* is an illusion, a construct of the brain."

Janet ran her hand along the wall on what should have been the other side of a door. "So, did the room ever exist?"

Tom laughed.

Janet turned, arms folded.

"Sorry," said Tom, waving his hands. "It's just, it took me a lot longer to ask the only question that matters. Shame you weren't at my place thirty years ago."

"I don't understand."

"For a long time, I assumed *they* stole rooms from our reality. But that's not it at all. The rooms are theirs, a little corner of their reality."

Janet shook her head, regretting the action as the room swam.

"Think of *them* as crab fishers, the rooms their crab pots. They take a bit of their reality, and they dress it up to look like ours. Then, they drop it into our world, sit back, and wait. Wait until the trap is full before—"

The old man snapped his fingers, startling Janet.

"But I was in the room. I saw it. I looked out the window into the garden. It was…"

"Perfect?" said Tom, looking out the window. "Nearly. You said it was too large. They miscalculated the dimensions."

Janet nodded. The more she remembered of the room, the more impossible it seemed, and the more stupid she felt. "It still doesn't explain why no one remembers my daughters?"

"Not just your daughters. Everything in that room. When they close their trap, it all ceases to exist. Not just now, but ever. Lance's crib was a valued heirloom, passed down through Erin's family for generations. Snap! None of her family recalled it once she was gone. Not one."

She'd searched everywhere for a scrap of her daughters' existence, even returning to their old home, much to the annoyance of the new owners. They'd threatened to call the police, but she'd seen what she needed to see. The old oak in the backyard once had four names carved into its trunk. Now it had only two, and she cursed the other name.

The old man walked around the bedrooms, and Janet followed, holding his tape measure when asked. Satisfied that what remained of the upstairs was real, they descended the stairs.

"Before you moved in. Was there anything odd about the property?"

"Odd?"

"In my experience, there's often a shadow over a house, and they prefer to drop their traps into dark places. My house had witnessed a murder and a suicide. Wish I'd known that before I bought it. That kind of thing leaves a stain."

Janet slumped on the stairs as the old man wandered off, returning a moment later.

"Janet?"

"It was cheap."

The old man grimaced. "Too cheap?"

Janet nodded. "It was a crack house. Before that, I don't know. I didn't want to know. Oh, God. The blood on the walls...I just wanted a new start."

"What?"

"My daughters, they deserved a new life."

Tom climbed the stairs, shaking his head. "No, not that. The blood?"

"There were symbols plastered all over the living room."

Tom rushed back down the stairs and into the front room. Janet followed and found him running a hand over the fresh paint.

"Do you recall any of the symbols?"

"No," said Janet, pulling out her smartphone. "But I don't need to."

She showed him the countless photos she'd taken, thankful that the flash had done its job.

"Oh my. Somebody knew what they were doing. This isn't just kids messing around. These are the forgotten runes. Whoa, go back."

Janet swiped to recall a photo showing the large boarded up hole in the wall.

Tom's finger stabbed at the screen. "There! That's our entrance."

"Entrance?"

The old man walked over to the wall opposite the kitchen. "Yup, right here."

◇◈◇◇◇◈◇

Tom fished into his carrier bag and, with a splodge, dropped a bag of blood on the coffee table. "Better hope that does it. I've called in my last favor with my nurse friend."

Janet climbed down from the stepladder, blowing an errant lock from her face, her slick hands holding a bloody brush and sticky pot.

"Erm, you got a little...something," said Tom, waving a finger at her forehead.

Janet wiped the back of her hand across her sweaty brow, unsurprised and unfazed to see a smear of blood. It had been a long and dirty job. Blood made for a poor medium, coagulating within minutes, making it difficult to recreate the runes. But after two days of painstaking work, she'd redrawn all but a handful of the strange symbols.

"That should do it. I've only got this corner left. A couple more hours."

"Good," said Tom, fishing into his bag to retrieve a can of tuna. "I'm going for a stroll around the neighborhood."

She swallowed hard, the raw taste of iron clawing at her palette.

Janet stared into glowering copper eyes. "There has to be another way."

From the address on Puffball's collar tag, Tom hadn't wandered far to find an unwilling sacrifice. The annoyed feline hissed and squirmed, desperate to break Tom's tentative grip on its neck.

"If we had time, maybe. But right now, if you want to see your daughters, the runes demand a sacrifice. I'll do the deed, but I'll need you to hold him. Do you want to see Sarah and Ann again?"

Janet took hold of the thrashing animal, prepared to do whatever it took to see her daughters.

"Okay, hold him still," said Tom, picking up the carving knife. "I'm sorry little..."

Janet screamed as Puffball broke her grip and twisting, bit deep into her wrist, front claws lacerating her hand as back legs tore into her forearm with vicious bunny kicks. Tom dropped the knife, moving to help, and Puffball launched himself at the old man, a whirling dervish of tooth and claw, spilling more sacrificial blood onto the hungry runes. A massacre, but not the one that Janet had imagined as she watched Tom tumble over the sofa, Puffball far from finished.

A shuddering groan followed by a deafening thunder crack silenced the vengeful feline, sending him fleeing. Tom's shredded face appeared from behind the sofa, and she followed his gaze to where the plaster crumbled into an expanding dark void, wind whipping at her hair.

Tom staggered to his feet. "It worked."

"Worked?" screamed Janet above the howl of crashing worlds. Blood, dripping from her arm, fell, never to touch the floor. Instead, rivulets of claret spiraled into the tempest, creating a pool that expanded to fill the void and quell the storm. "If this is working, I'd hate to see when it goes wrong."

Tom winced, dabbing at his face as he recovered the carving knife. "Seems like just fresh blood is the key. Wish I'd known that earlier."

Janet stared at him. How many unnecessary sacrifices had he made? Before she could ask, Tom ran across the room.

"Let's go. We don't have long," said the old man, stepping into the bloody portal, his passing leaving little more than a ripple.

Janet hesitated, fearing what fresh horrors lay beyond.

Tom's head momentarily reappeared. "Come on. This isn't going to stay open forever."

Janet crept towards the portal, poking a smiley tip of a bandaged finger into the crimson surface and watching the ripples before a blood-soaked hand dragged her from the world she knew.

⟡—◆———◆—⟡

"You don't need to hold your breath," said Tom.

Janet exhaled, steadying herself against the soft membrane of a long fleshy tunnel. Only the primal need to find her daughters stopped her jumping back through the semi-transparent, bloody portal to the safety of the front room.

"Okay, let's go," said Tom, leading the way up the ascending tunnel. "This is a blood vessel. What we want is an artery. That's where we'll find them."

"Them?"

"You'll see," said Tom, pushing his way along the moist passage. "Now, there are certain rules. Number one, if I say hide...hide!"

"Okay," said Janet, struggling to keep up, every footstep like stepping on a half-deflated bouncy castle.

"This place is not like our world; nothing here works the same. So, touch nothing, especially the doors."

Tom climbed out of the tunnel, turning to hold out a hand.

"Doors?" asked Janet, as Tom pulled her into the monstrous cavern.

No, not a cavern.

Another tunnel, an artery.

The sheer size of the space paled in contrast to what covered the walls. Doors. Thousands and thousands of them, end to end, edge to edge, a sliver of fleshy membrane all that separated them as they arched high overhead, taller than any cathedral. A sea of white and brown, dotted with rainbow colors, old wooden doors alongside new UPVC. Here and there, glass and metal glinted in the eerily lit space.

"Doors," grinned Tom, cutting a cross into the corpulent flesh. He placed a hand in the bubbling dark blood, drawing a large blue arrow before wiping his hands clean on his tattered shirt. "This is our exit. Don't lose sight of it, or we'll end up stuck here."

Janet nodded, barely listening as she struggled to comprehend the bizarre new reality.

"B...but...how are we going to find my daughters amongst all these?"

"That's why time is of the essence. Your daughters' room shouldn't be too high. Pulled doors drift away from their entry vessels, pushed away by new arrivals. It's only been a few weeks. They couldn't have got far."

Janet stared up at the doors on the misty ceiling, dismay overwhelming her.

"Ah, right," said Tom, taking her hand and leading her across the mosaic of entrances. "Remember, don't touch the doors. Watch."

The old man danced across the web of door frames, a masterful high-wire artist as Janet took her first few teetering steps. It took her several door lengths to gain her balance. When she caught up with Tom, he pointed back the way they'd come, the conduit with its blue arrow now halfway up the wall.

"Get it? Nothing here is like our world. Gravity included," beamed Tom.

Janet really didn't get it. It was impossible, reminding her of a film she'd seen where astronauts walked around the interior of a spinning space station. She shook her head.

As if she needed any more proof she wasn't in Kansas anymore.

"What color was your daughters' door? And don't tell me it was—"

"White," said Janet.

Tom sighed and scratched his whiskers.

"It had a big yellow and black "Private Keep Out" sign on it."

"Now that's more like it."

Janet scanned the cavernous tunnel. It still left a vast space to cover. "Should we split up?"

"That'd be a bad idea. But we can spread out a dozen doors. Any problems, shout. And remember—"

"Don't touch the doors. Got it," said Janet, tiptoeing further down the tunnel.

She'd gotten the knack of moving around the door's frames, an exercise in stepping on every crack in the pavement. The variety of doors she passed amazed her, no two the same. Each had something that made them unique. Most appeared to be interior doors, but sometimes she'd pass one with a house number, and she'd wonder if whole families could just disappear. She longed to know what lay beyond each door, convinced there must be others that could be saved.

"Keep moving. Keep searching," yelled Tom. He had an uncanny knack of sensing her thoughts.

Every few doors, Janet located the big blue arrow, now barely visible on the ceiling. A long way to run if Tom yelled for her to hide. She stopped at a door, sure that she'd seen movement in the narrow, frosted pane that extended its length. She placed a hand on the glass and stared in.

A hand appeared under hers with a thud, and she recoiled. Muffled voices proceeded excited shouting as other hands scrabbled at the glass, small hands, and with them a child's distorted face. When fingers rattled through the letterbox, Janet fell back onto a chestnut door, only to feel and hear knocking accompanied by more muted pleas. Janet leaped from the door, terrified it might swing open, sending her falling into...what? She didn't want to imagine.

Tom arrived a moment later. "What are you doing? Did you fall?"

She nodded, unwilling to admit she'd broken the rules. "There's people in these rooms. We have to help them."

"Damn it," said Tom, laying his hands flat on the spongy membrane between doorframes, fingers spread wide.

"Didn't you hear me? We have to help them."

"Shush," hissed Tom.

Janet's cheeks flushed, outrage taking over as she cursed the old man.

Tom held up a hand. "Shut up and listen!"

Over the banging and shouting, she heard another noise, a deep reverberating bass, like distant thunder rolling over hills. But unlike thunder, the sound rumbled on and on. A moment later, the stiffening breeze carried a new warning. The fetid stench of death made her gag as she stared along the tunnel, the approaching horror not yet visible as she turned to find Tom, gone, running faster than an old man had any right.

"Run!" he hollered over his shoulder.

Janet looked down at the door, at the fingers clamoring

at the letterbox, along the tunnel, back to the fleeting figure of Tom, and she made her choice.

It took her a minute to catch Tom, the blue arrow visible still high overhead. The air grew thick, dandelion-like spores choking her as they ran. With every glance along the tunnel, she expected to see death.

Tom abruptly stopped, sending Janet careering into his back.

"It's no good. We're not going to make it," he said, regaining his breath and his balance. He scanned the surrounding doors. "That one!"

The old man laid down parallel to an ancient wooden door, its green paint all but peeled. "Do what I do. Lay behind me and hang on to my belt. Hurry."

Janet didn't hesitate, the breeze now a warm breath on her neck as she perilously spooned the old man. Tom flung open the door and fell into the darkness, dragging Janet with him.

⬦━◦━━◦━⬦

Janet didn't know what to expect, but a moonlit ballroom had not featured in her wildest imagination. She landed upright, with little more than a jolt as Tom slid the door to behind them.

"Careful," he warned, eyes not leaving the narrow crack he'd left in the doorway. "It might still be occupied."

"Occupied?"

"Here, take this."

Janet took the offered carving knife and scrutinized the

shadowy room, eyes adjusting slowly to reveal a chequer-board of marble floor tiles. A grand piano stood at one end of the space, and at the far end, several chairs and two large sofas surrounded an ornate fireplace. Four large windows intrigued Janet, drawing her like a moth to a moon, larger than any she'd ever seen. They hung above a city torn from a Dickensian novel, gaslight and smokestacks stretching to the horizon.

"This is incredible."

"It's not real, remember. It's a trap. I only hope its victims—"

Plink.

The piano note echoed, and Janet spun, brandishing the knife. She saw Tom, finger on lips, slink down. The hairs on her neck bristled at the sound of creaking from behind her, and she turned again, knife pointed at the fireplace where two shadows rose from a sofa.

Plonk.

Heart beating out of her chest, Janet swiveled back to the piano, the upright lid hiding the awful pianist. She eased away from the window into the welcome folds of a heavy curtain as the figures glided on to the marble floor. In the moonlight, she saw a woman dressed in a voluminous ballroom dress and a man, a soldier judging by his tunic. The couple bowed before holding hands, ready to dance.

Janet looked to Tom for help. One glance through the crack in the door, and he gestured to her to stay put, not that she had any plans of going anywhere. The silent dance started, and something about the dancers made her skin crawl. Limbs that should have flowed twitched and twisted in quick staccato like over-wound clockwork.

Janet didn't notice the tip of her knife still glinting in the moonlight, not until an arm snaked from the shadows opposite, a bony finger touching the tip before tracing the blades edge. Hypnotized, she watched the digit rise into the air, a drop of dark blood welling, as a skeleton of a thing stepped from the gloom, a dusting of chalk falling from its disheveled wig. It grinned, a wide mouth revealing a row of sharp pointed teeth, the drop of blood falling onto an eager lashing tongue. The look of ecstasy in the creature's beady, bloodshot eyes sickened Janet, petrifying her until the creature leaned in and croaked.

"Voulez-vous danser?"

Janet screamed, waving the knife as she sprinted for the door, bowling over the dancers, sending them sprawling, long skinny limbs flailing.

Tom held up his hands. "We can't. Not yet."

She pushed him aside, throwing open the door to stare up into the underbelly of...

"What the fuck is that?"

"Them!" shouted Tom over the howling gale.

Janet glanced back into the room where the demonic dancers and Liberace's evil twin rallied, staring at them with hungry, glowing eyes. Beyond the door, a behemoth of a maggot wriggled down the vast artery, barnacle-like growths spewing green spores. Stuck between a rock and a hard place, Janet imagined squished to be a preferable end to the calculated tortures of the cast-offs of *Les Misérables*.

Plus, she was a terrible dancer.

She stepped out of the door, only to hover between competing forces of gravity. With a little effort, she hooked a leg over the door's frame and, throwing aside the knife, dragged herself up into the tunnel. Hot on her heels, Tom also chose to skip the dance, and Janet helped him up.

With the demons scurrying across the checkered dance floor, Tom leaned down, grabbed the doorknob, and pulled the door closed. An almighty crash threatened to turn the door to matchsticks, claws tearing at the wood as Tom and Janet fell about.

Janet lay on a cold metal door, staring up at the ass end of the undulating maggot as it made its way along the tunnel. She struggled to catch her breath in the thick smog of spores, banging and knocking coming from underneath her.

"You can fuck right off," she screamed, banging her fists on the metal door as she clambered to her feet.

"I tried to warn you," said Tom, retrieving the carving knife.

"Odd, I must have missed the bit about fucking demons," said Janet, brushing herself down and examining the permanent scars Puffball had left on her arms, thankful that the demons had no opportunity to add to them.

She watched the maggot's passing, long tentacles dropping through doors to retrieve struggling, screaming demons before lofting its victims high into the air, only to be silenced as they vanished into the maggot's gelatinous bulk.

Janet waved a finger at the abomination, unable to find the words.

"They harvest the ripe ones, the ones that have had time to marinate," said Tom.

Janet's arms slumped to her side as she braced herself for another diabolical revelation. "Marinate?"

The old man wiped his dry lips. "Marinate in their misery. That's what they do. That's what they feed on. Misery. Their victims don't die in their cells. They don't let them."

"The dancers?"

"Likely been stewing for a couple hundred years. Turns people into monsters, tasty morsels of concentrated evil."

Janet laughed, a part of her mind cracking at the unimaginable horror.

Tom wrapped an arm around Janet, her laughter snowballing into insane giggling, giving way to unstoppable sobbing as they watched the mammoth maggot rumble away, feasting on its demonic delicacies.

◇━◦━◦━◦━◇

Janet followed Tom, rescuing her daughters the only thought keeping her going, keeping her sane. They hadn't spoken for an hour, the blue arrow having long vanished in their wake as they pushed further up the tunnel. Tom glanced at his watch. He'd said nothing, but Janet guessed time was running out. She scanned the expanse of doors, hope all but lost, when a flash of yellow caught her eye. Heart leaping into her throat, she stumbled towards the door.

"They're here," she cried out, seeing the words "Private Keep Out."

By the time Tom joined her, Janet caressed a finger over

the two scribbled words "Ann's room." Tears streamed down her face.

"We've found them." She reached out to turn the doorknob only for Tom to seize her hand. "What?"

He stared at her earnestly, biting his lip.

"What!" screamed Janet.

"Nothing here is what it seems. Time included. You need to be sure...sure it's them."

She snatched back her hand. "They're my children. I'll know."

Tom nodded, his grip tightening on the knife.

Janet lay beside the door and turned the handle, letting the door fall away before taking a deep breath, closing her eyes, and rolling.

⬦━━○━━⬦

Hand held up, it took a long moment for Janet's eyes to adjust to the blinding daylight. She was back, back in the disputed bedroom, her daughters staring at her.

"Well?" asked Ann.

"Tell her, Mum. I'm the oldest," said Sarah.

Janet lowered her hand as she slumped to the floor.

"Mum! Are you okay?" asked Sarah.

Ann launched herself across the room, wrapping her arms around her mother, and Janet hugged her daughter tighter than she'd hugged anything in her life, any thought of demons dismissed by her daughter's unmistakable scent.

Sarah joined the scrum, and Janet plastered her in kisses. "What's up, Mum?"

"I...I...thought I lost you. I'm sorry. I'm so sorry."

She pushed them back, scrutinizing her daughters for signs of their captivity. But there were none, her children no worse for their ordeal. She glanced around the room, everything just as she remembered, her daughter's possessions still in their boxes.

"What day is it?" she said, pushing past to glance at the overgrown garden. It looked so real.

Sarah answered. "Moving day. Friday."

"W...When did you last see me?"

The girls looked at each other, confusion turning to concern.

"Mummy, you're scaring us," said Ann.

Janet rushed over to hug her daughters again. "Sorry, I'm being silly. I got spun around."

She might have believed her white lie but for Tom peering at her from the doorway, the curving ceiling, or floor, of the abyssal tunnel arching overhead.

Sarah followed her mother's gaze. "Who's that?"

"It's okay. That's Tom. He's here to help us get back home."

"But we are home," Ann insisted.

"Of course," said Janet, brushing aside a lock of Ann's red hair.

"We have to go," shouted Tom.

"Yes, yes. Okay, girls. We're going to play follow the leader. Tom has created an obstacle course, and he's quite the magician. It might seem scary, but remember, it's just a game. Okay?"

"Is there a prize?" asked Ann.

"Of course. The best prize ever."

"The room," said Sarah. "Winner keeps the room."

"Sure, but you have to do exactly what Tom does, step for step," said Janet. "Don't forget, he's going to trick you into making a mistake. Don't fall for it. Follow the leader. Right?"

The girls nodded.

"Okay, you first, Ann," said Janet, leading her to the door. The chaos beyond, coupled with the bizarre sight of Tom peering over the door frame, knife in hand, had Ann clinging to her mother's legs.

"Mum!"

Tom stared down at Janet. "You're sure?"

"Certain," hissed Janet.

Tom put the knife down, leaning in and extending a hand. Ann clung tighter to her mother's legs.

"Oh, come on. Don't tell me you've fallen for it already. I told you, he's a magician. It's just a trick."

Sarah had no qualms about taking Tom's hand. "It's going to be my room."

Tom hauled Sarah up, Ann's hands already clinging to the door frame when he looked back. With both girls and Janet free, they made their way back down the tunnel, Ann on Janet's back, Sarah watching Tom's every footfall.

◇————◇

"I spy something beginning with G," said Janet, distracting her daughters from their ongoing nightmare.

Sarah seemed almost oblivious to her surroundings, her focus on matching Tom's every step, desperate to win the prize. Ann, however, hoisted on her mother's shoulders, took it all in, her grip around her mother's neck tightening.

"Well?" choked Janet.

"A green door," said Ann.

"Right, again. Well done. Your turn."

"I spy...with my little eye...something beginning with L."

"L?" asked Janet, scanning the countless doors. "Lilac?"

"Nope."

"Lemon? Lime? Lavender?"

Ann giggled. "No. No. No. You're just guessing."

"Ah, I know...letterbox."

"Nope."

Janet shook her head. "I don't know. You've got me. What begins with L?"

"Lance's Room."

Tom froze, turning and glaring at the girl. "What?"

Ann pointed over her shoulder to an old graying door, a weathered sign emblazoned with butterflies declaring the owner. Tom scrambled, almost knocking Janet over. She lowered Ann, Sarah taking her sibling's hand.

"Stay here. Don't move," said Janet.

The girls nodded.

"Don't move," Janet repeated as she pursued Tom. She caught up with him kneeling at the door, brushing dust from his son's name. "Is it?"

Tom nodded, teardrops exploding on the peeling

paint.

"But it's been so long, Tom. Look at the door…"

Tom stood, wiping his eyes. "I know. But…but they're my world…"

"Were," said Janet, pushing away the offered knife.

"If it was your family?"

In his shoes, Janet knew nothing would stop her from opening that door. She sighed, taking the knife and hugging the old man.

"Get your daughter's home. Sell up. Move and never, never look back."

Janet nodded. "Thank you, Tom."

The old man lay next to the door he'd spent a lifetime hunting, and twisting the handle, he slipped away.

The soft chimes of a music box echoed through the tunnel, and Janet looked down into a gloomy, small box room, the only illumination from a child's nightlight. An empty rocking chair stood beside a crib. Tom stared down at a small mound and glanced back, a contented smile on his face. He bent down as the door began to slide closed.

Janet heard a gurgling. But what started as a baby's cooing ended in a death rattle, and Janet leaned out, desperate to see her friend. She held out a hand to hold the door, only for a pale face to appear. A woman with glowing red eyes glared through oily, matted hair, a broad grin stretching from ear to ear to reveal pointed teeth licked by a slithering, forked tongue.

"He's home," hissed the demon as the door slammed shut.

"Not far now," said Janet, dashing down the spongy access tunnel, Ann on her back and pulling Sarah by her hand. Any pretense of a game vanished the moment she'd screamed at what remained of Tom's wife. The girls had long given up asking questions. "Not far now."

It had become a mantra, the only hope Janet had left. Even when they found the blue arrow, she'd not stopped running, terrified that the portal home would vanish. But as she looked along the undulating tunnel, she saw a slither of light.

The knife skidded across the hardwood floor, and Janet followed, Ann tumbling from her back as Sarah fell onto the sofa. For a long moment, Janet looked up at the ceiling, ignoring the bloody runes, focusing instead on the joyful sounds of a world she thought she'd lost.

Panting hard, she pulled herself up to see the blood red portal vanish with a dull pop, leaving a large, jagged hole in the wall, a hole that went nowhere.

Ann had her back to her, something in her hands.

"Ann, what's that?" Her daughter turned, mouth dripping with blood, and Janet shot across the room. "Oh, God." Her fingers scrabbled at her daughter's lips, fearing she'd bitten her tongue or worse. "Open wide. Let me see."

Ann did as she was told, opening her mouth wide, wide enough to show all her razor-sharp teeth, wide enough to reveal a lapping tongue. Janet recoiled, seeing the bag of blood her daughter clutched in claw-like fingers.

"We're home, Mum," mocked Sarah, snatching up the knife. "And it's been so very long."

The thing masquerading as Sarah launched itself across the room, slashing and stabbing with the blade until Janet wrestled it to the ground. Even then, it fought tooth and claw with unnatural strength. All the while, Ann sat giggling, squeezing the last drops of blood from the plastic bag, not at all interested in helping its sibling. Janet pinned evil Sarah to the floor and knocked the knife from its clutches.

"Janet!"

Hand around Sarah's neck, Janet glanced over her shoulder to see her mother standing in the doorway as the demon bucked and thrashed.

"Mother! Help me. They're not my daughters," cried Janet, picking up the knife.

"No!" screamed her mother, joining the affray.

"They're not your grandchildren," screamed Janet, knocking her mother flying as she tried to stop the flailing demon from escaping. She raised the knife, stabbing the blade into the creature's face, missing by a hair's breadth.

Bag drained, Ann entered the battle, clinging to Janet's back and biting into her shoulder.

Janet screamed at her mother. "Help me."

The old woman scrambled to her feet and fled into the kitchen. Janet knew she was on her own. Tom had tried to warn her. A tricky punch to the nose threw Ann from her back, and with the knife in both hands, Janet brought the blade down on Sarah's snarling demonic face.

With a sickening thud, Janet's world exploded into

blinding white pain before darkness rushed in, accompanied by the sound of shattering glass cascading onto hardwood floors. The last thing Janet saw, surrounded by wilting flowers, was her mother, the blood-soaked doppelgangers hugging the old woman.

"Are you okay, Ann? Sarah? It's okay. Your mum just needs some help. It'll be alright. Come on."

"She's not taken her pills again," whimpered Sarah.

◇━◦━━◇━━◦━◇

"Janet, you've got visitors," announced the orderly.

Janet put down the jigsaw piece and looked across the sterile day room. "Me?"

The orderly gestured for her to follow.

It had been months, maybe years, since she'd arrived at the care center, and in all that time, she'd not had a single visitor. But her memory being what it was, she couldn't be sure she'd even remember. Post-traumatic amnesia they'd called it, and somewhere between that and the drugs, she'd lost track of everything.

The orderly led her down the corridor to an unfamiliar room. "In here."

"Thank you," said Janet, wandering into the meeting room, a large wooden table flanked by several plastic chairs. A window overlooked the hospital's lush green grounds, people enjoying the lovely summer's day.

"They'll just be a minute," said the orderly, closing the door. She smiled through the glass before leaving, and Janet slumped into a seat to attended to her graying split ends, watching a squirrel clamber down a tree.

The door opened with a click, and two women strolled around the table. Mid-thirties, dressed in smart suits like so many consultants she'd spoken to. She didn't recall seeing them on the ward. They stood smiling at her. The taller of the two women reminded her of faded old photos she'd seen of her mother.

The shorter woman brushed back her red hair. "Sorry it's been so long, but we've been so very busy."

"I'm sorry, have we met? My memory isn't what it was."

"Oh, come now, you can't have forgotten us," said the tall woman, crossing her arms.

"Not your own daughters," mocked the other.

In that moment, Janet remembered it all as if it had just happened, and she staggered from the chair to the door, rattling the handle, banging on the door as the world beyond the glass faded to reveal an arching mausoleum of doors.

Janet turned to see Ann's grin broaden until it reached her ears. "There you are. I knew you'd not forgotten us."

"Welcome home, Mother."

Chris Hewitt
About the Author

Chris lives in the beautiful garden of England and in the odd moment he's not walking the dog, he pursues his passion for writing fiction. With horror, fantasy, and science-fiction stories published in several anthologies from Eerie River amongst others. You can keep up with Chris' writing below.

Facebook: https://www.facebook.com/chris.hewitt.writer
Twitter: @i_mused_blog
Blog: http://mused.blog

WHO'S THAT TRIP TRAPPIN'
ALLY WILKES

Bank station gets its claws into you. Doesn't let you go without a fight.

It's a Monday, unremarkable in every way—grey stagnant clouds hanging low in the sky, blotting out the Shard, the promise of aeroplanes taking off from City Airport. There is nothing up there, just the mean face of the sky promising rain. She'd changed outfits twice before leaving the house, one too optimistic, the other—now—too pessimistic, because it's always too hot on the Tube. Everyone knows that.

Samantha—not Sam to her friends, not ever, she hates the feeling of being reduced—is sweating through her blouse and into her suit, crushed up against two tall banker-types with the long umbrellas that told everyone they barely had to walk more than a pavement-width between office and black cab. She tries not to make it obvious as she sniffs. She doesn't smell, not yet. But she's running late, will have to choose between a Pret almond croissant and escaping a lecture.

The Tube screeches around the curved platform like nails down a chalkboard, and Sam squeezes her eyes closed, feeling the beginnings of a headache.

As the train begins to slow, she surfs down the aisle, wobbling a little on stiletto heels, murmuring a constant refrain of "Sorry," "Excuse me," and "Thank you," as she butts up against similarly sweaty fellow commuters. The meaningless little "Open" buttons on the train doors hurry aside as the doors part, exhaling warm, damp air and sucking in the dull, dry underground-smelling air of Bank. People are already massing on the platform.

Samantha says, "Excuse me," again and, with a burst of irritation, decides to keep her elbows out, give anyone who tries to push past her a nasty surprise. A man swears, looks accusingly at her.

Good, she thinks. *Serves you right.*

"MIND...THE...GAP," says the ridiculously well-spoken man over the loudspeaker, and Samantha is buoyed up by the wave of bodies around her.

Suits and umbrellas and briefcases and—oh, horrors—wheelie bags. There's a bottleneck by the way out, and she finds herself trapped in the eddy of the crowd next to a large poster about a missing child. The picture is grainy, and the child is surprisingly ugly, wearing a cable-knit jumper and a little heart-shaped charm bracelet. Michelle has been missing since she was fourteen. That was nine years ago.

"Michelle is dead," Samantha mutters, thinking longingly of a flat white. It isn't a bad thing to think. It's simply the truth. Better dead than the other sad possibilities.

The stairs up to the next level are a seething mass of black and pinstripe, and Samantha's shoes click and scrape on the hatched metal. One of the heels has worn down to the nub, and that's it, she's going to have to get them re-heeled, and it's so unfair when there's barely a moment in Samantha's life that isn't Tube and office and gym and HelloFresh. There's just no time for chores.

She thinks that if she disappeared, it would take a bloody long time for them to notice.

◇━◉━◇━━◇━◉◇

Perhaps that's why she misses the interchange. The signs around Samantha go from black and green-yellow to red and brilliant cobalt blue. Gates are closed at the mouth of the Waterloo & City line, orange-jacketed staff with clipboards and walkie-talkies. She'd gone the wrong way, and she presses her mouth into a tight hard line and turns around.

"Hey!" someone says as Samantha swims against the tide, raises a hand in apology, and gets back on the escalator.

The crowd ebbs and falls with the arrival and departure of trains. This must be a moment of low tide, because no one else is on the escalator with her, except the tail-end of a school trip halfway up, the teacher looking ready to pack it all in before 8:00 a.m.

She pulls out her phone and says, "Shit," just loud enough for the children to hear.

One of them cackles.

And, coming from *under* the escalator, there's an answering laugh, dry as old bones.

Samantha looks at it with a flicker of interest, but the escalator is completely ordinary, grey marching stairs, worn-down yellow paint on the sides of each step, those hairy guard-things swooshing along at the side. She thinks, absently, that they must be doing repairs. Although, if that were true, the escalator would be closed.

She steps off at the top and scans the tunnels automatically. Back to the green-yellow. She follows the colours for a short distance, her hand clamped down on the phone in her suit pocket, her stilettos scrape-screeching on the tiled floor.

But she's gone wrong again, and that's the hell of Bank station: once you go wrong, you go *really* wrong, and it's hard to undo it.

"Shit," she repeats, then breaks into an awkward little flapping run—like a penguin, she thinks—arriving back at the same escalator.

It's going down this time, as if waiting for her.

There hadn't been any signs of this, and Samantha pauses for a moment before stepping back on. Plenty of people coming up. She's the only one going down.

This time, she's sure she hears something coming from the underside of one of those relentless mechanical steps. It's a woman's voice, far away but perfectly audible.

"Help me...please."

Samantha isn't a bad person. So she kneels—still going down, still descending—and peers into the crack between the stairs. There should be nothing there.

"Please."

She looks around. The commuters on the opposite

escalator look back—blank faces—although a few teenagers are sniggering. *Children*. She leans in closer, nearly at the bottom now, and puts her fingers, her aubergine-purple manicure, a few inches from the gap.

"Hello?"

She thinks she sees a pair of eyes.

⸻ ⸱ ⸻

Samantha wakes up alone.

She's lying on something hard. Tentatively creeping her hands out, she can feel it's a tiled surface. The cold seeps through her tights, numbing her legs, making her feel half-dead. It's so dark she wonders if there's been some sort of terrorist attack. She breathes out unsteadily, hand pressed to her mouth to stop herself from screaming. She won't give them the satisfaction, although she doesn't know who *they* are.

There's something wet under her fingers. Her face is bleeding, and she makes a small mewing sound, traces the flood upwards to her scalp. She's hit her head.

It feels...*wrong*.

Flat.

Flattened.

And there's so much blood.

Her breath comes in short, sharp bursts. As she explores the wound—clinically, as if it weren't really connected to her—she feels things moving on her skin. *Under* her skin. Bones rearranging themselves. A popping sensation she associates with the time she'd had labyrinthitis and had to stay in bed for a week because the floor was upside-down. Skin starting to come together. As she breathes, and breathes, she heals.

The blood stops.

The lights come on with a mechanical *buzzaw* sound. It echoes off the tiled floors and walls. Samantha sits up, fumbles to get a mirror out of her handbag. Her face is whole, but gobbets of dried blood are smeared around her temple and forehead. She uses a spare pair of tights to mop it up, throws them as far from her as she can manage.

She's in a tunnel. She's alone, completely alone. And she can't stop staring at the familiar ceiling—every third light dark, the others flickering subtly. At the walls lined with sunny adverts for *Mamma Mia!* and investment apps. The tiled floor is white, with a great deal of blood on it.

"Hello?" she calls. "Please? I think I fell."

It echoes. She wobbles as she stands up and steadies herself on the wall, slings her handbag over her shoulder. It's strange, the complete absence of people at Bank, the peak of Monday morning rush hour.

"Hello? I think I hit my head..."

◇━◇━━◇━◇

No, it had been worse than that. Because the gap between the escalator stairs had opened just a little, just enough for light and fingers to come through, a desperate face, blue eyes imploring.

"Help me," the woman had whispered to Samantha, every bone in her face visible,

Samantha would kill for cheekbones like that, and she'd bent down closer to touch the woman's fingers, tell her help would be on its way. She, Samantha, would be a hero. But the gap widened, and the little hairy guard-thing went *swoosh*, *swoosh*, and the stairs creaked. Suddenly, the woman's hand was there, grabbing Samantha's with such force that she could hear her fingers breaking.

"I'm sorry," the woman had said, then pulled.

Samantha's arm plunged into the innermost workings of the escalator. Something shone in her eyes, a heart-shaped flash of light, and the pain was exquisite. It was bigger and louder than anything she'd ever experienced. Her arm was being wrenched clean off her body. The woman was dragging her down like her life depended on it, and Samantha was screaming. She was still screaming when her hair came undone from its messy chignon and went into the belts that pulled and yanked and scalped her, dragging her face closer and closer to that widening gap.

She could see another Tube station through it— "MIND...THE...GAP"—and the escalator chewed once, a decisive chomp around her head and neck. Then she was falling, limp, to hit the tiled floor below on the *other side*.

WATER

"OWING TO WET WEATHER, THE SURFACES OF THE STATION MAY BECOME SLIPPERY," the man in the speakers says in his cut-glass accent.

Samantha's mouth is so dry she's eaten all her lip balm.

There's dripping water somewhere in the endless corridors. She follows the sound dumbly, shoes in hand, her feet padding on the cold tiling. The undersides of her tights are grimy, although the floor appears quite clean. And there isn't anyone else there. She's shouted herself hoarse, and that has made the need for water far more urgent.

The corridors she wanders through all look the same. They're indistinguishable from every Tube station she's ever passed through, with their low ceilings and occasional doors to nowhere. She's tried the doors; none will open. But she thinks the water is somewhere up ahead, because the sound of dripping is maddening, a slow relentless torment. She pauses to lick the inside of her lip balm tin. It's waxy.

She thinks she's been down there for several days already, and if she doesn't get water, she'll die.

"OWING TO WET WEATHER—" the man starts again.

"Yes, I fucking know!" she shouts back.

None of the station surfaces are slippery.

But there's a trickling sound as the echo dies away, and when she turns the next corner, there's a metal folding door, the sort they use to block off portions of the Tube for overcrowding. It's firmly padlocked, a metal chain so heavy it makes a sound like a bell when she drops it. In the corner of the door, a thin trickle of water snakes its way down.

It must be raining, she thinks. For a brief moment, she wonders whether she's really going to do this. She's Samantha Morton, thirty-five, works in investment banking.

She is *absolutely* going to do this.

The water tastes metallic but cold. London rainwater, seeping down hidden veins and passageways into the earth. It's probably dirty. It'll keep Samantha alive.

When she turns, face smeared with trickles of water, saliva, and tears, she can see the escalator, stretching up into the sky. But it's not a normal escalator. It doesn't start at the ground. It starts a good twenty feet high and marches away into nowhere. There are no handrails, no little guard thingies, no red buttons to stop it in emergencies.

She realises she's looking at its underside.

Speech

All Samantha's days are the same. At least, she thinks they're days.

She's relieved to find she's untroubled by hunger, then furious that another normal thing has been taken from her. She thinks about that Pret almond croissant, but she can't muster up anything except a dull sort of ache for water.

She walks around the corridors, always searching for the way out, one hand dragging along the wall to keep track. That hand is always dirty after a while, and she has run out of micellar wipes. Whenever she comes back to the folding door, she bangs on it and screams and holds her phone up in the air, trying to get a signal. But there's never any bars. The wireless won't connect, and her phone stays persistently on 4% battery. It's like that for days.

At least, she thinks they're days.

It becomes a routine. Samantha wakes when the man in the speaker says, "WELCOME TO BANK MONU-MENT STATION," and retraces her steps to the main chamber. She tries her phone. She tries the door. She drinks water if there is some. And she listens.

She's broken her nail file, though it would take an eter-nity, a fucking eternity, to use it to saw through the heavy metal chain.

Above her, the escalator moves quietly, like a heartbeat. For a few hours, which she counts by counting her breathing, she's able to hear voices and noise coming from above. Guitars if there are buskers. Laughter. Shouting. Sneezes. And then when the morning rush hour ends, it's all completely silent again.

And she wanders, talking to herself. Talking to the man in the speaker. He doesn't talk back except to say, "BEGGING IS PROHIBITED ON THE LONDON UNDERGROUND," as if she's done something to anger him.

⸏⸎⸏⸎⸏⸎⸏

She lies under the escalator sometimes, wonders if it'll ever open again. It's a kind of door, she supposes. As she was pulled down, someone else had crawled up—a woman, middle-aged, wearing old-fashioned Nikes and a feral expression. An exchange.

Some part of Samantha, some tiny flicker inside her mind geared for survival, for hunting, for fight-or-flight, gets it.

The escalator is one in, one out, like the tedious meat-market clubs around Cheapside on a Friday night. But that's such a ridiculous, horrible idea that she goes back to trying the chain and the tunnels. There has to be a way to escape.

Time

Her painted nails are a memory. She keeps her shoes, her impractical shoes, for times when the cold is particularly unforgiving. Her toenails have become hard and claw-like from padding around the corridors and chamber barefoot. She bites her nails into little peaks, spitting them out like curses, keeping them sharp so she can use them to rip and tear. The fragments of her nail file lasted perhaps a year.

Samantha knows the tunnels by heart. She sometimes walks along them, singing jingles, whatever she can remember from each advert as she passes. She particularly likes doing the "Go Compare" man, because the noise booms and echoes and crashes back around her, almost as if there's someone else down there. But she's started forgetting some of the words, and she pauses in front of something glossy about home insurance. It's like an itch at the corner of her mind, and she digs her nails under the loose edge of the paper, feeling around, getting a good grip on a whole strip of it.

She peels it back to reveal an advert for John Lewis Christmas, and Christmas songs keep her going for a good few hours.

Then she goes further back, *scratch-scratch-scratch* with the little jagged points of her nails, until she can get underneath.

As she rips, the colours change from wintery grey to burgundy, to the bright yellow of a Mediterranean sunshine holiday. She'd weep if she could; she hasn't seen sunshine in so long. She goes further, tearing and tearing and stopping to spit out her nails until she thinks surely this will be it; surely, she's down to plain wall...

But it's another home insurance advert, the same as the first. Policies purchased before the end of the month. The advert is from 2019, and her dizzying journey through time has just brought her back to the start again.

She punches the wall. It's not *fair*. Then she goes to listen at the escalator for the morning rush.

TRESPASSERS

She's been trying to find her way down to the tracks. Perhaps she could walk along them to another station. Or maybe there'll be an oncoming train.

That wouldn't be so bad, she thinks distantly. *Not now.*

There's a giant spiral staircase, wide and deep, that seems to lead to platform level. But at the bottom, as soon as she passes those schematic maps of the line, "Northbound" and "Southbound," the cavern becomes hotter than hell, and the tiled floor burns her feet like walking on hot sand.

The speaker man says, "DO NOT TRESPASS ON THE TRACKS" and "PLEASE DO NOT MOVE ALONG THE PLATFORM."

That last one is wrong, isn't it?

Isn't it?

Samantha binds her feet up and keeps going. The air smells of fire. Something floats past in her peripheral vision, and she turns, dream-like, to find it's a piece of floating ash.

"THE BRITISH TRANSPORT POLICE HAVE BEEN CONTACTED," he says.

Samantha croaks, "Well, lucky for me I *touched in.*" She cackles like a witch. Her Oyster card sits, useless, in her decaying handbag.

Around the next turn of the corridor—where all the

overhead lights are dark—something is coming for her. She can see it creeping forward, a tall dark shape, long limbs made of shadows, eyes burning coal-red in a featureless face. It's so hot she thinks her eyeballs will blister.

It reaches out. She takes a step back.

It reaches out and *howls*.

She stops running when she gets to the padlocked gate, coughing the taste of brimstone from her lips.

"PLEASE BE ADVISED," the man says, "THE BRITISH TRANSPORT POLICE PATROL THIS STATION REGULARLY."

"You've got to be kidding me," Samantha whispers. She laps at the water until her heart stops hammering. "*That's* the British Transport Police?"

She desperately looks around the chamber. If they come up here, there's nowhere at all to go, except into the escalator, if she can make it open enough for her to climb out. She thinks of the horrible pulling sensation, being rendered limb from limb, meat in a grinder. But she'd healed, hadn't she?

"Hello?" she calls up to the living world. "Can anyone hear me?"

⟡────⟡────⟡

She doesn't know why she thinks it should be a child. It just seems right. That's how monsters work. They take children. Some part of Samantha knows this.

And they've lived less up there. Maybe they won't miss it so much.

Every morning, she begs and pleads at the escalator. Sometimes, she's a frightened little girl crying for her parents. Sometimes, she gives dire warnings about stepping on cracks. Sometimes, she offers sweets or money. She becomes quite good at putting on different voices. They echo around the chamber, and she carries on for hours at a time, pausing only to braid her filthy hair back off her face, keeping it clear in case she has to make the journey through the machinery.

She doesn't walk the corridors. Doesn't seek out the platforms. Doesn't encounter the British Transport Police, made of fire and shadows, who keep her trapped like a very pissed-off genie in a bottle made of tiles and low-curved ceilings.

Samantha puts all her single-mindedness into finding the right child. The one who'll stop, look between the cracks, and reach out to her.

Christmas comes and goes, although she doesn't know which Christmas. She hasn't been paying attention. The children are bouncy and unbearable, all excited in their winter coats. Some wear earmuffs, making it even harder to hear her. Samantha grinds her teeth and makes herself bright and appealing like a little elf. She promises chocolate and presents. No joy.

Joy's in short supply.

She thinks it's February from the amount of rain seeping down into her little kingdom. She promises the children somewhere warm and dry. She promises somewhere wonderful.

One day, the sound of her voice makes something happen. She's lying on her back on the cold tiled floor under the escalator, in her nest made from discarded copies of *Metro*. She's looking up at the stairs marching onwards and upwards into the living world, marching away from her like everything else seems to have marched away from her, and then—

The stairs are right in front of her nose, and there's someone staring at her through the crack.

A girl, wearing a shaggy white coat, like a walking carpet.

She's young—although Samantha has no idea how to tell the ages of children—and has golden hair pinned back by a rainbow clip. She's very bright and very real.

"Who are you?" the child says, inches away.

Samantha swallows. Spider-like, her hands crawl towards the cracks in the escalator, which seem to have expanded like toffee. Time has stopped. She pokes her bony fingers through, swallows, tries again to speak.

"Help me," she whispers. "Please."

The child is clutching an expensive-looking phone. Samantha sees it with a spark of cruel envy.

"Help me," she says, stronger, and her heart beats a hungry *trip-trap* as she sees the child bend down, reach into the escalator, brush warm, firm, *living* hands against hers.

Samantha grabs and doesn't let go.

◇━◦━━━◦━◇

"Stupid!" Samantha screams. "Stupid, stupid, stupid!"

She hammers her forehead with the palm of her hand,

leaving greasy, bloody handprints on her own face. Then she squishes her face in her hands, taking in a big sucking breath between the flesh of her palms, smelling metal and death.

She kicks the wall with her bare feet, and it hurts. She thinks she feels a toe breaking. She isn't sure whether it'll heal.

"Stupid," she whispers, looking up at the escalator. It hangs up in the sky again, infinitely out of reach.

She doesn't turn around.

She doesn't want to face the memory of screaming, tearing, the hollow popping sound of limbs being torn from sockets. There was so much blood, more blood than Samantha had ever imagined. It sprayed into her face, got into her eyes, and she just couldn't let go of the child. She couldn't push past.

Above her, the little heart-shaped locket—stuck in the mechanism—winks dully in the dimmed lighting. Samantha hasn't seen true dark since coming down here, and it feels at once soothing and utterly alien.

There's a wet sound in the shadows, and her heart freezes.

She couldn't.

But she turns around to watch the child's broken body healing itself all the same. Samantha cries. She weeps and howls and yells at herself for being so bloody *stupid*, too cowardly to see it through. She should have known how bad it would be, how awful the price of freedom.

She screams, finally, into the darkness, just before the child's face is healed and the lights *buzzaw* back on.

BILLY GOAT #1

The child's name, she learns, is Amelia. She lives in West Kensington with her two mums. She has a cat but no dog. The expensive-looking phone is a model that Samantha has never seen, does things she'd never imagined, but it's exactly the same story. 4% battery, no bars of signal, wireless has been replaced by something else.

Samantha starts to ask what year it is, then stops herself.

Because the heart-shaped locket hanging in the sky had belonged to Michelle, the child on the "Missing" poster who'd disappeared nine years before. Michelle, the woman who'd dragged Samantha down.

She'd looked in her late forties, had clearly passed a lifetime under Bank station, however time worked...or didn't.

"Come on," Samantha says to Amelia, trying to sound happy because that's what children like. That's what they expect of adults. And she shows her where the water is, how to tongue it up from the groove between the metal door and the tiled walls.

"There's got to be a way out," Amelia says, her voice hoarse from crying. "There has to be."

Samantha won't tell her.

There's two of them now, down in the empty corridors, listening out for the voice of the speaker man, hiding from the British Transport Police. Amelia isn't growing up right. Or perhaps she's going to be stuck at eleven forever. Perhaps that's what happens if you don't crawl up through the escalator, making someone else take your place.

Samantha doesn't know.

But sometimes when Amelia sleeps, the troll sits underneath her escalator, waiting for Monday rush hours.

Waiting for the sounds of the living world.

Wondering if she can go through with it this time.

ALLY WILKES
ABOUT THE AUTHOR

Ally lives in Greenwich, London, with far too many books and an anatomical skeleton. Her short fiction has been published in Nightmare and Three Crows magazine. Ally's debut novel, All the White Spaces, will be out in January 2022 (UK) and March 2022 (US).

Twitter: @UnheimlichManvr
Instagram: @av_wilkes
Facebook: https://www.facebook.com/AllyWilkesAuthor
Website: https://www.allywilkes.com/

No. 43 Peach Street
Georgia Cook

No. 43 was a magnificent wreck.

Jamie paused on the pavement to gawp, his eyes moving from the sagging roof to the waterlogged gutters, to the overgrown mass of weeds and rhododendron bushes choking the front lawn. Ivy scaled the brickwork and enfolded the peeling window frames, shrouding the house in permanent shadow.

Peach Street was an affluent address, home to doctors, lawyers, and bankers, a far cry from Jamie's tiny third-floor flat. The houses on either side of 43 were tall and immaculate, boasting elegant front lawns and pristine white porches. What its neat, red-brick neighbours thought of No. 43, lurking between them like some sculking beast, Jamie could only guess.

Its windows were dark and empty, the path up to the front door thick with mulch. A large quantity of rubbish lay strewn across the front lawn—bottles and crisp packets, take-away cartons and bright plastic bags, alongside a child's upturned bicycle and what appeared to be half a chest of drawers.

Nothing stirred from inside; no shadows flittered behind the hanging net curtains. Jamie untucked the clipboard from under his arm and made a little mark in the box labelled "Unoccupied."

Good morning, Madam, what a lovely home! Do you have a minute to discuss your service provider? He was expected to make a stop at every house on the street, jotting down names and phone numbers, as much information as he could gather before the occupant closed the door. It was a conversation he'd had a thousand times, a script he could recite in his sleep, but something about approaching No. 43, dark and foreboding in a sea of such pristine grandeur, filled him with unease.

And so, satisfied with his own reasoning, Jamie turned on his heel, walked to No. 45 two doors down, and tried to put 43 firmly out of his mind. It loomed on the edge of his vision all the way down the street, growing smaller as he walked, but always present.

Unavoidably other.

It nagged at him.

Jamie couldn't help but wonder how houses became like that. Neglect? Abandonment? The sheer misfortunes of human life? There'd been a similar house on his childhood street, a tiny bungalow overgrown with brambles, its paint peeling, its roof sagging in the middle like an undercooked sponge cake. All the kids had sworn blind it was haunted, and an undisputed test of daring was to creep across the tangled lawn on Halloween night and knock on one of the grimy windows. Perhaps every street had a house like that. The twinge of nostalgia amused Jamie, and he put the thought from his mind at last.

◇━━◇━━━◇━━◇

That night, Jamie dreamed about Peach Street.

In the dream, it was early morning; Peach Street was empty and silent, its houses dark in the monochrome of pre-dawn, and Jamie was walking towards No. 43.

Without breaking stride, he opened the front gate and crossed the overgrown lawn, stepping over broken paving slabs and debris wrapped in weeds, picking his way between tangled lumps of foliage he could only half identify and was glad to pass without stopping.

Something glinted, off-white, between the bushes. Eyes peered from the depths as Jamie reached the front door.

He hadn't noticed it earlier, but in Jamie's dream, the door to No. 43 was bright, rich red, contrasting with the rest of the house's peeling grey exterior. It glimmered like a smear of blood in the darkness and, to Jamie's surprise, appeared perfectly maintained—almost new. The knocker was shaped like an owl's head, its beak clasping a thick bronze ring, its eyes round and unblinking.

In his dream, Jamie grasped the ring and knocked. The sound boomed through the house—once, twice, three times—before fading into silence.

And in that silence, deep in the gloom of dawn, surrounded by dust and brick and the sickly-sweet smell of old rot, something shifted within the house.

Jamie awoke to sunlight streaming through his bedroom curtains, the soft rumble of traffic cutting through the peaceful silence. He lay in the darkness, his heart pounding, the image of No. 43's bright red door burned across his mind's eye.

Even as he pulled himself out of bed, washed and dressed, gazed at his reflection in the bathroom mirror, the dream remained as fresh in Jamie's mind as it had upon waking. He wasn't frightened, he realised; there was nothing frightening about No. 43.

Instead, it filled him with curiosity, the same tantalising thrill he'd felt as a child, like the split-second terror before diving into a deep black lake.

Jamie spent the morning on Fairweather Street, another prosperous neighbourhood filled with handsome, identical houses, each with their clipped front lawns and sparkling windows. None of them resembled No. 43 in the slightest, but still Jamie found himself turning sharply at every door, half-expecting to catch that looming shadow on the edge of his vision, see the mess of overgrown garden, the patchy roof.

He never did.

That day, there were more streets to visit, more numbers to write, a parade of faces peering suspiciously from immaculate hallways. Through it all, Jamie's thoughts returned again and again to Peach Street and to that bright red door. Was it really abandoned? Neglected by some far-flung inheritor? Or perhaps home to some elderly shut-in, rich and ancient and unimpeded by the judgement of neighbours? Even in the brightness of daytime, Jamie couldn't shake the certainty that No. 43 *was* occupied; that it could be nothing *but* occupied. Something lurked between the crumbling walls, something as old and inevitable as the moss creeping up the front steps, the rain leaking through the gaps in the roof.

No. 43 was a place of residence. No. 43 was a *home*.

◇━◦━━━◦━◇

At noon, having exhausted Fairweather Street and the streets on either side, Jamie turned and headed back the way he'd come, intending to find his car and, hopefully, the sandwich he'd left in the glove compartment.

Instead, his feet took him down an unfamiliar side street, then left, then right, then down a tiny alleyway lodged between two houses, the walls rising high on either side, obscuring the gardens from view.

Jamie walked without really knowing where he was going but found he couldn't stop; it was like walking through a dream, down a pathway lost to childhood memories.

It was only when he arrived on the other side of the alleyway that Jamie realised he was back on Peach Street.

No. 43.

It stood just the same as the day before, its tangle of

trees rustling in the autumn breeze, its windows dusty and dark. A jackdaw hopped about on the high-peaked roof, uttered a loud screech, then dived out of sight.

The front door was indeed red. Jamie wondered how he hadn't noticed that before. He glanced at his clipboard. The box for 43 was still marked "Unoccupied." He'd be asked why he hadn't filled it in, why he hadn't checked. He could make something up, of course, but then...

Even then...

Jamie steeled himself. Then, he took a deep breath, pushed open the gate, and started up the garden path. Once upon a time, the path had been laid with paving stones, but the lawn had overtaken them completely, twisting up between the cracks to ankle height.

Something crunched underfoot. Jamie lifted his foot and found the tiny skeleton of a mouse crushed beneath his shoe. Its remains glimmered off-white between the slabs.

Jamie remembered the lawn in his dream, the strange lumps, too thickly tangled to recognise the shapes beneath. Had he seen flecks of white there too? Glimmers of bone and shadow, belonging to things much larger than mice?

Jamie lowered his foot and picked his way carefully to the front steps.

In the daylight, the door wasn't nearly as splendid as it had first appeared, the red paint faded to a greyish pink. There was no knocker, just a jagged little hole where presumably a knocker had once hung.

Despite his curiosity, Jamie didn't want to touch the door, didn't want the feel of it against his knuckles, didn't want to watch the paint flake away at his touch. He considered yelling his presence, but that also didn't appeal.

What if something yelled back?

Jamie shook himself. *What a stupid thought.*

He lifted his hand and knocked. The wood beneath his knuckles felt strangely spongey, riddled with woodworm.

There was silence from inside the house, and for a moment, Jeremy felt a surge of relief override his curiosity. *Of course,* it was abandoned. Of course, there was nobody home. God, why had he even thought—

He heard movement behind the door, soft, tapping footsteps, growing louder as they approached. A heavy bolt was drawn back on the other side, then another, followed by the soft click of a latch. Then, the door swung slowly open.

In the doorway stood a little girl.

She couldn't have been older than six or seven, with a tangle of dirty brown hair and dark, incurious eyes. She was dressed in a shapeless white smock stained here and there with patches of green and red and only one sock rolled up carelessly around her ankle. The other foot was bare.

The little girl stared up at Jamie with an expression of inherent disinterest, as if she saw him in that capacity every day and was now very bored with the whole affair.

Realising he was holding his clipboard in front of him like a shield, Jamie lowered his arms and plastered on his widest smile. "Good morning!" he managed. "Are your parents home?"

There was a moment of silence as the little girl considered it, then glanced over her shoulder into the darkness behind her. Not a single light was on inside the house, and the air smelt of decay and old dust. The gloom of the hallway seemed almost weighted, finishing just a few feet behind the little girl's ankles before trailing back into deeper shadow. It was a darkness caused by the copious trees winding up and around the doorframe, blocking out the sun—that made *sense*, that was *logical*—but Jamie couldn't shake the feeling that there was something crouched just out of sight back there, watching him.

He was aware of a sharp animal smell lurking below the moss and decay, acidic and strong.

At last, the girl turned back.

"No," she said.

Jamie blinked, his unease momentarily overwhelmed with concern. "You're here all alone?"

Another pause, another glance into the hallway. "No, there's Grandma here with me."

Jamie felt a rush of relief. "Well, can I speak to your grandmother?"

This prompted a third pause. "No."

"It'll only take a minute—"

"Grandma doesn't like talking to people."

"Well, that's—"

"Grandma doesn't like talking." The girl gave Jamie a severe look. Finally, she shook her head. "Besides, she's just had supper. You'll have to come back later."

So saying, she swung the door shut in Jamie's face. Jamie heard bolts sliding back into place, then silence.

The trees rustled overhead. Somewhere in the undergrowth the jackdaw screeched again. Jamie stared at the peeling woodwork, his heart pounding.

He didn't *need* the signatures. He didn't *need* the people in No. 43. But something had settled in his chest, that terrible curiosity again, pulling taut.

Not even concern.

Not even fear.

Just a terrible *need*.

As if something precious was barred from him as soon as the door closed. As if whatever lurked in the shadows of that deep, dark hallway was calling to him, pleading for him to see.

To *know*.

Jamie stood on the doorstep a moment longer, staring at the peeling red paint, then with considerable effort, he walked back to the pavement and turned to watch the house, searching the upper windows for some movement, some flicker of life, the little girl or her grandmother peering down at him through the net curtains. But there was nothing. The house stood silent, its windows as empty and dust riddled as before.

Jamie scribbled a fake number in the box on his clipboard, watched the house a further five minutes, then forced himself back down the street, the shadows looming large behind him as he walked.

It occurred to Jamie, briefly, that perhaps there was someone he should call, someone he should inform of the child and her grandmother, evidently living in squalor on a vast street surrounded by affluent neighbours. He wasn't sure why, but the thought prickled something strange and uneasy at the back of Jamie's throat, and he found himself reluctant to do anything.

Just in case.

Although, just in case of what, he couldn't possibly say.

⸻ ⸻

To Jamie's relief and disappointment, the following morning found him on King Lane, at least an hour's walk across town from Peach Street. King Lane was a much smaller, cosier neighbourhood, filled with leafy gardens and modern retirement bungalows. Jamie's supervisor had noted his lack of progress over the previous two days, and Jamie knew what an incomplete form would do to his work hours if he didn't buck up. He needed the job; he needed it more than he had ever needed anything.

Well...almost anything.

Jamie approached King Lane from the back, trailing from door to door, clipboard clasped in both hands, robotic smile plastered across his face, but for the life of him, he couldn't have described who he spoke to or even what their responses were.

Something else had caught his eye, growing larger as he neared the far junction.

King Lane had an abandoned house all its own.

No. 5 King Lane sat behind a low wooden fence, obscured in a bowl of arching trees, long and squat, with a gabled roof and a raised American-style porch running along the front. It was much smaller than No. 43, resembled it in no discernible way, and yet Jamie felt himself drawn across the road with the same breathless fascination. As he approached, he realised what had first caught his attention.

No. 5's door was red. Bright red.

Jamie froze on the pavement outside. It was just the sunlight, of course, just an evening glow across faded paint. And if not, who cared? Plenty of houses had red doors.

But even so...even so...

Jamie had already swung open the gate before he knew what was happening, started down the scattered pebble path. A set of narrow wooden steps lay ahead of him, leading up to the porch. They creaked dangerously under Jamie's weight, smelling of woodworm and rot, but he kept walking. Overhead, up in the roofspace, something hooted.

The screen door was sagging in its frame, revealing nothing of the house beyond but darkness, and it was indeed red, a soft peachy pink made crimson by the sunset. Feeling rather foolish, every nerve tight with adrenaline and uncertainty, Jamie knocked.

Silence from inside. Only the rustling of the trees overhead and the soft rumble of building work in the street opposite. Jamie almost laughed with relief and disappointment.

Then, a pattering of feet in the hallway, the soft click of a lock. Slowly, slowly, the door creaked open.

"Oh," said a familiar voice. "It's you again."

The little girl in the grey dress squinted up at Jamie from the doorstep. The hallway behind her was dark and long—impossibly long. Surely, he should have been able to see to the end of it? Surely...

"H-hello," Jamie managed, feeling the knot in his throat begin to tighten.

"Are you still here to see Grandma?" asked the girl.

Jamie opened his mouth. Why was he there? Why did he want to know? What drew him to those abandoned houses with their bright red doors? Why couldn't he leave it all alone?

Are you here to see Grandma?

"Yes," Jamie replied, realising as he said it that it was true. "Yes, I am."

The little girl studied him a moment longer, then shook her head. "Sorry," she said. "She's still not ready." She moved to close the door.

To his surprise, Jamie flung out a foot and jammed it between the frame and the door, stopping it from closing. The girl stared at him without surprise.

"I-I want to know," he said. "I-I want to know what's back there. What's inside! What *is* this place?"

What lived in those places? What lay beyond that long, long corridor, perched between pristine homes, ignored entirely by its neighbours. Did it create the abandoned houses, like urban camouflage rippling across an animal's back, or did it merely occupy them? A house-shaped Cuckoo in a nest of brick and picket fences. Was it one creature or many? If he'd stayed long enough to peer through those grime-flecked windows as a child, would he have seen the pale form of a little girl in a grey dress, peering back at him?

Did those places call so sweetly to others? Filling them

with the same mixture of dread and anticipation?

As if sensing Jamie's desperation, the little girl smiled. "Why, it's home, of course," she said, and closed the door.

⊹━◦━━◦━━◦━━◦⊹

Jamie didn't return to his car after that. He threw his clipboard into the nearest bin and started off through the streets, winding up pavements and down again, searching for another desolate house, another bright red door, but nothing came. No new ruins loomed out of the dusk, calling to him with their deep dark windows and rampant lawns. No sign at all of a little girl in a grey smock dress and her hidden grandmother.

He was so close, Jamie knew. *So close.*

⊹━◦━━◦━━◦━━◦⊹

That night, Jamie dreamed of Peach Street again.

He was already walking up the garden path, the gate swinging shut behind him. The door to No. 43 lay open ahead, a pitch-black hole in the grey morning world, and Jamie was drawn to it inexorably through the tangled lawn. He felt a shiver of anticipation, the clawing need in the pit of his stomach.

Finally, he would know.

Finally, he would *know.*

Without breaking stride, he stepped over the threshold and into No. 43.

The little girl was waiting for him inside the hallway.

She seemed smaller in the darkness, as insubstantial as shadow. Her eyes were beetle black, her little hands wrinkled and clawed like the feet of a bird, and in his dream, Jamie wondered how he had ever thought she was human, how he had ever assumed that place was a house at all.

The hallway walls were narrow and dark, lined with something that could never have been wallpaper, leading back and back into an impossible deepness. A breeze whistled through from somewhere inside the house, tinged with a cloying dampness.

Jamie remembered the bones of the tiny mouse out on the path. He remembered the owl head knocker, with its blank bronze eyes and sharp bronze beak. He remembered the animal smell, so strong in the gloom.

There was a word for the things left undigested by an owl's stomach, debris of a tiny animal swallowed whole, spat back out in a ball of bones and hair and stringy fibres like rubbish littering a tangled lawn.

The little girl turned to Jamie.

"Are you here to see Grandma?" her voice was whisper quiet.

Something shifted in the shadows beyond the hall. Something with beetle-black eyes and rusting feathers. Something with a glittering sharp beak and towering, bristling wings. Something older than Peach Street or King Lane, older than the city, older than anything could be or ever had been. Something that had lived there for a long, long time.

Jamie nodded wordlessly.

He was. God, he was.

The little girl took Jamie's hand—gently, gently—and led him inside No. 43, down the hall, and into the shadows.

Did the mouse know, before the owl swooped down, what was coming for it on midnight wings? Did it glimpse the needle-sharp claws and marvel at their beauty? Did it peer upwards at the rustling branches and wonder what it might find inside...

Did it think, in its final moments, that it could ever have escaped?

Georgia Cook
About the Author

Georgia Cook is an illustrator and writer from London. She is the winner of the LISP 2020 Flash Fiction Prize, has been shortlisted for the Bridport Prize and Reflex Fiction Award, among others, and has written for the horror anthology podcasts 'Creepy', 'The Other Stories' and 'The Night's End'.

She can be found on twitter at @georgiacooked and on her website at https://www.georgiacookwriter.com/

TILL DEATH DO US PART
DAVID GREEN

"Can you turn this crap off? Put something else on... maybe a tune written this century."

Kate scowled at the road as she drove, bit her lip, and cranked up the volume as Waylon Jennings crooned "Ain't Livin' Long Like This." Maybe fate laughed at her; the song's title matched her thoughts all too well. She looked at Dan from the corner of her eye.

His frown matched hers.

"My truck, my rules. Don't like it, get out."

Dan rolled his eyes and shook his head like some kind of overgrown bobblehead. She hated it when he did that.

"Relax," he muttered.

Relax. Kate despised it when he told her to do that, too. Her fingers dug into the steering wheel, afraid she'd sink them into Dan's face if she let go. Everything about him irritated her, and she knew her presence had the same effect on him.

They'd reached that part of their relationship.

The end of it.

Ain't living long like this, Kate thought, trying to lose herself in the song's rhythm instead. *Wonder what it'll take for one of us to walk away.*

"Why do you even listen to this country trash, anyway?" Dan whined, throwing a sullen look through the passenger window.

"My daddy loved it. You know this."

"Yeah, well, my old man loved racial slurs, misogyny, and alcohol. Doesn't mean I have to."

Kate ground her teeth. "Not sure liking Waylon Jennings compares to those, but whatever."

Dan didn't reply. The tension that had grown between them settled in for the drive, making the silence heavy. Deep down, she still loved him. He just made it so goddamn hard.

That's not fair, Kate told herself, just as she did every day.

The year before had pushed them both; Dan lost his job, then his parents. Though his relationship with them had never been strong, it hit him hard. And now with finances tight, Kate and Dan's home looked as unfinished as it did when they moved in two years prior. The couple turned thirty within weeks of each other: broke, angry, and without the family they'd longed for.

Kate sighed and flicked the radio off, sparing Dan from any more Waylon Jennings.

"Thanks," he murmured, reaching out and touching her thigh.

She noticed his hesitation. They'd grown awkward together.

"Where do you want me to drop you off?"

Kate's courier work would keep her busy most days, long hours for low pay, but they needed it. Dan spent his time job hunting with little success.

He tries, Kate thought. *Every damn day.*

She peeked at him from the corner of her eye. He had a little more grey in his short, brown hair, a few more lines in his boyish, open face. At that moment, it looked like stone as he psyched himself up for another day handing out resumes.

"Anywhere here will do."

Kate indicated and pulled in, thinking of what she could say to make things better, anything to close—just a little—the canyon that had formed between them.

Dan opened his door and hung one leg out of the car.

"Hey," Kate smiled, taking his hand in hers. "Let's get takeout later. Couple of beers. I hear that new Marvel show's pretty good. Maybe we can watch a few episodes."

Dan blinked in confusion. A quick smile lit up his face. "Yeah, sounds good. See you later then?"

Kate leaned over and kissed him on the cheek. She felt his lips brush her skin.

"Go get 'em, Dan. You got this."

She watched him leave and returned the wave he threw over his shoulder. Kate felt lighter, positive, a sensation that had been alien to her over the past year. Smiling, she flicked Waylon Jennings back on and checked her route for the day.

"Mr. Paul Holloway, looks like you're up first." She smiled as she drove past Dan, a grin plastered on his face, resumes clutched in his hands.

Her thoughts turned to their evening plans. It had been months since they watched a show together, even longer since they shared takeout.

"Think I'll order pizza. He always loves that."

⋄────⋄────⋄

"Two stops left." Kate smiled as she parked outside of her latest port-of-call, a Joseph Collins, whose delivery took up most of the room in her truck. His house—more a ranch on the outskirts of Portland—lay the furthest from her starting point, too, but the remaining two stops were on her route home. Her stomach fluttered a little, nerves from her upcoming house-date with Dan. "Let's get this done."

She hopped out of the truck and glanced around, the day's heat still lingering well into the late afternoon. After turning off the main route, she hadn't seen another vehicle. Her job took her to all sorts of places, but something about remote locations like that one always gave her pause. More often than not, she'd scoot a package up to the front door and leave without a signature, marking the delivery as "not at home."

But Kate couldn't do that.

The recipient left instructions saying he had to remove his delivery from the truck and count each item. It happened now and then. Kate knew folks could get really particular.

Didn't mean she had to like it.

Sighing, she flicked her blonde ponytail over her shoulder, wiped a sheen of sweat from her forehead, and plastered a smile on her face. A fence ringed the ranch, and a stone path led towards its door. Kate followed the walkway, eyeing the surrounding tall trees.

"Pretty," she muttered, pushing away thoughts of people watching her from behind the trunks. "Might be nice to live out here, if you enjoy the solitude."

The steps to the ranch groaned with her weight. A CCTV camera stared down from above the mahogany-coloured door, an intercom next to it. With a shrug, Kate pressed it.

"Hello? Can you see me? Delivery for Joseph Collins."

Kate tapped her foot as silence answered her.

She lifted her fist, intent on knocking, but a sign reading "Visitors Please Use The Intercom" made her hestitate. She glanced around again; aside from her truck, with its engine idling beyond the fence, she appeared alone.

"Maybe he's gone out. Don't see a car."

She fished her cell out of her pocket. *4:00 p.m. Damn. Want to get home before six, order the pizza before Dan arrives. Could just leave this dude's boxes here...No one will nab them, right?*

Kate nodded, her decision made. She had tried to follow her instructions, but it wasn't her fault Collins didn't answer. She'd load up the dolly, drop off the delivery, then hightail it out of there.

Back to civilisation.

She turned and took a step towards her van, but a *creak* made her freeze.

"Hello there. You caught me working in the basement. Thanks for waiting. I'm running low on supplies."

Kate looked over her shoulder at the voice. A grey-haired, bespectacled man in beige overalls smiled at her, wiping his hands on a rag. She felt the weight lift from her stomach as she returned his grin.

She enjoyed chatting with old men. They reminded her of her dad and how she missed him. She and Dan waiting so long to marry, not having her father walk her down the aisle, stuck out as the biggest regret in her life, one she punished her husband for, which she knew wasn't fair. She'd delayed their wedding day more than he had.

"Hey, no problem. My docket says you want to count the inventory?"

The man hesitated, blinking, then looked away from her face.

"You okay? You're Joseph Collins, aren't you?"

He stuffed the rag into his pocket. "Yes, that's me. Sorry, it's just...Don't get many visitors out here. Counting my order, hope that isn't a problem?"

Kate smiled again. "No, happens all the time. It's in the truck."

His footsteps followed as she walked down the stairs, a spring in her step. She'd be on the road again soon, and that meant just two more stops before a night in with Dan, saving their relationship. Kate's stomach twisted at that prospect. How had they let it drift so much? When had they stopped communicating, other than the endless sniping and passive-aggressive remarks? She didn't know if they could go back to the start again, didn't know if it were possible, but she wanted to try.

Joseph's voice caught her attention, but she missed the words. "Sorry, miles away."

He laughed. "No problem, miss. I just asked, 'you had a busy day?' "

"Sorry, things on my mind. Quiet out here. Makes my thoughts wander."

The old man chuckled once more as she led him to the back of the truck. "Sure, plenty of time to think out here, no doubt about that. Say, what's your name?"

She paused at the vehicle's rear, eyeing Joseph. He stared back, face open, an amiable smile twinkling his eyes.

"I guess I know yours. What's the harm? Name's Kate."

Joseph's face slackened, just for a moment, so fast she thought it could have been her imagination. That steady grin swam back to the surface in the blink of an eye.

But she saw it.

"You okay?"

"My wife's name is Kate."

"What a coincidence, huh? She gonna come out and help you count?"

His eyes didn't leave hers. He didn't even blink. "She's dead."

Despite the sweltering heat, Kate's skin chilled. The way he stared at her, the flat tone in how he spoke those words, like a reflex. She could sense Joseph's pain on the still air, and she'd put her foot right in it.

"I'm sorry," she stammered. "I didn't mean anything—"

"How could you know? Please, don't worry about it. Years have passed." Joseph nodded at the truck. "My delivery?"

Kate fumbled for her fob to unlock the doors. *Change the subject. Anything. Just say some words that won't remind him of his dead wife.* Images of Dan swam into her mind with the unbidden thought of losing him forever. She shoved that away.

The doors swung open, revealing two stacks of boxes for Joseph, twenty in total.

"Ah...I don't make a habit of asking, but what is this? Had me curious since they loaded my truck this morning."

She watched as Joseph ran his eyes over the delivery, counting each box, before he nodded. "Borax. You know what that is?"

Kate fired up her handheld scanner, prepping it for his signature. It so happened she knew the chemical. "My daddy used it to treat fungal infections in horses' hooves, but I don't see any around here."

Joseph chuckled and took the device, their fingertips brushing. He didn't seem to notice. He squiggled his signature and laid the scanner back in the truck on top of a pile of old paperwork. "That's one use, sure. It's versatile, quite a marvellous substance. I need it as a preservative."

With a sigh, Kate pulled her dolly from the truck and hauled the boxes on it. It would take her two trips. "Taxidermy?"

"Sure." Joseph eyed the boxes again. "Do you have a spare dolly? I can take the other stack. It'd be my pleasure."

"You don't mind?" Kate asked, already pulling her spare from the back. Joseph *did* offer, and the day's heat made her shirt stick to her skin. "Thanks."

They made quick work of stacking the boxes of borax and were soon wheeling them back to Joseph's house. Kate didn't look forward to hoisting them up onto the porch, but she'd be back on the road in no time. The next two drop-offs were small enough to slip through a mailbox. Traffic permitting, she'd be home in time to freshen up and order food before Dan returned.

"How long have you been married?" The question made her stumble as they approached the porch. "Forgive me, I saw the wedding band on your finger."

"An eye for details, huh? Guess that comes with the taxidermy. Three years in September."

"Kate and I were married for forty years."

The dollies crunched in the dirt as they came to a stop before the porch. Kate's heart went out to him. She remembered her daddy when her mom had passed, how he lived like a shadow until he followed her.

"You must've got hitched young."

Joseph picked up the boxes, four at once. Kate's eyebrows rose. The old man was stronger than he looked by far.

"Teenagers, both just eighteen, high school sweethearts. These past five years have been tough, but my work distracts me well enough. Do you mind helping me bring these into the house? My wallet's in there. You deserve a tip."

Kate grabbed two boxes and followed him up the stairs. It looked like he could carry more with ease, but she didn't see the harm.

"It's not company policy, but what they don't know..." Her words broke off as she and Joseph approached the open front door. Familiar music drifted out from inside. "You like Waylon Jennings? No way! Me too."

Joseph shrugged and paused as Kate moved ahead of him into the house. "My wife and I saw him live plenty of times. Have a few of his LPs signed, too. Would you like to see them?"

Kate bit her lip. Her eagerness to get back on her route and finish her deliveries nipped at her, but how could she say no to *signed* Jennings LPs? It wasn't like she could get any of hers autographed. He'd been dead almost twenty years.

A record player stood near an armchair in the corner, shelves with LPs and books surrounding it. Wood panels lined the walls of the large, open-plan living area, and a cozy-looking maroon carpet ran across the floor. Kate spied two archways leading off into the back of the house and a white door in the far corner. Even from where she stood, she saw the latch and bolt locking it.

"Where do you want these?" she asked, glancing over her shoulder.

"By the door over there."

Kate nodded and glanced at the walls again, a missing detail jumping out at her. "That your workshop? I thought you'd have this place filled with animal heads and all that."

She laid the boxes down by the door with care and a sigh. She spun around, hands on her hips.

Joseph stood a step toward her, his hands behind his back.

"I never said I was a taxidermist."

Kate had no time to react. He threw himself at her,

slamming her into the white door. It rattled with their impact. She thought she heard muffled screams from the other side, but Joseph's hands grabbed her head, a cloth in his hand pressed against her face.

Waylon Jennings continued to croon. Her thoughts swam as she struggled, images of Dan arriving home, finding it empty.

Strength left her limbs as she faded into darkness.

⸎

Kate sat up with a jerk, chains rattling against stone as she tried to scramble to her feet. The restraints fastened around her wrists and ankles cut into her skin and sent her crashing to the icy floor, pain blooming in her face as her cheek slammed against the surface.

She peered into the darkness, eyes wide, searching for anything to tell her where she lay. To her left, she discovered a door, a red light above it the only source of illumination she could find. But it gave her something to look at other than pitch-black.

Kate stared at it, drinking in the details to stop her hammering heart, the rising panic in her chest that made her want to scream her lungs dry. She remembered the other door, the one Joseph had slammed her into before knocking her out. The one in front of her appeared to be made from the same material, but it didn't have a bolt that she could see.

In the red gloom, it seemed to pulsate in her vision. She wanted to look away, close her eyes, do something other than staring at the crimson-hued door, but Kate knew the alternative would swallow her. She glanced at it, the black claustrophobia threatening to overwhelm. Her heart rate picked up; her breathing quickened. Kate focused on the door again.

Then she remembered the muffled screams.

"Hello?" Her voice cracked and fell flat in the smothering gloom. "Is anyone there?"

Silence answered.

She shifted to her back, clinking chains disturbing the quiet, and reached out with her fingers. The stone felt smooth, cold, but the chains felt like ice when she found them. Kate followed them towards the wall and moved her body that way, pushing herself into an upright position with her back flat. Her face ached, as did the part of her skull that smashed against the door.

"Dan," she whispered. "Come find me. Please."

Her mind whirled. Someone would come looking. They'd have to. Kate's route that day had left a trail, one anyone could follow. When she didn't return, Dan would call the police, and her company would see her last delivery point.

Simple.

She just had to stay alive.

Kate eyed the door again. The hope surging in her chest tapered off. Whatever lay behind there turned her stomach to water, her imagination whispering dark thoughts that she tried to ignore in the corner of her mind.

"I heard screams. I know I did. That sick bastard had someone else down here before me...What happened to them?"

The door didn't answer.

Kate tested her restraints, wincing as each pull dug into her flesh. She gave up with a snarl; the iron felt tough and well-fixed into the wall and floor.

Thoughts played in her mind; she'd watched her fair share of true crime documentaries, read the books. Kate shut her brain down before panic at what Joseph could do to her sent her crazy. She should have seen the signs—an old man, alone, living on a big ranch in the middle of nowhere. Only, those things happened to other people, faceless strangers she never met and only read about online.

Not her.

But now it had.

The door opened, and Joseph, bathed in the blood-red light, watched her.

Kate shrank back, pressing into the wall, making herself as small as possible. He leered at her, a smile plastered on the face she once considered friendly, now psychotic, one detached from reality. She'd just seen the old man, looked past his dominating height, the broadness in his shoulders. Kate had seen him lift four boxes filled with borax like a package of feathers and knew he could have lugged more without breaking a sweat.

Her job took her to all kinds of places, made her meet all sorts of people. She'd dropped her guard, a cardinal sin when alone and dealing with strangers, letting daydreams of her evening with Dan take over her judgement.

Tears welled in her eyes, and still, Joseph didn't move from where he watched, framed in the red light by the darkness behind him.

"What do you want with me?" Kate's voice shook as tears ran down her face.

Joseph cocked his head, a slight V forming between his eyebrows. He took a step forward and closed the door behind him, locking it with a key selected from a bunch he slipped into his pocket.

"I'm sorry, Kate. You're safe now. With me. Where you belong."

He shuffled forward, heading down the stairs, a shadow in the darkness. He knelt before her, and Kate could see his eyes shining, glowing with fever.

"No, no, no. Please, let me go." She held out her hands, the chains rattling. "I don't belong here. Let me go, before people come looking. I promise I won't tell anymore."

Joseph chuckled in response.

"Who do you suppose will look for you, Kate?"

"My husband. My company will know where I am. They'll check the delivery logs." She forced warning into her voice, tried to make it sound like she had his back. "You're in big trouble, but if you let me go, it'll all be okay."

A bright light startled her, causing a scream to escape her lips. Kate blinked as Joseph held a small torch in her face. She twisted her head away from the glare, but he reached out and caught her chin, held it still like a vice.

Her eyes streamed as he emerged from the spots swimming in her vision. Joseph peered at her, head cocked, smile fixed in place.

"You're so much like her, you know. You even have the same name. You're a little shorter, of course, and you don't wear your makeup the same way. That can all be fixed."

"Fixed?" Kate spat, twisting her head from Joseph's grip. She glanced around the stone basement, empty other than the red-lit door and a flight of wooden steps leading upstairs. "Didn't you hear what I said? My husband will come for me. The police. You're screwed."

Joseph sighed, then pushed himself to his feet.

"Do you think I am a fool? You have slept for hours. I completed your rounds and ditched the truck. When any-one comes out here, they will have no reason to suspect a thing. You are not the first guest I have had in my home. Oh, no...you are not. But I very much hope you will be the last. So much like her. Kate." Joseph closed his eyes when he spoke her name, then licked his lips like he savoured each letter. The finest bite he'd ever had.

He spun on his heel and climbed the stairs, the wood complaining under his weight as Kate sobbed, alone in the darkness with only the crimson door for company.

Time passed in a haze. Kate either wept until she thought she'd drained her tear ducts or slept in a half-dream, one where Dan's face would emerge from the gloom, leering at her until it changed into Joseph's. Sometimes, she'd open her eyes and the old man would be there, watching her.

Twice, he'd brought her a bucket to relieve herself, turning his back when she did. A part of her—a fraction of her being that disgusted Kate—felt thankful to him then, that she didn't have to urinate on the stone floor like a dog.

She hadn't even waited for Joseph to leave before the tears flowed.

Joseph brought her food, too, a simple ham sandwich with the crusts cut off, served on a plastic plate meant for a toddler.

"Eat," he said the second time, that feverish glow making his eyes bright. "Please. I don't want you to starve."

Kate turned away in silence and waited for him to leave before gorging on it, her wrists screaming at the heaviness of the restraints.

She stared at the door to pass the time. Before, she'd shied away from what lay behind it. Now, she tried to guess, her thoughts turning darker each time she considered the red-hued portal. At first, she'd have put money on it being some secret sex room filled with lurid devices to turn Joseph on, get him off. But he had made no advances on her; in fact, their interactions remained asexual. Instead, he treated Kate with a perverse reverence which grew each time he visited her. The old man stared at her, eyes bright, drinking her in. She knew he saw his dead wife.

The last time he brought her food, he pondered her wedding band, his face slack and without expression.

"It is not the same," he mumbled, a shadow passing over his face, twisting into a hundred expressions all mixed together. "Take it off."

"I can't. I don't want to lose it."

And she didn't. She wanted to cling to it, to feel it pressing against her bone, a reminder of Dan, a metallic memory of her marriage. One on the edge of failure, but they *could* save it. If only she could escape. Kate didn't want to anger Joseph, do something that sent him over the edge of violence, but she couldn't take it off. It would feel like giving up.

"But it is not the one I gave you."

She met his eyes. Joseph looked at her, but she got the impression he didn't see *her.* He saw a different time, another life.

Someone else.

The other Kate.

She tried to smile, hoping the old man would ignore the fat tears falling down her cheeks.

"Maybe soon," she whispered through the fake simper that hurt her face. "When we know each other better, I'll take it off."

Joseph blinked and surged to his feet, his surprising speed making Kate flinch, but she didn't want to look away. She stared at him, her lips still fixed in a smile she felt he wanted to see.

"Of course."

Joseph strode to the door, unlocked it, and slipped in. A light blinked into life in the room beyond it as he did, but the doorway closed behind him before Kate could make out what hid there. A sterile, clean smell wafted over to her, and she drank it in, if only so a fresh scent could mask the stench of sweat and fear pouring from her.

She'd fallen into a fitful slumber since, but Joseph hadn't come out of the room. Kate didn't know how much time had passed, and she'd long given up trying to judge it.

She tried counting the toilet breaks, the amount of food Joseph had brought her, but they all merged. It could have been days, might have been a week.

"Dan, I hope you're looking for me. Please don't give up."

Kate turned towards the door, watching, wondering what her captor did behind there. She hadn't forgotten those screams she'd heard. She stared, her eyes growing heavy again, lulled by the red light.

She thought her imagination played tricks on her at first, or that her brain craved some kind of noise so invented one in the silence, but she sat a little straighter and strained her hearing.

Her eyes widened.

From the other side of the door, she heard it. A faint whirring sound, like an engine. A machine, at least. Maybe a paper shredder, of all things. It buzzed a little while longer until it cut off with just as much warning as it had started.

The door swung open, and an iron grip squeezed her heart, stole the breath from her lungs. Joseph stood there, lit by the room's white light, his clothes and skin caked in blood, his face like stone. He closed the door without turning, locking it with the key he carried, then stomped toward her, his heavy footsteps echoing against the stone as the basement plunged into darkness once more.

Kate whimpered, shrank against the wall as he came to her.

This is it. No, please, no. Dan, I'm sorry. I'm so sorry.

The stairs leading upstairs creaked as Joseph ascended them.

She sobbed, confusion and relief exploding from her. "Please, let me go. I've done nothing to you. Everything hurts. I'm scared. I just want to go home."

She heard him stop moving. Kate flicked her eyes to the red light above the door, just for something other than complete darkness to stare at as she listened to his breathing break the silence.

"You promised you would never leave me, Kate. Just as I promised you. We won't break our word, will we?"

Her limbs shook with built up fear and unspent adrenaline as Joseph resumed his climb, leaving her alone with the door once more.

◇━◦──◦──◦━◇

"Kate, I have something for you."

She struggled to open her eyes, lost in dreams of her former life. They hadn't comforted her; they'd appeared too realistic, letting her relive her hours of work, the tension at home with Dan, the nights spent in separate rooms. The things left unsaid. Kate woke with longing inside her, a wish for things to be different, and regret.

"What is it?" Her dry lips cracked as she spoke. She ran her tongue over them, but she had no moisture in her mouth.

"Water. Food. A change of clothes." Joseph flicked his torch on, illuminating a pile of assortments by his feet. "Look, it's that dress you always loved. You look so beautiful in it, even though you told me you would not wear it anymore, that you were not a young woman, no matter how much I begged you. Would you wear it now?"

Kate eyed the pile. Beneath the sandwich on the plastic plate and a bottle of water lay a floral dress that looked like it had been left in a time capsule from the 1970s. She had no idea how long she'd worn her clothes, and she didn't want to give the old man the satisfaction, but the idea of getting out of the chains, even for a few minutes, tempted her.

"Joseph," she smiled, meeting his eyes. They burned with that familiar bright fever. "The chains...I can't change with them on."

She watched him study her ankles and wrists, his breath catching as he lingered on her wedding band.

"Of course," he muttered. "I've brought a salve for your skin. I am sorry I had to do this, Kate, but you haven't been yourself in quite some time."

She hesitated. How had she missed the sheer craziness pouring from Joseph when they met? Had he hid it so well, and now she'd peeled the corner of his sanity and saw it all, revealed without limits? It seemed he *believed* she and his Kate were the same person.

"I know. I'm sorry. I promise I'll do better." Her mind whirled as she thought of an angle, any way she could escape. "The salve sounds great. My wrists and ankles really do hurt, but that isn't your fault. It's mine for not doing as I'm told."

Joseph nodded as he fished the keys from his pocket and selected a small one from the ring. "You have always been spirited—one of the reasons I love you—but sometimes you do take it too far. It is what these chains are for, remember?"

He popped one from her wrist; relief flooded through her limb, along with pain as the blood rushed freely into her hand. She fought the tears back from her eyes and the urge to wince, not to mention the desire to hit Joseph with all the strength she had. No, Kate would wait for the right time to act. He continued to unfasten her, pins and needles making her feet ache.

"I remember," Kate bit out, rubbing her wrist, massaging some life back into them. The skin felt chaffed and blistered beneath her fingers.

Joseph reached out and took them, his grip gentle but firm.

She watched beneath her brows as he rubbed the salve into her wounds, working with care like he would on a frightened animal. *That's what I am. That's what the other Kate was. Possessions to him. Ones to do as we're told, to be looked after.* Another thought dawned on her. *The screams... could that have been her? No, she's been dead five years. Hasn't she?*

"There," he murmured, inspecting the chafe marks on her wrists, "much better. Would you like me to turn my back while you change?"

Kate eyed the pile of clothing, worried about how far she could push her luck.

"Would you mind going into the other room? Just to give me some privacy. I've been in these clothes a while. Might not be a pretty sight."

Joseph crouched in front of her, unmoving, watching. She held her breath, not knowing how he'd react.

"You won't try anything funny, will you?" he asked, eyes narrowed. The V between his eyebrows formed again. Joseph pointed towards the stairs. "I locked that door behind me. There's nowhere for you to go. I am trusting you, Kate. Do not let me down again. You know how it disappoints me."

Kate shook her head, frightened to make a noise in case it made him change his mind. Nodding, he stood up and approached the red-lit door, unlocked it, and passed through. Before closing it, he paused.

"Knock when you are ready."

The lights inside the room blinked on as he walked in, though the closing door plunged the basement into darkness again. A shuddering breath escaped from Kate's lips, her limbs watery and weak. For the first time in days, chains didn't restrain her, though she still remained trapped.

"Progress," she told herself, leaning on the wall as she stood up on unsteady legs, like a newborn foal.

She inched her bare foot forward, and her toes touched the pile. She peeled the clothes from her skin, shuddering as they clung to her, and tossed them aside before grabbing the water bottle. Kate took a mouthful before pouring the liquid over her. She scrubbed at her body as best she could, picturing days' worth of filth running off her.

Next, she gathered up the dress and pulled it over her head, then bent down to retrieve the sandwich, jamming it into her mouth. She thought about running to the stairs, trying the door above, but she knew Joseph would have locked it. *Might hear the steps creak, too.*

Instead, she approached the other door, the one the old man had disappeared behind, the one he spent so much time in. Rubbing her wrists and grimacing, Kate considered her position. Unchained, dressed in fresh clothes, fed and cleaned. She'd made progress on getting Joseph to drop his guard. She just needed to keep hers up and play him. He'd make a mistake, and she'd capitalise on it.

"Slow and steady wins the race," she muttered, standing in front of the door, the light above turning her bare skin red.

Kate reached out and knocked twice on the door, then stepped back.

It swung open, like Joseph had waited on the other side, hand on the handle. He closed the door behind him but didn't lock it. Not that time. Under the red light, Kate could see his feverish eyes fixed on her, tears welling in them as he drank her in.

"Perfect," he whispered, cocking his head to one side. "You haven't aged a day since you last wore this, Kate. How is that?"

Careful now.

"It's just the light, Joseph."

"No." He took a step forward, trembling hand outstretched. "It's more than that. You're—"

An alarm from the room behind the door blared, cutting him off. Joseph swung his head that way, then towards the stairs leading to the house above.

"What is it?" Kate asked, daring not to hope.

He scowled, the red light above him reminding her of

the time he stalked by her, caked in blood.

"A visitor. Stay here. I will make sure they leave and that you are safe."

Hope rose in her chest as he walked past her. Had someone come to look for her? She listened to his footsteps as he ascended, waited until the door closed behind him, the sound of the bolt sliding shut.

Joseph hadn't locked the other door.

She bit her lip. What harm could a look do? She could glance around the room, see what her captor hid there, and have the door closed before he returned. There might even be something of use inside.

Kate approached, grasped the cold handle, and pulled. As she passed under the red light, the darkness inside the room disappeared as automatic lights turned on and took her breath away.

It resembled an operating theatre mixed with a mausoleum, one designed by a madman.

In the centre of the room lay an empty table, one with restraints. A trolley with trays lay next to it, filled with scissors, scalpels, and other types of operating utensils, jars of borax stacked beneath it. To the left sat a large, stainless steel meat grinder. Blood leaked from the sides and dripped to the otherwise clean floor. Vomit rose in her stomach as she stared at it, but something else had stolen the breath from her lungs.

A display lined the back of the room. She approached it, legs trembling. As she passed the tray, her fingers worked of their own accord and snatched a pair of surgical scissors, the blades the size of her palm. Kate continued to walk, transfixed by what she'd found.

Standing upright in plastic coffins, eyes closed, were the preserved bodies of women, like collectible Barbie dolls.

Wearing various shades of makeup, differing hair colours and fashions, the women stood, untouched by time. Icy fingers crept up Kate's spine, her eyes wide as she took in the details. The women couldn't have looked more different—some slim and petite, others tall. She approached the one in the centre who looked older than the rest. A stitched wound stood out angry across her throat. Kate's gaze fell to a wedding band on her finger.

None of the others wore one.

A part of her mind whispered that the woman's eyes would snap open.

"The original Kate," she murmured, squeezing the scissors as she held them against her chest. "He killed her. He murdered them all."

"Because none of them were you, Kate."

She spun, hiding the scissors behind her back. Joseph stood in the doorway, his face blank. The look made her want to scream.

"You didn't lock the door." She took a step back and almost jumped when her shoulders rubbed against the display.

Joseph jerked forwards. "A visitor came. Looking for someone who went missing. A delivery driver, can you believe that? I sent him away and told him I hope he finds who he is looking for."

Dan! Kate felt tears sting her eyes. Her husband could still be upstairs, so close to her. She just needed to run. Escape, as fast as she could. She gripped the scissors so hard her forearm shook.

"Who are all these people?"

Joseph's eyes flicked over the display lining the walls. "Her. Though none of them are Kate. Just you."

"None of these women look like me!" Kate threw a look over her shoulder at Joseph's dead wife. "I don't look a thing like her, either. You killed them all!"

He moved forward again, head cocked to one side, a confused look in his eyes. "They all said they weren't you, Kate. But I knew they were. Though some...some, I could tell. I fed them to the meat grinder. I had a guest just before you came home, Kate. She wasn't you."

Her stomach flipped.

The screams.

Joseph had a woman chained when she'd arrived and ground her bones to a bloody paste as Kate lay in the next room. Her vision spun and panic pulsated within her. Kate wanted to sink to the floor, to cry, to give up. But Dan had come for her, and she needed to escape. She wouldn't become another doll preserved in a madman's basement.

"Come." Joseph took another step forward and held out his hand. "You should not be in here. This is my private place. You know better. Back to the chains until you learn. You will learn, won't you?"

A crash echoing from above stopped Kate from answering. Joseph's face shifted, turning from blank to stone in seconds. He spun, heading for the door to his chamber, keys in hand.

Kate ran and leapt at him.

She crashed into him, knocking him to the ground face-first, and plunged the scissors into where his neck and shoulder met.

He screamed and tried to push her off, but she held on and, with a snarl, stabbed him again, deeper. The scissors stuck out of him as Joseph howled in pain, blood spurting from the open wound in his neck onto the white floor, splashing across Kate's face. The will to live took over, pushed away the repulsion she felt at plunging metal into another person's body. He deserved it.

She snatched the keys from his slack grip and surged to her feet, slipping a little in the blood. She hurried up the stairs, taking two at a time, heading for the door above. As she reached it, it opened.

Dan stood there, anger turning to astonishment. "Kate?"

"Dan! We've gotta get out of here. Now!"

"I knew you were here. Knew it! I worked through your delivery route, but that old guy...mentioned your name, showed him your picture. Thought he wasn't gonna give it back to me."

Kate smiled, tears running down her face, mixing with the blood. "Dan, I love you, but we've gotta go. Now!"

A noise whistled by her head, like the sound of wind tearing.

He jerked, eyes wide, and stared down at his chest.

The bloody pair of scissors stuck from his sternum, blood blossoming and turning his white T-shirt red. Dan opened his mouth, and his brow furrowed as they both stared at the silver handles protruding from his flesh. He looked at Kate and sank to his knees.

Rough hands grabbed her ankle and pulled. Yelling, she crashed onto the stairs, the wood groaning with the impact. Blood splashed into her eyes as her head smacked against a step. Dizzy, she glanced behind her. Joseph, crimson pumping from his neck wounds, held one of her ankles, his teeth bared.

"You swore you would never leave me. You swore it! Yet here you are, leaving me again. I cannot allow that, Kate. Do not make me punish you again."

She felt his fingers crawl up her leg as he pulled her back down the stairs towards the basement, toward his room filled with dead dolls. Throwing a wild look upwards, she saw Dan's chest still rise and fall as he breathed. With a snarl, Kate kicked with her free leg.

She felt cartilage crunch as her foot connected with Joseph's nose, felt his blood and snot leak onto her bare sole. He cried out, but still he held on. Kate kicked again.

And again.

And again.

Screaming the hatred, frustration, fear, and grief out of her body, she hammered her foot into Joseph's stubborn face until, at last, his fingers slipped from her leg.

She scrambled to her feet, back towards Dan. She had to work fast. The bastard who'd kidnapped her wouldn't stop. Not until he owned her. Or put her on display in his psychotic mausoleum. Kate knew that, but she couldn't leave Dan.

"Come on, Dan. Lean on me."

His groans answered her as she, stumbling under his weight, hoisted him up. She steadied herself and swung the door shut, fumbling the key into the lock. Her unsteady hand betrayed her, and she kept missing, the metal sliding around the keyhole.

Joseph screamed her name. The wood creaked as the old man came for her.

She closed her eyes. Dan's heavy weight leaned on her, and his body juddered as he tried to breathe, blood leaking from his chest, warming her. Opening her eyes, she jammed the key in the lock and turned it.

"That'll give us time," she snapped, spinning around. "Let's get out of here."

Dan gurgled in response. She glanced at him as she hauled him through the living room—no Waylon Jennings this time—and forced the panic down deep into her stomach. His skin had turned paler than a bottle of milk. Sweat beaded all over his skin as the blood pumped from his body. She pulled him through the doorway and saw Dan's car waiting at the bottom of the path.

The sun beat down on her, just as it did when she first arrived at Joseph's ranch, but she paid it no mind. She had to reach the car. She knew the wound in Dan's chest would kill him without getting help.

From behind, the door to the basement rattled. Then

it boomed.

"Shit," she screamed, pulling Dan across the gravel.

A thought popped into her head.

A sick little idea that made her stomach flip.

She could leave Dan and run. Get into the car, escape. Kate rejected it as she ground her teeth and pulled harder.

When she was around twenty paces from the car, Joseph destroyed the door in a loud *thump* of exploding wood.

"Kate! You are mine! No one else will have you. You do not get to walk away again!"

Blind panic moved her limbs, added strength to them. With a scream, she half lifted Dan the rest of the way, shuttling him to the car. They thudded against the passenger side as she fumbled in his jeans pocket, him groaning in pain as she jostled him. Her fingers made contact, and she unlocked the vehicle, shoving him with as much care as she could into the rear seats. She flung herself into the driver's seat and stared through the side window.

Joseph staggered through the house's entrance, stumbled down the porch. Even from that distance, she could see the ruination her foot had caused in his face, the blood making his flannel shirt stick to his body. Even with his hand pressed against his neck, holding his life source in, the old man still came for her.

Kate blinked through the blood sliding from the cut in her head, stuck the key in the ignition and turned. The engine spluttered into life. She jammed her foot on the accelerator, and the car screeched as she spun the wheel, turning and aiming it at the house.

It crashed through the wooden fence, sending splinters in all directions as she headed for Joseph. Before she crashed into him, she saw his feverish, bright eyes open wide.

Her triumphant grin as she bore down on him the last thing he ever saw.

The car jerked as the hood slammed into Joseph, sending his broken body spinning into the air like a rag doll. He crashed onto the windscreen, the impact of his head against the glass sending a spiderweb of cracks across it. The blood oozing from his forehead left a stain.

Kate put the car in reverse and screeched away, his lifeless body dropping to the gravel. She spun the car and headed away from the ranch, her foot floored, the windscreen wipers smearing Joseph's blood.

"Hang on, Dan," she cried over her shoulder. "I'll get you to a hospital. They'll take care of you, and I will too. I'll never leave you, Dan. I promise."

Just what Joseph wanted you to say to him, a small voice in the back of her head whispered to her.

She bit her lip and glanced in the rearview mirror, squinting. Through the dust trailing behind her car, she thought she saw a figure in the distance, a hand pressed to his neck, watching her race away. She blinked, and the figure vanished, if she'd ever seen it at all.

Dan coughed and gargled as the car bumped down the dirt road.

"Hey," she called, accelerating, her eyes flicking to the rear mirror. She saw *something.* "Stay with me. Remember, we promised we'd be together forever, right? I'm not letting you break that. Not today. You're not going to die, Dan. I won't let you."

She gritted her teeth as she sent the car spinning onto the highway and smooth asphalt, ignoring the whispering voice in her head.

Now you sound just *like Joseph.*

David Green
About the Author

David Green is a writer of dark fiction. Born in Manchester, UK and living in Galway, Ireland, David grew up with gloomy clouds above his head, and rain water at his feet, which has no doubt influenced his dark scribblings. David is the author of the Pushcart Prize nominated novelette Dead Man Walking, and is excited for his fantasy series, Empire of Ruin, debuting in June 2021 from Eerie River Publishing.

Newsletter: https://tinyurl.com/y6ah8brp
www.twitter.com/davidgreenwrite
www.davidgreenwriter.com
https://www.facebook.com/davidgreenwriter

THE SWIRLY PEOPLE
PAUL O'NEILL

Cuthbert Watson wasn't sick. He was the only one in his house who could say such a thing. His dad's racking cough barrelled down the hall as Cuthbert lay on his pillow, arguing with himself about phoning an ambulance. As long as he could hear his mum and dad spluttering the night away, they should be fine, he hoped. It was when silence fell that worms seemed to wriggle under his skin.

He clutched the top of his covers, an electric buzz swarming inside his skull. The sound built as he clenched his eyes shut.

"Go away." He punched himself in the head as he spoke. "Go away. Go away."

The noise melted away, and the pressure in his temples faded. Sounds of distant coughing and spluttering returned.

Since they locked their home off, shutting out the outside world, Cuthbert tortured himself, imagining they'd cough their souls right out of their bodies as he dialled for an ambulance, watching them perish one by one. In his mind, the ambulance always arrived too late. Then, he'd be the man of the house—a mantle he did not want.

Duncan, his older brother, slept on the bunk below him. Cuthbert leaned over the side of the bed, hanging up-side-down, blood pressing in his temples. Dunc's sweaty face glowed in the streetlight that spilled in through the drafty window.

Cuthbert focused on Dunc's chest, unable to detect any movement. He narrowed his eyes, ignoring his pulsing, protesting brain. He'd never seen his brother look so pale, so weak. Dunc snorted, and Cuthbert almost fell off the bunk.

A giggle escaped him as he sat back up in his own bed, the edges of his vision pulsing in the aftershock of his fright. He tasted the salty stench of sweat and dirty tissues as his breath returned to normal.

Rest was what his family needed. Since the bug descended on the house four days before, he'd barely slept two hours at a time, bursting awake at every cough or wheeze.

His brother continued to haul in wet breaths as Cuthbert gazed up at the white ceiling. His eyes went wide as he stared and stared, not blinking, wishing with all his bones that his family would wake the next day feeling spritely, ready to leave the house and take in the Scottish springtime air. He longed for a kick about with his dad. He'd even settle for a bruising from Dunc, as long as they were outside.

The white landscape above shifted and swirled as his eyes went dry. Cascading dots of light fell down like rain. A wave of dizziness crashed into him, eyes screaming for moisture.

He ignored the pain, continuing to stare. From that spot on the top bunk, he could almost touch the ceiling. It was one smooth lick of white paint, but when his eyes gazed into it, it changed. Swirls and grooves transformed, shifting around like thousands of fingerprints twisting, pushing down on the ceiling, reaching for him.

He hauled his race car duvet over his head. In his mind, he could hear the moist rubbing together of those shapes like maggots squirming over each other.

"Pull yourself together, ya idiot. They don't exist," said Cuthbert, sour breath steaming in the darkness under his covers. "You're not a kid anymore. They don't exist."

The Swirly People—that's what he'd named them when he was a wee boy. They'd always been there, their faces swirling and dancing above him. His mum wrote it off as some weird version of an imaginary friend.

"Go play with your Swirly People, sweetie," she'd say whenever she wanted rid of him.

They were a trick of the mind, a childish fancy. On New Year's Day, he'd resolved to rid himself of them, to finally grow up. Since that day, the Swirly People came every night, screaming their mute agony down at him.

He pulled the covers down below his eyes, something inside still curious as to what the creatures were. If he squinted the right way, he could see into their pulsing, static universe.

A face burst down at him. The contours of the ceiling ran over its toothless gums as if someone held a plastic bag over its head, suffocating it.

He hauled the covers over his head. The contents of his stomach were ready to catapult out of his mouth if he made the slightest movement. Under the thick cover, he realised he couldn't hear Dunc or the rest of his family.

He cursed the stupid illness that held his family in its grip. As soon as Dunc had taken to sleepwalking in his feverish state, Cuthbert swapped bunks with him, assuring him he was fine to sleep up top after refusing for so many years.

Oh, the Swirly People? They don't exist anymore. They never did. Just a fragment of his imagination is all they were.

He whipped the covers off, keeping his eyes closed, listening intently, relief flooding him when he heard his brother's pig-like snoring. He slowly opened one eye.

A hand pressed down from the ceiling as if the roof was white cellophane. It shook with effort as it reached, its long fingers splayed like it would burst through and grab him, crushing his skull into dust.

He leapt from the bed. A little *oomph* of pain jangled up his spine as he landed on the balls of his feet. He glanced at his sleeping brother, checked that he still breathed, then tiptoed out of the room to check on his parents.

◇━◇──◇━◇

Cuthbert glared at the ceiling in his parent's bedroom. It'd been years since he spent any proper time in there. Running the length of the ceiling was a minuscule crack. As he concentrated on it, the familiar wriggling patterns emerged, shadows dancing around like shapes behind static snow.

The Swirly People phased into life, pointing and

screaming down at his father. He'd never seen them outside his own room before.

Cuthbert held his breath. The muggy air of the hot spring day mingled with the harsh scent of cigarettes. Broken shapes slithered about on the ceiling. Handprints pushed down. The ceiling bowed under the pressure as if it were melting toffee. Pointed edges like alien fingers almost pierced their way through it, ripping into the real world.

"Spider up there, dude?" said his dad, struggling to sit up on his elbows, a dazed light in his normally bright eyes.

Cuthbert shook his head. The falling shapes vanished. He turned his attention to his bare-chested father, at his stubble of a beard that grew in rough patches like sickened clumps of grass.

"No," said Cuthbert. "Just...never mind."

"Huh. Minds me how you used to be terrified of—" A gargling cough erupted from his dad, his face turning beetroot red. He whacked at his thin chest and lay back on the bed, catching his breath. "You were just a couple of months old the first time. Screamed so loud I was running before I realised I was even awake. You just...gazed at the roof, all dreamy eyed, you know? Like you hadn't just screamed your lungs out. Had to shake you out of it. Never quite knew what you saw up there. Took you a while, but I'm glad you're over all that."

Molten pain built in Cuthbert's temples. He slammed his eyes closed. A murmuring, shifting noise built inside his head. They weren't real; they couldn't be real. Just a leftover from his childhood imagination, that's all. He was over all that now.

"You need anything from the kitchen?" said Cuthbert.

"No, I'm—" Another cough exploded from his dad. "No."

Cuthbert walked out the room, pausing in the doorway. "Dad? You'll shout on me if you feel any worse, right?"

He waited. The tension in his shoulders felt like two boulders hunched beneath his skin. He focused on the puddle of sweat that shone in the centre of his dad's chest as his lungs sucked in air like they'd forgotten how it was done.

He strode through to the living room where his mum slept fitfully on the couch, the alkaline odour of snotters and saliva lining the air. He didn't like that his parents slept in separate rooms. They'd decided not to "share each other's germs" so they didn't keep each other sick.

"What?" his mum croaked, sitting up, chucking her covers off. "Tell me it's not got you, too? My strong boy."

Cuthbert stared down at the discarded tissues dotting the carpet like sick snowballs. He wanted nothing more than to fold himself in the crook of his mother's arm and have her hum gentle melodies in his ear.

"I'm fine, Mum," said Cuthbert. "It's—"

She sighed. The act of keeping her eyes open looked a monumental effort. "Your father said you were the weakling. Sure proved us wrong, eh? You've been a superstar. Doing a fine job of being the man of the house."

Cuthbert cleared his throat, puffing out his chest. "As soon as you're all fit and ready, we'll take a nice long walk. As a family. That's my orders."

"That's my boy."

She closed her eyes and collapsed back onto the couch. Cuthbert hauled the covers over her, tucking her in. Her skin was hot enough to alarm the empty pit of his stomach.

He did his best not to look up, but soon his neck hurt as he glared at the moving ceiling. He could almost taste their dead earth smell as they raved above.

He marched into the kitchen. A wooden seat creaked under him as he stared out the window. He longed to run outside, the fresh air swirling around his bare neck, the green pine scent of the forest enveloping him as he entered the cool shade of the trees.

In the forest, he'd be free of the constant weight pressing down on his shoulders. Were the Swirly People there to take his family away? Was it a punishment for attempting to banish them from his life?

"You're making it up, Cuthbert," he said to himself. "No such thing, young man. You're letting your imagination run away with itself—that thing always had legs. Just another few days and we'll all be out of here. Just a few days, that's it. Don't lose it. They're relying on you. Step up, man."

He dug his nails into the palms of his hands, white crescents staring back up at him. "They don't exist, silly bones."

From down the hall, a nightmare whimper came. From his dad or Dunc, he couldn't tell. He stood, hovered for a second, then sat back down.

"There you go again, ya big bairn. No need to jump at every wee sound. They're fine. Everything will be fine." He tugged at his nest of hair, a sharp pain burning his scalp. "Get your act together."

It was his job to make sure death didn't claim any of his family. He was on watch, the "man of the house" as his mum had said.

White pain lit the centre of his forehead. He closed his eyes, rubbed his temples, wishing away the flood of heat that built up inside his skull. The scent of oil and iron was strong on the air.

Again, the nightmare groan came to him from the hall like a ghostly breeze.

"Dunc?"

He ran, shoving the bedroom door open. Dunc stood, swaying beside the bunk beds, his neck craned up at the ceiling. The strong, pungent sting of pee tweaked at Cuthbert's nostrils. A dark stain appeared over his brother's crotch, a growing oval spreading down one leg.

A sack of taut, translucent skin dropped from the ceiling. Swirling masses of agonised faces pressed against its rubbery surface. Their shrieks punctured his brain. The sack dropped inch by slow inch like melting rubber, as if some alien creature was about to give birth.

"Dunc?"

Cuthbert stepped forward. Shivers jolted up his arm as he held Dunc's wrist, his slow, weak pulse on his fingertips. He blinked away a heavy, dizzy spell.

Dunc's arm tensed. His entire body vibrated like he'd stuck a finger in a plug-socket. His eyes rolled in the back of his head, and he toppled back. Cuthbert held him upright, tightening his grip.

"You can't have him!" Cuthbert roared at the ceiling.

"What's that?" mumbled Dunc. "I won, didn't I? Now, I get my prize."

"Did you talk to them?"

"I don't wanna be here no more, all mushy inside. Take me..."

"Take you where, Dunc?"

Dunc pointed up, his head lolling like it was too heavy for his shoulders. "Up there in the forever place..."

The drooping mass had vanished. The ceiling was a smooth desert of shifting white sand. Hands slapped the other side of the ceiling, a sound like an army on the march.

"Snap out of it!" said Cuthbert, shaking Dunc.

Dunc convulsed, a shudder running all through him as he jolted awake. He glared at Cuthbert, a nasty bite in his eyes. "What is it, ya wee pillock?"

"The Swirly People, they—" Cuthbert looked up, his mouth hanging open as his words fizzled out.

Nothing.

"They were right there, I swear."

Dunc tugged at his oily hair, then drummed his fingers against his wet trouser leg, his eyes going wide. He darted under his covers. He'd smelled like an unwashed sock soaked in piss.

"Dunc, I'm sorry. I can't just let them take you."

"I'm sick of your crap about those damned people. Know how childish you sound? Wake me again, ya prick, and I'll knock your teeth out the back of your head, got me?"

Cuthbert glared up at the unending white of the ceiling, clenching and unclenching his fists. He felt his eyes go together. If he focused hard enough, he could see what was *beyond* the ceiling.

Shifting faces appeared, flying around like ghosts yelling in the night, mouths hung open in endless screams. A buzz like white noise filled his skull. One face peered down at him, the swirling mass of it drawing closer, its flame-like tail of a body trailing off like glistening waves.

"Numb-skull. Get to bed," whispered Dunc.

Cuthbert let go a breath. His family needed him. Needed him to grow out of that nonsense.

He stepped to a chest of drawers, took out a pair of Dunc's pyjama bottoms, and lay them on his pillow. Cold from the metal steps buzzed through his soles as he climbed into bed.

He closed his eyes tight, promising he wouldn't open them until morning.

"You never existed," said Cuthbert. "Now, go away."

⋄◦◦─◦──◦─◦◦⋄

In Cuthbert's dream, he ran through a white world of shifting quicksand, the blank sky making his stomach twist and turn. The ground enveloped him as he waded through the mushy surface. The harder he tried, the harder it pulled him down. Soon, it covered his neck. No Swirly People gazed upon him with their screaming, desperate faces.

He gasped in a final breath, sinking. He hammered against the hard bottom of the world, slapping his palm against it. With all his might, he shoved down. The ground turned to goo under his touch. He was almost able to touch his own sleeping face.

"Dunc…" he whispered, his mouth full of bitty, tasteless sand.

Four Swirly People huddled around Dunc's bed in the real world below him, touching his sweaty face with their blank, white fingers.

They snapped their attention up at him, pointing.

He fell through the ceiling, springing awake in bed, sending his covers cascading down to the floor. He leaned over the side of the bunk bed, blood rushing to his head as he hung, staring at his brother.

Dunc's covers moved with each irregular intake and release of breath, a nasty click sounding in his wide-open mouth.

Cuthbert grasped his hair with both hands, hauling at it until his follicles screamed fire at him. Tears sprung to his eyes as he slowly glanced up, his neck muscles protesting. Empty eye sockets pressed against the white, warping the ceiling. The faces bumped against each other, fighting to push through.

He climbed out of bed and set a hand on his brother's quaking covers. He picked up a tissue and wiped the thick mucus that clung to his brother's chin.

"I can't be the man of the house anymore," said Cuthbert. "I need you to wake up strong and look after everyone, alright?"

The faces continued to shove their slow way through the ceiling. A noise like a pelting thunderstorm echoed inside Cuthbert's skull. His mind skittered, the image of those empty faces reminding him of playing whack-a-mole at the arcade. A giggle escaped him as his sanity threatened to float away like a black balloon.

Cuthbert bolted down the hall, almost able to taste the VapoRub scent on the air.

"Dad?" He pushed his parent's door.

His dad lay on his back, eyes open, his skin a moth-ball shade of yellow, the scratchy fuzz of his beard growing on a jaw that hung open wider than Cuthbert thought possible. His father's chest didn't move.

Cuthbert stood by the bed, his hand covering his mouth. He held his breath, praying at his dad's chest, his feet stuck to the ground as if encased in concrete.

"D-dad?" said Cuthbert. "No..."

His dad's hands shot up. He gulped in a huge, gasping breath as if breaking out of water into fresh air. Pain crawled up Cuthbert's arm as his dad grabbed his wrist, drawing him close.

"Can't," said his dad, eyes still fixed on the ceiling. "Can't..."

"I'll get an ambulance. Sit up. Breathe, alright? There you go. Breathe. Dad? Look at me. Breathe. I-I'll be right back."

He wrangled his way free of his father's clinging grip. He gazed up at the ceiling, fearing what he might see, helpless to look away. Eight points jagged the surface, pushing down, almost ripping the shiny material of the thin veil that held the Swirly People in their own world.

The creature's mandibles and eight bulbous eyes shoved down in the middle of the ceiling. He fled to the living room, seeking his mum's phone to call an ambulance.

"Mum? Where's—"

He could almost feel the two halves of his brain being yanked apart. He stood, looking down at his unconscious mother on the floor, her legs cocked at an unnatural angle like she'd slipped off the couch, the fall not enough to wake her from her slumber.

Her phone lay on the floor like a black pebble. He picked it up and dialled 999.

"H-hello?" said Cuthbert.

The voice hazed through the phone as if the woman spoke through a marshmallow. "999, what's your emergency? Hello?"

"Yes, hello? I need an ambulance. They've come…"

"What? You're breaking up, kid. Say again?"

He nearly said the Swirly People were there. That'd be a fine way to deny an ambulance when his dad lay choking on his own breath, and his mum lay unmoving.

"Ambulance. My dad. He's choking, can't get a breath. 27 Kirk View. Mum's hurt too. Hurry."

"Kid? You still there? Kid? If you're there, press a button for me, will ya?"

Cuthbert's forehead creased as a spike of squealing feedback sputtered out the phone.

"H-hello?" he said, clenching his teeth as he put the phone back against his ear.

Fetid breath steamed out of the phone. The velvety voices made a shock of squirming electricity jolt down his neck.

"What did we ever do to hurt you, Cuthbert?" they said. "We'll kiss your family, one by one."

The red end-call button warped as he pressed it. He launched the phone across the room. He backed away, and his back hit the wall. A seething giggle spewed from the phone in the room's corner.

He clamped his hands over his ears, drowning out the demented screams. Faces pressed against the living room ceiling, their cavernous mouths upturned in promising smiles.

"Go away!" he shouted.

"Oh, do shut up, Cuthbert," his mum said, head cocked round to near breaking point. "Leave us to sleep. There'll be time to be a selfish wee brat later."

He hauled his mother up on the couch, then he burst out of the living room, stumbling over his own feet, the sludgy nightmare settling over his shoulders like a cold blanket.

Dunc stared at a drooping sack that came down from their bedroom ceiling. Its swirling mass danced like ants gone crazy as it lowered itself inches from Dunc's nose.

He grabbed Dunc's arms, leading him back to his bed. Dunc mumbled something as he set him down on the pro-testing mattress, shoving the covers over him.

The tear-shaped thing bubbled down from the roof, almost reaching the floor. Beyond the thin membrane, faces and hands punched out, nearly bursting through. A long finger pointed at the bed.

He looked at his brother who slept on his back, his chest hitching as his lungs clawed desperately for air.

Cuthbert turned to the mass, now inches from his face. Its smell reminded him of the taste of bitter cellotape. He leaned in, peering into its depths. A face screamed at him, almost touching his nose. He stumbled and fell on his backside, a small jolt of pain running up the length of his spine.

He punched the floor and got back to his feet, glaring at the monstrous Swirly People trying to reach his world.

"Take me instead."

✦—◦———◦—◦—◦✦

Dunc walked into his bedroom, the sour stench of sweat and other unfortunate stinks on the air. It'd been a few days since he'd snapped out of his funk. His inner oven was back to normal, no longer flipping from Antarctic freezing to hellish fire every two seconds.

The wee guy had come through. If it hadn't been for his little brother calling an ambulance when he did, their mum and dad would probably have died. It still plagued him how frantic Cuthbert had looked.

Untrustworthy, fevered memories played in Dunc's mind like a broken film. White beings had hissed at him, begging him to come up. He recalled the urge to hug his wide-eyed brother as he'd stood by the side of his bed. In his snot-addled condition, he chose not to comfort Cuthbert when he'd needed it most.

He stroked the covers on the top bunk where Cuthbert had slept, giving up his usual spot on the lower bunk despite being terrified of the ceiling. He'd given it up, all for him. It was Cuthbert's sacrifice that saved them from being overcome by their mysterious illness, keeping the family tethered together.

Dunc let out a long, shaky breath, running his hands through his recently washed hair, locking his fingers behind his neck. He felt like a new person when he'd gained his strength back. The scent of coconut shampoo smelled like heaven compared to the reek coming off him when he'd first came back to his senses.

A twitch of movement like a snake sidewinding across sand caught his eye. He blinked, not able to shake the feeling he was being watched. He peered at the ceiling, the blank canvas transforming into swirling fuzz.

A face appeared pressed down, its mouth twisting out silent screams.

"It can't..."

He stumbled into a lopsided chest of drawers. Rivers of ice shot up his legs, darting up his spine.

Dunc shoved his hands over his ears, a sound like teeth grinding together itching the centre of his brain.

"It was all real..."

"What was?"

Dunc gasped, his heart flashing in alarm. "Cuthbert...y-you scared me."

"You're being awfully strange, Duncan," said Cuthbert, tilting his head.

Dunc looked at the ceiling, hot blood throbbing in his ears.

Nothing but smooth white.

He let go a giggle as he turned his attention back to his little brother—the rock of the family.

Dunc felt shame stab him as a sickly feeling waved over him. An icy breeze trickled over the back of his neck.

He couldn't explain it, but Cuthbert had changed. Maybe he'd grown up a lot over the past few days. The way Cuthbert looked at him with vacant eyes—

"Duncan?" Cuthbert smiled. "Whatever is the matter?"

Duncan. He'd called him Duncan. He never called him that. Dunc or booger-face were firm favourites, but never Duncan. His voice lacked the sizzle and pop Dunc was used to hearing. It was as if his vocal cords relaxed too much when he spoke.

"Still a little woozy from being sick, I guess," said Dunc. "Say, Cuthbert? Know how you used to go on and on about those Swirly People? W-when I was sick, I think you shouted at me to get away from them. Did...did that really happen?"

Cuthbert's smile warped into a grimace. "No, it did not."

"I saw you in there." Dunc pointed up. "I swear it was—"

"We don't look up anymore."

"I saw you."

"You must've imagined it, Duncan."

"But I sa—"

"Don't turn into a big baby. There's nothing up there, okay!"

"Right..." Dunc stared out the window at the bright day that lay ahead, the trees at the edge of Kirkness swishing back and forth like a green sea. "Mum's out of the worst of it. Says we can go out again. Let's get the fudge out of here."

"Out there? Outside?" whispered Cuthbert.

"Just to the forest for a wee walk. Fresh air. I haven't

been out in so long; I might get drunk on it."

Cuthbert clutched at his T-shirt, his eyes almost jumping out of their sockets. He ran one hand over his face, clawing his cheek, pulling that side of his face down. The pink part of his lower eyelid unfurled as he wrestled with himself, his eyes darting to the ceiling, then down again.

"We can't go outside," said Cuthbert. "It's too...*big* out there. You can't make me." Cuthbert dropped to the floor, clutching at his knees, dragging them close to his chest. His small body rocked back and forth, grinding his teeth like a fevered rat. "Don't make me. Don't make me."

Dunc walked over, throwing an arm around his quivering shoulders. "I'd be worm food if it wasn't for you. You saved us all."

As his brother buried his face in the gap between his knees, Dunc stared up at the ceiling. Figures rippled across the white, screams dead on their faces. They swarmed around a lone figure who flailed, batting them away.

It was Cuthbert up there. The shadow of his little brother punched a hand toward Dunc, his bony fingers digging through the latex-like substance of the ceiling, reaching.

"Cuthbert? What? I—"

The hand retracted as the other Swirly People clawed their arms around Cuthbert's neck, hauling him away, up into their own universe. The ceiling returned to its blank white nothingness.

"Whatever is the matter," said Cuthbert, standing inches from him. "Brother?"

Paul O'Neill
About the Author

Paul is a short fiction writer from Scotland. He is a PR / Internal Communications professional who tries not to let the horror of corporate-speak seep into his stories. His tales have appeared in Scare Street's Night Terrors series, Purple Wall Stories, and Fae Corps Press' Nightmare Whispers anthology. As a child, he spent far too much time staring at his ceiling.

Twitter: @paulon1984

Moss

Benjamin Alloco

Jared slaps me in the back of the head as the bus pulls away. The force pops an earbud out. It dangles across my collarbone, and I go to reinsert it, but Jared's hand yanks the cord from my phone. My sanctuary of music is gone. They spread across the road and throw my headphones back and forth. The cord twists in the air like a writhing snake.

This has happened many times.

I will have to buy another pair of cheap earbuds later.

"Hey, Blowjob, I fingered your slut girlfriend and couldn't get the stink off for three days."

"Hey, Blowjob, you see what they wrote about her in the bathroom? *Call Churchy for fresh sushi.*"

Hey Blowjob.

There are three of them: Jared, Alex, and Carl.

It is springtime. Everything is wet.

Churchy is not my girlfriend.

My first name is Brian and my middle is James and together that makes BJ.

I focus on my phone, the glowing screen, the text box. I

want to text Churchy, but there is no point. What could she say to help? I can't type anyway because one of Jared's hands is digging into my shoulder, his other slapping the phone out of my grasp onto the asphalt. I scramble for it, but he wrenches my right arm behind my back, forcing me upright.

Alex swoops in and takes the phone.

"Give it back," I say. My voice is not commanding. It is small. It squeaks.

Alex grins and throws the phone over my head. He is two years younger than the rest of us but still bigger than me. Jared catches the phone and waggles it, mocking me.

"Look at this faggy shit," Jared says. He scrolls through my messages.

I start toward him. He backs up. Alex loops around and stands between us.

"Give it," I say.

"*Give it,*" Alex mocks.

Through all of this, Carl hangs to the side and watches his feet.

"I'm gonna tell Churchy he's a fag," Jared says.

Almost two full years of this.

They are less awful in the morning. At least then I can stand apart and wait for the bus. But they might get behind me and grab my ankles as I climb the steps. Real funny. I avoid them at school, keep my head down. But the afternoon torment is clockwork.

The neighborhood is a suburb nested in a forest. Wherever there are not houses, there are trees. They are tall and thick, and they cover everything in shadows and keep the mosquitos breeding. Right in front of the bus stop is an empty lot full of tall grass, a swamp the size of someone's yard. The forest picks up behind it and goes for a long, long time. Jared types into my phone and laughs and types more.

"She's buying it! Here's what she said. 'Beej, I accept whoever you are and whatever you find attractive.' "

A string of cackles follows.

I don't particularly care about this line of attack. Let them see through me, out me, call me whatever they want. I'm only bothered that Churchy doesn't recognize an imposter. Can't she tell the difference between me and him? Doesn't she know what I sound like?

"Look at this, Blowjob. I'm saving you the trouble. I'll just go through your contacts and send a mass text. How's that sound?"

I move forward. Alex gets me in a headlock. Carl stands by.

There is nothing I can do.

Jared types and laughs, types and laughs.

I hear myself grunting, overpowered.

I decide to fight.

When Alex lets go, I sidestep and charge for Jared. He laughs and runs through the empty lot, beelining for the woods and kicking up mud and water. I chase. The water comes over my ankles, ruining my dress shoes. I mindlessly pursue through the empty lot, rage burning bright.

Something is growling, and I realize it is me.

I kick through the brush at the edge of the woods and stop in my tracks.

Jared has been crucified upside down to an X of fallen logs, arms and legs spread. His genitals have been sliced off, leaving a pink slash, and they have been placed in his mouth. There is a flash and some kind of world-shaking stutter, and Jared is zigzagging through the woods, still laughing.

The X is gone. Dead Jared is gone. Never there. He is alive and has my phone.

When I catch up, he stands in front of a huge dead tree with a hole in the bark as big as a basketball. He giggles. His pupils have dilated, and he's breathing hard. On the football team, he is something called a halfback, which means he gets the ball a lot and is very fast. He's practically foaming at the mouth.

"Fetch," he says and throws my phone over his shoulder into the tree.

It thumps somewhere inside the hole.

I hold back a scream.

Hands shove me from behind. I go facedown into pine needles and rotten leaves and something else—something acrid, cold, and wet. When I look up, Jared's face leers inches from mine. His smile is deranged, and I am certain that he's about to produce a knife, that he'll cut my throat and leave me here in the woods, bleeding.

Something twists inside of me. Something terrible awakens, an anger I've never known. Like a wild animal, I bare my teeth and snarl.

"Kick him," Alex says, somewhere above me.

Jared considers it. He studies me on the ground.

Twigs snap behind me.

Jared looks away, and the moment is broken.

"Let's fucking go," Carl says from the distance. "My shoes are ruined and it smells like shit."

The mad glee in Jared's eye blinks out. He shakes his head as if to clear it. "Yeah. Fuck it."

I hear Alex back off. Jared arcs a wide circle around me. I listen to their footsteps fade in the distance.

I remain where I fell, lying on something worse than garbage, worse than shit. I feel it below my chest, slick and cold and soft as gelatin. When the trio is out of sight, I roll away and force myself to see what is on my shirt. It takes a moment for the bile to work into my throat.

I cannot tell what animal it used to be, but it has been dead a long time. A soup of flesh and gray guts surround yellowed bone and needle teeth.

I puke across a pricker bush.

◆━◦━━━◦━◦━◆

Once upon a time, Carl—who these days watches his feet as I get the shit kicked out of me—was my best friend.

Then high school.

He was talented. A rising star quarterback. Like me, he had always been quiet. For him, this was perceived as humble coolness. For me, awkwardness. It started in gym class, when Jared and his jocks and their new friend Carl witnessed my inability to catch a ball or make a basket. This surprised me as much as anyone. I was not always this way.

Summer before freshman year, my body betrayed me. I did not grow into a chiseled block of sex. I evolved in reverse.

My legs trembled, and my hands sweat. The boys around me seemed to grow tall and thick, while I stayed skinny and frail. Gym class spilled into taunts in the hallway.

Jared's favorite line was, "Give me the ball, Blowjob," a reference to my clunky hands.

They threw things at my head: in gym—footballs, basketballs, baseballs; in class—pencils, pens, erasers. Once, someone's dirty sock. Carl did not encourage them, but neither did he say a word to stop it.

This is what I think about as I reach my hand into the tree trunk, feeling crumbled wood and bark and something wet and furry. I flinch back. I cannot get a good angle. The hole is head-height and goes all the way down, the base of the tree hollow. I can't reach my phone.

I give up and sit down, putting my back against the tree, thinking maybe I'll get lucky and it will fall on me. I want to talk to Churchy, but I don't want to talk to Churchy.

My heart feels sideways.

What's really messed up is that Churchy dated Jared for a month last year. It was before I knew her, but still. She tells me he was a jerk, but she won't say more. I think she feels bad for him. She won't tell me why. They had sex, which, despite wanting to feel otherwise, makes me wary of her and a little disgusted. If she can give her body to someone like that, be taken in by him, what does that say about her? Could she turn on me like Carl did?

Is it horrible of me to think this way?

Am I horrible?

Something knocks against the tree, right in the small of my back.

I think for a moment someone has thrown a stone at me and missed, but there is no other sound or sensation. I lean forward, away from the bark, much of which has peeled off, leaving reddish-green stains beneath.

I wait and listen. Maybe a squirrel or chipmunk. I look up at the branches. I do not know what kind of tree this is, but the limbs are skeletal and bare.

There is another thump. A sharp knock.

I back away, scooting through dirt. I turn to eye the tree, as if it might raise itself on its roots and lumber toward me. There are no living plants around it. The sky is filled with its spiky bows, blocking the sun. It stands in the center of a circle of rotting plant life, as if a tiny nuke went off, the tree ground zero.

Something wizzes past my head, lands on the leaves beside me.

I see it from the corner of my eye, allow my vision to drift to it.

My phone. There on the leaves.

My phone came flying out of the tree.

There is no breeze, but I hear a low *shush* in the air around me like the shimmying of leaves, yet all the nearby trees are still or bare. The hair on the back of my neck stands rigid. Like magnetism, the hole in the trunk draws my attention. It seems to ripple or shift, like I'm seeing it through a haze.

Something tells me I should go to it. *Come nearer.*

I don't feel scared. I feel peaceful.

I could cut them into pieces. It is like a dream thought passing over me.

I shift on the ground to see better into the hole, and my screen catches a glint of light through the branches. The light sparks in my eye. I blink. Why am I so calm? Trees should not look this way. Trees should not *feel* this way.

Has the hole grown larger? Are the edges...pulsing?

I can do it, if you tell me.

This is not my thought. It comes from somewhere else.

I dive for my phone, snatch it up, and split for the edge of the woods, back the way I came. The whole time, I sense something close behind me, within arm's reach. I splash through the abandoned lot and leap onto the road as if solid ground is all I need to be safe.

◇━◦━━◦━◇

"What happened to your shirt?" Mom asks.

I'm only wearing my undershirt, and there is a smear of rotten guts on my chest. I tell her I spilled something at lunch. Must have left my button-up on the bus. Really, I stuffed it in the trash at the end of the driveway.

"If your generation would carry backpacks, you might not lose things so often." She clucks her tongue. "Speaking of losing your shit, your father called. Know what he said?"

Mom is a rail-thin woman with a tangle of blonde hair and pockmarked skin. She is not what you would call pretty. She smokes and stinks of smoke, and so does our house, but there is a steely toughness to her. If I told her about Jared and the others, she'd want to grab a baseball bat and stand at the bus stop every day. She works two jobs. She'll make dinner, then leave.

I tell her I don't want to know what my father said. She tells me anyway. Something about wanting to see me more, and they need to take my feelings into account from time to time. They have been divorced for three years, and the fighting has not diminished. Dad says it's too hard to keep track, and if things were steadier, I could be there more. I don't know what this means.

I head upstairs. Mom keeps talking as if I'm still in the room.

My phone won't turn on. I settle into my gaming chair and load up a shooter. Every kill is Jared or Alex or Carl. This fantasy calms me. Mom calls up that dinner's ready. I say nothing. Half an hour later, she knocks on my door and says stew and salad is in the fridge. I don't like stew. I play my game so long my eyes hurt.

Sometime after dark, a chat pops up on screen: *HEARD YOU LIKE IT IN THE BUTTHOLE LOL.*

I slide off the bed, approach the TV, and stare at the message. The username, *BroncosFan1414,* is so generic it has to be Jared. My stomach twists in knots. I ball my fists. I am so very sick of all this. I just want...I just want to—

My phone buzzes, shimmies on the nightstand. There is no notification of an incoming call. Nothing. Yet it buzzes. Moisture from the tree got inside. It's just malfunctioning.

My skin prickles. My window is dark.

I sense eyes out there, watching me.

I grab the phone and the buzzing stops. I press it to my ear.

I hear static. I hear wind. I hear what sounds like someone sighing.

"Hello?" I say.

Aaaah.

My worries dissolve. My trembling hands still. I wait.

The voice is there. Faintly. It breathes moisture in my ear like cupped lips.

It says, *I can cut them into pieces.*

So calming, this voice, this sentiment. I melt into the words and they into me. This is a love song. It warms me.

That is what you want.

"Yes," I say.

Tell me I can. The voice deepens, lowers, almost a groan. Pained. *I can hurrrt themmmm.*

"Yes," I say. "You can hurt them."

Aaaaah. Mmmmm.

My phone goes dead. A hunk of black glass and plastic against my ear. I'm so heavy, so tired. I can't be on my feet anymore, and the room is getting blurry, and there's someone standing in the corner with a pale face and a black shroud. I find the edge of my bed. I lie down.

⊰–•–——–•–⊱

Mom doesn't usually make breakfast, but when I go downstairs, there's a note on the microwave: *You didn't eat dinner! Eat breakfast!!!!*

A plate of pancakes sits inside, but I have no appetite. She'll be pissed if I don't take her gesture, but I'm still not hungry. I feel weird.

It isn't until I go upstairs to get my phone that I remember last night—the bus stop, the woods, the phone call.

Thinking about it hurts my head.

Outside, a cool fog hangs over the neighborhood, the sunrise hidden behind trees. I move down the street like I'm waiting for something. I don't know what. My soggy shoes go *squish-squish*. The crows usually perched in the trees are not in the trees. It feels like the aftermath of a big storm. The intersection at the bus stop stands empty. A few buds in the forest are in bloom as spring returns. Nature waking from sleep. I watch the abandoned lot, expecting Jared and the others to jump out jeering.

I can still see our tracks in the long grass. Crooked lines where the weeds have been matted. On the street, there is some discoloration. Lichen or moss has grown out of the lot and spread across the asphalt. It appears fuzzy and green, accented with deep reds.

I hear a voice in the distance. A call. Wordless, but human.

Then again. Louder. Sudden, then gone.

A yelp. Someone crying out.

The bus's airbrakes shriek as it slides around the corner.

Of course that is all it was.

⊹⊱─⊰⊹

I hide in the back of my homeroom. Churchy finds me. I keep my chin on my forearms and my eyes closed, but I hear her sit beside me. She pulls at my eyelid.

"Can we talk?" she says.

I say nothing.

She sighs and leans back, crosses her arms.

Churchy is annoyingly pretty. It's difficult not to resent her for it. The school says girls have to wear skirts or loose slacks. She wears skirts. Today's is checkered blue and white with black stockings and these chunky red clogs that should violate dress code, but all the teachers like her. Her hair has been pulled into a ponytail. All the boys love her. I am, of course, invisible to them or worse. It's a small town, a small school.

"Don't be a turd. What happened yesterday?"

I say nothing.

"Fine. You don't want to talk, we won't. I'll just sit here."

She does. She sits there until the first bell sends her to homeroom. She stands and sighs, and her chunky shoes *click-clock* out of the room.

I am not socially connected enough to have a direct line with the rumor mill, but I hear things nonetheless—whispers in the cafeteria, between classes, winding through the desks.

Carl and Jared are missing, along with a kid from the middle school.

That would be Alex.

Their parents are freaking out. Kids have been questioned.

Someone mentions mold growing in the hallway.

Jared's locker is smack in the middle of the second floor—next to Carl's. I know this because Jared tries to trip me and says, "Give me the ball, Blowjob," whenever I see him. I therefore avoid this area, preferring to take an unnecessary trip to the third floor and back down the other stairwell to avoid a chance encounter. Out of habit, I follow these rituals today, but between Spanish and chem, I make a special trip.

What I see stops me in my tracks.

Seniors bump into me and grunt. I drop a notebook. Someone stoops to grab it and hand it back, but they stand there with the book outstretched and me staring at the wall until they mutter something and drop it at my feet.

Twin smears of green and red work their way out of two lockers, climbing toward the ceiling. The pattern resembles smoke damage. A custodian drags over a stepladder, climbs up, and scrubs the growth with a sponge. It peels off in fat strips, leaving brown smears.

The custodian sees me, turns. "You're gonna get in trouble."

My face gets hot.

"You're late for class."

The halls are empty. In my daze, I missed the bell.

<hr>

After school, I wade through the empty lot, trembling but not cold. Pretending I am brave. I part the final strands of grass and head into the woods.

I am no tracker. Should I be looking for drag marks?

What trail might a monster leave behind?

It doesn't matter. It's not a trail I discover.

It's the X. It is slightly taller than me. Moss covers the logs. They could be ancient except they weren't here yesterday, and they aren't really logs, but branches or roots or tree trunks growing crookedly out of the ground. At the joint, they've grown into and through each other.

I shut my eyes and shake my head and will it to be gone, but when I open them, it's still there. I force myself not to run. I have to look. I have to check. Just this one thing. I do not breathe. I wait for a shadowed arm to grab me from behind. And when I see what I'm looking for, I throw a hand over my mouth and force myself not to scream.

I don't run. Panic is a wild thing. If I run, it will pursue, and it is faster than me.

I look at the ground and I don't take my hand from my mouth until I'm in the abandoned lot. I only breathe once I reach the road and kick the water from my shoes and tell myself I imagined it.

Mom watches me come in, lips pressed into a white line. She blocks my way to the stairs.

Not now. I can't do this.

"Do you know what gratitude is?" Her voice is flat, firm.

I try to focus.

"I said, do you know what gratitude is."

"I heard you."

"And do you?"

"Yes."

"Then you aren't grateful, are you? If you were, you might take care of yourself. If not for yourself, then out of respect for the people who care about you. For the person who is trying but apparently failing to raise you the right way."

This is because I didn't eat her stupid breakfast.

"Are you listening to me?" she says. "Hello?"

I shove her out of my way.

I have never shoved my mother. I feel her boney shoulder under my hand, lighter than I expected. She steps backward, her mouth hanging open, and I pound up the stairs and slam my door. She screams that I am just like my father.

I shut her out. When I close my eyes, I see holes. Holes in the ends of those deformed branches of the X, one hole at each end, puckered like irritated flesh, as if nails had been driven into the wood and removed.

Holes stained red.

Mom leaves without a word. The door slams. I surf the web, looking mindlessly at sites I don't read. I want to shut the world out. I close my laptop and pace.

I picture the X, the puckered holes.

I walk down the hall and take a shower, stand under the faucet till the water goes cold. I dress and go back to my room and pace till my feet hurt.

I drop into bed with a sigh, let my eyes drift closed.

I see the X.

Something growls to my right.

I shoot upright. The growl comes again, lessened, intermittent.

Nnnnnn.

Nnnnnn.

Nnnnnn.

My phone. I dig through the pile of clothes on the floor and find it in my pants. My body relaxes as I study the display. I deleted his contact info last year but will remember the number forever.

Carl.

Of course it was all a prank. The three morons hid to freak me out. They've set up a webcam somewhere in the house or on the street and have been recording my weird behavior all day. Now he's calling to taunt me. Except when I press the phone to my ear, there's only static on the other end, like someone blowing into the mouthpiece. The static fades, grows, rises, falls.

It isn't static or wind.

My hands go clammy.

I am naked head to toe, my towel around my feet. Helpless as a pink-skinned baby.

The breathing pauses. *Who else?*

My chest spasms.

Who. Else?

Lightning sparks outside and a heavy rain splats against the window.

"Leave me alone," I say.

I can hurt them. Tell me—

I rush to the window, jam it open, and fling my phone into the night.

❖━◇━━━◇━❖

I can't sleep. I recite prayers I stopped having faith in years ago. I will God or anyone listening to come down here and stand by my door. But there is no savior. There is only me shivering in bed with the sheet pulled to my chin. I stare at the overhead light, a round globe.

It flickers.

Thunder racks the walls. And again, louder, closer. The bed shakes.

Something about this thunder is not right.

Through the window, I hear only a gentle dripping. And when I crane my neck, I see a sliver of moon. The storm ended hours ago.

My light winks out, and the door to my room rattles.

I whip the covers over my head and hear the door creak open.

There are no footsteps, but I feel it moving closer. I smell its foulness, concentrated rot.

I beg my body to be invisible.

A sudden pressure on the sheets pushes on my stomach.

There is a clicking sound, like sticks knocking together.

Who else? It presses harder.

I feel a pinch. I can't move. Only my lips and tongue are free. It wants me to say.

I can't say.

I won't.

I can cut them apart. I can open them.

The voice is deep, throaty. It bubbles from some drowned place.

The pain in my guts is electric, shooting through me.

I can take their eyes. I can separate the bones.

It penetrates me, stabs. It happens all at once, my body giving over. A finger made of bone or wood pops through my flesh, wiggles around my organs. That's all I can take.

I give in, rattling off a list of names. All the people who ever insulted me, however insignificant their trespass. An unkind word or look. A misunderstanding. A gesture from a moving car.

I name everyone I know, and then I move on to strangers, describing them the best I can. Anything to stop the pain, the hurt, the violation, the agony. I give them over, and it's almost a relief even before the splinter pulls from my body.

I fade into blackness.

⬦–◦⊶–◦–⊷◦–⬦

Morning. The sheets cold with sweat. The door stands open, and I can see into the dim hall. I peel the covers back and ignore the hole in the sheets, edges singed with something green and red. I study my stomach for scars but find none. I blink at the ceiling light, back on, a dull yellow in the morning haze. I dress. My phone sits on the nightstand. I leave it there. There is an earthy smell in the air like fresh loam.

In the hallway, thick gobs of moss hang around the edges of my mother's bedroom door. It grows along the walls and floor, bursting through the seams where the wood comes together.

Mom was right. I have always been ungrateful.

I try the door, but the moss holds it shut. I put my shoulder to it. It takes five or six lunges before the door bursts inward. I stumble into a room dripping with decay.

The rotten bed dips in the center, the sheets greenish

yellow and shoved to the side. The carpet squishes cold and wet through my socks. Downstairs is much the same, the rooms overtaken by moss. Dishes in the sink rusted through, moss crawling out of the drain, hanging from the ceiling fan like foam, coating pictures on the wall. The frame around the front door's latch has been blown inward.

That was the thunder I felt.

Before I leave, I slide on my boots.

◈━━◇━━◈◇

The fog is thicker today. My stomach sinks as I move through the streets, what could be a town abandoned for a hundred years. The houses crawl with greenery. Their siding peels and the roofs sag, lichen smearing the windows. The school bus sits on the corner on cracked, empty tires. The moss has consumed it, as it has consumed the pavement below me. I circle the bus and search the windows, but it appears empty. It must have pulled up to the stop just minutes ago, but it looks as if it's been sitting here twenty years.

The water in the abandoned lot comes halfway up my shins. I splash across, and at the edge of the woods, I nearly fall to my knees at the sight of what lies before me.

Bodies laid out in welcome.

Some have been tacked to the trees with wooden stakes, through the hands, through the torso, through the neck. Many are naked, their pale faces agape. The kids from the school bus hang from a maple, hairy vines around their throats. Some of their shoes have fallen off and lie useless on the dirt. I spot one of my neighbors, Mr. Landau, on the low branches of a pine tree. His arms and legs end in gory stumps.

I vomit, then dry heave and force myself forward. I pass piles of flesh and bone. Kids I recognize from school but whose names I never knew.

This is my fault. That knowledge is all that keeps me from turning back, from falling face down and screaming till my mind leaves me. I'm too horrified to cry.

My fault. *Mine.*

Jared and Alex's remains have been placed on either side of the hollow tree. Their heads rest right-side up on the dirt, and behind them, their limbs are neatly stacked. They look surprised.

The base of the tree is larger than before, rounded like a pear. The hole has warped, the top and bottom unevenly folded like uncertain lips. Moss radiates from the hole and climbs the trunk. As I watch, the moss undulates and spreads, drawing more of itself out of the hole. The branches droop with its weight. Wet red bulbs hang from the tips of these spindly sticks, some nightmare fruit that will soon bloom.

I grip the bottom of the hole. The bark crumbles under my hands. Something warm coats my palms. I turn them over and find them slick with blood. I wipe them on my pants and reach inside again. I lean forward, kick against the bark, and roll my body over the edge into the chasm.

I tumble down an incline, limbs and skull rapping on firm ground. When I come to a stop, I lie on my side in a fetal position, expecting blows or hands or roots to wind me up and pull me apart. I hear water. The gentle sound of lapping waves.

I open my eyes.

I'm on an island in the middle of a swamp. The island consists of carefully stacked boulders, all fuzzy with moss. I seem to have stepped right off the large flat boulder above me. On top of that boulder, a stone archway, slightly larger than a regular door, has grown seamlessly out of the rock. Through the arch, I see a distorted image of the forest I came from.

The swamp surrounding this island is an endless plane of scummy water peppered with dead trees. The trees are massive—unearthly. They climb for hundreds of feet before their tops disappear into fog. They have no branches, more like giant spears than plants, and there are yellow-white protrusions in various spots around their trunks.

Whatever or wherever this place is, it's not the world I've known.

I make my way down the slippery island and ease into the freezing water. It rushes into my boots, rises to my knees, then my thighs. I wade forward, sending ripples radiating. Driven by guilt, I press forward. As I pass the first tree, I see that the yellow-white protrusions are bits of skeleton held in place by stringy vines.

Here, a fractured skull.

There, a forearm and a few remaining fingers. A dangling leg. A ribcage.

Many are too strange to place. The bones twisted, skulls adorned with pretzeled horns. The remains of otherworldly lifeforms. The fog swirls, creating a tunnel here, a clearing there. I follow where it leads, playing by its rules.

When I hear the first scream, I freeze. When it comes again, I remember that this is what I came for. I pant and splash and give up on stealth. The waterline drops as I approach the source of the screaming, down to my knees, then my ankles, and as I slog endlessly onward, a hump of dry land appears in the mist. I climb a gentle slope, but my foot catches in the soil and I drop face first, hands absorbed to the wrists in a coil of plants, dirt in my mouth, a coppery taste.

I roll and wipe the mud from my face and scoot to my left where a skinny tree stands. I get a hold of it and pull myself up and look to see what I fell on—a bone, half buried.

It's not the only one.

All along this new island, bones protrude from the filth. I spit and wipe my mouth and taste that coppery taste and realize how red the mud is, the distinct shapes in it. The coils I fell into are not plant life, but intestines. I recognize other organs from biology texts and pictures in doctors' offices.

Liver, spleen, kidney, lung.

I dry heave until my muscles are ready to give out.

Another scream pulls me onward.

The gore transitions to packed dirt. Shapes ahead. Structures in the mist. A cluster of those twisted Xs. I can't make out details at first, just their clothes, the vague shape of their faces hanging upside down. I stumble closer, manic, eyes burning with my own sweat and tears and the clinging filth of the swamp.

My mother and father are dead. I recognize them only by their clothes and hair. The skin has been peeled from their faces and hangs off in pale sheets. They have been disemboweled. I look away. A pathetic whimper escapes me.

I go to Churchy first because her mouth is open and her head is rolling from side to side. She wails, but she doesn't see me when I drop in front of her and mutter words I only half hear myself. I put my body between her and what lies in the center of this stage: her little brother, her father, her mother.

I touch Churchy's face, wipe at the grime but only manage to leave more. Unlike the others, she has been secured to the X with some kind of twine-like vines. I pull at them, calling her name, telling her foolishly that she is okay. The twine is too tight. Her hands and feet have turned blue.

I worry at the knot until it frays. I bite at it and finally get the knot loose enough to slip one hand free. It takes a long time, but I slip her other limbs loose. She crumples onto the dirt. I whisper and hold her head in my lap, cry and tell her "I'm so fucking sorry," but she needs to wake up.

Her eyes roll and come to rest on Carl still hanging on his rack. He is shirtless. His upper body resembles torn fabric. The flesh of one arm has been sliced into strips to reveal pink muscle and bits of tendon and bone. Lateral slats of ribcage show through his upper chest. His breathing is shallow. In a sane realm, he would be dead.

I crawl to him. Thick wooden spikes secure his wrists and feet to the wood. The only way to free him is to yank his limbs hard enough that the spikes tear through. I grip one limb at a time and pull. His wounds don't even bleed anymore. He is empty. I lay him out and try to slap him awake.

Churchy watches, face slack with shock. I sense something watching us from nearby.

We have to go.

I drag Carl several feet by the ankles. Churchy doesn't move.

"Come on, Churchy," I grunt. "Help me."

Churchy says, "Come on, Churchy. Help me." She frowns, touches her lips with two fingers.

I wave for her to follow, but she gives me a quizzical look. "Please."

She just looks at me.

Carl coughs and spasms, and I lose hold of his feet.

The spasms quit. His chest hardly moves. If I get him back to our world, the sane world, how long will he last?

I leave him.

I stand beside Churchy and take her left arm over my neck. We stumble a few steps and go down in the dirt. I haul her back up. I whisper that we are going to safety.

I don't look back at Carl.

⬦◄━━◄━━►━►⬦

The fog has become agitated. It spirals and twists. We walk a long time. After a few minutes, it becomes clear that something is following us. Ripples collide with ours, and I hear splashing and gasps from behind.

The closer it gets, the louder I speak to Churchy. I tell her we're in a dream, and we'll wake when we reach the island. I'm on the school bus, napping, and when I get off the bus, Jared will slap me in the back of the head and take my phone and taunt me like usual.

My hell will be contained inside me, where it belongs.

The stone island looms. I hardly notice the figure halfway up the rocks, black shroud whipping in the wind. Churchy buries her face in my shoulder. I feel its stare more than I see it. The cloak obscures its features, but the stark white skull centered in its hood is unmistakable.

I lower my shoulders and push forward.

Waterlogged and heavy, we heave up the first layer of rocks. I avoid its gaze but feel the monster—my monster—smiling on me. We stand dripping and shivering. There is one way out, and he blocks it, waiting for us to crawl into his embrace.

This has all been a taunt. It gave us hope just so it could snatch it away.

A disturbance in the water, a series of splashes close by.

The thing that followed us.

An impossible figure slumps up the shore, rags of flesh. Carl rises to his mangled feet and glares at the figure and releases a howl that is more animal than man, a roar. The monster loves it. Carl turns to me, his one remaining eye telling me all I need to know, and my heart breaks into a thousand shards.

I want to tell him I didn't understand, but he turns back to the monster who still stares, still grins without grinning. Slowly, deliberately, Carl crouches and searches along the ground, one mangled hand patting the moss. When he finds what he's looking for, he stands and steps back, pulls the object to his chest and cranes his neck.

His final play.

He winds up and fires off. The rock is not large, but the throw is perfect. It hits the creature squarely in the forehead, knocking the hood back to reveal a hairless dome which snaps to the side and springs back, focused on Carl.

Carl climbs slowly, hampered by his ruined body.

I take Churchy's weight and pull her up the rocks, keeping one eye on Carl. He limps toward the back of the island, and I lose line of sight. When I see him again, I am halfway to the creature, and he is level with it.

He charges from behind. He connects hard and low, dislodges it from its purchase. They roll, black cloak wrapping them. I see hands with long fingers and yellow claws. I see these claws digging into Carl's back, pulling out handfuls of flesh. They tumble past us, bones snapping. Grunts and hissing, what I recognize as the sorcerer's voice, a whisper in my head.

You can suffer more. Tell me you can suffer more.

Not much farther.

Churchy covers her ears. I shove and yell and tell her not to listen. None of it is real, and I tell her that she is my friend, that she is my friend, my friend, my friend.

Somehow renewed, she climbs. When I look back, I see what I know I will see.

Pieces of Carl scattered among the rocks.

The creature rises toward us. It doesn't walk or climb. It levitates, its arms slightly out from its sides. Its black eyes hold on mine. I look away, but I hear it whispering in my head. I climb, and Churchy calls. The sorcerer drifts up behind me. I slip and crash to my side, and the wind goes rushing out of me.

A few feet ahead, Churchy climbs to the top of the island. I feel relief. She's going to make it, dive through the portal and escape. She turns to face me. Her eyes are wild, and her hair whips around her head in a sudden rush of wind. She reaches for my hand.

"Go!" I tell her, my voice weak.

She doesn't go.

I scramble forward and give her my hand. She pulls me up to her level, and then she freezes, her eyes huge and focused on something over my shoulder.

I shove her hard and send her backward into the portal.

I turn.

Its face is right up to mine.

It was never human. Not this thing. Where there should be eyebrows, bones covered in white flesh protrude and entwine. The eyes are solid black and set far in their sockets. There is no nose. For a mouth, slivers of bone humped around a black opening. So close, its vileness comes off in waves. It studies me. I reach out my right hand and push on the front of its cloak, over its chest. The body beneath the shroud sinks inward like the surface of a mushroom.

It grips my wrist with huge, spidery fingers. At its touch, my skin mottles green and red. I try to wrench my arm free, but its grip is too tight. I feel no pain as the moss moves up my arm, toward my elbow.

I stare into those black, hungry eyes—and I understand.

It does not feed on physical pain. It is only me.

What I have given it—my anger, my fear, and my rage.

I woke it while I fumed, while I wept in my room, fantasizing death, wishing the worst on those who wronged me. All these deaths are only to fatten me further, to baste me in my juices.

It lowers the rotten mouth to my hand and inhales. My fingers crumble, the moss dissolving into green flecks of dust that disappear into the cavernous, lipless mouth.

The moss bites deeper into my arm, sliding up and around my elbow.

I close my eyes. I picture Churchy. I can almost hear her voice as she stands over me in homeroom, asking me what's wrong, her care for me approaching something like love, and me turning her away out of selfishness, embarrassment, anger.

I push that anger aside, and I am thankful for her company in that moment, in all those moments. I picture Mom and Dad in our kitchen, tossing bits of cereal at each other and laughing. I see Carl on the playground in sixth grade, hanging by his knees from the jungle gym, pretzel sticks poking out of his mouth like walrus teeth.

"I am Walrus Batman," he says, barely comprehensible. "I cannot fight crime, for I am too fat!"

I think of his sacrifice in this place, dragging his collapsing body across the swamp.

For these things, I am grateful.

Happy.

Something hitches in my arm. I open my eyes to see that the sorcerer has swallowed half my forearm. The creature shudders again, its body jerking as if something is caught in its throat. I hold on to my images of Churchy and Mom and Dad and Carl, and now I picture Jared and Alex and my neighbors and the kids at school I know and don't know.

I am so sorry. I am sorry and I love you and it's okay. It is a great relief, and the sorcerer releases me and drifts down the rocks, those black eyes glaring, accusing.

I feel myself falling through space. Spongy earth slams against my back, and I lie blinking at a gray sky through the branches of a dead tree.

It is okay. I love you. I am sorry.

✧────◇─────◇────✧

I cannot find Churchy.

The town is the same as when I left. The moss has consumed it, eating through the metal and wood of the structures like algae on an underwater wreck. However long I was in that other place, enough time has passed for many buildings to collapse. My house still stands—for now.

I slumped out of the woods, back the way I came, into the sodden core of my room where I lie on my damp mattress and feel the moss creeping along my flesh, deeper into my bones and blood. It has made its way to the base of my neck and spreads like sepsis through my veins, etching dark lines along my chest.

I hope Churchy is okay. I have this terrible feeling that she was dead when I found her. I can see her crucified upside down with her abdomen open and empty. I don't know if this is my imagination, a memory, or something in between. That other place is not real the way this world is real. Perhaps I conjured it, invented it, willed it into being the way I willed this town to its destruction. And if so, could I will Churchy's future into existence too? Could I will them all back to life, to some perfect existence where none of this happened?

The ceiling drips a brown liquid that splashes across the corner of my mouth. It tastes like nothing. I try to spit, but my mouth is numb. My vision has blurred. A figure steps out of the corner near my window. I hear wind. It's Churchy. I did it. I conjured her. I knew I could.

She moves closer, leans over me. She looks strange. Her hair frames her face like a shroud, and she smells like the swamp.

She lowers her lips to mine, and breathes me in.

BENJAMIN ALLOCCO
ABOUT THE AUTHOR

Benjamin Allocco is an author, podcaster, and occasional musician. He lives in the Syracuse, New York area with his wife and their two rambunctious cats. His first novel, Deathform, was released by Severed Press in 2016. His second novel is forthcoming from Black Rose Writing in 2022. He prefers his fiction dark and his monsters ravenous.

To keep up with his writing and more, visit www.benjaminallocco.com.

On the Other Side of Time
Richard Clive

03/02/2030

"God," shouts Wright over the din of the helicopter blades. "It's...*beautiful*."

Mackenzie snaps a magazine into her assault rifle and swallows hard, gazing at the horizon through the chopper's window. The small hairs on her arms prickle. The air feels charged.

Obscured by tendrils of mist, the pyramid-shaped craft hovers above the mountain, inverted so its lowest vertex points down at the snow-dusted peak, the ship gently spinning on its axis by centripetal force.

The craft's three black faces are as smooth as glass, mirroring Snowdon's rugged terrain, and blinding white balls of light orbit the ship in dizzying, elliptical arcs, stitching the sky with bright trails.

The chopper thunders towards the mountain, transporting the three soldiers, the smouldering cities and graveyard towns now miles behind. The villages below, though, lie in ruins. Mackenzie stares down at a collapsed farmhouse and imagines people crushed beneath the building's brick and beams, the blackened bones of men, women and children buried beneath rubble.

The scale of decimation in the past twenty-four hours is incalculable, and she's almost grateful for the internet dying, for the worldwide blackout. Who wanted to see the destruction of humanity on YouTube? She closes her eyes for a moment to shut out the world because the sky-blue clarity of daylight is difficult to bear. But her mind remains filled with fire and death and screaming.

"Saw a documentary years ago," says Wright, looking at her with his one good eye, the patch affording him the look of a bandit. "The ancient Egyptians, they knew."

She had visited Cairo as a child. But the upturned pyramid that slowly rotates in the sky dwarfs even those ancient tombs. The sheer size and scale of the thing is, quite simply, preposterous...yet it's there, and so is she. Her whole life has railroaded her to this point. She feels her blood pumping, her heart beating hard, adrenaline surging, time ticking... moving further away from the day she lost John...and...

...the baby.

The day *her* world had really ended.

Yet when she woke earlier on her bunk at dawn, she was filled with an unspeakable sense of dread. And a strange sense of hope.

A knowing.

Because, she thinks, the universe has clocks, pendulums, mechanisms, and this morning she had felt something click, like teeth interlocking, the gears of a great machine turning, engineering her arrival, bringing her here.

Nearer to the end.

Closer to death.

Closer to John.

"The Aztecs too," says Wright, playing with the silver crucifix around his neck. "Only took four thousand years for the shit to hit the fan."

"You reckon."

"I know," he says.

"Know?"

"This shit's been a long time coming. You know, this mountain's a prehistoric volcano, and then there're the ancient myths."

"*Myths?*"

"King Arthur...*the Druids.*"

"You sound like someone I used to know."

The chopper passes over a forest and a rocky ford. In the distance, a lake glitters beneath the hazy plumes of drifting clouds that cast thin shadows on the jagged and calcareous cliffs. Snowdon is majestic, the mountain range a stunningly bleak panorama, populated only by the occasional flock of sheep.

"Sorry you volunteered?" says Wright.

"*Volunteered?*"

"*Right,* fucking suicide mission."

"Today's as good as any."

"How old *are* you?"

"Rude to ask a lady her age."

"*Lady?*"

"Fuck you."

He smiles again. "You got balls, Mackenzie."

"Quit flirting," shouts Smith, fixing his helmet cam. "Get ready to rock and roll."

She adjusts her own helmet.

"Put her down here," shouts Smith into his headset.

The copter's pilot obeys. The chopper swoops low, and the ground rushes towards them, Mackenzie's stomach in freefall, the force of air from the rotor blades flattening the surrounding brush. The landing skids touch the rocky ground, and the three soldiers climb out of the chopper, carrying their gear and weapons.

From a distance, much of the tetrahedron's huge form had been visible, but they are now too close to observe its entire shape. Instead, its mass fills the sky, casting the steep slopes in gloom. The craft's smooth surface, though, is even more evident. Mackenzie remembers visiting a shipyard years ago where cranes assembled plates larger than buses, the panels welded together to assure buoyancy. This ship has no such seams, no irregularities or evidence of construction.

The helicopter ascends, leaving the three soldiers standing at the foot of the mountain. They watch as the chopper fades into the horizon.

"You know the drill," says Smith. "Get up close, get the footage, and report back. *That's all.*"

"Chopper could have taken us closer," Mackenzie says.

Smith pulls out a small pair of binoculars and hands them to her, pointing beyond the track ahead. "*Look.*"

She does. Dozens of small drones litter the uplands like

dead flies on a sill. She hands the binoculars to Wright.

"Electrical field. Nothing can get close," says Smith. "With the satellites down, we got to do it the old-fashioned way. But this is a reconnaissance mission. Do not engage with the enemy. We get to the top of the mountain, scout the area, and return to the rendezvous point, *here*."

Smith sets the pace, marching some fifteen feet ahead, and lazy wisps of cloud drift in, thickening to a white sea as they ascend.

"Where did that come from?" says Wright.

"Weather changes quick up here," Mackenzie says, wiping her nose on her smock's sleeve, pulling the hem up her arm.

"Your tattoo?" says Wright, noticing the ink inside her wrist.

Still holding her assault rifle, Mackenzie turns her left wrist and reads the italic font:

John
02/02/2020.
"John?"
"My...*husband*."
"You never—"
"Another life."

02/02/2020

"Will you get a move on? We're going to be late," shouted Jo, throwing her bag in the car's boot. Manchester was a two-hour drive away. The wedding started in two and a half.

No answer.

"*John.*"

Jo marched down the drive, burst through the front door, and found him kneeling in front of the TV, the remote hanging limply in his hand, unconcerned about the creases and carpet fluff he'd picked up on his fresh-pressed suit.

He turned around, wearing a wry if slightly guilty smile. Then he frowned. "This virus," he said. "I'm telling you, Italy is in trouble. Feels like the bloody apocalypse."

"If you don't get in the car...*now*...you won't have to worry about the *bloody apocalypse*. It's my sister's wedding. I'm not missing it because *you* didn't get up early enough."

"Need my beauty sleep."

"You didn't look too pretty, way you were snoring this morning. Still had red wine on your teeth," she said. "You can't drink that way once the baby arrives."

He grinned. "You think parents don't drink?"

"Not the responsible ones, not into a wine coma."

"I'll cut back. Months yet."

"*Seven.*"

John walked over and kissed her forehead, rubbing her belly tenderly as he did.

"I'm sorry."

She smiled. "Move it."

"Yes, sir, Sergeant Mackenzie, Sir."

"That's ma'am to you, dickhead," she said, trying to contain a laugh.

He switched off the TV with the remote and squeezed past her to get to the door. She playfully slapped him on his backside. She had once dreamed of joining the military, but at twenty-four, she already thought she was too old—not to mention too pregnant. That ship had sailed. The last thing she wanted was to enlist with a bunch of spotty teenage lads who couldn't tie their shoelaces. And John wasn't cut out for military life. While she was punctual and efficient, he was late and scatty, always daydreaming about something or other. His present hangover and dawdling had already cost them a precious twenty minutes, delaying their journey with every subsequent toilet visit and forgotten toothbrush or comb.

When they finally hit the road, the drive was smooth, the expressway clear. They passed a few coaches crammed with travelling football fans, overtook a few long-distance lorries, and that was it. Despite running late, they were making good time, listening to Radio Two at John's insistence, humming along to Fleetwood Mac, Spandau Ballet, and Tiffany. John sat in the passenger seat, nursing his hangover.

"God, you're old," she said, eyes fixed on the road ahead. "*Thirty*."

"Old," she repeated. "This music, it's—"

"Better than the crap you listen to," said John. "What's

his name, *Stomzy*?"

"Now you sound seventy."

"Respect your elders."

"Could understand if you were even...forty."

He laughed, and she felt irked by his dismissiveness. The least he could do after making them late, after making *her* drive—pregnant—was let her choose the radio station.

"Special day today," he said.

"Yeah, my sister's getting married."

"No, I mean the date."

"Your brother's birthday? *John*, you forgot last year."

"I posted a card," he said. "Think about it, the date."

"February 2nd, *and*?"

"And in numerical terms, that's 02-02-2020."

"So?"

"It's called a palindrome," he said.

"*English?*"

"It means the date reads the same backwards as it does forwards."

"Point?" she said, checking the rear-view mirror.

"Palindromic numbers are said to be significant, that's all. Time...space...everything, it's just numbers."

"What the bloody hell does that mean?"

"Time hinges around the year zero. There's before and after and—"

"Oh, *John*."

"No, there's symmetry in everything. The universe has strange...mathematical consistencies. Take a snowflake—"

"You know what I think?"

"Huh?"

"That you should get to bed earlier."

"No, you don't—"

"I get it. Life, it's all a video game, *right*?"

"I'm telling you: everything happens for a reason. There are some people—scientists, physicists—who believe in the concept of a multiverse."

"How did we jump from your brother's birthday—?"

"Imagine every time you make a choice, no matter how insignificant, the universe splits off in a new direction."

"You stay up too late, drink too much, watch too much—"

"It's like parallel universes. Imagine other versions of you...other versions of *me*."

"One's enough."

"Imagine every choice you didn't make playing out in some alternate reality. Sometimes I wonder—"

"That's dangerous."

"—about that saying: if you had an infinite number of monkeys and an infinite number of typewriters—"

"Go on."

"Well, maybe somewhere we get it right. Somewhere the world's perfect, for all of us."

"Nothing's perfect," she said.

"Apart from you."

"*Creep.*"

"Love you too," he said.

She gave in and smiled.

"I think time's an illusion."

"Tell that to my sister," she said, putting her foot down on the accelerator. "We should have left earlier."

"You know, some physicists believe the universe is tenseless, that the past, present, and future are equally real, that there's no end," he said, "that alternate realities happen concurrently."

"Bollocks."

"Based on science."

"Whose science?"

"I don't know...*NASA*?"

"Based on *Sci-Fi Channel* rubbish," she said.

"There's a prediction an asteroid could hit us in 2026."

"Six years! You'll be lucky. This virus has its way, the apocalypse is already here," she said, momentarily taking her left hand off the wheel and resting it on her stomach.

He smiled, then changed the subject. "The baby, how big do you think he is?"

"What makes you say 'he'?"

"A feeling."

"See it in the stars, did you?"

"No."

"Ancient Mayan prophecy?"

"It just feels wrong calling *him* 'it'."

"*He's* about the size of a walnut," she said, laughing.

"And you haven't felt him kick?"

"No," she said, checking her mirrors. "That doesn't happen until five months, or so I've read. I've not been pregnant before, you know."

The grey sky started to spit, rain lightly drumming

the windscreen. She turned on the wipers. He turned up the radio. Coldplay's *Clocks* was playing. Maybe it was her hormones, but she was finding the old music increasingly irritating.

"I meant what I said, about the drinking."

John remained silent. The atmosphere changed as if by the flick of a switch.

"*John.*"

"Heard you the first time."

"I know what you're like when you get together with Tom," she said. "The last thing Jade wants is her groom paralytic on her big day."

"Okay."

"I'm not doing this alone. I can't cope with a baby screaming the house down while you're at work all day, and then the second you get home, you—"

"—*try to unwind.*"

"Going to the gym is unwinding, or watching Netflix, or reading a book. Drinking a full bottle—"

"You make out like I'm a heroin addict."

"Maybe you'd snore less on smack."

"I work hard."

"More to life than work and—"

"Let's just leave it, *okay.*"

Jo bit her lip. The rain was coming down harder now. She turned the wipers to a faster speed.

"This is important, John."

"Can you just drive and get us to the bloody wedding."

"So you can get sozzled again," she snapped. "Great

wedding this is going to be."

"Great wedding, *indeed*."

She scowled at him, catching his eye in the corner of the rearview. She checked the outside lane was clear, indicated, and overtook another high-sided lorry. She remained in the outside lane.

"What do you mean by that?" she said.

"By what?"

"Sarcasm doesn't suit you."

"Couldn't think of a better way to spend my Sunday," he added.

"*Our* Sunday," she corrected.

Bill Medley was warbling on the radio about having the time of his life. The music was *really* getting under her skin now, the speaker's hum vibrating in her bones. Wasn't the song from that movie, *Dirty Dancing*? The film sickened her. *Misogynist crap.* And wasn't Swayze playing a man in his thirties, preying on teenage girls at a tacky summer camp? The film should have been called *Dirty Bastard Dancing*, as far as she was concerned. Or—what the hell? *Sex Predator.*

"You know, you didn't have to come," she said at last.

"Wanted to," he mumbled.

"Sounds like it."

"I just..."

"Just what?"

"Never mind."

"No, John, go on."

"Why would anyone choose to get married on a Sunday?"

"Because it saved them money," she said, sighing.

"And cost *me* time."

"Time...*really*?"

"Yes, really. I get twenty-five days annual leave a year and—"

"And you don't want to spend that time with me?"

"Yes, but—"

"But what?"

"Having to book tomorrow off, I don't get much annual leave, it's—"

"You talk about symmetry," she said. "Pretty ironic. There's a pattern forming here too."

"*Pattern?*"

"Your drinking, your dismissiveness, your utter selfishness."

"*Selfish?*"

"Yes, *selfish*."

"I don't see how that's selfish. I've given up my Sunday—"

"God's sake—"

"Time *is* precious."

She turned and flashed her eyes at him, meeting his.

John's face was cast in a conceited expression of self-satisfaction. Jo felt the thin line between love and hate narrow, and all the things she loved about him became the things she suddenly despised. She risked a second glance, challenging him. His deep blue eyes, usually piercing and honest, appeared self-important and cruel. His slightly large nose, which she usually thought of as endearing and masculine, now gave him the appearance of an ugly and pompous man. For that split second, she resented carrying his child.

"The only thing that's precious is you," she snapped, holding his eyes for longer than she should.

The white van pulled out. Time slowed inexplicably. Jo noticed the thick grime of dust on the van's rear windows, saw the rusted exhaust pipe spouting filthy black fumes; she read the bumper sticker: "MILF Hunter Onboard" it proclaimed.

She slammed on the brakes.

Time unspooled, and the world became a series of juddering flashes as the car skidded, righted, skidded—and then thumped into the van's rear, the windscreen exploding in a shower of glass.

◇—◇——◇—◇

"Weather's come from nowhere," says Wright.

Not weather, thinks Mackenzie, wishing for the clear skies and clarity that had been so difficult to bear.

Thick fog rolls down the slopes in a vapour avalanche, consuming the mountain. Lightning pulses, each flash transforming the topography of the pregnant black sky into an unnatural and sinister miasma. Above them, the ship gently spins, its vertex barely visible amidst the storm that seems to spread from the craft with increasing malignancy.

"Keep on," says Smith from behind.

Mackenzie leads, and as they ascend, nearing the mountain's peak, the lower-lying cloud also thickens, and they reach a knife-edged arête. The narrow ridge is perilous, separating the two steep-rising valleys on either side, the traverse requiring them to frequently scramble on all fours.

She sidles along...and sees a figure in her periphery vision. But by the time she turns her head, there's nothing but tendrils of pale vapour drifting over rock. The stress, it must be getting to her, playing tricks on her mind.

She climbs on.

Again, the figure appears, standing at the apex of a distant outcrop of rock. *John*, she thinks and slips, losing her footing, sending a mini avalanche of rocks cascading below. She steadies her breathing. Looks again.

Nothing.

But the figure's after image remains stark in her mind, the slight slope of his shoulders, the cock of his head.

John?

She flips down her night-vision goggles and scans the slopes, expecting the thermal imaging to detect a spectrum of shifting orange-red light.

Nothing...

She plants her feet wide apart and unslings her rifle, finger poised on the trigger. Then the sound of loose scree behind her—*a cry*. She turns and finds the thermal imaging of one man where there should be two.

"*No*," he roars.

She flips up her goggles.

"Gone," says Wright, kneeling over the drop on his right side, his face as pale as the snow. "He was standing right there...I told him. *I fucking told him...The ropes...*We should have used the ropes."

But far below them, where the cloud is lighter, only jagged rocks sneer.

"Shit," she shouts, her heart beating wildly, feeling a pang of guilt for being grateful the sergeant's body is out of sight. The drop at this point is almost vertical, the ground hundreds of feet below. Survival would be impossible. She imagines the shell of his skull cracked and leaking, his limbs shattered.

Wright wipes a glob of snot from his nose. Silence reigns.

They had both lost comrades before, but she had never got used to it; mourning, though, would have to come later.

"Thought I saw someone...*something*...up ahead," she says finally with urgency, pointing. "*Up there.*"

Wright flips down his own goggles, clearly still struggling with shock. "*Human?*" he asks, surveying the slopes ahead.

"I don't—"

"*Sheep?*"

"I don't know...*maybe*," she says, doubting herself.

They mark the spot where Smith fell with a small pile of rocks. Wright says a prayer. Reluctantly, they clamber on until the track levels out to firmer ground, their path widening, the inclination softening.

Both soldiers have the high conditioning of elite athletes, yet Mackenzie feels the strain of the climb on her calves. The air is thinner at this elevation, and the constant rush of adrenaline in her blood, too, coupled with a build-up of lactic acid, is causing her legs to cramp. She realises she needs glucose, electrolytes.

"*Refuel*," she says.

They rest, leaning against a shelf of rock where a hardy if delicate-looking species of alpine plant sprouts. Its purple flower is the only colour in a world that is eerily grey and silent.

Lightning, or something like it, continues to pulse above them, but no thunder follows. Both the mountain's peak and the craft's form are now hidden by cloud. Mackenzie gulps down a small bottle of orange juice, feeling its goodness infuse her. She takes two pieces of chocolate from her supplies, feels the spike of sugar replenishing her tired limbs.

"We met at basic training," Wright says, gazing absently into the snow-dappled rock. "He was like a brother to me."

She unwraps another piece of chocolate.

"You were going to tell me about your husband?"

She looks to the ground, says nothing, and when she finally raises her head, her gaze settles on his eyepatch for a split second longer than she'd intended.

"A scratch," he says. "Training Kurdish security forces. IED."

"I see."

"*I don't.*"

She smiles, grateful for his humour; she understands, in some ways, their morale is as implicit to their survival as the laser-sighted SA80 she carries on her back.

A sudden gust of wind brings a thick spume of fog, but the scream that follows is as piercing as it is unexpected, the mountain acoustics causing an unnerving echo, as if rebounding from the deepest gorge.

A shiver creeps up Mackenzie's spine. "*Alive?*" she says, feeling her neck hair prickle with goosepimples.

"*Impossible,*" says Wright.

"*That* word ceased to have any meaning about twenty-four hours ago."

"Come on," he says with a brusque nod.

They hurry, retracing their steps down the mountain slope, loose stones shifting beneath their boots like gravel. They scramble their way back across the ridge and stare into the ravine where they had assumed Smith had perished.

"Sarge?" Wright shouts.

No answer.

"*Sarge,*" he roars.

Only the mountain answers. When Wright's echo finally fades, the silence is eerie. The wind, though, continues to wail like a grief-stricken mother.

"Going down after him," says Wright.

"The ropes aren't long—"

"I'll climb."

"*Think,*" she snaps. "You can't lift him out of there, not alone."

"I can try."

"You'll die."

"If he's injured—"

"He has morphine...*supplies,*" she says. "You go down there, you're disobeying direct orders. We're talking about the entire fate of the human ra—"

"I can't leave him."

"We're nearly at the top. We get the footage, get back down, get a rescue team. We can be back in hours."

"He might not *have* hours."

"Climbing down there, *if* he is alive, will *delay* him getting proper help."

"No," he says. "You go on, get the footage. I'll take care of Smith."

"I'm not—"

"*Go*," he says.

She watches helplessly as he hurries, fixing his carabiner to the anchor, unravelling the rope from his pack, readying to make his descent.

"You only need to capture a few minutes' footage. Stay low, get what you need, and get the fuck away," he says. "Meet me back here. If I'm not back, get help."

"I can't—"

"Go," he says. "Finish this."

And within the flicker of an eye, he's gone. And she is alone, listening to the crumbling scree as Wright descends, lowering himself deep into the mouth of the chasm.

She turns back towards the mountain's peak. She grips her weapon tight and disappears deeper into the fog. Visibility is practically non-existent, and her eyes play tricks, the faint, ethereal shape of a man she once loved guiding her.

She feels the ascent, the strain on her knees, the increased resistance on her tightening buttocks as her muscles work. If she keeps climbing, she'll arrive at the summit sooner or later. But with every step, she fears the edge of some unseen cliff. Again, she imagines Smith's split-open skull, warm blood coagulating on the cold slate.

He had cried out, hadn't he?

Hadn't he?

Something had.

Still the lightning—*not lightning*—flickers, and so do memories in her mind's eye: from a decade before, John's blue eyes, his last lingering glance, regard her the second before the car slams into the back of the van, and the cold wind brings a flurry of hail, grazing her cheek like glass.

❖━◦━━━◦━❖

She woke covered in fragments of the shattered windscreen, pinned to her seat by the inflated airbag, the scent of petrol bringing her around, sharpening her senses. How long had she been out? *Seconds? Minutes?* Time had ceased to exist, yet that confounded radio station continued to blare.

Her head pounded. In the rearview mirror, the pale, bloodied face of a woman who looked ten years older stared back, regarding her with incredulity.

Ahead, blue lights swirled somewhere beyond the crumpled carnage of the pileup in which she was entombed. The electromechanical whine of a short-circuited car horn blared. Her crotch felt wet.

The baby...Oh God...The baby...

Pushing free of the airbag, she turned her head towards John and saw the ruin of the face she had loved for five years. Both her car's bonnet and the white van's rear had crumpled on impact like accordions, sending a steel rod shooting from the other vehicle's back window like a projectile through their windscreen.

She vomited, spewing the greasy contents of her stomach—the omelette John had made her for breakfast—all over the dashboard.

"Oh God, John...Oh God, no," she whimpered, drooling, acid burning her throat, the stench of puke filling her nostrils. "*John.*"

The scaffolding pole—*the spear*—separated the driver and passenger sides, pressing what was left of John's head into the cushion of the car seat. She could see in high definition the abrasive surface of the rusted steel. And she wondered how many damp days and how many wet weeks and how many miserable months and passing years had caused that corrosion. Decades maybe, the rust thickening, becoming more calloused with every drop of rain.

Time conspired.

Fate was patient.

The pole obscured much of John's face from her line of sight. But as well as her vomit, she could smell the copper tang of thick blood oozing from the ragged flap of skin that hung, exposing the layer of yellowish subcutaneous fat of his cheek.

John wheezed, trying to speak. "Lo...love..."

"I know," she said, trying to swallow.

She attempted to stretch and touch his hand, but she was still trapped by the airbag and the suitcase that had flown from the back seat on impact, wedging itself between the dash and the two passenger seats.

Blood bubbled on John's lips. "Together..." he gasped, his words trailing off. "Somewhere together...world...perfect..."

He was dying a terrible death in this sick-stinking car, and his final comfort, it seemed, was the suspect astrophysical theories of dubious internet forums.

Jo was too choked up to speak, tears streaming down her face. She reached again and managed to take his hand. She squeezed.

Oh, God no. Not John. Panic surged through her.

"Help," she screamed. "Somebody, *help!*"

When her husband finally took his last gurgling breath, she sat staring into his vacuous eyes, bleeding from her crotch as they cut her from the wreck. Removing John was a more delicate operation. Flecks of his grey matter had spattered the car's seats. Later she wondered how well they had cleaned up, how much of her husband's brain tissue that had once contained his hopes and dreams had gone with the old Nissan to the wrecking yard.

She bled for two days. When the miscarriage was finally over, she flushed the pre-foetal form down the toilet like a dead goldfish, imagining birthdays and Christmases and bad crayon drawings that would never be.

She drank herself into the worst condition she'd ever been in during a pandemic that was killing people by the thousands. Her kidneys hurt. Her skin was blotchy. Every morning, she wiped her sleep-crusted eyes and recuperated just enough to poison her body once more, only to fall asleep drunk and sufficiently numbed until morning.

It was the military that saved her.

Basic training was easy.

She embraced her physical suffering, her blistered feet, her aching muscles. Pain became her. It masked deeper wounds. With exhaustion came sleep, and three years passed in a regimented blur.

After thirty-eight months in the Royal Marines, she was encouraged to try for the Special Air Service. Forty-day marches, sleep deprivation, climbing perilous cliff faces without a harness, it was easy. The hardest part was not swallowing a bullet. Every time she considered this, her memories of John guided her.

On a cold autumn day in October, Joanne Mackenzie passed out for the SAS. Two years later, she was selected for an elite, highly covert squadron reserved for only the most dangerous of missions.

◈━◈━◇━━━◇━◈◈

Mackenzie checks her helmet camera is recording and emerges from the thick fog. The craft darkly glimmers above, its revolutions churning the cloud, the vortex pulsing with white light.

The peaks below are sheathed in a grey sea of fog, and heavenly crepuscular sunbeams fan outwards as the sun sinks below the horizon, the red sky silhouetting Snowdon's crest...

Where the heads of her comrades are mounted.

The spike has pierced Smith's thick head at an angle, hideously warping the features on his blood-drained face;

Wright's is a vapid mask, mouth hanging open above the ragged root of his neck.

Then she sees them: seven black shadows circling the decapitated remains. Cloaked in monastic robes, they raise their arms as if in ceremony towards the craft and the whirling vortex above. The creatures' eyes burn as bright as stars from deep within their cowls, and their serrated mandibles faintly gleam, gluey secretions dribbling between labia-like mouthparts.

Pumped with adrenaline, she aims her assault rifle, but a sudden shift in air pressure causes excruciating pain to erupt outward from her sinuses. Her ears pop. She presses her palms against the sides of her head, dropping her weapon, blood running down her neck.

The air beneath the rotating craft is shivering like a summer heat haze, and the bright balls of light are orbiting the ship at quicker and quicker speeds, the surrounding storm, too, a cosmic swirl.

Then the thunderclap booms in old-testament fury, the sky shattering as violently as a windscreen in a high-speed crash. Shadows bleed from the hole that has appeared in the atmosphere, ribbons of darkness unfurling like ink in water.

Rock cracks and splits, fissures spreading on the mountainside as if disturbed by a tectonic shift; impossibly reddening veins of magma appear like branches of arteries, steam rising in the cold air, melting the last pockets of winter snow.

She hears the rhythm of distant drums beating from beyond the hole in the sky, the mournful sound of a battle horn...*marching*...the legion advancing. She hears this even before the portal's gate is breached and their blasphemous banners emerge at the mountain's summit.

She scrambles on her knees for her weapon, only for it to be kicked away. The seven are upon her, surrounding her, long robes billowing in the sulphur-smelling wind.

Their dialect fills her head like a radio transmission, planting vivid pictures in her mind's eye: she sees ruined cities beneath strange skies; she sees endless rows of towering pyramids and granite-built columns; she sees great lunarlike vistas and endless deserts; she sees boundless, roiling oceans and planets with seven suns. She sees fire, she sees death, and she sees whole worlds burning in the flicker of an eye. The creatures push her mind to its limits, manipulating her neural processes beyond the point of sanity.

By the time her bladder lets go, Hell's army is flooding the mountainside, the horde's dreadful percussion louder now than her fast-beating heart. Their tune is maddening, the whistle of their pipes infecting her aspect as nightmarish, birdlike shadows move past her in the falling dark. One soldier plays a wind instrument fashioned from a human torso; another beats a drum sculpted from a head with sticks made from bone.

Her place in the universe feels small, inconsequential; her death will be an irrelevance, and as the hot wind whips up to a human-like scream, she imagines a million others crying out in protest at the planet's annihilation.

The nearest creature unsheathes its blade, eyes glittering blindingly bright, and her only comfort is the long silence she hopes will follow the end of her days.

0Ɛ02/20/Ɛ0

John sat in the passenger seat. He turned up the car radio. Coldplay's *Clocks* was playing.

"Do you have to?" said Jo.

"What, the radio?"

"Yes, *the radio*. I can't hear the satnav. Going to be late for the church. The last thing I need is to get lost."

"Loads of time," said John.

The sky was a grey slate, rain spitting at the windscreen with every gust of cold wind that brought a swirl of red and brown leaves.

"I meant what I said," Jo said, watching the road, "about the drinking."

"Haven't touched a drop in—"

"I know," she said, indicating before pulling out. "But I know what you boys are like, especially when you get to-gether with Tom. It's a *christening*, a family occasion, not an excuse for you to go quaffing booze like you're twenty-five. You're forty."

"Don't I know it."

She smiled in the rearview. "You okay back there, Wal-nut?"

"Don't call me that," said Will, scowling, his concen-tration directed at his games console. Strapped into the car's backseat, his upper lip was stained with chocolate milk-shake, giving him the appearance of a younger boy. He was growing up so quick. Sometimes she felt she lost more of him minute by minute, time stealing the baby they'd made.

Jo said, "Walnut, it's what we called you when—"

"Heard it a million times, Mum."

"*A million*?" she said.

"Six noughts," said Will, looking proud.

"Very good" she said.

"Well, now you've heard it one million and one," said John, flicking through the radio stations. "How many noughts has one million and one?"

Jo watched in the rearview mirror as Will furrowed his brow in concentration.

"Five noughts and another one," said Will.

"Spot on...and that's a palindrome," said John, turning his head around his seat to acknowledge his son.

"What's that, Dad?"

John said, "It's a—"

"Story for another day," interrupted Jo. "We've a christening to get to. I can't hear the satnav with all the blabbering, and we are running out of—"

"Classic," John said, ignoring her protests and turning up the radio.

Bill Medley was warbling about having the time of his life.

Jo swore under her breath, but she thought she might be having the time of hers too. Life was hectic and unpredictable, but on days like this, when the three of them were together, things couldn't have felt more perfect, and if they *were* late, well, it wasn't the end of the world.

RICHARD CLIVE
ABOUT THE AUTHOR

Richard Clive is a writer, journalist and editor living in the medieval town of Conwy, North Wales, with his wife, daughter and pet Labrador. Richard studied film and scriptwriting in Manchester and describes himself as a horror and science fiction writer. His passions include books, old horror movies, long walks and tea. Richard's story Made in Hell was published by Sinister Smile Press in its If I Die Before I Wake: Volume 5, and his story The Fever and The Thaw features in Skywatcher Press's Pandemic Unleashed anthology. Find out more about Richard here:

https://www.facebook.com/richard.clive.332
https://www.amazon.com/-/e/B098PHRD4K

OFFICE EDUCATION
STEVEN STREETER

Brent sat in the back of the bus and stared at his smartphone. The GPS application told him Shannen was already at the Education Development Unit (EDU) offices. He shook his head and watched as the world whizzed past. The traffic seemed heavier than usual, but that was probably just a simple matter of perception; he was running late, and everything felt worse than it really was.

The phone blipped, and he stared at it.

A message from Shannen. *ETA?*

He grimaced. The only reason she would have sent that was if all of them were already there and waiting for him, and because of his position as secretary, they really couldn't start without him. But at least she could see he was on his way. They shared the GPS app so they could see where one another was without having to send messages or make calls, which could have made things awkward with their respective partners.

That evening was actually an official work function.

5 min, on bus, he quickly typed.

She responded with a smiley face emoji.

He decided not to reply. All he needed was for Shannen's husband to find something he sent. And with that in mind, he deleted her messages, just in case. Not that Alyce seemed to suspect anything. She was a teacher like himself, and meetings of various professional groups like that one were par for the course. But he could never be too careful.

The bus stopped, and he climbed off, then started to jog in the direction of the building where the Math Teachers Association met. He rounded the next corner, and there it was, nestled between a delicatessen on one side—already closed at that time of the night—and a yellow building on the other, which housed the headquarters for an art collective underwritten by one of the state's universities. One day, he would gather the courage to go inside and have a look at that place. It had always intrigued him.

He paused briefly in front of the stone walls painted such a bright yellow they almost glowed. The dull, rhythmic thud of music being created somewhere inside it pummelled the air while a young couple sat close to one another out front, sharing a cigarette and a painting easel.

He smiled and nodded in their direction. They returned the gesture, and he grabbed the handle of the door to his building.

◇──◇────◇──◇

Shannen stared at her phone, watching the yellow marker emblazoned with Brent's number getting closer, and zoomed in a little. He had stopped next door. Maybe one of the university kids had asked him a question or something.

"So, where is he?" growled Marcia.

"It's not his fault," Shannen shot back, her glance shifting to the glass door. The windows that made the front of the building were covered in EDU sponsored advertising, obscuring all movement outside.

"I know. I know. Stupid bloody public transport," Marcia replied.

"I had a kid an hour late for school last week because the bus driver took a wrong turn," one of the others said.

The discussion quickly turned away from the lateness of the committee's secretary to the problems with the government. Shannen, though, was concerned. She looked back at her phone.

Brent's GPS signal was now blue and flickering. Low signal strength? Was his battery running low? Well, that wouldn't matter; he'd be there soon enough.

◇━◆━━◇━━◆◇

Brent pushed down on the handle and entered the front foyer of the building, closing it behind him with a loud click.

His hand jerked away from the handle, and he looked down. *An electric shock? Where did that come from?*

He shook his head, then stopped short. It was dark. *Where is everyone? And where are the lights?*

He turned and looked behind himself at the windows. Black paint had been splashed over them, but through multiple scratches in the enamel, he could see that wooden boards had also been placed on the other side of the glass, completely enclosing the place in gloom.

That was ridiculous.

He would surely have noticed planks of wood hammered over the windows as he came in. In fact, he was positive he remembered seeing posters advertising the union's latest pay claim that blocked anything inside from being visible.

He shook his head and walked across to flick on the light.

The switch moved freely, but there was no clicking sound, definitely no illumination. He shook his head. *Why wouldn't they have told me about a change in venue?* Shannen would have made sure he knew, unless everyone thought everyone else was going to tell him. Not unheard of in groups that came from so many different worksites. He pulled his phone out and looked at the screen.

His flag was right where he expected it to be. But it was blue. *What happened to the normal yellow?* He wracked his brain and then looked at the screen once more. Blue meant poor signal. But it had never been poor in the middle of the central business district before. His battery indicator told him he still had three-quarters power, so it wasn't the battery. Maybe it was the phone itself, but why would it lose signal so suddenly? *Is there some sort of interference in the building?*

He looked at the screen again, then tapped to zoom in closer. Where was Shannen's yellow flag?

He removed his own indicator.

Her yellow flag stood there, unmoving.

Shannen's position was, according to the screen, right where he was standing.

He stopped, holding himself completely still.

A single thump, like a bass drum, came from a long, long way away. A second or so later, it was echoed from even further afield.

That was it.

Where is the traffic? The rhythmic and constant drumming from the gallery next door? The sounds of the city in general? Brent had heard of silence being deafening, but he had never understood just what that meant before.

He was in the EDU offices, in the middle of the city, had just caught a damn bus in heavy traffic to get there. None of it made any sense whatsoever. He looked at the phone once again, but his hand was shaking so much he was having trouble seeing the screen. His own position indicator once more covered Shannen's completely, still blue, flickering to deep purple.

The colour of last known position, no current signal at all.

A drop of sweat ran down his nose and splattered on the corner of the screen. He swallowed and licked his lips, then tapped Shannen's number.

It took him two attempts to get it.

He hit the dial key, held the phone to his ear, and waited.

Shannen's phone rang in her hand, and she jumped a little. The name "Brent G" flashed up on the screen. She lifted the phone to her ear and moved away from the rest.

"Where are you?" she hissed.

"I'm here."

She could not believe how shaky he sounded, as though he was freezing.

"Where?" she demanded.

"Right...ere...fron...yer...are...what...no...ing..."   And with that, his voice cut out completely.

She stared at the screen. "Signal Lost." The GPS indicator was still there, but Brent's flag was deep purple, indicating a last known position.

And that position was right there, with her. As she watched, it flickered blue, but the flag did not move.

As far as the smartphone was concerned, he was in the building.

"Was that Brent?" Marcia demanded.

"No, wrong number," Shannen heard herself say, unable to take her eyes from the screen and the anomalous reading that confronted her.

◇━◦━◦━━━◦━◦━◇

Brent ran his hand over his face, wiping away the nervous sweat that was building up too quickly. The phone had cut out, but he had made it through to her. Talking was not going to be possible, but...

He looked at the screen and saw his flag turn from purple to blue. He had a signal, and he quickly started to type.

Where the hell are you?

He waited, looking around in the gloom. A notice on the wall behind him indicated the emergency evacuation procedures, the same notice he had seen in every government building he had ever worked in. *Make your way down the stairs. Do not use the elevator. Use the exit door for your assigned area.* In texta after that was written, *Ground floor exit door is main front door.* Then the regular printing once more, *Gather on the sidewalk. Make sure you cannot be seen from the air. Obey the instructions of the armed supervisors. If confronted, run.*

He nodded at the comforting words he had seen a hundred times before.

He stopped.

Cannot be seen from the air? Armed supervisors? Run if confronted? What in the hell? Some sort of bizarre joke? He read it again, confirming that he had been right the first time, and even noted that the insignia at the bottom of the poster was the usual seal of the state government.

The phone in his hands blipped, and he fumbled it briefly before looking at it.

We are all here in front foyer. Where R U? GPS says UR here.

He tapped the screen.

Mine, too.

⋄━◇━━◇━◆⋄

Shannen walked away from the group towards the rear of the front foyer. She was having trouble thinking, and her breathing became constricted. Her hand fell to her pocket where her asthma inhaler nestled comfortably against her thigh. She sat down on the bottom stair of the flight leading to the offices of staff who worked there during the day.

She stared at the screen, dominated by Brent's *Mine too* message. She looked around, knowing it was futile. *Where could he be?* Her attention was caught by the poster beside her.

Is there a teaching poster next 2 the stairs? she tapped quickly.

Yes.

The one here says, Teaching – the real oldest profession.

She winced even as she typed it. It was the union's latest attempt to get attention for their pay negotiations, and it had certainly done that. Everyone in the city knew about the campaign. The amount of parents complaining because they had been forced to explain to curious children what the "oldest profession" meant—and if it wasn't teaching, what was it—was legion.

The response took a long time to come.

⁂

Education – the difference between Us and Them.

Brent looked at it even as he finished typing and hesitated before hitting the send button. *What in the hell does that even mean?* It was like something out of a 1950's propaganda piece, but the design, the photograph of the stern looking teacher—he guessed—at the left, and the way the whole thing was put together looked much too modern to be from that bygone era of "Reds under the Beds" paranoia.

He closed his eyes, listening to the nothing all around him, and then hit the send. The beep echoed through the entire structure, and he winced a little.

He lowered himself slowly onto the stair and watched his phone's screen, waiting for a response. He gazed at the door in front of him, shaded from the outside world by black paint and wooden boards.

Maybe he should have a look out there.

Maybe he had unwittingly stumbled into some sort of art installation designed by a university student with a warped sense of reality.

He tried the handle, waiting for another electric shock that never came. It turned. He exhaled slowly, not even realising until then that he had been holding his breath. With his weight pushed against it, it moved only a fraction, and what sounded like a nail in wood protested against him. Apart from that, it held fast.

He manoeuvred himself around to peer through the crack in the door.

The street was dark, and no lights were on. It wasn't nighttime. Where had the light gone?

But even in the darkness outside, he could see that the trees, which should have lined the street, were not there. And he was sure he could make out a car skewed across the road, no glass in the window that he could see and possibly no wheels either.

He fell back, panting, the gap in the door closing as he did so. As though moving would leave behind the view of outside, he looked at the handle and backed slowly away, hoping it would all cease to exist.

Because it could not exist.

He laughed at himself and went back to the stairs to sit down. He'd fallen asleep on the bus, and it was all some bad dream borne of too many recent late nights.

It had to be a dream because it could not be real.

The phone blipped, and he jumped and grabbed it.

What the F U talkin bout???

He could even hear Shannen's anger in that brief text message. If he was with her, he'd be wincing at the force of her words, and he would know that their stolen moments would stop for a few months at the least. But it was serious because that text message and what he was feeling was telling him that, if it was a dream, it was a lot more realistic than any he had ever experienced before.

His every sense was working overtime, the silence punctuated by sounds, what he could see around him, the mental shock of it all. It was all too real.

He inhaled deeply. The air had the hint of smoke and dampness, even the faint taste of something foul on the wind. He ran his finger over the wall beneath the poster, leaving behind a smear in the caked-on, damp dirt, feeling it like a moist film of slime.

Yes, his every sense really was working and telling him that where he was was not only real, but was somewhere he should not be.

Blip.

brent.

He stared at the phone and watched as his blue flag changed to deep purple again.

No signal.

And he suddenly felt indescribably alone.

⟡⸻⟡⟡⸻⟡

Shannen hit the send key again, but the response "Could not be sent" flashed onto her screen. The message was terse and angry, but that was how she was feeling. She glared at the screen.

"What the fuck are you up to?" she whispered at it. But the GPS app still told her his phone was right there, in that building, matching the position of hers as near to exactly as the device could ascertain.

She felt her chest tighten, and she rammed the inhaler into her mouth. Two deep puffs and inhalations, eyes closed...relaxation. She needed to relax.

Her gaze moved upwards. She did not know how, but that was where he had to be. He was right above her on the next floor.

Some joke.

He was going to cop it.

Why she had ever allowed herself to become involved with that arsehole in the first place, she would never know.

In her pocket, the phone's screen changed.

"Message Sent" flashed across it.

⟡⸻⟡⟡⸻⟡

Fuk U!

Brent stared at that message for a long time. The smartphone told him she was so incredibly close, and yet he had no idea where she was. And then that message. She clearly felt he was playing a joke, a bad one. The meeting was running late, and she was probably copping all the flack for it.

Not that the others knew the truth of their relationship, but still...

He could not blame her. Would he have believed her if she had told him that she was going through something similar? He looked at the phone again. She didn't believe him—hell, he didn't believe him—but he had to make her understand.

Am sitting on stairs. Windows black. Cold. No one here. Where are u?

A simple explanation, but he could not think of anything else. What could he say? *I'm in the Education Development Unit offices, and I'm all alone, and there's nobody anywhere here.* Well, that would just about cover it, but it certainly would not make any sense.

A low droning sound came from somewhere above. A flash of light made its way across the top of the stairs, then disappeared, and the droning noise faded. *I'm not alone?* Brent slowly climbed to his feet. He opened his mouth but thought better of it and slowly made his way upwards.

He moved carefully and silently, helped by the fact the stairs were concrete, built into the wall when the place had been constructed. But the higher he went, the colder it grew. The smoky smell and that foul taste in the air grew thicker and thicker. The stairs ran to the left, and he paused at the landing, staring upwards. He could see the roof of the building, but a breeze hit his face. A cold breeze.

The droning sound came again, and he waited briefly. So much louder, and he saw the light enter the rooms above before disappearing behind the roof above him. Brent just stared at its path, swallowing hard. The chill that ran down his spine was not due entirely to the cold.

His phone blipped, and he cried out a little. He reached into his pocket and pulled it out.

Wat th F U on about?

He groaned. She was not seeing it. He shook his head. The poster in the corner of the landing caught his eye. "They hate Us," the legend declared. And in the background of the poster—torn at the bottom but lacquered well to the wall— was a picture of a child no more than ten or eleven, laying on his back on a swing, covered in blood.

Brent shivered again. The image was well done.

Very well done.

In fact, if he did not know better, he would swear it was real, with the little flaps of skin around the wound in the neck, the trickles of blood coming from multiple little cuts. He looked closer; the head looked like it had been almost completely ripped off. The bones protruding from the chest looked like white sticks, not ribs. The photoshopping on it was intense and really disturbing.

Really, really disturbing.

All too realistic.

That was not something he ever expected to see on an

Education Department poster.

He shook his head. If only Shannen could see that, then...

He looked at the phone and cursed himself. He made his way halfway back down the stairs and aimed the smartphone at the front of the building. A few taps on the front of the screen and a flash of light told him that the photograph had been taken. He nodded to himself and quickly sent it on.

An error message flashed up on the screen. "Signal lost—transfer incomplete."

He shook his head and slammed the phone into his pocket, retracing his steps back to the landing halfway up to the second storey. The disappointment of his failure faded from his mind as he looked up at that darkness above him, only to be replaced by fear.

He knew he should, at the very least, see what was up there. He had to go. What other choice did he have, apart from cowering like a child in the front foyer and waiting for the sun to come up?

In his pocket, the phone's screen flashed into life briefly. "Image PSM12-670 sent."

⬥━━◇━━━◇━━⬥

The second storey was made up of a single large room with a smaller kitchen and bathroom—including a shower, Shannen noted with amusement—with several desks dotted around the walls, a large whiteboard on one wall, lots of computers, half a dozen full bookcases, and a wide empty area in the centre of the floor.

But she also saw no sign of Brent anywhere. She looked at her phone again and saw that his signal was blue, that he was right where she was. That would mean the only other place he could be had to be the roof. But that was even too much for Brent, whose sense of humour was not something that endeared him to her.

Her anger was quickly being replaced by worry. Really, what was he doing?

The phone gave a dinging sound. *A multimedia message?* A sense of foreboding hit her hard, and she apprehensively looked at the smartphone's screen.

The picture was dark, but she recognised it. The dull red carpet, the beige walls, the poster off to one side—that was everything downstairs. She started down the steps and paused at the landing. She looked down, then moved a few more steps, gazing at the view before her and back to the one on the phone. He had taken the picture from there. The timestamp told her that it had been taken less than three minutes before, sent through the same communication tower that her phone was using. Was it Photoshop? Was he really pushing the joke that far?

She tapped the screen and zoomed in on the picture. The poster was not the one she could see in front of her, and it was obvious even at that angle. She could make out the start of the word "Education" and "Us and," just like he had said.

It was damned advanced digital manipulation, and as

good as he was with electronic gadgets, it was not something he could throw together in a few minutes.

Come on – where are YOU!? she typed, making her way back up the stairs, away from the others whose agitation was growing increasingly vocal.

◇◈◦ ◦────◦ ◦◈◇

Brent ignored the phone as he approached the top of the stairway.

He could see the sky, a thick cloudbank of black and grey moving with the wind, blocking out the sun or moon or whatever other celestial body was supposed to be shining down on them all. Most of the roof and wall at the front of the building was missing, and the smell was like the odour of rotting vegetation. The large, single room up there was empty, with the remains of a whiteboard hanging from one wall by a single screw. But what he noticed above all was the scene in front of him.

Where was his city?

He should have been able to see the high-rise buildings from there, the church steeples, the tall trees. Instead, it looked like every building had been cut off at three storeys, and the roofs of every structure he could see had been punctured in some way, like the one he was standing in. Trees had been ripped out of the ground and dumped, cars dotting the roads in various states of destruction. And flying above it all were objects he could not really make out, except that each of them shone a beam of white light down into what was left of the city.

A red glow fell from one of them to the ground below, landing with a percussive thud and a flash of light like a brief explosion. The shaking hit him again, coupled with the need to throw up. *This can not be real. No way...no way...*

He did not bother to read the message sent to him as he set up another photograph showing the hole in the building and, he hoped, the city beyond, quickly forwarding it to Shannen. The flash took on the magnitude of a lightning strike in the complete darkness.

Almost immediately, the droning sound grew quickly closer.

Brent knew instinctively that he did not want to be caught there, and he darted back to the stairwell, laying on his stomach on the steps, eyes looking through the cavity above him that should not have been there.

He saw the light first, a single beam of white scouring the area. It slowed as it reached the EDU building. That gave Brent the opportunity to see its source. It was oval shaped, maybe as large as a family car, coloured dark grey with lighter grey markings. There were no rotor blades, no engine exhaust, nothing to give an indication of any means of propulsion, just an oval vessel with a spotlight beneath. It was like nothing he had ever seen before. He moved backwards a step, sliding uncomfortably on his stomach and chest.

The light stopped at the edge of the building, but Brent could not see what it was focused on.

A red circle opened up in the bottom of the hovering craft, and a figure was lowered by a cable from it. It looked like a headless silver bat or bird, and when the cable detached itself, it hovered in the air. A series of circles opened around the body of the object, each red and each shining its own beam of light across its surroundings.

Brent slid down the stairs, bumping his way down until he reached the landing, and managed to make his feet. He ran down to the front door and grabbed the handle, pressing his whole bodyweight against it.

◆━━━━━━━◆

Shannen looked at the picture that suddenly reached her. *What in the hell is that?* She stood at the top of the stairs, facing the wall whose windows gave a view across a city she knew well.

The image sent to her was that same city, taken from that same spot, but it was not the city she was seeing in real life.

She did not care about anything anymore. It was not anything she should be seeing. But it was where Brent was.

Her Brent.

She tried to make the call.

"The number you are trying to reach is out of service range," came an automated voice, and she hung up immediately.

She tapped her message urgently. *Get the FUCK outa there!!*

◆━━━━━━━◆

The smartphone blipped, and Brent risked looking at

it. He managed to smile a little.

"That's what I'm trying to do, Shan," he whispered.

He started to put the phone away again but then paused. He glanced behind him at the stairs but could see nothing out of the ordinary.

Luv U, he tapped quickly and sent it before he could change his mind.

Then, he pulled the phone out once more and brought up his messages again. He grimaced a little and wiped a tear from the corner of his eye, sending the same message to Alyce, his wife of seven years.

He hoped he would get the chance to explain it to her…

◇━◦━◦───◦━◦◇

Shannen looked at the message and leant her head against the wall. Tears quickly welled up in her eyes.

"I love you, too," she whispered to the message as she slid to the floor, just staring at those two little words.

◇━◦━◦───◦━◦◇

The red glow on the walls was accompanied by a deep buzzing noise. Brent watched as the light came down the stairwell, and then the silver bat-thing came into view. From that angle, it looked as though it was metallic, but apart from that, Brent could not work out what it was. It stopped moving.

One of the red lights shifted and illuminated Brent's face and chest.

He froze and felt his heart speed up. He readied himself and then darted to one side, aiming for any of the three meeting rooms through the door beside the stairs.

The flying thing anticipated his movements and blocked his escape before once more shining that red light on Brent's body.

The crackle of lightning came from the tips of both wings as Brent tried another sideways movement. The electricity that charged the air grazed across Brent's back. Tingling ran through his body with a burning pain in the muscles across his shoulders. The smell of cooking meat rose quickly, coupled with the feel of wetness dribbling down his skin.

Brent allowed himself to fall to the floor, and he glanced sideways at the thing. The red lights were duller, but the glow was gradually increasing. He assumed it was recharging. That gave him a small chance, and he grasped the door handle, ramming his shoulder and hip against it. The wood outside started to give with a distinct *crack*. The pain in his shoulder running from the burns on his back was excruciating, but he knew he had to fight through it as hard as he could. He did not know what was going on, or what he was facing, but he knew his life depended on it.

He risked a glance at the thing, moving his body as he did so. The arcs of electricity struck the door right where he had been standing, one of the unnatural lightning bolts searing right through the palm of his hand as it rested on the metal handle.

Brent screamed and clutched the hand to his chest as

the handle exploded, along with the black-painted glass and some of the wood on the other side. The lights of the flying object were once more dulled, and Brent knew that was his one and only chance. He stepped back and then ran at the door, hitting it with all his weight from a poorly timed jump.

The door flew open, and he spilled out into the street, tumbling across the footpath before tripping and landing on the bitumen of the road, sliding across it painfully.

A car skidded to a sudden and loud halt, the squealing tyres sending up a small cloud of acrid grey smoke. The two young people using the shared easel in front of the gallery came to Brent's side.

"Where the hell'd you come from?" one asked as the driver of the car showed a single finger and drove around them.

Brent looked wildly about, then down at his hand. Blood was oozing out of a hole in the centre of his palm as large as a coin, and his fingers twitched uncontrollably. The pain in his back burned hotter, and skin had been scraped from his legs when he had been hurled outwards across the road.

He sat up suddenly and looked all around, at the buildings, the cars, the trees, the people. And he started to laugh wildly, hysterically.

The door of the EDU building opened, and Shannen sprinted out to his side. "Christ, Brent, what happened?"

He just shook his head.

"Oh fuck, look at you," she whimpered, touching the bloodied hand. She leant her forehead against his and whispered, "Really, what happened?"

He closed his eyes and felt the tears running down his cheeks. "No idea," he replied as the rest of their committee joined them in the middle of the road, all anger dissipating when they saw the injuries that marred his body. Too many questions were thrown at him for him to answer, and he just let his body collapse a little.

Many hands lifted him to his feet and almost carried him toward the offices, but he barely noticed them. He opened his eyes and found himself frantically scanning the skies above them all. But as they reached the door, he recoiled in horror.

"No," he begged, pushing away from the building. "Please no..."

Shannen was at his side straight away and saw his eyes once more look skywards. The others did as he asked and lowered him to the ground while Marcia rang for an ambulance on her phone.

Confusion reigned.

But all Brent could think about was the sky...and what it held...

STEVEN STREETER
ABOUT THE AUTHOR

Steven Streeter is from rural Australian and has been writing since childhood. He is a former professional wrestler, with two children, and is currently completing his third university degree. An unabashed fan of pulp fiction and escapist entertainment, he has a number of books waiting to come out through various publishers around the world.

Twitter: @Streeter_Writer

THE GRAND FINALE
STEVE NEAL

"There's two ways this morning goes." The officer stood in the lobby of the inn, blocking the route to the sole exit. He was a portly, elderly gentleman with a handlebar mustache that curled inward toward cracked lips, grey hairs stained yellow from tobacco use. "You and your... companion...follow us back to town, and we talk this out in front of the station, or you wake up in the back of the wagon. Your choice. This isn't strictly an arrest."

"Yeah," the other officer snarled. A lanky, younger man, clean-shaven and scowling, he tapped his baton against his right shoulder, pressing it down like a caveman carrying his club.

Bernard didn't bother conferring with Alfred, his driver and confidant, before nodding. "We'll follow. We don't want to cause any trouble." He spoke with an Italian accent. It was an affect adopted for his stage persona, Davide Dolos, which he maintained when around anyone aside from Alfred, out of earshot from anyone who might expose him for a fraud and not the well-traveled magician he claimed.

"Wise choice. I'd prefer if this didn't end in more bloodshed," the older officer said, garnering a grunt from his underling. "After you."

Alfred led the way out of the inn's lobby, a drab, grey room of stone and oak support beams, void of any decoration aside from an ash-filled fireplace and small wire-haired rug by the front door with its bristles caked in mud. Outside, the day greeted them with a soft warmth and subtle golden glow, a still summer morning where the night's chill lingered, not yet warmed by the cresting sun. Aside from the crunch of their footsteps on the gravel path that led around the side of the inn, the world remained quiet, the birds and insects yet to wake and start their chatter and chirping to fill the countryside.

The path led them to the back of the inn where Alfred parked the stagecoach and stabled the horses the prior night. In front of the gate, the officers had parked the police wagon sideways to take up most of the path, ensuring it was difficult for a person to squeeze by, let alone for a stagecoach and a couple of horses to make an escape. The pair inched by without commenting on it, knowing that anything spoken out of turn might result in a baton crashing into the base of their neck or side of their knee.

Alfred led the way through the gate, heading to his horses to release them from their stables, strapping them into the front of the carriage, while Bernard tossed his steamer trunk into the far door of the coach, unwilling to let the officers get a free view inside. He hopped up onto the bench where

Alfred would spend the long hours driving, prepared to ride alongside him, a rare occurrence left for the sunniest of days or special events. He tried to act natural, settle into the cushioned seat like hours of travel molded it to his buttocks, to look like he belonged and was comfortable high up, exposed to the elements.

Alfred didn't make eye contact as he attached the horses to their reins and prepared them for the trip ahead. He took his seat next to Bernard, smacking the horses forward towards the gate, stopping them a few feet in front of it.

"Ready when you gentlemen are," Bernard said to the officers who stood on either side of their own carriage, the lanky one still clutching his baton as if loosening his grip would allow the pair to make a daring escape across the surrounding fields of cows and crops.

Neither Bernard nor Alfred said anything as the officers prepped their horses for travel, nor when they moved forward down the gravel and out onto the dirt road. It was not until the wind whipped into their faces and they were at a full canter that they felt the safety necessary to speak freely.

"You need to tell me exactly what happened last night," Alfred said, staring forward at the road, a hint of fury cracking through his usually deferential demeanor.

"I don't know. They just...went crazy. Stormed the stage a few seconds after the finale."

"But why? They're going to question us, and if I don't have the answers...Listen, they're polite now, but that's out the window when we're in their town. It'll be the gallows, and I don't want to hang next to you if you fucked this up." Alfred paused and finally turned his head to talk to Bernard eye to eye. "No offense."

"The door." Bernard didn't want to keep eye contact, happy to focus on the passing trees lurching over the road, curved at their halfway point, forming a tunnel over the road that blocked out the sun. "I don't know what happened, don't know what it showed them, but whatever it was, they didn't like. Started yelling, throwing stuff—"

"What is it?" Alfred cut him off.

"I couldn't tell you. Honestly, I've not the foggiest. This isn't magician's code horseshit; I have no idea. It was in the corner of Horatio's warehouse with a sheet over it, no documentation, and you know what he was like with that stuff. Figured it was something half-cocked he never finished, looked it over, couldn't find any wires, no holes or slits. Seemed perfectly normal. So, I opened it, and Alfy... it's impossible. I couldn't see the warehouse through it, just a meadow, but it looked real, alive. It moved, and I swear, up and down, I swear that I could see the blades of grass moving, could feel the wind that made them sway. And there was two people, arm in arm, rolling around, laughing. I heard them. Don't know what they said, not a language I've ever heard, but it was noise. They made noise. Do you know how incredible that is? Without anything visible. They looked at me, made eye contact, and both of them looked lifelike, like I was staring at them from fifty feet away. It unnerved me, frankly. I've never seen anything like that, not from up close. If I was looking at the door from across the warehouse, sure, he could fake that. An inch in front of my face? I don't know. I don't possibly know. All I was certain about was it had to be part of my act. Something that incredible? I had to. You understand, right? It's the kind of thing that'd make me national news."

"And I think it might," Alfred grumbled. "That doesn't tell me what happened. That doesn't explain what happened out front last night."

"Out front was nothing. Yeah, they spooked the horses—"

"You didn't see it. You were safe back there." Alfred spoke fast to cut him off, his nose scrunching up as he suppressed his anger and kept his voice low as to not let it carry forward to the officers ahead. "They were fighting in the streets. Trying to climb up here, clawing at the horses." He leant across and lowered his voice even further. "Had to twat a guy around the head, climbed up next to me with madness, pure madness in his eyes, pupils wider than a shilling. Don't tell me it was worse inside. We barely made it out alive."

"I got out of there quick, the second it started...but I saw...look, when I opened the door, I opened it toward me, showed it to them, never saw inside. But I heard it. That language again, a man speaking clearly, proudly. And the audience dropped. No wonder, no amazement, just terror and disbelief. Some ran for the exits. Some started down the aisles. I signaled for the curtains to be closed, and I bolted."

"Because they rushed the stage?"

"Because of how they did it. They didn't charge at me. They dropped to their knees, crying, begging for mercy and for forgiveness. They were screaming about their sins, how they weren't worthy, and…" Bernard's head fell into his hands, needing a momentary break to collect himself.

In the shadow, he saw the scenes replaying, the writhing mass of bodies crawling over one another down the aisles, scratching at the faces of those below them, the streams of blood pouring from gouged wounds and split lips. And then the darkness, the increasing blackness of wide pupils that inflicted all of them. He yanked his head upward, back to the light, away from the visions.

"They didn't care who or what was in their way. They just crawled, slapping and scraping their way down the aisle. Whatever the door showed them…it wasn't what I saw in the warehouse. I don't have a better answer for you."

Alfred grunted. "Coppers won't accept that. True or not, they're gonna wanna know. If we don't have our story straight, they're going to have us swing. And I ain't. I fucking ain't."

Past the farmhands plowing fields, through the thin, winding country lanes that sauntered beneath the boughs, the pair tried to conjure an explanation for the night's events, something that'd leave the officers angry but sated, a tale that would earn a lifetime ban from the town but avoid the gallows.

Whatever Bernard came up with, Alfred poked holes in, tried to assume the role of an officer looking for the slightest reason to execute them. Nothing worked. Everything always led back to the same result.

"Show us then," Alfred groaned after the sixth time

repeating it. "It's unavoidable."

The town's meager silhouette appeared below them as they crested a hill, nestled between more empty fields and dense woods, bisected by a slender, sinuous river, void of any identifiable factors or points of interests. Even its focal point, the church spire that loomed over the rest of the town, was a duplicate of myriad others across the south of the country. Behind it, billows of smoke filled the sky, dark plumes befitting the great industry of the far-off coastal towns despite not a single smokestack on the horizon.

Time ran thin, less than twenty minutes before the officer's wagon led them through the cobble streets, still drying from the night's bloodshed, and to separate cells for interrogation.

"Maybe that's not a bad thing," Bernard said with the finish line glaring at him.

"You can't be serious."

"Let them look. Either they see what I saw, and the trick is safe—we're safe—or they see what the audience did... well...I don't think they're going to be much of an issue."

Alfred blustered, opening and closing his mouth multiple times before sputtering out, "That's murder," as quiet as he could with it still making it to Bernard's ears.

"Is it? We're not doing anything. Hell, we don't even have to open it ourselves. But if we don't stop them...are we culpable?"

"You can't justify that with a technicality. You know what it'd be. I know what it'd be."

"If it's that or hang, which would you prefer?"

Alfred didn't respond, some combination of the town's increasing proximity and the unwillingness to admit compliance aloud silencing him.

The horses slowed to a trot, the thud of their footfall turning to clacks as their hooves hit stone for the first time in miles. The streets, though deserted, appeared normal at first. Row houses nestled side by side, three stories tall and thin enough to cross in under ten steps. A pristine if boring town, quaint if solemnity were of the highest importance, a place where people could grow old and wither away without any disturbance. Well-maintained gardens sat out front the properties, manicured lawns demarcated with rose bushes and pansies, others with sprouting carrots and cabbage. The idyllic town rotated from Bernard's sight as they followed the wagon's turn from the street.

Storefronts came into view, brick constructions with plate windows showing off their wares. They passed the butcher, then the baker, a tailor, all closed. No one walked the high street or peered into the unlit shops, checking their watches for opening times. As they passed the grocer's with its smashed window pane and the remnants of glass that sparkled on the pavement's stones, Bernard understood why the town was deserted.

Some of the cobbles out front were dull compared to the others, marred, a brown tint across the grey. Every few feet, a new stain spread across the pavement, countless crooked circles of blood. Splatters blemished brick walls while dried copper marks ran down shop facades. The further down the street they moved, the more remnants of chaos appeared.

Detritus flowed across the street, shattered wood and bent metal impossible to mentally piece back together into their original shapes. Everywhere Bernard looked was more evidence that the riot continued long into the night.

"Shit," Alfred muttered as they came upon the theater.

The marquee that previously displayed "Davide Dolos" was in charred pieces on the ground out front of it, the rest of the facade blackened, only hints of its original royal crimson paint still visible, burned to an unrecognizable state.

"We can't," Alfred whispered.

"I think we might have to," Bernard said as his head scanned the carnage, realizing that the officers weren't going to go light on them.

They turned down another street, one that was not as destroyed as the other but still showed the lingering signs of a crowd gone mad. As they passed homes, curtains shifted, eyes peering out the glass to see those courageous enough to brave the outside world. The police wagon stopped outside a building identical to the row homes around it, aside from the white double doors that took up most of its width with a stone plaque above it, carved with "Police Station."

"Stick with the truth," Bernard said as he saw the elder officer clambering down from the passenger side of the police wagon.

"We weren't properly introduced. I'm Constable Jenks," the man said as he approached the horses, rubbing one of them on its muzzle as he passed by. "Officer Harrison over there is my deputy. I'm sure you'll understand that you're now in our jurisdiction. As such, you'll be doing as I say, understand? If I could get you both to come down and talk to me eye to eye?"

Jenks showed no emotion on his face as he spoke, pacing in front of the horses, a nervous energy about him, a hint of eagerness to avenge the loss of life from the prior night.

The pair hopped down from their seats in tandem, landing on the hard stone. Before Bernard could straighten himself up, Jenks was at his side, clutching his arm with a grip hard enough to assert dominance, light enough to not leave a bruise, the experience of a man who manhandled countless drunks and miscreants and knew how to obfuscate his abuse.

"Driver, go over to Harrison. He'll be talking to you. You, sit over here." He pointed toward a waist-high brick wall enclosing the police station's neglected front garden. He released Bernard, allowing him to walk over to the wall under his own volition and take a seat. "I want this to go easy. I want you to be truthful." He put his hand on his baton, suggesting the outcome if he deemed any answers unsatisfactory. "From what I understand, your little magic show is responsible for this. We had to cremate over a dozen people as a result of your little stunt."

"You've had to burn—"

Jenks cut him off. "You saw the smoke. I'm asking the questions. Now that you're here, in my gaff, I can say that there's a good chance you'll swing for this. Lots of people want retribution, understandable?" The first hint of emotion flashed across the man's face, a clenched jaw, teeth pushing into one another. "But I'm a nice man, so before we make this official, why don't you tell me what happened? Tell me what you think. And maybe we can work something out between us."

Bernard recanted the night and the door's origins as honestly as possible, explaining every detail, even giving away some secrets behind his other tricks in order to get the man on his side. Officer Jenks held his eye contact the entire time, rarely blinking to break the contact, surveying Bernard for any hint of deception.

"And we ran. Got out of here as fast as we could," Bernard ended.

"You want to tell me that you own a genuinely magical door, and that *it* is responsible for last night? That's really what you're going with?" Jenks nodded and walked closer to Bernard, closing the distance between them, bending at the hip so their faces were only a few inches apart. "Witchcraft," he whispered before standing up straight, taking a step back. "That's what I think. Some kind of spell you've put on these people. Work of the Devil. You have one final chance. Tell me what you did and tell me truthfully. Tell me how to fix these people I have downstairs."

"What people?" Bernard dropped his Italian accent around a stranger for the first time in years, raising his palms outward as both defense and a plea of innocence. "Look, this is a misunderstanding. I'm Bernard Morris. I'm from Birmingham, for God's sakes. I'm a magician. It's an act. It's all tricks. What—"

After a stifled chuckle at the revelation, Jenks bared his teeth and stopped the man in his tracks. "They don't stop, rambling and violent. You crack 'em in the head, and they pop up a few minutes later. Don't waste a bullet on 'em. They'll be rampaging around like nothing matters. Burning 'em put an end to it, finally, but a few of 'em we've managed to round up. I want to fix them, return them to their families as they were. It's the only thing keeping you alive at the moment. So, I don't give a fuck what your name is, where you're from, or who you're shagging. Fix these people, and I'll let you go. Keep up with this nonsense charade, and I'll let each person in this town spit on you before we kick the trap door out from underneath ya."

"I swear." Bernard looked exasperated, desperate that the man would believe him. "Whatever happened happened because of the door. Maybe if we destroy it, if we open—"

"Oh, so that's your game. Get us to look? Escape while we fall under your spell? Sneaky prick. Yeah, we'll open it. Harrison?" Jenks turned to the side, yelling out to his partner. "Bring him over."

"What? No." Bernard stood in protest as he saw the lanky officer apprehend Alfred, wrapping his forearm across the driver's neck and marching him forward like a human shield.

Officer Jenks' baton swung from its sheath and smacked into Bernard's gut in one swift motion. Bent over from the strike, Bernard couldn't struggle away before handcuffs clicked into place around his wrists. The back of his hands shoved together as Jenks pushed him back down to sit on the wall.

"Let's see what happens, shall we?" Jenks smiled as

he said it, baring each crooked and yellowed tooth in his mouth.

The grip around Alfred's neck was tight enough that his face turned a shade of purple. Harrison held him in place next to the stagecoach's door. Jenks walked over and opened the carriage.

"Of course. You travel around with such a dangerous and unpredictable piece of equipment laying on the floor. Such a threat that there's not even a weight on it to stop it from opening during travel. Right," he scoffed before reaching into the stagecoach, dragging the door out with complete disregard to its or the carriage's construction.

He used nothing but brute strength, pulling it out onto the street, banging it against the sides, practically tossing it out onto the stone, only stopping it from tipping over with a colossal grip on its frame.

"Like this?" he mocked as he stood to the side, holding the tarnished doorknob in his hand with an outstretched arm.

"Don't look, Alfy. Whatever you do, keep your eyes closed," Bernard shouted before turning his head to obscure the door from his own view while keeping an eye on everyone else.

When the door opened, the cacophony immediately started. A hundred voices yelling at each other, speaking over one another in a myriad of languages. He recognized Italian, French, German, and English, but most of them were incomprehensible to Bernard, forgotten and foreign languages from every corner of the Earth. Above the rest, spoken with a clarity the others clamored for, the language he'd heard the other times.

They spoke with anger, a clear disgust that overruled all language barriers and comprehension. An immediate warmth filled the street, turning the soft English morning balmy, more befitting somewhere in the tropics, a humidity that stifled even the shallowest of breaths.

Alfred kept his eyes clamped shut, hard enough that his nose scrunched up and brow furrowed. Behind him, Officer Harrison hadn't taken the same precaution. With wide eyes, he stared into the door's scene, mouth agape and spit falling from it uncontrolled. Alfred began to struggle as the grip tightened around his throat, the forearm digging deeper into his Adam's apple until he began to flail around, slapping at the officer's arms and begging for respite.

Entranced by the door, Harrison didn't relent. His mouth started moving at a rapid pace, constant speech inaudible among the other voices. His eyes grew blacker, pupils growing until they swallowed his iris entirely and leaked out into the whites of his eyes. Unwilling to watch his companion choke to death, Bernard launched himself from the wall, running the few steps necessary and throwing himself full force into the pair, knocking everyone down to the floor. He landed facing away from the door, Harrison's feet next to his head. Closer to the man, he could pick out his voice among the others, speaking the nonsensical language of the door, speech that sounded reversed, consonants and vowels jumbled without reason.

Another voice joined the fray behind him, Alfred's,

as he also started to speak the incomprehensible tongue. Unwilling to turn and confirm that he'd jolted Alfred's eyes open with the impact and inadvertently subjected him to the door's effects, Bernard rolled onto his knees and attempted to scurry away down the street, any way to increase his distance from whatever hell spoke to them. He fell repeatedly, unable to stand in a panic without his arms to brace him. Bernard only gained a few feet of distance before he felt a hand clasp around the collar of his shirt and hoist him to his feet at a full sprint. Stumbling and struggling to match the pace, Bernard found himself floating in the air for half-steps, hoisted by the hand around his neck, forcing him toward the police station.

"Get inside," Jenks yelled at the top of his lungs, barely audible among the babbling, as he tossed Bernard forward into the closed door, smacking his cheek against the solid wood before he opened the other side and threw Bernard unceremoniously onto the wooden floor of the station's foyer.

Two officers looked down on him from a staircase to his left, stood staggered on separate steps with scowls on their faces. A thin hall stretched down to the end of the house in front of him, undecorated and uninviting, barely lit by a circular window on the back wall. A myriad of blows struck his shins and feet, causing him to reflexively pull them in toward his body.

When the door slammed shut, the chorus of voices became dulled by the brick and wood dampening their sound, muffling their words into a murmur. A secondary, smaller chatter took their place, not as clear as the sound on the street, as if a handful of people somewhere in the building strived for attention, clamoring for supremacy over one another in the same garbled tongue.

"Holloway, get the Webleys, axes, whatever you can find. We need ear protection, too," Jenks barked. "Prescott, move one of them downstairs. Need a cell free."

The pair ran off, practically falling over themselves in their haste. Jenks lifted Bernard up by the back of his shirt and began leading him down the hall by a knuckle dug into the small of his back. The corridor was tight enough between the staircase and the wall that Bernard's shoulders brushed against both as he marched forward.

"I don't know what you did, but I'm gonna destroy that fucking thing, and when I do, you're next." Jenks punctuated the sentence with another prod into the back, sending Bernard stumbling a few steps forward.

At the end of the hall, the wall to his left turned into a banister surrounding another set of stairs going down. Jenks pushed him toward them, giving him no choice but to start his descent. From the first step, it was clear that the new chattering came from down there, at least four people talking at a frenzied pace. Bernard tried to halt his descent, but Jenks kept him moving toward the bare stone of the basement floor.

"Who is that?" Bernard asked halfway down the steps when he could make out the various tones and inflections in the speech.

"That's your doing," Jenks grumbled.

As they neared the bottom, Prescott appeared, clutching his forearm, a steady stream of blood pouring out from underneath his fingers.

"She fucking gouged me," he said through gritted teeth.

"Wrap it and help Prescott. Not the time for your whining," Jenks responded as they passed onto the basement's stone flooring.

The basement was dimly lit, a sole lantern lighting the pallid stones with an effulgence too weak to illuminate every crevice and crack of the room, leaving the corners engulfed in shadow. Once at the bottom step, Bernard saw the purpose of the basement. Four cells were crammed into the tight quarters, two on each wall, rooms too small to be considered anything other than a brutal punishment. If standing in the center of one, Bernard could've touched all four sides.

In the low light, their stones appeared grimier than those outside of them. Hints of mold and awful stains blackened by time covered the mortar and overflowed onto the stones themselves. A cot in each room served as further disrespect to the occupants, too small for any adult to find comfort in and void of any blankets or pillows. Well-dressed but disheveled people occupied all but the nearest cell, yammering to themselves incessantly, heads all tilted upward, unaware or indifferent to Bernard's arrival.

Jenks marched Bernard to the nearest cell, tossing him inside without care of how or where he landed. Bernard bounced off the back wall, taking the hit to his shoulder in time to see Jenks slamming the bars shut and locking them in one swift motion.

"Maybe seeing them up close will make you have a change of heart," Jenks growled before sprinting off toward the stairs to join the others in arming themselves.

In the cell next to him, a woman and man walked in circles around one another, heads tilted upward toward the ceiling as they spoke. In the cells across, two men acted much the same. One appeared to have a broken leg. The limb twisted from the knee down at an unnatural angle, yet it didn't slow the shuffling in the slightest.

Beyond their chatter, Bernard heard the men upstairs sprinting around, heavy footsteps on wood boards echoing around the stones, amplifying them to an uncomfortable degree. Bernard sat on the cot, rocking backward and pulling his knees up to his chest so that his wrists could slide over the back of his thighs and over his feet, bringing his hands in front of him, a motion he'd practiced and performed a thousand times in various escape routines.

In a more comfortable position, he stood and started to pace, his mind racing with ways out of the cell, out of the building, out of the town. The thought of Alfred outside chattering along with the others, at the whim of whatever stood inside the door, attempted to haunt him and distract him away from concocting a plan, but there wasn't time for it. The quiver in his lip would have to wait. No time for mourning when inaction meant the end of his life.

"Can you understand me?" he said after another minute inside the cell. "Do you hear me at all?"

The woman in the cell next to him gazed down for a second. Dark hair framed her face. What might've been a well-manicured styling the prior night now sat in thick, matted clumps decorated by gravel and other unknown pieces of debris. Her eyes were blacker than Harrison's, no hint of any humanity as she looked in his direction.

"Oh you," she spoke with an unexpected clarity, a slight hint of an upper-class upbringing in her accent. "How lovely to see you again, dearest. Look everyone. He's back."

The others didn't react to her, content to stick in their spiraled babbling.

"I owe you so much, dear. Thank you, truly, thank you."

"For what?"

"For saving us, showing us the light, showing us Him and His."

Through the floorboards, Bernard heard shouting before a loud thud and the stomp of feet. The assault launched on, the war raging.

"Miss, could I ask you a favor? Do you have a hairpin?"

Her head cocked to the side as if she were trying to remember the concept, let alone if she had one on her person. Bernard scanned the mess of hair on her head, searching for a pin that he could use to pick his cuffs and make his escape. Something shimmered in the low light as her head tilted, camouflaged in the darkness of her hair.

"Could you come here a second?" He motioned her towards him.

"Of course, dear." She stepped forward, walking straight into the bars as if she'd not seen them, not reacting to the impact.

"Could you tilt your head down for me?"

"Of course, dear."

Loud claps came from outside, what Bernard could only assume were gunshots, the situation growing more dire every second. Despite her civility, he didn't trust the woman, politeness used as a predator's mask, luring prey in with a lowered guard.

"Sir, the other fella in the cell, do you understand me as well?"

The man stopped his walk and lowered his head, staring across the cell at Bernard with one darkened eye, the other a bloody socket with no remnants of the eye visible. He smiled softly.

"Mr. Dolos." He sounded as well-to-do as the woman, but his jaw made over-exaggerated movements with the words as if the motions were unfamiliar or unnatural. "What a pleasure it is to see you. You've been mentioned—"

Bernard cut him off. "Could I ask a favor of you? It would help me greatly."

"Why, of course. Anything for the man who has brought—"

"The woman there has a hairpin, the thing sticking out of her hair. Do you see what I'm talking about?"

The man nodded. "Absolutely, what can—"

"Could you grab that and slide it through the bars to me, please?"

"It would be my pleasure." The man moved with the fluidity and grace of someone with all their faculties. He plucked the pin from the woman's head with ease, skidding it across the stone with a deft touch. The bent metal pin stopped an inch short of Bernard's shoe.

"Thank you," he said as he sat on the cot, grabbing the pin and beginning to fiddle with it. "You can go back to whatever it was you were doing."

The man went right back to his yammering and circling in the cell, while the woman looked up at him with the strange approximation of a smile, as if her muscles didn't quite remember how to make one.

"Okay, dearest. Are you planning on bringing them to us? It'd be lovely to see them face to face again."

"Exactly, yeah."

"Oh, wonderful. How wonderful," she said as she stepped back from the bars. Her head snapped backward toward the ceiling, and she continued her spiraled march around the cell.

More gunshots boomed from the outside, ferocious volleys of sound that mimicked the worst of thunderstorms. It made his palms sweat, loosening his grip on the pin. He knew that something was worth shooting, a physical being from the door worthy of a hail of bullets.

Bernard tried to steady his breath, knowing that he'd picked dozens of police handcuffs over his life, even though he usually hid the key in the roof of his mouth for escape tricks. The knowledge was there. He just had to feel the tumblers inside, balance them properly, and they'd click. The cuffs loosened, the latch inside releasing them and allowing him to pull his hands free of the restraints.

He ran the two steps to the cell door and thrust his hand and forearm through the bars disregarding any pain. With his arm through, he easily angled his wrist to repeat the trick on the door, a simpler act with his hands free. Once the door unlatched, Bernard bumped it open with his shoulder.

The gunfire above ceased.

Whatever battle transpired had undoubtably concluded with untold amounts of blood pooling in the streets, creating meandering streams between the stones. As he sprinted up the steps, he heard the front door slam closed. On the ground floor, he turned the banister to see Holloway hunched over, heaving with breath. The sound of Bernard's footfall caused the man to look up as tears streamed down his face. All he did was shake his head before he raised his pistol up to his own temple.

Bernard averted his gaze before he heard the clap of gunfire and the heavy thud as weight crumpled to the ground. Outside, the myriad voices were louder than ever, spoken with a vociferousness that neither stone nor steel could hinder. The winner of the battle was undeniable. Exiting through the front of the building would be impossible, lest he wished to turn into one of the mindless devotees of the door's occupant.

The window in front of him seemed too small to fit his shoulder through, too high to properly climb through, but given the other option, Bernard acted. He removed his shirt, wrapping it around his hand before he punched into the glass with all his might, shattering the pane and littering shards on the floor and sill, leaving jagged teeth surrounding the circular frame. The mess of words came louder, a crescendo growing more extreme with each passing second.

Bernard tried to punch out the remaining shards of glass and wipe off the sill as fast as possible to ensure he wasn't flayed when squeezing through.

The job was far from finished when he laid his shirt on the window frame. Dozens of serrated teeth waited to dig and slice into his flesh, but the situation hadn't afforded him time for perfection. Bernard felt his palms punctured as he hoisted himself onto the frame. His shoulders were scraped and torn in jagged lines as he wriggled them through the tight space. He bit down on his tongue, unwilling to scream out in pain and alert the horde of voices to his location.

By the time he'd forced his torso through the gap, the hundreds of languages felt as if someone screamed them inches away from his ear, the agony almost on par with the wounds inflicted from the glass. When his waist passed, Bernard collapsed to the ground in a heap, hitting the lawn of grass and tiny shards flat on his back, knocking the wind out of him.

He looked up at the sky, at what had been a clear and gorgeous day, and saw it replaced by solid white. At first, he thought it to be a blanket of clouds rolling in over the town, not atypical for the countryside, but noticed a lack of texture, no bumps or dips, no breaks that let the sky's blue shine through. Nor had the world darkened any.

As he rolled to his side to stand, he saw that not a single shadow cast across the ground. Light permeated every angle and corner, blades of grass lit on both sides, leaves in nearby bushes bright underneath. The sight paused him on all fours, but the growing conversation spurred him back into action.

Bernard scrambled to his feet and headed towards the wall at the back of the property. Pain slowed him as he scurried over top of it, landing again in a crumpled heap in a bush in someone's back garden. With grunts and whines, he rolled out and up to his feet again, rushing toward the side of the house and into the street beyond it.

People lined the pavement. Some stood on the steps of their homes, others peering out of windows, but all had the same expression on their face, open-mouthed fear as they looked to the sky behind Bernard. He didn't notice if their pupils were growing or if the ones that saw it first were beginning to mumble the dead language.

In his fright and exhaustion, he turned his head, glancing over his shoulder at the sky above the police station, believing the door blocked by walls and homes.

It floated, slowly, high above the town, six huge wings that should've cast an all-encompassing shadow across rooftops. Each wing had an abyssal eye where it joined the central mass, a solid black orb that shimmered with flecks of gold and silver inside of it. The wings all connected to a mound of colorless flesh, an eyeless face, with a mouth that contained a thousand tongues, all endlessly flapping, expelling their message in all languages, known and unknown.

When he met its gaze, Bernard understood every one of their words, all of them speaking the same message as he stared gormlessly at it.

"His time is now. He has returned."

STEVEN NEAL
ABOUT THE AUTHOR

Steve Neal is an English-born writer currently surviving the summers of Florida with his supportive wife and less supportive cats. As a lifelong horror fanatic, he enjoys poking at the unknown and seeing what comes crawling out, as long as it isn't spiders.

Follow him on Twitter @SteveNealWrites

THE ARTIST IS NOT PRESENT
JENNIFER QUAIL

The challenge of *Door* was this:

You enter the gallery alone, and the guard locks the door behind you. There is only the artwork to study and a bench you can sit on. You're free to get up, examine it more closely, step back farther, sit on the floor, stand on the bench, study it upside down if you like, but you must keep looking at the work. You do this for fifteen minutes.

At that point, the door will unlock.

No one had made it to fifteen minutes without begging to be let out.

I knew there was some sort of trick to it, of course. There had to be. The lights were dim, but it was not pitch-black. They specifically warned you—*warned* you—there would be no one in the room with you. There was no sound in the exhibit, no strobe lights, nothing in the waiver you had to sign that suggested anything dangerous.

I'd been to installations where the waiver wasn't a joke. What I hadn't encountered before was the condition that no one who entered the installation, not even a critic, was permitted to describe what they saw inside. No joke, the waiver included a condition of entry that the viewer would not reveal any details of the art, gallery, or the rules. Doing so would irreparably destroy the work.

I gave it to Molchalin—the sales pitch alone was worth the price of admission.

I had no intention of honoring that clause, of course. The job of the critic is to critique the work, and vague platitudes that force the audience to see for themselves are nothing but a trick to turn an honest review into free marketing. I didn't write anything for free. But I certainly admired the chutzpah.

Normally, I wouldn't have even bothered with such an obvious stunt piece, least of all from a crank artist who wouldn't give interviews, allow anyone to observe their process, or even identify themselves as man or woman or xi or zir, just Molchalin. One of the paper's interns dug up that the name was Russian, but since it meant *silent*, odds are it was another affectation. Probably some washout from a studio arts program who couldn't get a gallery show any other way.

I certainly didn't believe the story that someone who'd attended a Molchalin installation titled *Mirror* walked out of the show, stood in the middle of the road for ten minutes, and then threw themselves in front of a streetcar.

Still, that's the kind of thing a nobody artist would want going around, and I'll admit it worked. The buzz around *Door* meant I was lucky to get a preview invitation.

The strange conditions, including the staggered arrivals so I couldn't see or speak with anyone who'd already seen it, were all part of the show.

Everyone was going to love the review. I'd probably be able to live off the ad-click revenue for a year. If I set the record, say, twenty minutes, or even a half-hour, ArtNews or Art World might come calling, and it would be goodbye, student shows and third-rate openings, hello, champagne receptions in Basel and Hong Kong.

The gallery attendant was a typical college kid in a cheap museum polo, who probably would have been on his phone if there weren't security cameras to keep him honest. He droned through the same rules from the waiver I'd already read.

"Remember, fifteen minutes until the door opens," he said in the dull monotone of someone who's said the same scripted line a hundred times. "But if you want out sooner, knock loud. I almost didn't hear the last one in time."

I ignored him and barged past, plunging into the dimly lit gallery, ready for my first look at whatever wannabe masterpiece Molchalin made the focus of the stunt. I hadn't realized the door closed until I heard a click and instinctively looked over my shoulder. The door I'd entered through, part of the heavy, temporary walls built around the installation, not only locked, but it had no handle or bar or even any visible hinges. In the darkness, it was almost impossible to find the crack in the dull black wall.

Something about that sent an unsettled twisting through my stomach. I shook it off and composed my opening sentence. *The entrance to the enigmatic artist Molchalin's new installation* Door *is ironically unprepossessing.*

Unprepossessing and *enigmatic* were the kind of words serious publications like *Momus* or *Ursula* would use.

Black walls contrast with—I looked up—*a dark gray drop ceiling made of translucent cloth that seems to suggest an overcast twilight. Muted lighting at the edges of the ceiling creates a feel of encroaching darkness, suggesting an oncoming night.*

They'd eat that up with a spoon at the *New York Times*.

The darkest wall was the one I'd entered through, and it *did* give the uncanny impression of oncoming night. I turned away, resenting that Molchalin had achieved at least one of his-her-its aims just by painting a wall so dark it drank up the light. Obviously, a lazy trick with that super dark paint Kapur likes. What kind of skill did a paint roller really entail?

The darkness is cheap, as Dickens once put it, playing on a child's fear of the closet at night. A good literary reference always looked smart.

It did get brighter toward the other end of the gallery. It was bigger than I'd expected, and while it might have been a trick of the lighting, it seemed to taper, too, the far wall narrower than the one behind me and much more illuminated. The bench intended as my vantage point sat two-thirds of the way in, the same sort of backless seat as in any gallery. It was just long enough two people could have sat on it comfortably, even though the terms of admission allowed only one viewer at a time.

A commentary on the dwindling audience for museums? Or a statement on the self-absorbed modern human, using an object made for two alone?

You could have—if you wanted—sat on the bench and not faced the work. I was tempted, as a nice little "fuck you" to Molchalin's cheap manipulation. But manipulative or not, the darkness worked. From that distance, I could barely distinguish the wall from the shadows. It might have been there, or it might have been a void where nothing existed at all, not even the void staring back.

The black paint and trick lighting suggest a cheap evocation of Nietzsche, hoping we will stare into the abyss until our mind tricks us into thinking it stares back.

There was nothing there to stare back.

The other side of the wall, the ticket kiosk, and the surly teen didn't even exist anymore.

I shook off that thought hard. Another point to Molchalin—haunted house stunts with Blackest Black sometimes work. I checked my phone, a prohibited item I'd cheerfully lied about not having. Two minutes in. Time to take a good hard look at *Door.* I straightened my shoulders, stepped in front of the bench, and turned around.

And laughed.

And after all that build-up and the lazy attempt at existential dread, Door *is...literally a door. A well-painted door, to be sure, but a gunmetal gray, institutional door painted on the wall. Or possibly on a board. There's some depth to the edges. I'll give Molchalin the point that it's an exceptional example of tromp l'oeil. The lock has a dull brass sheen, and the keyhole looks depressed into the plate. The paint texture is the same pebbly enameled metal as fire doors the world over. There's no knob or bar on this side, but there's a small peephole, like the outside of a hotel room. Molchalin even makes the glass look convex, as if it's reflecting light, and has painted a hint of light showing underneath. Well played, a master technician, even, if you like realism, but almost pitiably obvious. You came in one portal you can't see and are confronted with one you can't use.*

I checked my phone again. Nine minutes until the door unlocked.

Something about that caution suddenly seemed off.

"After fifteen minutes, the door will unlock." I said it aloud, but my voice didn't echo. There are sound-damping panels, I assume, to make sure all you hear is your own breath, heartbeat, rumbling gut. There is a thudding in my ears, and I give Molchalin another point.

Which door?

That's stupid. The door in front of me was a painting. It was on the wall, not in it. It was a painting, a technically excellent one, but only a painting. The glitter of light on the peephole is a well-executed trick, like the gleam from the bottom crack. The only thing behind the thin layers of hardened paint is the wall itself. There's nowhere for light to come from.

So why did I see a shadow flicker across the bottom?

Much as I hated following Molchalin's directions, I sat down on the bench, facing the door.

It was a trick, a combination of my eyes adjusting and the brighter light around the painting, but the dark end of the gallery felt as if it came all the way up to my back and pressed against it. I made myself look for the brushstrokes and air bubbles and tiny little pores in the finish that revealed the trick.

The technique is almost too flawless to be impressive. Like hyperreal pencil drawings, there is something to be admired in such a photorealistic rendition of an object, but is it really art? Even presented in the manipulative environment Molchalin has constructed—

My mental first draft was interrupted by the realization that my heartbeat wasn't all I could hear. Somewhere in the room, there was a low, steady hum I hadn't noticed when I entered. Maybe it was just the gallery's HVAC turning on. I didn't feel any air moving, though. Come to think of it, the room was almost humid, as if the air was getting heavier around me, like the dark behind was gaining mass as it crept closer.

I spun around in my seat. The light illuminating *Door* was affecting my eyes, and I didn't give them time to adjust, so there was only impenetrable dark.

When I turned back, the shadow flickered under the door.

It didn't. My eyes weren't adjusting. *The low-frequency noise is calculated to contribute to disorientation. But as I pass the fifteen-minute mark, it remains relatively easy to remain oriented in spite of the artist's haunted house intentions.* I checked my phone, wondering if I hadn't heard the click of my release or if the disinterested attendant had been Face-Timing and missed the time

Eight minutes until the door unlocked.

I didn't realize I'd jumped up until I noticed I was standing much closer to the door, the painted door. How had that only been a minute? I blinked, held the phone up to the light, turned the screen on and off.

Two minutes until the door unlocked.

I heard a soft shifting sound, a faint patting, distant hands on metal.

It was coming from behind the door. Behind the thin layers of paint on the solid wall.

The bench was shrouded in shadow but hadn't been a moment before. Five minutes? Beyond it was the blackness, making the light around the door seem even brighter. I didn't feel like sitting back down. If I sat, I'd pitch backwards, the heavy pressure of the hum and the weight of the blackness throwing off my balance, tumbling me into the abyss.

I looked at the floor which I hadn't examined. "The waiver leaves out the stage lights and the use of subsonics to create an oppressive atmosphere, which, combined with the imposed countdown to release, create a sense of impending doom." My own voice falls dead against the air, like standing in a closet lined with soundproof panels. "Cheap theatrical tricks take a mundane, realist work and impose a forbidding nature—"

The peephole in the door flickered, throwing light into the room.

I jumped backwards, my legs colliding with the bench, and I wound up sitting whether I wanted to or not. I could *see* something moving behind the painted glass, blocking light that had no source, covering and uncovering the peep-hole.

As if someone kept looking, turning away, looking again.

One minute until the door unlocked.

Which door?

I forced myself to stand. "The use of sound effects"—I composed to fill the silence, hoping I remembered it all later—"combined with trick lighting, create a visceral dread that no doubt has led to no one but this critic reaching the fifteen-minute mark. The monster in the closet, the doctor in the asylum...we start to question who is locked in and where? Molchalin's mundane realism is raised to at best a Halloween funhouse by their use of carnival sleight of hand."

There was a solid, settling sound, someone leaning on the other side of the door.

Thirty seconds.

I stepped forward. Another step. I could smell linseed oil, spirits of turpentine, see the tiny lines in the glaze from the last pass of the brush. Deep below the brass and bronze colors that created the rim of the peephole was a faint ghost of pencil tracings. My article would expose the fraud, spread across the art world, expose Molchalin for what they were. *From inches away, the trickery's exposed, ordinary ability masked by Hollywood tricks...*

The glass is an optical illusion, the movement in the depths just my vision adjusting from dark to bright to dark. I leaned in, the urge to "peep" overpowering even though it was all layers of paint. My hands pressed against the door, and I felt only the slightly tacky surface of paint on the wall.

Fifteen seconds.

Which door?

Hands braced on the other side; a body pressed against it at the same place as mine, pushing towards me. I couldn't lean away. The dark closed in against my back.

Ten seconds.

Which door?

I squinted into the peephole.

Five seconds.

Which door?

The eye looking back blinked.

Three. Two.

There was no other door. Only the dark.

I felt the other move.

The slam of a bolt in the painted lock.

The door cracked. Air rushed around the seal.

I ran.

I should have stumbled across the bench, but it wasn't there. My eyes couldn't adapt fast enough, and I plunged into the darkness, hands flailing in front of me. My phone hit the floor, but I ignored it. The kid could get it after he let me out. The door had to be only a few feet in front of me. Even if it was still locked, I could pound on it until someone heard. I was running, but the wall wasn't there, only the dark so thick I could feel it choking me.

Nothing but the dark, and I was sinking through it.

My hands slapped flat on a door.

I traced the edges. It was cold metal, coated in pebbly

paint, the seams flush to the wall. I couldn't see the color. I couldn't see anything. There was no knob or handle or lever, only a bolt for a lock that refused to turn no matter how hard I tried. My palms were sticky from the tackiness of almost-dry paint.

I think I screamed, but I couldn't hear myself in the sound damped silence.

Scrabbling frantically, my fingers brushed a small metal circle.

There was a peephole.

I pressed my eye to it.

On the other side of the door, I saw a dimly lit gallery. There was a bench half-illuminated, gloom-shadowed, the same sort of backless seat you find in every museum. The edges of the room were touched with a muted twilight glow that faded away until the other end of the room was lost in velvet black.

Muffled through the wall, far away in the dark, I hear the creak of a door.

I hear the bored voice of the attendant.

"Fifteen minutes until the door opens."

Jennifer Quail
About the Author

Jennifer Quail is a writer of fantasy, horror, and mystery, a wine-tasting consultant, trivia geek, and owner of two of the world's cutest dogs. In December 2019 she achieved a life-long dream of appearing on Jeopardy! without embarrassing herself in the process. She enjoys travel, art, and excessive amounts of coffee.

Find more on Facebook at /AuthorJenniferQuail or on Twitter @jenniferquail

MR. HOBB
AISLING CAMPBELL

The rain started almost as soon as they got in the car. Colours faded; sounds were drowned out. Sophie started to draw patterns in the newly forming condensation. Her finger, still greasy from their lunch, smeared the glass.

"Stop that," Hannah said, starting the car. She looked over her shoulder as she started to reverse out, straining to see amidst the downpour. The air was misty, all the sunshine the forecast had promised gone. She heard Sophie's arm flop down onto the seat.

A sulk.

Perfect.

"Soph, you see anyone coming?"

The little girl wiped the window with her sleeve. She shook her head. Hannah eased up on the clutch.

Brakes squealed.

"Jesus fu—"

The other driver thumped their horn as Hannah crawled back into her space to let them pass.

"I asked you if…Jesus Christ, Sophie." Her hands shook. She looked across at Sophie. The girl looked back, wide-eyed. Hannah couldn't tell if it was from shock at the near collision or hearing her mother swear in the confines of the car.

"I didn't see," she whined, eyes glistening.

Hannah recognised that cadence, an omen of quiet, guilt-inducing tears. She yanked the gearstick and pulled out.

⬥━◦━━◦━⬥

They drove in silence. Hannah might have turned on the radio, but that felt like an admission of defeat—an acknowledgement that the snuffling next to her was getting under her skin. She drove slowly. The rain was coming down in sheets, the sky even darker than before. She might have believed it was night had the clock on the dashboard not told her otherwise.

14.36.

Hannah repeated the number in her head, tracing the digits over and over in imaginary red ink. It was good to keep track of time. It kept her away from the empty place where the seconds meant nothing more than aching.

14.37.

They'd be home by 15.50.

She had to call her sister, ask her about the holiday, parry the usual questions. They'd had a big lunch at the park, so maybe just some fishfingers and peas for dinner. There were still some left in the freezer. She'd leave Sophie to watch cartoons, then she could call Matt. She smiled, then bit her lip, the guilt needling at her. She hadn't told her sister. Hannah knew what she'd say—that it was much too soon.

Movement in the passenger seat caught her attention. Sophie's head bobbed as she squirmed against her seatbelt, stretching towards something on the back seat. She bumped Hannah's elbow.

"Sophie." It came out sharp and cutting, like diamond on glass.

Sophie flinched.

Hannah clamped her mouth shut. She glanced up at the rearview mirror and saw a lump of orange and pink bobbled fabric sprawled across the back seat—Fliss, Sophie's raggedy cat. One orange wool leg dangled over the edge of the seat, brown button eyes staring towards the windscreen. As the car rounded a corner, Fliss slid back across the seat, out of Hannah's sight. Sophie started to fidget again. Hannah pulled over to the side of the road and stopped the car. The road was wide enough and empty.

"Go grab her then," Hannah said, hating the way Sophie had looked at her as the car had slowed.

Like it was a trap.

Her voice still sounded shrill in her own ears, taut like a bowstring. If she tried to smile, she'd look like a lunatic baring her teeth, unable to hide. She stared ahead at the grey static of the rain while Sophie undid her seatbelt and reached into the back. She sprung back quick, Fliss held in a headlock. Hannah leant her forehead against the window-pane, listening to the *thunk* of Sophie's seatbelt sliding into place. She sighed, and condensation formed like a mask next to her mouth. The figures on the clock blinked somewhere out of her sight.

Home by 15.50. Dinner at 17.00. Minute by minute, hour by hour, day by day. Baby steps back to normality.

Hannah sat up and twisted the key in the ignition. The car lurched, rocking her so hard the seatbelt locked across her shoulder. The engine made an unfamiliar sound. Hannah tried again. A smaller jolt, a scraping sound, and then nothing. She wanted to try once more. Three was the magic number after all, but that sound stuck in her ears.

She reached for her phone.

"Mummy?"

"Just a breakdown, Soph. Be quiet for a minute, yeah?" She lifted the phone to her ear, drumming her fingers on the steering wheel.

⋄—◈—◇—◈—⋄

Thirty minutes, they said. Hannah left her phone on the dashboard where she could see it, now that the clock was as dead as the rest of the car. She couldn't turn the radio on even if she wanted to. The rain was coming down harder. Looking out through the windscreen was like looking into a stream. She half expected to see fish slapping against the glass.

"Did you have fun today, Soph?"

The little girl looked up from her lap and mumbled something. She squeezed Fliss's paw tight in her fist.

Hannah felt the beginnings of an ache at the base of

her throat, a tightening around the eyes as she blinked. She dug her nails into the steering wheel, breathing in deeply. She watched the frown on Sophie's face, the deep furrows it left in her plump cheeks. Hannah looked away, out of the driver's side window into the woods. The trees looked like faded smears of paint, melting together into a green-grey blur. Without the sound of the engine drowning it out, the droplets coming down on the body of the car took on a new rhythm. More static beating down overhead.

"Mummy, I need a wee."

Hannah recalled the startlingly-blue slush drink Sophie had downed, the cup wrapped around with napkins so the ice wouldn't sting her hands. She listened to the rain and shut her eyes.

"Mummy..."

"Fine. Brilliant. I get it." She opened the car door, unhooked her seatbelt, and stepped out.

The rain wrapped itself around her like a cloak. By the time she made it to the boot of the car, her bra was sodden, water trickling over her skin, her clothes heavy. She rummaged around, scattering magazines, a tire iron, upholstery cleaner, and wet wipes, until she unearthed a bundle of dark blue nylon. She cast around, looking for the second anorak, but the rain was biting, and the other square of brightly coloured plastic was elusive. She slammed the boot and sloshed back to the car door with the one raincoat clamped under her arm.

Her wet hair slapped against her back as she pulled open the bag and handed the folded raincoat to Sophie.

"Put this on."

It dwarfed her, her pink face poking out amidst a sea of deep blue material. The sleeves were far too long. Hannah helped her roll them up.

"Leave Fliss here, Soph. She'll get all wet."

The little girl was trying to stuff the doll into a pocket. At Hannah's words, she stopped and looked at the toy in her hands.

Hannah stepped out into the downpour again. She hurried around to Sophie's side, yanking open the door. Sophie jumped out, the anorak falling past her knees.

Hannah led the way to the edge of the road where the trees started. Sophie glanced over her shoulder, back at the car.

"Go quick then," Hannah said.

Sophie darted behind an oak tree.

"Can you still see me, Mummy?"

"I'm closing my eyes."

She listened to the rain hitting the leaves. It was different to the metallic drumming against the car roof, more... zen. Zen was the word which came to mind, if it was possible to feel zen while damp and chilled and standing in the mud waiting for your six-year-old to finish pissing behind a tree. The cold was snaking in.

"Sophie, you almost done?"

⋄━◈━◇━━◇━◈━⋄

She thought she'd remember those moments for the rest of her life. Panic so strong it was like something outside of her, pressing in, crushing like a vice. She called Sophie's name—once, twice, three times—each time stranger to her own ears. By the time it sunk in that Sophie wasn't there, wasn't emerging sheepishly from further in the trees, she sounded like a banshee, like something out of folklore.

Conscious thought dropped out, and Hannah ran into the trees, twisting and turning and shrieking to be heard over the rain.

She hoped it was a game, cruel and ill-thought-out but still just a game. She tried to turn at that point, to go back to the car. If it was a game, then Sophie might be there, shivering and sorry. She got just a few steps before she realised the trees seemed just as thick behind as in front. She looked down at the ground, hoping for a trail of her own footprints to follow, but in the gloom, she could hardly make out what were footprints and what were just natural depressions in the ground. Puddles had sprung up everywhere, drowning out her trail.

Lost.

Her hand went to her jacket pocket, feeling for the smooth cover of her phone. Instead, all she touched was the lining. The phone was still on the dashboard in the car.

Her head throbbed.

It wasn't possible. How could she have run far enough to completely lose sight of the road? She'd turned around, back the way she had come. Perhaps she'd made a mistake, gone at an angle, ended up running lengthways through the woods. She'd come to a fence soon enough, some farmland or a housing development. Those were no wild woods, just trees on the side of the road. So, why did they seem to stretch on so far, like a fairy tale forest straight from a children's book?

There was still no hint of light in the distance, nothing but trees and fallen leaves. Hannah started to cry. Her face was already streaming from the rain. It barely seemed to matter if she added a little more moisture to the mix. She couldn't even see the sky clearly to orientate herself, to assure her she was going in a clear direction rather than just meandering steadily in circles.

The cold rushed in all at once, as if it had at last found some crack to seep through. It lodged in her chest, trickling down towards her gut and sucking the strength from her legs. She staggered, hands braced against wet bark. Shivers rippled like sobs under her skin.

◇—◦—◦———◦—◦—◇

It'd been nice out, one of those rare gems of British summertime. They'd sat outside at the garden table, Hannah with her book and Sophie with sketchpad and pencils. There was a big jug of squash on the table to ward off dehydration. Hannah had kept making sure Sophie's glass was topped up. She had sunscreen smoothed into her skin. Then, the phone rang. Hannah had been comfortable where she was, book in hand, the sun soaking warmth into her, but she was waiting on someone—solicitor, sister, doctor, boss.

She'd got up without a word, gone inside. She couldn't even remember which of them it was, hurried on in to answer it. She'd put the phone down on the kitchen counter when she'd heard the shattering of glass.

When she ran back outside, she saw Sophie curled inwards on herself, arms up, trying to cover her face, writhing from side to side. Saw one wasp crawling on her cheek, another on her wrist, the shattered pitcher on the patio. The one on her cheek must have stung her then because Sophie flinched and threw her head back, looking up at her mother. She hadn't called out for her, hadn't screamed. Like she thought she wouldn't come running, that she wouldn't help.

❖—◦————◦—❖

The fence came out of nowhere. Hannah staggered into it, banging her thigh against the post in a shower of rotten wood. It looked old, the wood soft and the wire rusty. But she followed it, grabbing onto the metal as she continued crying out into the trees.

She knew she should try and turn back around, head for the car, call the police. They'd be able to find Sophie, and maybe she'd be cold and scared, but she'd be okay. It didn't happen there. You couldn't lose children in the woods on the side of a road no more than fifteen minutes from a town. You couldn't get lost yourself. Maybe somewhere in the Highlands or one of the Moors or the New Forest, but not *there*.

Thirty minutes. That was what the man on the phone had said. A repair man would come, and he'd see the empty car with the phone still sitting on the dashboard. He'd call someone.

How far could they manage to get in thirty minutes?

Her fingers were bleeding, pulled raw by the rough metal of the fence, but the rain washed them clean over and over.

She stumbled, hitting logs and falling again and again until her jeans were stained through.

"Sophie!"

The ground sucked at her shoes, trying to tear them from her feet. It reminded Hannah of when Sophie had clung to her legs, giggling, while Hannah hauled her around like an iron boot.

She was so focused on her feet, she didn't see the way the fence dipped, disappearing as the ground fell away. It ripped her foot free of the clutch of the mud, and she fell into the pit.

✧⊶◦⊷◦⊶◦⊷✧

Her fingers tingled, palm stinging with the remembrance of the slap. She told herself she hadn't meant it. Told Sophie she didn—

She thought she was paralysed as she first came to, too cold and stiff to feel. She had to start from the fingers and toes up, wiggling them until she finally felt able to raise herself up out of the dirt.

Rain still pelted her, feeling like pins and needles over her back. She could taste blood. Probing with her tongue revealed a chipped tooth and small gouges in her cheek. The pain was exquisite—multi-layered and piercing like an ice pick to the head. The one upside was that it brought her back, reminded her of where she was.

Lost. Woods. Sophie.

She twisted in the mud, trying to ignore the aches and pains. Her left knee felt swollen, painful under pressure, but she managed to get onto her front. When she looked up, she saw the door.

It was like something out of a fairy tale, wooden and circular, painted forest green with a black iron handle and latch. The kind of door faeries, gnomes, and sprites would live behind. Hannah looked around, wondering if she'd fallen into the remains of some children's play area. It seemed like a strange place to put one.

She crawled closer.

Child-sized, an adult would have to crouch to fit inside. The ideal place for a scared, cold, little girl to hide.

Hannah pressed her palm to the puckered paint, dry and slightly warm to the touch. The door swung open, revealing a dark corridor with wooden floorboards and faded wallpaper.

She called out once, and her voice echoed down the corridor as her eyes adjusted to the light. She could see the corridor curved slightly to the right. A faint, flickering glow seemed to be coming from somewhere around that bend.

Hannah dragged herself over the threshold, out of the rain for the first time since the whole nightmare had begun. Her knee throbbed with the increase in activity, and Hannah found herself wriggling across the floor like an insect. By the time her feet had made it over the threshold, she was exhausted, shivering, and close to tears with pain. She couldn't crouch, couldn't put any more weight onto her injured knee. She had no choice but to continue dragging herself across the floor by her hands and elbows.

Somehow, she made it to the turn, enough to look and see the corridor carried on, lit by tiny oil lamps, a faded, red carpet runner ending at what looked to be another turn. For a moment, she thought she heard voices coming from somewhere up ahead.

"Sophie!" she called, manoeuvring around the twist, her clothes scraping against the floor. She almost screamed when she had to bend her knee, the cramped tunnel seeming to get even smaller as she dragged herself forward.

The sounds ahead remained fuzzy and undecipherable. They might simply have been the rain drumming down somewhere—because how big could the playhouse really be?

"Sophie?"

"Shh!"

Ice travelled down her spine as Hannah looked for where the hiss had come from, so loud it could have been right beside her. She glanced back over her shoulder at the faded wallpaper. Two muddy child-sized handprints were planted across it. Had those been there before? Had she looked at that wall as she'd crawled by?

A trickle of mud-tinted water ran down the wall, and none of the shivers wracking Hannah's body had the slightest thing to do with the cold.

"Soph, please sweetheart. Let's just go back to the car, yeah?"

Hannah's heart thudded in her chest. She'd heard no

footsteps coming up behind her, nothing to suggest someone else was in there with her.

A bang echoed through the little corridor, the vibrations making the paintings tremble in their frames. What sort of kid's playhouse had miniature paintings on its walls? It took Hannah a few moments to realise that it was the sound of the front door crashing shut.

She'd already started to try and back up when she saw movement ahead of her. A dark blue beyond the archway at the end of the corridor, the light sound of a child's footsteps pattering by.

"Sophie…"

She couldn't go back, only forward. Slow, slow progress, dragging her shivering body across the floor towards the arch. Beyond it, the corridors continued. A painting hung on the wall beyond the arch, a portrait. As Hannah edged forward, she focused on the figure, trying to keep her mind off the pain and discomfort. It was a woman, or so she thought, with long pale hair and grey eyes. There was something off about the features, too sharp in some places, too wispy in others. The eyes, which had seemed at first to be staring into the distance, now seemed to be staring back at her. The more she looked at it, the more it made her skin crawl. She almost didn't want to go closer, but there was no other way to go.

She looked down the right-hand corridor where the flash of colour had disappeared to. A set of shallow stairs descended into the chill gloom.

Hannah followed them, whimpering at first, then crying as her knee bumped against every single step, the pain never having a chance to subside.

* * *

"What?"

She regretted that barbed tone, her own inability to build walls between what she felt and what came out of her mouth.

Sophie stood, holding a book—Hannah couldn't remember what it had been—dressed in her pyjamas. Hannah sat on the sofa, skin itching with all the words in her husband's infuriating, damn sanctimonious letter. *This situation has become intolerable...I am sorry, but I will not be returning.* Like they were strangers. Like eight years of marriage was just so much dog shit on his shoes, and he couldn't wait to be rid of it.

"Daddy always reads me a story," Sophie said, extending the book towards Hannah.

It went flying, pages torn as Hannah flung it at the wall.

She'd never really thought hard about those words, that moment, preferring to block it out, but it was back. At the time, she'd heard an accusation—*it's your fault he's gone, Mummy*—but she realised now that there was another way she might have interpreted it. The way she should have interpreted it. As an invite. An opportunity to forge a new bedtime tradition together.

If only she'd seen it then.

* * *

Her knee was bleeding, the fabric of her jeans stiff with blood. She pulled herself forward with her fingertips, the continued impact of stair after stair imprinting new bruises.

She kept going forward, going down, and the way ahead was dark despite the small mushroom-shaped lamps set along the panelled walls. Hannah watched them, grunting as her body thumped onto the next step, the dim glow appearing out of nothingness, lighting up as she moved. She looked at the carvings which ran along the walls. Ivy and oak leaves, apples and pears, with little faces peering out through the gaps. Curious, laughing faces.

She didn't have the strength to look back, knowing that if she did, it would be to see the way out shrouded in darkness.

Her arms felt like there was fire wrapped around her bones. How far had she come? A mile? Maybe more...

But if she stopped, she might not be able to carry on.

Hannah closed her eyes, thinking of Sophie safe, of the two of them tucked up under a blanket on the sofa with the central heating on and dumb animated movies on the telly. Her fingers shook as she grasped the next step, and Hannah pulled hard, kicking her good leg against the stairs above to give her a boost forward.

So focused on forcing her body onwards, she didn't see the gap between the stairs, the yawning maw which swallowed her headfirst before she had a chance to save herself.

⟡━◦━━◦━◈⟡

Her injured knee split on impact, the sour taste of vomit rushing up her throat at the wobbling, writhing pain of it. Hannah coughed up stomach acid and the liquid remnants of the sandwich she'd had for lunch, so long ago it might have been another world.

No light, not even a sliver.

Besides her knee, her right wrist throbbed, it hurt to breathe, and there was pain like a line of fire running down her back. When she tried to move, it spread, licking along nerves like they were candle wicks.

The air was thick with a fetid stench, a musty, mouldy smell.

She reached out with her left hand, screaming behind gritted teeth, and her fingertips brushed up against slimy stone. With a sob, she lowered her arm, her palm hitting the floor—more porous stone—with a smack.

It was cold in the dark. She felt faint, exhausted down to her core. Hannah shut her eyes, curling inwards as much as she could bear, all her tears spent.

⋄━◈━⋄━━⋄━◈━⋄

The sound woke her, a slow creak of hinges and light in her face. She could smell wood smoke, cooked apples, and burnt sugar. Warm, hearty, homely scents.

She could scarcely feel her body, her skin as cold as the stone she lay on top of. The various breaks and fractures seemed tipped with ice, crackling lines of pain in an otherwise numb existence.

"H-help..." Hannah raised her head, blinking in the rich glow.

Her baby was there, dressed in soft red fabric with her hair neatly braided and twined with ribbons. Warm and clean and safe, all a mother could hope for.

Standing beside Sophie was a man. A strange man. His skin was sun-browned, furrowed with age, and yet he held himself just as straight-backed as any man in his prime. His eyes were dark, the light glinting off them like a pair of pinheads sunk in pitch. Sharp when they fell on Hannah, gentle when they met Sophie.

"So-Soph—"

Sophie looked towards her mother with a wary, watchful expression, the one Hannah had always hated. *It had only been the one slap*, Hannah wanted to yell. Why couldn't she just forget?

"You have to choose, child," the strange man said. He sounded like the scents floating through the air—like warmth and safety. Like being indoors while the snow came down outside. A voice far more ancient than the trees somewhere overhead.

Tongue heavy, lips cracked, Hannah tried to explain, to apologise. But even as she half choked on the syllables, Sophie was already turning away, back to the strange man with his ragged garments and comforting voice.

"I want to stay here, Mr Hobb. I want to stay with you."

"Are you certain? Once the decision is made, you can never go back."

Sounds crackled and whistled through Hannah's mouth, but no words came out.

"I'm sure," Sophie said, a smile on her lips. It had been

so long since Hannah had seen one like it.

The old man reached out a trembling hand and petted the child's head, tender and gentle. When he spoke, his voice wavered as if coming from under an aeon's span of grief, a grief at last lifted.

"Welcome home then at last, my dear daughter."

As he knelt to embrace the child, he made a gesture with his right hand, and the heavy door swung shut, leaving Hannah in the dark with the cold once more.

⟡━◈━━◇━━◈━⟡

Hannah glanced at the clutch of trees through a rain-spattered window and shivered. In the dark, they looked like the sprawling forest from some fairy tale, big and deep enough to lose a child in. The sort of place where Hansel and Gretel's cruel stepmother had left them to die—to the elements, to the animals, whichever came first.

They'd found their way back though, hadn't they?

The little children returned rich to their widowed Papa, ready for their happily-ever-after with just the three of them.

Hannah twisted the knob for the heater, disappointed but not surprised when it didn't work. There was a chill, a cold well-settled on every inch of skin, sunk through her ribs and lodged there.

She wrapped her arms around herself, craning her neck back to see if she had a jumper or a jacket left on the backseat.

A pair of brown button eyes stared back at her, belonging to an ugly, woollen toy cat. A friend's kid must have left it behind. Maybe one of Maura's twins the last time Hannah had taken them to a swimming, dance, or gymnastics lesson, or to and from school—car packed full of excitable six-year-olds. Maura's two girls, and who were the others? Mia, the next-door neighbour's child, in between the twins in the back. Loudest of the lot. And then, in the passenger seat?

Hannah had a hazy impression of a quiet girl gazing out the window, as blurry as the world beyond the glass.

Orange lights flashed in front of her as the repair van crept to a stop. She rolled down the window with a smile for the mechanic.

There was nothing else to do except sit with her thoughts while the mechanic worked, going back to worry over the vague memory like it was a loose tooth. She almost had it. In her mind's eye, the little girl was turning her head, turning to look at Hannah and—

The bonnet closed with a clunk, the mechanic tapping on the window to tell her she was all set to go.

Hannah just wanted to get home. She had things to do. Fishfingers and peas for tea. Cartoons. Bed. She frowned as she twisted the key in the ignition and drove off.

That wasn't right.

Tea. Phone calls with her sister. Her boyfriend. A bath, then bed.

That sounded better.

She wasn't sure where the other stuff had come from. The faint impression of another routine sat next to her. She pictured her house, going through room by room. Hallway then living room. Kitchen. Bathroom. Up the stairs now. First was Steven's office, full of all the crap he hadn't wanted to take with him when he left and which Hannah hadn't managed to get rid of. The upstairs bathroom. Hannah saw plastic boats and rubber ducks sitting on a shelf next to bottles of brightly coloured baby shampoo.

She wrinkled her nose and tried to concentrate on the road in front of her, on the twists and turns and the rain lashing everything. Her mind carried on to her bedroom. She'd stripped it all back, gone minimalist in her attempts to purge Steven from her life. Across the hall lay an empty room. In Hannah's mind's eye, the door was ajar, small holes in the wood where a nameplate of some kind had once hung, impressions worn into the carpet from furniture no longer there. The walls swallowed sound, quiet as a tomb.

Something was missing, something vital.

But no matter how hard she tried, Hannah couldn't recall it.

Aisling Campbell
About the Author

Aisling is a British writer from a seaside town in southern England. She studied English with Creative Writing at the University of East Anglia, graduated, promptly had two near death experiences and now writes like the Grim Reaper is two steps behind her. Her work has appeared in the anthology 'C is for Cannibals' and her short story 'Swallow' is available on The Dread Machine website.

Instagram: @aisling_the_horror_hag

HOLLOW
ADAM DOUGLAS

It took over an hour just to find the entrance. Kyle had to double back twice. Weeds hid the sign for the house, and the dirt track was almost invisible at the side of the road.

He winced at the gravel pelting the wheelhouse of his Corolla. It was a shitbox car, but it was *his* shitbox car. And it wasn't like he could afford repairs or body work on it.

At least not yet...

A telltale *clink*, *clink*, *clink* reminded him he had forgotten his bong on the backseat floor. *It'll probably be broken by now.*

The trees were densely packed on either side of the narrow road. The sky wasn't there under the canopy, for all Kyle could see. He had to turn on the headlamps to avoid potholes and large rocks as he drove.

Why would the guy choose to live out here, especially now? Such a remote location, an hour away from Saint John, in an area that was thinly populated, was hardly accommodating to someone with severe health issues like Bob. As he drove, Kyle rarely saw houses or any signs of civilization. It was fairly typical of Charlotte County, New Brunswick, a few run-down towns sporadically dotted with shut-ins and survivalists who liked the isolation.

The potholes seemed to get worse the longer he drove. He slowed the car down to a crawl. He wondered, not for the first time, if the trip was the right thing to do.

There were mixed feelings about his uncle. As a kid, he thought his UncaBob was the coolest human he knew. Everyone in Saint John knew his car commercials, the catchy jingle—"Drive your way to a new daaaaaayyyyy..." The kids in school, who were easily impressed at that age, considered Kyle to be related to a celebrity.

Bob was charming and good-looking, too. Other members of their family paid him respect, even if it was grudging, tinged with jealously. Kyle's Dad once said that Bob could sell porn to the Pope.

But all that was before the scandal.

Finally, the dense trees gave way to a clearing, and Bob's house was revealed.

Kyle stopped the car, shocked. *Bloody Christ...what a dump!*

There were many old houses built in the nineteenth century and beyond in the original section of Saint John that radiated out from King's Square. Those homes were beautiful, the best his city and province had to offer the world in terms of architecture and culture.

Bob's old house was the opposite.

Its paint was almost stripped bare by the elements. The

teardrop shingles on the roof were mostly missing. There were some gaping voids on the twin turrets in front of the house where you could see right into the attic. As he observed the house, a crow flew out of one of those holes and into the woods, cawing, its black wings spread wide. Weeds were choking the grounds and trying to strangle the walls.

Again, Kyle debated turning around and heading back.

But then he recalled the phone call from his Uncle and remembered the note of desperation in his voice. *Jesus, kid, I know what you all must think of me. But I swear to you, this is the most important thing in my life right now. One day, one visit, that's all I'm asking.*

The Corolla idled roughly at the edge of the clearing as the house loomed in front of him. Kyle shook his head, shifted the car into gear, and drove forward.

◇━◉━○━━━○━◉━◇

He had to watch where he stepped on the rotting porch, afraid it wouldn't hold his weight for long. The front door had a stained glass window set in the centre with several colored panes cracked or missing. He knocked.

When the door opened, Kyle thought it was a stranger who had answered. The last time he had seen his uncle, Bob had an athletic physique, like a swimmer. The man who answered the door was a shadow of his uncle. He was very gaunt; he had probably lost sixty pounds, maybe more. His once immaculately coifed hair was ragged and falling out, and his eyes were sunken and rheumy. He was an old man at fifty-five.

But the most alarming aspect of his appearance was the cuts and scratches that cross-hatched his face and hands. Ugly red lines and gouges peppered the exposed surfaces of his grey, sallow skin. It was as if his divorce really had been death by a thousand cuts. Kyle guessed a bad fall or similar accident. But if there had been any doubt whether Bob was truthful about it being near the end, it vanished as soon as he saw him.

"Heya, kiddo." Bob smiled in a weak yet relieved way. "Wasn't sure you would show up."

"UncaBob," Kyle greeted him, repeating the old joke, hoping it hid his shock well enough. "I said I'd come. I meant it."

Bob extended his hand, and Kyle shook it. The grip was firm, but Kyle recoiled slightly at the bony, dry fingers. *Touching death,* a voice said in his head. He ignored it. There was a distinct smell of booze on his breath. *At least some things haven't changed*, he thought.

"Come in, kiddo." Bob moved to the side so Kyle could enter. The wallpaper was threadbare on every wall, and there were signs of decades of neglect everywhere he looked. It was as if no one had lived there for at least sixty years before Bob showed up.

"Not much, I know," his uncle said as perhaps a kind of apology. "But the real value is in the land. Let's go to the kitchen. I gotta sit down."

His uncle moved slowly down the hallway. They ended up in a kitchen lit by a single bulb hanging from a broken fixture on the ceiling. A wooden table sat next to a steam radiator with two chairs. Bob sat, groaning slightly.

"Death sucks, kid. Try to avoid it." He laughed.

A manila envelope lay on the table next to a bottle of Wild Turkey and two glasses. He pulled it toward himself. An ashtray filled to the brim with butts and ashes sat next to his elbow with a half-used packet of DuMaurier's open nearby. Bob opened the envelope and pulled out some official-looking papers.

"Just gotta put your name here, and everything goes to you. Like I promised."

Kyle grimaced. "Hey, you don't have to do that right away. I mean, that's not the reason I'm here. Not the main reason, anyway."

Bob looked at him and smirked. "You don't have to pretend. It's ok. Your mom would probably shit a kitten if she knew you were coming to see me. I really don't care if it's just for the money. I'm just glad you're here."

Kyle sat opposite his uncle. "No, I'm serious." He took a deep breath. "Look, I'm not going to lie. I almost turned around when I came here. I mean...I'm just as mad at you as everyone else is, okay?" Kyle wasn't looking at him while he spoke, but he could tell that the man grew very still. "But you treated me pretty good when I was younger, talked to me like I mattered, like I was an adult. That meant something to me." Kyle paused. "What you did to Aunt Toni was pretty fucking horrible. I'm not letting you off the hook for that, no way." He looked at him now, but Bob's expression was unreadable. "But, when it comes down to it, I came here because...I think...well...no one should have to die alone. If you can be there for someone in their final days, you should be with them no matter what went on before. That's why I'm here."

Kyle had said it so well, he almost believed it himself. Who knew? It might even have been kinda true.

Bob didn't move or say anything for a few minutes. Finally, he said, "Damn, kid. Damn." He filled in Kyle's name on the will. Then he signed it at the bottom, pulled a cigarette from the pack, lit it with a lighter from his pocket, and dropped it on the table. "I knew I was right about you."

They smiled at one another, Kyle more shyly than his Uncle. Kyle tried hard not to think about the money, how much he needed it, even if it wasn't going to be very much. To think about the money at that moment seemed like a betrayal.

Finally, Bob said, "I did, however, lie about something."
Kyle's smile fell. "What?"

"The value of my estate. Toni got pretty much everything in the divorce. What was left over went to medical expenses for me and then buying this house. Speaking of which, yeah, I know, it's total shit. I didn't buy the place for the ambiance.

"You'd probably have to pay to have it knocked it down, no value here. I also said the land here, about fifty acres or so, might be worth about a hundred thousand or more. That ain't exactly exact."

"Bob, I really don't care—"
"It's likely worth millions. Billions, maybe."
Kyle had no idea what to say to that.

Bob grinned. "Let me take a couple of the pep pills my doctor gave me. They should give me just enough energy for us to go for a walk. I've got something very important to show you. It's the most important thing you'll ever see in your entire life."

⸻ ◇ ⸻

Even after his "pep pills," the man was pretty slow on his feet. He had to stop every so often to rest against a tree or stump as they walked down the path. The smell of damp pine and cedar filled Kyle's lungs. The afternoon sun was warming when it managed to peek through the trees. You could've called it a nice day, if not for all the dying going on.

"Do you know why I bought this place?"

"No."

"I'm surprised. I would have thought Toni would have told the whole family the story. Listen, what do you hear?"

Kyle cocked an ear and listened. "Cars."

Bob nodded and pointed back towards the house. "Highway One is just down that way. This house is at the top of a cliff; it likely had a pretty good view of the ocean at one time before everything grew over. When the lights are on in the upper floor of the back turret, you can see it easily from the highway and vice versa.

"Teenagers used to break in and party here before I bought it. There's graffiti all over that room. Toni saw lights up here one night as we drove by and said it was the perfect example of what a haunted house should look like.

"It became a bit of a joke with us. Every time we drove

by, I'd point out the house and make up a story I heard about how the police found a satanic cult here where human sacrifices were performed, that sort of thing." He chuckled as he worked his way down a slope between two large pines. "I used to think she was such a pussy, so afraid of anything scary. Sometimes, I used to push her buttons, telling myself I was toughening her up. Really, I was just amusing myself by being a bully.

"You know, it shocked the hell out of me when she filed for divorce. I didn't think she had it in her." He kept his pace steady as he walked, stepping over exposed roots carefully.

"She didn't know I was sick, by the way. I hadn't told her my diagnosis yet. I hated to think of her seeing me weak."

Only a weakling could beat a woman like that, Kyle thought bitterly. He had seen the photos his mother texted to him, heard the stories. Apparently, the beatings had been going on for years. His mother's sister was a sweet, gentle person. It was an abomination to hurt a good person like that. *Yet, here you are,* he thought. *Here you are.*

Bob went on. "Why did I buy such a shithole, you may ask? I bought this house as revenge. I actually thought...I *actually thought this,* you understand...that if I told her... this is embarrassing to admit...every time she drove by the 'haunted house,' I'd be in that window at the back turret, watching her, cursing her as I lay dying, drinking myself to death. I thought she would be wracked with fear, guilt, and remorse."

He laughed heartily. "What an idiot!" He looked back at Kyle. They had been walking for about ten minutes by that point. "You have to understand, drinking at the same time as I was talking my medications turned out to be a really bad idea. You make some seriously dumb decisions." He chuckled. "She laughed at me when I told her. *Laughed* at me."

"Served you right," Kyle said aloud, surprising himself.

Bob didn't miss a beat. "Fuck, yes. Absolutely, I deserved it. I was a monster to her. A death like this, it's what I deserve."

"Well, I don't know..."

His uncle ignored him. "She married Evan, I heard. He used to work with me, you know? At the dealership. Nice guy. No hard feelings there whatsoever." Despite his words, Kyle thought he detected a hard edge in his tone. "Have you met him? Evan?"

"No," Kyle lied. In fact, he went to their wedding. Evan Takiyama was everything UncaBob was supposed to be—honorable, dependable, and admirable. Maybe a little dull and reserved, especially for a car salesman, but everyone could tell how much Aunt Toni adored him. She deserved some genuine love for a change.

Bob looked at his nephew. "Do you believe me? When I say I wish them all the best?"

"Well...," he said vaguely.

"It's true. After she laughed at me, I saw her in a new light. I would have left this treasure to them if they would have taken my call, which I'm sure they wouldn't. Toni's away for a week at your grandmother's place in Arizona, anyway, so it wouldn't have made any difference."

They began walking into a large crevasse in the forest floor, a fissure that began more than a hundred feet wide but gradually narrowed as it descended deeper into the earth. The rich odor of soil and rain-coated granite was pervasive.

"So, my great plan of revenge had failed. I had nothing to do, nowhere to go. Drinking myself to death isn't as much fun as it sounds. On days when I had the strength, I wandered my useless property. With any luck, I told myself, maybe I could fall down a sinkhole and break my neck."

He pointed ahead. "But then I found this, just around the bend here."

There was an enormous finger rock, like a pillar, blocking their way forward. The crevasse had narrowed to the point where it was only about three or four feet across, and the tangled foliage walls on either side of them were at least twenty feet high.

"I found out later that the house on this land was built in 1879 by a guy named Mitchell Warring, the patriarch of one of the wealthiest mining families in all of Atlantic Canada. He would often spend several weeks here during the summer, hunting deer.

"Or, at least, that's what he told everyone he was doing. In reality, he must have been dealing with this!"

They had to shuffle sideways to move past the enormous rock. As soon as he was on the other side, that's when Kyle saw the door.

It was obviously very old, over a century. The dark, grey wood planks were weather-beaten to the point where the gaps between the boards were wide enough to slide your hand through. Moss caked the whole structure, but it still looked solid enough to hold for another ten or twenty years.

"This," Bob said, breathing hard, "is where everything changed."

The iron hinges groaned as he pulled the wooden handle with all his waning strength. A pitch-black tunnel angled downwards. Stale, cold, damp air washed over them.

"A mine?"

"That's what I thought at first. It's what the Warring family was into, after all, mines. But I doubt they even dreamed what they were gonna find down there." Bob reached into his pocket and produced a couple of small flashlights. He handed one to Kyle.

Kyle switched it on and shone it around the entrance-way. There were support beams of heavy timber just on the other side of the door. Burned into the wood were strange symbols that Kyle didn't recognize. There were crude stick figures of humans intermixed with other characters that looked almost like hieroglyphics but with a Native American twist. None of the stick humans looked too happy. In fact, many of them seemed to be writhing, twisting in... ecstasy? Pain?

"It's not too far inside. Just a little further." Bob hobbled down the tunnel.

Kyle, wishing he had brought a warmer jacket or worn a sweater, followed close behind. The damp chill of the earth began to seep into him almost right away. He shivered, but he wasn't sure it was the cold that was making him do it. The whole situation was beginning to creep him out.

They walked in silence for a few minutes, crouching low to avoid hitting their heads on the low ceiling.

"Mind you don't tread on Bugs," Bob said suddenly.

Bugs? Kyle thought. He had visions of an Indiana Jones-type swarm of millipedes, mantises, and other crawlies on the walls and floor. He swung his light beam about, afraid he'd stumble into something nasty.

When the beam found it, he let out a little shout of alarm. A large mass of brown and white, about the size of a loaf of bread, lay a few feet in front of him.

It took him a few seconds to figure out what he was looking at. It was a rabbit, very dead. Its skull had been smashed apart, and its grey, rotting brains were peeking out of the gap. The eyes and mouth were wide open. Kyle had the distinct impression it had been screaming.

"I'll tell you about that in a bit," Bob said conversationally. "You'll understand once you see it." He hobbled on.

Kyle looked back the way they had come. A slight curve in the shaft meant that he could no longer see the entrance anymore. Sweat had broken out on his forehead despite the deep chill of the mine. He didn't know why he was so nervous all of a sudden. Something felt very wrong.

"It's just over here, kiddo. Don't wuss out on me now." Bob's voice floated from the darkness ahead.

After a few seconds, Kyle followed it.

Bob had stopped just past another archway of heavy timber. Kyle saw similar runes and markings on those beams as well, but several had rotted away from decades of damp and decay.

He saw that his uncle was standing in a crudely hewn room of about ten-foot cube. Under his feet was a makeshift flagstone floor, and just beyond him was a second archway at the other end of the room, framed by the same thick timbers.

"This is it," said Bob. "This is what I needed to show someone before I die." He reached down around the opposite side of the timber and switched on an LED lantern. The area was filled with bright light.

Confused, Kyle looked around. The room was rough, carved from the hard New Brunswick granite. It must have been challenging to create, he guessed, but he didn't think it was all that remarkable.

Bob looked at him. "Go over to the archway and take a look." He indicated the far exit.

Beyond the second archway, Kyle couldn't see anything at all. He walked over to it and shone his light into the space beyond.

What am I seeing? He couldn't tell. His mind couldn't wrap itself around what his eyes were telling him.

Beyond the archway, the light from his flashlight was... *absorbed*...by the darkness. There was no other word for it. It was as if the beam couldn't pierce the shadow there.

It almost seemed solid, the darkness. It had a distinct edge, a point where the light just stopped...yet he wasn't sure it was solid at all.

"Touch it," suggested Bob.

Kyle looked back at him. Bob was grinning wryly, obviously enjoying himself.

"Don't worry," he said with a laugh. "It won't bite."

Fascination overcame creeping dread. He slowly, gingerly reached out with his fingers.

Gasping, he pulled his hand back as if it had been burnt. What he had felt was like nothing he'd ever experienced before. There was no sensation at all.

No, that wasn't right.

It was a complete and utter absence of feeling, or sense of anything. As soon as his fingers pierced the darkness, he had the sense his fingertips had been amputated, immediately and painlessly. It was like they didn't exist anymore. Only by looking at his complete and seemingly unharmed fingers could he believe that nothing horrible had actually happened to them.

His rapid breaths were shallow. He felt unsteady on his feet.

"Hey," said Bob.

Kyle turned to look at him. His uncle was holding a large stone in his hand, about the size of a baseball.

"Check this out." He threw the stone at him, hard.

The rock sailed past Kyle's head, missing him by less than a foot, and he whirled about just in time to see it vanish into the ink-darkness.

Without realizing at first, he instinctually was waiting for the telltale note of stone striking stone, echoing off the walls that must be there. But no sound—nothing whatsoever—echoed back.

"What is this?"

"I haven't the faintest idea," Bob said with a tone of

amusement that Kyle didn't care for. "It's not just shadow. It sure the hell doesn't feel like it, like you just found out. Get closer to it and listen. Tell me what you hear."

Slightly dazed, Kyle moved towards the edge of the darkness. More sweat broke out on his brow, and a droplet trickled down along the inside of his right eye. He placed his hand on the timber arch to steady himself, fearful that he might accidentally touch the blackness and feel the same, terrible absence of sensation.

He got as close as he dared. The border of the strangeness was not quite as sharp as he first thought. There was a subtle rippling haze along the dividing line between the absolute darkness and the harsh light of the lantern.

He turned his head and listened.

It was genuinely unnerving, an absolute absence of sound. But it was more than that. His other senses, like smell and the tactile nerve-endings on his skin, began to react. Each neuron throughout his body seemed to cringe, to cry out meekly, submissively. He began to tremble.

Suddenly, he became aware of something behind him and felt a grip on his shoulder.

He turned sharply and gave out a little cry of alarm. Bob was right there, inches away. His hand—surprisingly strong for a dying man—had a firm grasp on Kyle's shoulder.

For a horrible split second, he thought Bob was going to shove him in there, into the darkness. For a fleeting moment, he was sure he saw it in his uncle's eyes.

Murder.

But the hand pulled him back away from the edge.

"Easy there," said Bob, smiling. "You don't want to take a tumble in that, trust me."

Still trembling, Kyle moved away from the darkness. He sat down on the cold floor on the other side of the room and stared at it. Bob joined him, sitting with difficulty.

"I've been down here several times," he said, "fascinated by this...*whatever*. Once, I dared to stick my whole arm inside. It felt like I had suddenly become an amputee."

He reached into his jacket pocket and produced a cigarette. He lit it and blew smoke. The smoke, Kyle fancied, moved away from the darkness as an act of will, of self-preservation. Not even fire wanted anything to do with that hideousness.

"I did some other experiments, too," he continued. "There's no gravity in there. I'm not kidding. I brought some rope and began throwing objects into it, trying to gauge where the bottom might be. It didn't matter how heavy the object was or what it was made of. It would just float inside that, suspended. Utterly still. There was no movement at all! No waves, no...whaddayacallit? Vibrations. I pulled it out like it weighed nothing at all. And then, at the edge, it was like it suddenly remembered it had mass and would fall to the ground with a crash."

Bob blew more smoke into the room. "Then I wondered, what if you put something alive in there?"

Kyle turned to look at him. His expression was unreadable.

"That was Bugs, the rabbit back there, in the tunnel. I bought him at a farm supply shop in St. Stephen. Nice little guy, very easygoing. Didn't fuss at all when I tied the rope around him and tossed him inside."

Bob took a deep breath and closed his eyes for a moment. "It couldn't have been more than five minutes before I pulled him out.

"At first, he was so still I thought he was dead. Suffocated, I thought, which made sense. If there's no gravity, surely there's no air. Poor Bugs's eyes...wide. So wide. They looked utterly terrified.

"But then he spasmed. Violently. God, it scared the bejeezus out of me! Bugs began to thrash about on the floor like someone had hooked up a car battery to him. And he was screaming. A mad screech that you couldn't believe could come out of such a tiny body.

"I got scared. I tried to get out of here as fast as I could. I only made it partway up the tunnel when I heard it scrambling behind me.

"I turned and shone my light on it just as it attacked. Its eyes...my God...they were insane, beyond insane. Blood was streaming out of his mouth. It leapt at my face and began biting and scratching me with a ferocity..." He indicated his many scratches and wounds on his face and hands. "Well, you can see for yourself. I'm sure it would have blinded me if I hadn't got lucky. I finally managed to grab its hind leg and smash it with all my might against the wall.

"Bugs finally went quiet. Th-th-th-tha's all folks!" He laughed.

Kyle looked back at the darkness.

Bob went on. "Nephew, I have no idea what's in there. I

don't know if it's a mistake, maybe? A space that God forgot to finish when He created the world? Or maybe it's some sort of astrophysics phenomenon kind of thing, I don't know...

"Regardless what it is, I cannot fathom how that rabbit, or anything that breathes air, could survive in there. And I never want to find out." He stubbed his cigarette out. "Thank God for death, eh?"

They were sitting back at the kitchen table again. Kyle had a double shot of Wild Turkey in front of him in a mason jar glass that was not too clean. He couldn't have cared less about the cleanliness as he drank it. His hands had finally stopped shaking.

"Somebody will want to study it," Bob was saying. "Science-types. Ministry of Environment. Defense for sure. NATO, maybe. You see what I mean about this place worth millions now? If you lease it out to them, you could set you up for the rest of your life."

Kyle understood. However, if he was genuinely inheriting the place, he was certain of one thing: he was going to sell it as soon as possible. Even if the government offered him a pittance for it, he'd take it. He wanted to be rid of that blackness from his life as soon as possible.

He had another drink, then another after that. Bob had several himself.

Pretty soon, the cloudiness of the bourbon began to

obscure the horror he had felt under the cold ground. He began to relax. Bob talked about old times, family get-to-gethers. They reminisced about this aunt or that second cousin. Bob hadn't kept up with the rest of the family since the falling out and kept asking questions about who was doing what and with whom. They laughed.

Pretty soon, Kyle felt the need to piss. Bob directed him to the upstairs door, second on the right, but cautioned him to beware of the third and seventh stair, as they were pretty rotten.

Kyle paused at the bottom of the stairs and regarded the rickety-looking climb. The night hadn't cooled off yet, so he turned around and walked out the front door.

Weaving his way unsteadily away from the house, he headed for the shed that was just at the edge of the path towards...No, he didn't want to remind himself of that. He just had to find a place to piss that was quiet, not on the house he was about to inherit.

He sighed in relief as the warm stream struck the earth. The moon was full and bright. He glanced down to avoid wetting his shoes and saw something in the shadow of the shed.

He thought it might be a memory at first, a flashback. It was a rabbit, a different one. Just as dead, its head smashed open and its eyes wide like the first in the cave. Kyle looked at it confused, unnerved.

He quickly zipped up and walked back to the house. Bob was still in his kitchen chair, opening a second bottle.

"Why is there another rabbit?"

Bob looked at him, surprised. Then he looked away. "Ah," was all he said.

"You never mentioned it. Why? How did that one die?"

Bob smiled again. "Peter," he said. "Bugs's brother. He was the first experiment." He motioned to the chair for Kyle to sit. Kyle complied.

Bob got up unsteadily, drunkenly, and walked over to the counter. "I bought two rabbits, Bugs and Peter. Not the most original names, but what the hell." He opened a drawer and withdrew something that Kyle couldn't see. He turned and walked back to the table. "Peter sure surprised me, I can tell you that."

Kyle caught the briefest glimpse of UncaBob's arm swinging towards his face before the world went black.

◇━◦━◦━━━◦━◦━◇

His head was pounding. The light hurt his eyes. Kyle's first thought was his brain had turned purple, then thought, *what an odd thing to think*.

He tried to sit up, but his arm wouldn't move right. Blinking to clear his head, he saw his wrist was chained to the base of the radiator heater. It was a short length of chain with a simple keyed padlock securing it.

Bob was seated at the table, looking much worse than before. The friendly uncle was nowhere to be seen in that face; the joking man reminiscing about family get-togethers had fled.

In its place was a stranger, a man with similar features

but whose eyes had been replaced with something that re-minded Kyle of the darkness in a cave not too far away. Bob looked at his nephew and did not smile.

"Peter..." he began slowly, "was the first experiment." He took another drink of bourbon. His hand was shaking.

"Bob...what the hell—"

Bob ignored him. "I couldn't get the rope around Pe-ter; he was squirming too much. I got frustrated, angry. He pissed me off, the little shit." He gave a short, sad laugh. "I just threw him into the blackness."

He drained the glass and poured himself another. "Ah well, I thought. Wasted a good bunny there. Good thing I had a spare, eh?"

He looked directly at Kyle. "But," he said with an anger that was also full of fear, "he came back."

"W-what?" Kyle was still groggy. He wasn't sure what he was hearing.

"I was sitting in the living room. Drunk, of course. I heard a scraping at the door. Then I heard the screaming. The same screaming that Bugs did when I pulled him out.

"I don't know how, but Peter managed to get into the house. Like Bugs, he was insane, completely focused on one thing, attacking me, getting at the one who put him into the darkness.

"I managed to kill it, finally, just like Bugs. I put the body out by the shed. I guess you saw it."

Kyle gently touched his temple, feeling where he had been struck. It ached viciously. "Jesus, Bob, I don't get it. Why would you do this to me about a goddam rabbit you tortured?"

Bob cut him off again. "I'm a hell of a salesman, you know that? I was gonna get into politics, too. Mr. Kirkland, my boss, was going to help bankroll my run for mayor. I would have probably won, too, if not for this fucking illness." He took another drink before he went on. "I can sell anything to anybody. Like you. Dangling the promise of a cushy inheritance to a loser stoner like yourself was just too easy."

Kyle was caught for a moment between being offended and terrified.

"But I had to use all my talent, every molecule, to convince Evan, my wife's new husband, to come out here. It took every skill I ever learned to get him to follow me down that tunnel and see that abomination under the ground."

A silence settled over the room. The only sound was the *drip, drip, drip* of a leaky faucet at the kitchen sink.

"At the edge of that darkness, your knees go weak. You felt it. I could tell. I felt it the first time I saw it. And *that little shit who was fucking my wife* felt it." He moved closer to Kyle's face. Kyle could smell the sour stink of booze on his breath, the rancid stench of sweat, sickness, and hate. "Weak as I am, it was almost too easy to push him inside."

Kyle felt sick to his stomach. "Holy shit..."

"Toni's probably frantic right now, wondering why he hasn't called back, texted at least." He wiped his mouth with his scratched and scabbed hand. "And I thought I had gotten away with it." Bob's eyes suddenly went wide with terror. "But Peter came back!" he screamed.

"What...what do you mean?"

"Don't you understand? That fucking rabbit...*some-how*...came out of there. Either on its own or...Think about it. An idea came to me, and it will really screw with your head. *Maybe* something pushed it back out!"

Kyle began to shake. His ears were ringing, probably from concussion. He wasn't sure what was real and what might be a nightmare.

"I truly don't know what that blackness is, nephew," he hissed. "It might even be a gate into hell, kid. A nothingness of pure madness. Where you float without sense, without feeling, but still aware, still alive!"

"Jesus Christ, Bob..."

"Exactly right, boy! A resurrection from hell! It took three days for Peter to make it out and try to kill me." He paused, licked his cracked lips. "I pushed Evan into that void three nights ago."

Kyle began to push himself back from his uncle. He yanked at the chain binding his wrist, futilely trying to break it. "What the hell do you want from me, dude!" Kyle twisted his wrist, writhing, straining to get free.

Bob laughed again, but that time it was manic, crazy, almost hysterical. "It was hilarious, you know, that little speech you gave at the table when you first got here. That stuff you spun about being there for someone, so they don't die alone? What a load of shit, by the way. Never try to con a conman, kiddo." His grin was Cheshire-like, completely mental. A thin rivulet of drool snaked down his chin. "But you were right about one thing. No one wants to die alone.

Bob reached behind his back and pulled out a large

kitchen carving knife about eight inches long. The blade shone weakly under the single bulb of the kitchen light. "Any minute now, Evan, or something that used to be Evan, is gonna come for me. We can either kill it together, or we can kill each other." He giggled insanely. "Either way, I ain't going gently into that good night. You get me?" Then he dropped the knife at Kyle's feet.

Kyle snatched it up and pointed it threateningly at Bob. "Get this goddam lock open, you psycho!"

Suddenly, there was a terrible, inhuman scream from outside the house. It came from the direction of the back door, the one closer to the path.

They both turned and looked that way as if trying to see through the walls and trees. A second scream cut through the night. It was a terrible sound, alien and drenched in violence.

"Shit, shit, shit," said Bob. "I was right. I knew it..."

"What the fuck! Is that...?"

"It's him. My God, it's him. He's out!" He turned back to Kyle; his expression was of utter terror. "Do it. I tried. I can't do it to myself."

"Untie me, you son of a bitch!" Kyle bellowed, waving the knife at Bob.

Another scream sounded from the woods, worse than before, closer.

"Yes," cried Bob. "Do it! Then you can do it to yourself! We don't have to die alone! We don't have to go into the darkness alone!"

Kyle looked around for something to wedge against the

radiator. Maybe he could break the pipe and slide the chain off? There was another scream from the thing that might be Evan.

It was much, much closer.

Bob grabbed Kyle's shirt and pulled him close. "Look, you little shit. You're the most useless thing I ever laid my eyes on. I couldn't believe something as pathetic as you could possibly be related to me. For once in your life, do something right! Grow some balls and stick that knife into me before—"

He didn't finish the sentence.

The back door burst open, the doorframe breaking apart like it was made of balsa wood, and the door hit the floor with a crash. In the weak light of the kitchen bulb, Kyle saw a mockery of a human being. It was beyond pale, ghost white. Its clothing was torn and bloody from a dozen cuts and gashes after tearing mindlessly through the woods. Its eyes were wild, bright red, and utterly devoid of humanity. Blood coated its mouth. Kyle saw it had no tongue and believed that it had chewed it off while floating in the infinite darkness.

Bob gibbered and fell back on his side. Kyle screamed as the thing fell upon Bob, its fingers clawing, its mouth gaping to bite at his uncle's flesh. As it landed on Bob, the thing's shoulder slammed against Kyle, knocking his head back against the radiator. For the second time that night, the world went black.

The sun was shining through the dirty windows when Kyle came to. He had vague memories of Bob crying out for his mother. There was a bloody trail leading away from where he sat to the back doorway, in the direction of...

He stayed chained to the radiator for three days and nights. He didn't have his cell phone. His repeated cries for help went unanswered.

On the third night, desperation forced Kyle to use the carving knife to sever his own thumb, allowing him to slip free of the chain. With his hand a bloody, mangled mess, he somehow managed to drive himself to the hospital, but not before using Bob's lighter to set fire to the living room curtains.

The old house was already engulfed in flames before it disappeared from his rearview mirror.

The police questioned him about his injury, whether he knew anything about his two missing relatives who had seemingly vanished without a trace. Kyle maintained his hand was an accident with a bandsaw and he knew nothing about either uncle's whereabouts. Eventually, the case went unsolved.

About two years later, he learned that the land where the house used to stand had been fenced off with industrial chain-link topped with razor-wire. A sign was posted on the fence saying the area was government property.

There were many rumors about it, that site.

One story reached Kyle's ears.

The authorities found something in the woods, something they couldn't figure out, no matter how hard they tried, no matter how many tests they ran. It remained a complete mystery.

In the end, all they knew was that they had a handy place to put the worst of their undesirables...just so long as there was a very, very secure door at the entrance.

Adam H. Douglas
About the Author

Adam is an award-winning storyteller who lives in eastern Canada with his wife, three dogs, and five cats - one of whom is very evil. His forthcoming debut novel, "Welcome To Roofoland" is a horror story about escapism and parenting.

Twitter: @adamhdouglas

THE BLACK ROOM
MASON GALLAWAY

"Oh my God. Here it is."

Maddie stepped into the large attic. Her eyes hardly saw the dusty floor, the antique furniture, the crumpled boxes. All other features of the room she noted out of obligation, a way to form the backdrop for what she was really there to face.

What Maddie saw was the door.

A wall divided the attic into two rooms. In the center of that wall stood the door in question. Her eyes fixed on it. It was closed, as she had prayed it would stay forever.

But she knew, as fear coldly caressed her spine, that it would soon open again.

Maddie's husband, Beau, entered the room behind her.

"Whoa." His eyes jumped around, landing on every dusty, decaying piece, as if wondering where a child could have possibly fit in. "You stayed in here?"

"It was slightly cleaner back then," Maddie said faintly. She was just inches from the door. Her fingers brushed the knob gently, testing its realness. Then she took hold of it, awkwardly, like a bad handshake, too fast and too hard, showing no intent to actually turn it. Instead, she clinched the knob as if to keep it from turning on its own.

Beau went straight for the window that looked upon the neighborhood. He crouched and peered out at the yard below and the street beyond, both still radiant with healthy, sane afternoon light. A mower droned from somewhere. The yard across the street was deserted, but there were toys littered about, waiting for a child to play with them or a grumbling parent to pick them up. The yard over was free of people and toys but held flower beds bursting with color, tulips and poppies maybe.

"Wow, I bet this was something," Beau said absently. When he turned back to Maddie, seeing her at the door, he flinched. Suddenly, the attic seemed bigger to him, his wife smaller and farther away.

"I mean, it could have been."

He nervously wiped his mouth and went to her, a graver tone creeping into his voice. "This is the big, bad door, huh?"

Maddie didn't look at him, but she nodded. She lifted her hand and pressed two fingers into the striations of the wood, listening to the whispers emanating from it. There was no yield whatsoever. The door might as well have been stone.

Beau sighed and looked at her. "I still can't believe your grandmother did that. What a terrible thing to do to a child."

Maddie just nodded again.

Beau turned and pointed to the area directly across from the door. "There?"

Maddie didn't respond for a moment, then she blinked and sniffed out of her torpor.

"What?"

"Was it there? That you had to sit?"

Maddie turned and took a deep breath. "Yep." Her more casual response dissolved some of the tension in the room, and Beau relaxed his posture.

"If I left my toys out, that's where I'd sit," she said, her eyes spacey. "If I looked at her wrong or coughed wrong, that's where I'd sit." Suddenly, Maddie shifted and stepped back from the door, watching it as though it might open.

Beau's eyes also went to the door, but he tamped down the unease welling within him. "How the hell did she ever dream of such a shitty thing? To tell a child, no less?" he said, shaking his head.

"Dream of it?" she asked. Her eyes narrowed and her brow creased.

"Yeah. I mean, a room of complete nothing. Blackness. But from it comes what? Monsters, ghosts, demons? That's so awful to tell a child."

"It was no dream or lie. It was real, Beau." She looked at him as if he'd torn up something she'd drawn for him or had spat in her face. She'd never looked at him that way, and he sucked in a breath.

"Maddie," was all he could say.

She wiped her eyes and laughed nervously, realizing

she'd lost herself for a moment. "I'm sorry. It's just this room. I haven't been here in so long."

Beau stepped forward and placed a hand on her back. "It's okay. I know. When you're ready, you can tell me what happened. We can talk about it."

Maddie's eyes began to drift around the room again. "I think I'm ready now."

There were two objects across from them, objects made amorphous and ghostly by their sheet coverings, either sheet-covered chairs or the hands of giant monsters waiting to sink their claws into unwary asses. Maddie had initially overlooked them upon entering the attic. Maddie walked over to one and pulled off the sheet. Chair indeed. Beau did likewise.

The chairs seemed to have been set out just for them.

He smiled and then looked at her.

"You sure?"

She gave a tepid smile and blink-nodded a yes.

"But right here?" he asked.

She smiled brighter, the corners of her mouth twinkling with eagerness and sadness. "Where else?" She bent down and swept her palm over the seat of the chair, brushing away any dust that might have settled, and then sat down. "If we're going to at least try to make this house work, I've got to face this."

"But facing it is—"

"Talking about it. I know." She felt her eyes begin to frost with anticipation and fear as she gazed at the door.

"Did she ever put you...in there?" he asked.

"No. It was never about going in. It was always about what might come out."

Beau reached over and placed his hand on Maddie's. Both of them gripped the armrests with their free hands.

"She called it the 'Black Room,'" Maddie said, more to the room than to Beau. "Whenever I was bad, or whenever she thought I was bad, up here is where I'd go. Here's where I'd sit, sometimes for no discernible reason. This wasn't always my bedroom, you know. Just a regular attic, like this. Maybe not as full, a bit cleaner, but an attic just the same. And it was my punishment place. So, she'd take me up here, and I'd sit, with my back to the door. The chair wasn't like these. It was a rickety wooden chair. I'd sit there, facing where we are now, away from the door to the Black Room."

She paused, taking reassuring breaths, looking ahead. The dark, innocent eyes of her younger self looked back at her from the hard, wooden chair, wondering about the open door behind her, the things it held, the things it might release. Where all her innocence would be sucked inward to die.

"Then what?"

"Then, my Nan would crouch down close to me. Her eyes would go hard and sharp, and they'd jump from me to the room, and back to me again, like she was making sure something wasn't creeping up behind her. She'd whisper in my ear, '*The Black Room, the blackest of all, as deep and dark and endless as small. Don't turn around. Don't let it see. The blackness of your eyes—open doors they be...*' I think that's it. She'd open the door to the Black Room, and she'd hurry out of the attic. I'd be alone, with the open door behind me."

It was silent as Beau processed what she'd told him. He sat back in his chair, and his eyes held a curious, inquisitive sparkle. He turned to her with caution.

"So, after she'd leave?"

Maddie pulled her eyes from the door and met Beau's gaze.

"Well, not much would happen at first. I thought she was just trying to scare me, trying to add a nasty edge to time-out or something. But after a few minutes, when the afternoon light began dying out, something would change in this room. The air would become thin and chilled. I'd shiver, have trouble breathing. At first, I thought I was just imagining things, but I could sense something. And before long, I could actually feel the darkness behind me, its pull, its depth, its endlessness, something like the end but an end that led to so many horrible beginnings. I didn't conceptualize all that then, obviously, but that was my kid interpretation. I just knew, at any moment, that dark would either suck me in or let something nasty into this room with me. I would see some horrible monster, and my eyes would be like an open door for it to come in and…"

Maddie's breathing began to quicken, and she clinched her eyes shut.

"Jesus, look at me," she said.

"It's okay. We can move on."

Maddie shook her head. "

"No, I want to get through this."

"Ok, so you'd experience that. What would actually happen?"

"I don't really remember. I'd panic, and sometimes I'd black out."

"Shit."

"Call it relief, but that may have been the worst part actually. After blacking out a few times, losing memory, I started to wonder if it was the actual darkness getting me somehow, having its way with me. I don't know."

"Good Lord." Beau squeezed Maddie's hand. "That's pure psychological torture, like the cleanest kind." Beau grunted and huffed like a beast as he looked to the ground. "Your grandma was a real fucking witch."

"She was ill, Beau."

"Whatever." He turned to her, then swept the walls and ceiling with his eyes. "You sure you want to keep this house?"

"I'll be fine. I managed to sleep in here, for God's sake. The weight of it all didn't hit till later. But I can actually think about it now without panicking. I'm not really afraid of the dark anymore. I even sat in our closet that entire time. I almost fell asleep."

Beau snickered. "Just remind your doctor it was your idea and not mine."

Maddie laughed. "Hell, she suggested it. But coming up here was the last step. Really."

They looked at one another, a long glance. Then Beau turned away and slapped his palms against the wooden arm-rests of his chair. "Well, in that case. It's time."

He pushed himself up out of the chair and walked towards the door to the Black Room. When his hand touched the knob, Maddie screamed. The sound was so strident and forceful, Beau jumped, feeling as if something sharp had been driven into his ears, meeting his brain. He ripped his hand away from the knob and cupped his ears, cowering.

"What!"

Maddie halted her scream. Her eyes were wide, and her mouth was open, though it was now covered by her hand. She felt even more shocked than Beau looked.

"I don't know what hit me."

"I was just going to..." Beau gestured toward the knob.

"Don't!" She shot up from her chair.

Beau backed away from the door.

"Okay. Okay. So maybe we still have a ways to go then?"

She shook her head fiercely, then she looked at the window. A drape of dust-speckled afternoon sunlight hung through the glass. The light had waned since they arrived, but it still kept the shadows of night in the corners. Through that window was a world full of things, full of light. Dangers and surprises, no doubt, but only those that could be seen and felt and possibly understood and overcome with time. She turned back to Beau and the Black Room.

"It's not me, Beau. It's you I'm worried about."

"Me?" Beau asked, his face wrinkled with puzzlement.

Maddie closed her eyes, and her body tensed and rose with breath. "I said I never turned around, that I never saw the room. I lied about that."

"What did you see?"

Maddie began rubbing her forehead, coaxing the memories loose. Then, she opened her eyes, peering into the hollow, shadowy stacks of her mind. She turned to Beau and looked through him, through the door, into the other room.

"Only blackness. It really was...a black room."

"You mean it was dark."

Maddie shook her head. "No."

She walked toward Beau, still seeing beyond him, not noticing him shuffle out of the way. Her gaze was locked. At the door, she stopped and leaned in close enough that her ears almost touched the grain. She swallowed hard and cleared her throat of whatever fear had lodged itself there. But she didn't move.

"I mean it was *black*. I got close enough to see in. It was a day like today, just as bright. Some of that light should have at least crossed the threshold, but it didn't. The darkness remained, solid yet full of space. And it had a pull. I couldn't tell if it was a physical suction or just my mind being drawn to something so beyond."

She suddenly pulled away from the door.

"What? Did you hear something?"

"I got away that time. And I never looked in again. I knew that if I ever did, I'd be lost forever. And I know you would be too." She turned back to Beau. "But yes, you can hear something. It's more of a feeling maybe, but it's there. Go ahead. Try." She motioned for him to step forward and listen as she had done.

With reluctance, he stepped forward. Constraining him was both skepticism and fear. Either his wife was telling the truth, which would be bad enough, or she was not--by intentional deception or outright delusion. He put his ear to the door.

Maddie watched him and the door, knowing that Beau would soon know what she knew so well.

What Beau heard was not surprising at first. There was a faint whir, the sound of gentle movements. Various natural forces running through the house's interior, against the exterior. Gentle air currents moving and dancing through the room, eddying in its corners, sweeping across the door. Emptiness but not true emptiness.

But after a moment, that ordinary hollowness expanded and began to pulsate, becoming more of a feeling than an audible sensation. There was a deep breathing sound, not the breath of life but the breath of violent potential. The door seemed to vibrate, but it was a fine vibration. So fine it tickled the hairs of his face, his nose, and his eyelids. Then he heard the voices. An unintelligible, muffled mess of voices at first, but then they gelled and clarified.

And they spoke to him. Saying his name.

Then the voices shrunk to one voice. A tender, playful voice, full of softness and light and innocence. It was a child, calling for his brother to come and play. To hurry. There wasn't much time. Because time was stupid, and life ended way too soon. Beau's little brother who drowned in the bathtub was calling for him to help him finally get out and dry off.

Beau gasped and pushed himself from the door. His eyes remained locked on the door's grain, his mind still echoing traces of that strange, expansive breathing sound and the lilting syllables of his dead brother's call.

"Holy shit," Beau said, out of breath.

"What?" Maddie said, going to him.

"I just thought I heard something. Just psyched out." Beau turned to Maddie, his face strained with shock and stony understanding. She nodded.

"And I heard my parents. That's what got me to turn around, to go to it. But when you get close enough, it pulls you in for good." Maddie's voice had taken on a soft, childlike quality but with none of the cheer and innocence. She twitched her head, sensing herself regressing. Her voice became emboldened. "I mean, that's what it does. It draws you in by making you think it's full of the things you miss, yearn for. Things you need. Things you want to do over again."

Maddie's brow wrinkled with thought, and she continued.

"I can't face it. Not really. And neither can you. But we don't have to see it to face it." She went back to the chairs.

Beau watched her, still shaken.

"I don't know. I'm not even sure I—"

"Do it for me?"

Beau smiled, melting some of the shocked chill in his face. "Of course."

They both grabbed their chairs and spun them around to face the eaves of the attic opposite the door. Then, they slid them back a foot or so, to where Maddie had sat as a child. She eyed the chairs and then the door for reference. After adjusting the chairs a couple inches forward, a few centimeters backward, she nodded in satisfaction.

"Okay," she said, looking at Beau.

Beau made to sit in his chair, as did Maddie. Maddie halted before settling.

"Oh! Damn," she said, snorting a laugh. She walked around the chair and approached the door. She put her hand on the knob and told Beau to turn around. "I'm going to close my eyes and run to you."

She watched him sit down and face the other way, not seeing Beau's lips rise in a half smile, one of anticipation and amusement flecked with fear, imagining his wife clinching her eyes shut and scampering away from the scary door like a child playing a game. Or a child terrified of getting too close to the always reaching, always hungry dark.

The knob hissed as it turned, the door sighing and grunting as it opened. Maddie whisked back to her chair and dropped in it with a squelch. She opened her eyes.

"Just look ahead," she said.

"Okay. I feel a little silly, I have to admit."

Maddie took a deep breath as the moment settled upon her.

"You okay?" he asked, turning his head and eyes just slightly.

"Shh! Yes," she hissed. "Just wait."

For a moment, Beau felt like a person sitting in an attic with his back to an open door. To a room that probably contained nothing more than shadows, dust, and forgotten junk. Maybe a skeleton or two. Maybe even actual skeletons. But then Maddie's breathing began to accelerate, growing deeper and more rapid. It was the respiration of fear but also, oddly, of sexual anticipation. Though there was no arousal in the air. And he noticed his own pulse, his own breath, quickening.

There was no sound, no sensations other than what they'd already experienced in the main attic. But Beau's mind was suddenly being pulled toward the room, a room that could have held nothing or many things. Many benign and innocuous things or many grim and eldritch things. Terrible secrets. Or, as its namesake suggested, so much nothing a person's mind might implode seeing it.

Still, he felt his consciousness drifting toward the room, trying to conjure images of what could be in there but coming short. There were quick reels of an ordinary room, then a room not so ordinary, but not at all preternatural, with bones or bloodied clothes and things that wanted to stay hidden. Then a room with nothing but blackness, a blackness that breathed eternal emptiness, that pulsed with the somethings that only nothing could become. Somethings monstrous. Somethings painfully, mournfully endless.

Suddenly, Beau was afraid. Terrified. He couldn't tell Maddie's hyperventilation from his own. And it didn't matter. Their fear breathed as one. There could be a truly black room behind them. All kinds of terrible somethings or horrific nothings. Or maybe he was just disturbed to his core by sitting in the attic of a deceased, witchy woman, reliving his wife's psychological abuse, with his back to an open room that held God-knew-what.

Then his brother's voice rose again, calling for him, for both of them. Faint and breezy. Could have been a draft or his own wheezy breath. And for an instant, Beau wanted to fly from his chair and go to him, find him in all that blackness and tell him that he meant to save him, that he never wanted him to die, and really did like playing with him. To pull him from the engulfing dark to finally take that desperate breath.

Beau's eyes opened, and his grip on the armrests tightened, readied to propel him upward. That's when he realized the sounds he heard were not his brother but his wife. Maddie was whimpering, uttering what sounded like words that wouldn't fully materialize. Her eyes were closed, and she was in some kind of a trance.

Beau turned completely to look at her, to see her face. A single tear rolled down her cheek, and tears were brimming in his own eyes. He could also see the room in his periphery. Though it was out of focus and the attic was shadowy, what he saw his was nothing short of a deep, rectangular black.

A portal to nowhere.

A nothing that wanted him.

That wanted them both so, so much.

Maddie's eyes flew open, and more tears rolled down her cheeks. But her eyes were bright with relief and maybe even joy. She was smiling.

"Babe, are you okay? We can stop this."

"Don't look," she said, pushing his gaze away from her, away from the door behind them.

"Enough? Is this enough?" he asked.

"I'm just happy that you're here. It feels just like it did when I was kid. Just as terrible." She paused and rested her hand on his arm. "Only this time, I'm not alone, and that's a good feeling."

Beau took her hand, more deliberately this time. They both squeezed with so much force their hands should've hurt, but they didn't. Then Beau let go and got up from the chair.

"Fuck this," he said.

"No!"

"I'm going to the door, and I'm looking in. And then I'm going in. This all has to end."

"You mean you don't believe me?"

"No, I do believe you."

"Then prove it."

⟡⸺◇⸺◇⸺◇⟡

Maddie and Beau stood before the open doorway of the Black Room. They kept their eyes closed tight before the blackness, the endlessness, unseen beyond the darkness of their eyelids. They both felt the room's breath, its pull, and they heard its calls. But they did not back away from it.

"You ready?" Beau asked.

Maddie only nodded but hard enough to send an affirming shudder through her body down to his hand.

They took deep breaths, and together they walked into the Black Room.

They felt no fear.

Because whatever terrible somethings or endless nothings they might face, they would face together.

Mason Gallaway
About the Author

Mason Gallaway is a writer of dark, weird, and scary stories. His short fiction has appeared in various publications, such as Dark Moon Digest, Calliope, It Calls from the Sea from Eerie River Publishing, and Dates from Hell from Hellbound Books. He began writing seriously after reading Stephen King's Night Shift and thinking, like a fool, how hard could it be? He lives in Tennessee with his wife and their peculiar pets.

You can catch him on Instagram and at MasonGallaway.com
https://www.instagram.com/masongway/
https://masongallaway.com

RINGING THE BELL
RACHEL UNGER

When things went wrong, it happened fast.

I knew—we all knew—we shouldn't go into the abandoned mine. But Shane was going deeper in, almost out of sight, and someone had to call him back.

Or maybe it was just that we had to see too. Maybe we had to test ourselves, the way we were always testing ourselves, and the mine was the latest way to do it.

Or maybe it was the mine itself, pulling us in.

"Wait for me if you find something cool!" Henry yelled as he bolted back outside, heading for his "good" camera in the rental car. If he'd had the better camera when we found the clearing, he and Shane would have competed for first into the mine, but photography had always come first for Henry.

"Damn fools going in all freaking directions," Mel huffed, slumping into the wall beside her. "Shane doesn't even have a headlamp and—"

And then part of the ceiling collapsed.

We came from everywhere. That season had rafting guides from places like Vermont, San Diego, and British Columbia, but we had more in common than whitewater and muscle tone. Once our company-given camping spaces were set up in the bush, we had little to do except figure out just how far we could push ourselves.

Well, we could drink, and we did, but mostly it was about pushing the envelope. One of the old-timers—on his fifth year of guiding tours, which made him nearly thirty—had a thing for rock climbing. Within a month, we were constantly on the lookout for new things to climb. On rainy days, we'd drive into town for the climbing gym, roping in and racing each other, seeing who could be the first to ring the bell at the top of each route. Sometimes, it didn't even have to be raining.

Ringing the bell was addictive, and we had the money for gas and day passes. We bouldered, too, any time we were conscious and not on a raft with tourists, but it was ringing the bell whether we were indoors or out.

When the drought closed up the shallower parts of the river, our hours dried up with it. The company let us use the campsites until the end of the season. And then Mel found cheap tickets to Seattle.

Mel was lean and savvy about anything wilderness related. If you wanted a fire built or a river investigated before taking a tour down it, you asked Mel.

"There's a rainforest in a national park up there, Kat,"

she said. "Jesus, look at this!"

She knew about my plan to hike all the national parks. Hell, everyone did. I wasn't shy about it. Between her enthusiasm and mine, five of us threw camping gear in backpacks and went to the airport. Mount Rainier was covered in clouds when we arrived, but we hopped ferries and asked about breweries.

Eddie took the wheel the second morning. "I lived here for a bit when I was a kid. If I can find it, we're going somewhere else first," was all he said.

Once we got into the forest, the service roads had numbers instead of names. The road climbed, and the trees closed in. We stopped complaining about the hallucinogenic rainforests we were missing because the sun was out and the mountains were amazing.

We parked at a trailhead, and Eddie's sly grin became enormous. "So," he said. "Do you want to see the crashed airplane or hike a mountain pass?"

We ran the first mile, leaping downed logs or running along them, shouting at each other and at the wind. We took some daypacks with water and food, but the bulk of the camping gear was left in the trunk.

Eddie slowed at a spur off the main trail. Shane dropped into some impossibly difficult yoga position, mostly to prove he could do Flying Pigeon and we couldn't. He admired his new shoes once again while down there. God, we were all sick of hearing about those shoes, but Shane was obsessed with them.

Eddie glanced down both options for the path and

then pointed along the main trail. "Let's go this way," he said, and away we went.

We were still laughing and pushing each other when we came to the entrance of the mine. The shadowed gray stone framed an open tunnel plunging back into the rock. The ferns around the hole were almost as dark, as though the sun looked away instead of shining on their leaves. Even the birds were silent.

"Cool," Henry whispered, already reaching for his camera, and so we walked closer.

I didn't want to. Something about it was repellent, though I couldn't figure out why. Hundreds of people had probably gone into it on a daily basis, back when the mine was running. It was basically just an open door.

The air was so still that my skin tingled.

There was probably a moment when someone could have spoken and stopped us, but it passed by in that stillness.

Mel looked as intrigued as Henry, but Eddie seemed weirded out.

"I don't..." But we never found out what he was going to say, because by then, Shane was inside.

"Guys! Come look!" he called.

We really shouldn't have gone in. I don't know what we expected, but what we got was the stuff of posted warnings and common sense. There was a *clack-thunk* of rock shifting, and we were stuck.

Instinctively, I pressed back into the wall, curling my arms up to protect my head. A yell lurched out of me before I could pretend to be completely cool. And then everyone was slapping at their phones to get flashlights on, then swinging them around.

Mel coughed. "What the hell! Eddie! Shane! Kat!"

Everyone but Eddie answered. All of our headlamps had gone off, but I started mine again. I must have turned it off when I covered my head before. I felt dumb and still freaked out.

Dust settled, though the air was murky. I found Eddie huddled against the wall, wild-eyed. I touched his leg.

"Eddie? Are you okay?" I think I was asking myself as much as him. He flinched and looked like he might lunge away, so I tightened my grip. "Eddie!"

Something in my tone must have gotten through because he made eye contact and his shoulders started to come down from his ears. He was the best of us with heights, completely unafraid in any rapid you'd care to name, but apparently, he didn't do well in enclosed spaces.

Shane was swearing about ten feet farther in. He pointed at the dim light filtering between two dislodged rocks behind us.

There was no way any of us could fit through that gap.

Mel put a hand on the pile of rock, and Eddie spoke up. "Don't!" he said sharply. "Do you want more to come down?"

She glared at him but took her hand away. "Henry, if you're there, go get help!" she yelled.

There was nothing but our breathing in response. Shane didn't have a headlamp, and Eddie's wouldn't work, but Mel cajoled hers into producing light. Since signal had dropped to zero as soon as we went inside, everyone put their phones away to conserve battery.

"Two headlamps should be enough," Shane said in a dubious tone.

The walls were dark gray and brownish black, and the treacherous ceiling was a little low. Some timbers along the floor lead away from us into the dark, probably the remains of a set of rails.

The headlamps created as many shadows as they banished. With the shifting beams of light, lumps of rock on the walls seemed to lurch from side to side. Down the tunnel, the shadows merged into one.

Eddie released a shaky breath. His hands were fisted between his body and the wall behind. His lips moved but no sound emerged.

"Eddie?" I asked again, and then we heard it.

"Hello?"

The voice came from farther down the tunnel. There was a suggestion of faint light too.

Was it Henry? It didn't quite sound like Henry. Something about the voice made all the hair on the back of my neck stand up.

"Henry?" Mel called, her voice uncertain.

Shane looked back at us and shook his head. "Doesn't sound right," he said very quietly. "I don't know who or what that is, but it doesn't sound right."

Eddie yelled back. "We're here!" His voice was tight and higher than usual. "Is there another way out down there?"

The answer came immediately. "This way," the voice said.

Eddie was scrambling over Shane before any of us had time to do anything but notice that the voice hadn't answered "Yes" to Eddie's question.

Shane reached out and hauled Eddie back. "Would you wait?" he demanded.

Eddie fought to get free, but Shane had him. "Let go!"

Shane shook Eddie. "*Slow down*!" he snarled back. "We don't know where we're going, and you're going to bolt and leave the rest of us because you can't keep your shit together? What if the tunnel *branches*? We don't even know who that is!"

This was rich, coming from Shane, but he also wasn't wrong.

"This way!" the voice called again, and Eddie's struggles increased.

Shane shoved him back to Mel and me.

"Screw this," Shane said, "I'm leading. Maybe you can keep him from freaking the hell out." He strode forward, leaving us to either calm Eddie down or at least slow him up.

"What the hell is wrong with you?" Mel yelled, trying to stay upright as Eddie pushed past her. "You haven't even got a headlamp, moron!"

"I'm just seeing if—" Shane called back.

Then, abruptly, nothing.

"Shane?" I called, but he didn't answer. My stomach went into free fall.

All three of us ran for where he'd been. We came

around the corner fast, but he was gone. There was just the gray rock, speckled with chunks of black, and a lone shoe lying near the wall.

Those damn shoes. Shane never would have left a shoe behind. Ever. All the air rushed out of me, and my first few tries didn't seem to suck anything breathable back in.

Ahead of us, the faint light flickered like a beacon.

I grabbed one of Eddie's arms, and Mel grabbed the other. He dragged us both along, heedless of what must have just happened to Shane. The headlamp beams danced crazily over the walls. Eddie pulled us around another curve, and then suddenly, there were two tunnels headed in opposite directions. I hesitated, wondering if Shane had darted down one of them instead of just disappearing, and stumbled over a rock that Eddie neatly avoided. I let go of his arm to stop myself from going face-first into anything.

Mel hauled back, planting her feet, and for a moment she almost had him.

"We're nearly there!" Eddie panted, yanking his arm free. "We just have to get to that light!"

Mel grabbed two fistfuls of his shirt and shook him. "The tunnel has curved and we still haven't come across anything that's lit up! Where do you think that light is coming from?"

But it didn't matter. Eddie wrenched loose and ran into the dark after the tiny little glow. We heard his footsteps and his voice calling out to someone. Both sounds faded into the distance faster than we would have liked.

Mel yelled profanities after him until she ran out of

breath, and then she looked at me. "Do you want to go after him or go back and wait for Henry?" she panted.

My heart hammered in my ears. I considered both tunnels in front of us and then looked back. Everything looked bad. "Do you think Shane took one of these?"

"I have no idea," she said in a small, frustrated voice.

"People don't just vanish," I said, trying to convince myself as much as her. "He's probably trying to freak us out. You know what he's like. He's got to be down one of these two tunnels, and he's just waiting to laugh at us for being scared." And I *was* scared. The ceiling collapse had happened fast, but the rest of it was slow enough that panic had caught up.

Mel nodded—as though we were both calm, as though all of it was reasonable—and then we stared at the two tunnels. We edged closer together.

"We know Eddie went left," she said at last, and that was that.

I mean, we could have gone back, but there was that light. There was that voice. It was creepy as hell, but what if there really was another way out? We followed. I used the time to try and slow down my breathing. It didn't really help. The walls almost loomed out at us with each corner we took, and the adrenaline continued to thrum through me.

We called for Eddie as we went, and once or twice, he even answered.

When he stopped, Mel said, "He's probably just out of earshot. That's good, right? Maybe he found a way out." She didn't sound like she believed it either.

After an hour, the tunnel continued on, brown or black where it wasn't gray, getting smoother as it went, almost washed clean of dust. Throat-like. We walked deeper into the mine.

We spoke less and less. I was breathing more shallowly, as though it were important to be as quiet as possible. I knew the tautness of Mel's features in the light of the headlamps had to be mirrored on my face. Every few minutes, we would pause and listen, Mel's hand on my arm or mine on hers. My bones were nothing more than cables stretched to the breaking point.

Then our lights picked up Eddie sitting and leaning against the wall just up the tunnel.

"*Jesus Christ*, Eddie!" Mel exhaled loudly. "You *asshole*! You scared us half to..." She didn't finish, because by then, we could see him clearly.

I don't know how he could have been beaten so thoroughly without us hearing a sound. There was blood splashed on the wall near him, probably from when his nose and half of his face had been broken. There was blood pooled around him too. His arms were both mangled. When I realized the pointy bits in his leg had been bone, I lost the contents of my stomach.

What had done that to him? What the hell was down here with us? My stomach continued to try to crawl to freedom through my mouth. My heart was like a jackhammer, tenderizing my flesh for whatever was out there.

Eventually, there was nothing left to throw up. When I looked up, Mel was blinking rapidly, her hands shaking. She exhaled sharp little puffs of air as though she were running instead of standing still.

My gaze went again to Eddie's body. I couldn't help it. The blood pooled around him seemed less somehow, and I trained my headlamp on it. It took me a moment to realize it was seeping into the rock. And then, no more blood, just dry, clean gray rock.

There was a small noise, like a pebble being kicked or a stomach rumbling. It could have been a gunshot from the speed at which we both snapped to alertness.

Mel looked at me, eyes wide and teeth bared in a snarl. I couldn't tell if she was more angry or terrified. "We can't go back," she whispered after a moment. "We'd be trapped."

I felt trapped already, but before I could say so, the voice came again.

"Here! This way!"

The light came again, too, but stronger. Closer, maybe? It was hard to tell in the darkness. My heart went back into overdrive, pummeling me into some kind of decision. *Fight, or flight?*

Mel's eyes narrowed. "Oh, we're coming," she hissed, and she dug in her daypack until she pulled out a Swiss army knife. It stayed in her left hand as she put the pack back on. She gestured down the tunnel with only her gaze.

The light stayed ahead of us, but we moved more warily anyway. Eddie had run, heedless of danger. We weren't going to make the same mistake.

We crept around a curve and came to another branching set of tunnels. Though the light continued down the righthand branch, even brighter, we peeked into the left option.

We found Shane.

It had popped him like a balloon. The only recognizable thing was the foot extending into the corridor, still wearing that damned shoe.

We bolted. There was no room for wondering how he'd gotten that far, why he'd left a shoe behind, or why the light seemed to get brighter yet stay just as far away. I kept seeing his shoe in my mind and all the blood seeping into the gray rock. Sheer terror made the walls seem to breathe around me. I couldn't have stopped running if I'd tried.

We burst out into an open space, and for a moment, I nearly wept because it was an alien sky above us. There were no recognizable stars, only endless darkness.

Then, I realized it wasn't the sky.

It was just a cavern, tall enough that we could barely see the ceiling.

The sweat on my forehead turned icy for a moment. I craned frantically around. The rock there was different, still dark but undeniably red. There were some white streaks and some grey, but we were surrounded by walls that looked bloodied. The color went all the way to the ceiling.

There was a grinding noise in the tunnel behind us. Across the cavern, the light flickered brightly.

My forehead got colder again, and my hair brushed my cheek. *A breeze?* I looked up again, and I saw a small opening situated high above the tunnel we'd come in by. I didn't know how small, but it was open to the sky. A faint, cloudy light came from beyond the red rock.

"This way!" the voice called, and it was perceptibly louder.

Was it gleeful?

Mel shrugged out of her pack, knife in hand, pivoting between the voice ahead and the noise behind. She wasn't going down easy, whichever direction she was attacked. I grabbed her arm and pointed up.

"*Ring the bell!*" I gasped, dropping my pack. Then, I hurled myself at the wall. It took Mel a fraction of a second, and then her pack thumped to the ground. I heard her starting to scramble up behind me.

The two of us raced up the face, trying to go faster, trying not to think about what could be down below.

Trying not to think about what would happen if we fell.

We'd climbed with headlamps before but only at the climbing gym because we knew better than to boulder after the rocks had been heated by the sun. You never stuffed your hand into a place you couldn't see, not outdoors. But there was no time to consider what could be living in the crevices. There was just the climb.

I no longer thought I was going to live to see the end of that vacation.

I just wanted to live a little longer.

I pulled my shoulder hard when a foothold crumbled under me, and I had to support my weight over too large of a span. Broken rock skittered down the wall and onto the floor below. I didn't care.

"Hurry!" Mel snapped from right behind me.

I clambered into the opening, which was just barely large enough to squeeze through. I crawled the few feet forward onto actual dirt lit from the world above and hauled myself out into the air. Glorious, fresh air. I sucked in a lungful and then another as I scrambled forward and then flipped around, crablike, to look behind me.

The hole wasn't empty, and I fumbled for anything to use as a weapon, but it was Mel, dragging herself out as I had. Her headlamp was a dim third eye askew on her head. I sagged in relief, the soft earth cushioning my body.

Mel lay panting, face down. Behind us, the opening beckoned. Warm, dark, a place to rest. *We all return to the earth eventually*, it seemed to say. I shuddered and looked away.

It was daytime. We were on a slope with trees all around. Looking down the hill, I could see a clearing holding the skeleton of an airplane. It must have been the B-whatever Eddie had remembered.

Then Mel screamed, body stiffening as she yanked at her leg. A shadow had reached out of the hole to curl around her foot, and she began to slide back. There was a snapping noise. She clawed at the ground, still screaming, her foot twisted.

I lunged forward. I think I got lucky. I was still wearing my headlamp. As I leaned over her leg, shoving the heel of her shoe loose, the light fell on the shadowy arm. It faded and then retreated.

It took Mel's shoe and her sock, leaving only the

crushed brown foot behind. We both shoved ourselves away from the hole in the earth, nearly tumbling backwards down the slope.

Not being sure how far was far enough, we stumbled down the hill as well. We didn't stop until we were on the grass in the clearing. Mel used her heel as much as she could, but she growled in pain almost all the way down.

Clouds hung over the treetops like distant, uninterested bystanders. We'd get no help from them. My pulse throbbed in my ears as I waited, almost lightheaded with fear.

Nothing more came out of the hole. We were alone.

Mel got over to the wreckage with some help. My heart rate slowed down a little. I thought about Eddie, how he'd barely remembered the place but had brought us unerringly to the trailhead. I thought of Shane, first inside the mine. I looked at the broken spine of the B-whatever-it-was on the clearing floor, and I had no trouble believing that the thing in the mine had pulled it right out of the sky.

We didn't have our packs, but we had each other, and we got creative. We lashed Mel's bad leg to one of my good ones with our belts. It was an awful three-legged hike back to the car, treating obstacles like rapids to be navigated. It took hours, but we didn't dare stop. We rested when we had to but never for long.

Eddie had the keys to the rental, which we only realized when we were standing next to it. We had signal at the trailhead, and we called 911. They said it would be a while, but once we knew they'd arrive before dark, we were fine with waiting, as long as it was during the daylight.

We called Henry. He didn't answer.

Henry had made it back to the car only to remember Eddie had locked it, so he trudged his way back to the split in the trail. He wouldn't be able to do the image he thought of with his phone camera, the long exposure with the group of them walking away, lit only by their headlamps. They'd have looked like ghosts vanishing down that tunnel. He sighed and headed uphill to the mine. There would be other pictures.

When he got back to the opening, he discovered it was nearly blocked by rubble.

What the hell? When had that happened? Henry pushed experimentally at the top boulder, and it rocked back and forth before he could pull it free.

He leaned down to the hole. "Guys?" he called. "Are you okay?"

A faint voice came through the gap. "Here!" it said. "In here!" He couldn't tell who it was.

He worked at the next rock down and the next until the gap was larger. "Is anyone hurt?" He called again, but there was no answer.

Crap. They probably need help. Carefully, Henry turned on his headlamp and squeezed himself inside.

Rachel Unger
About the Author

Rachel thinks that now is an excellent time for us all to be kind to each other. Yes, really. She spends her days excavating stories from the dirt, staring down a microscope, and daydreaming about her next bike ride.

You can find her online at www.fictionbuffet.com.

Thanks for Answering
Michael Gore

The day they put it in, half the darn street came to see it. They all looked at it, gobsmacked, and slapped Pa's back, laughing as they held the pepper-shaker-sized thing to their ears.

She couldn't understand why Pa was so darn excited to have that...thing...in their kitchen. Even though there were seven adults, all chortling and trying the new phone, making the kitchen feel tiny, Josie felt alone, very alone. She always felt alone. She was the only kid on the street after all. The girls at school either didn't like her or lived too far away to play with.

A big set of gruff hands pushed her towards the phone. Everyone suddenly looked at her with giddy anticipation, and before she could protest, Pa took the receiver and put it to her ear. The black-painted brass was warm, and it felt sticky and gross.

Who would want to push something against their ear like this? It's like a wet willy, she thought as Pa urged her to speak into the part that looked like the horn on their record player.

"Speak!"

"Say something!"

"Talk, Josie."

"Just say hi, for cherry's sake!"

"Anything would do. Just talk, and you'll hear them talk back."

"Oh, don't press her. She is scared."

"Kid don't understand how gal darn astounding this is."

"Talk, Josie. Talk!"

"Speak."

"Speak!"

The words slammed at her from every which way. She had no clue who was saying what, why they were they being so bossy, but everyone yelling at her made her face hot and tied her tongue.

It was almost impossible, but after the twelfth cajole, she eked out a tiny, shallow, "Hello."

Seconds later, Josie was on the porch, bent over Pa's knee, stockings and underwear pulled to her shoes, her buttocks exposed for everyone to gawk at.

And they gawked, all right. All seven of them came out to watch her get punished, every last one of them.

Whack, whack, whack.

The spankings always hurt, but that time, Pa had a callus on his palm at the base of his pointer finger that was rougher than normal, and she could feel it scratching her skin with each slap.

There were mumblings and angry comments. A few

told Pa it was enough. Another spoke up and said it wasn't, that the phone was worth more than Josie's whole damn life.

But all Josie could think of were the words that awful, awful voice had said to her that caused the knee-jerk throwing of the ear piece to the floor.

It was a voice of pure evil.

Deep, gravely, and almost hypnotic. The vibrato made the words quiver into her ear and down to her ear drum like some sort of intelligent snake that knew right where to slither. The words scared her.

Your pa killed your ma.

In Sunday school, she was told stories of Satan, how he could try to trick and entice her, but she never thought they were true, let alone that he would talk directly to her.

No one talked to Josie.

⟡⎯⎯⎯⎯⎯⟡

Josie brought Pa his evening drink as he sat in his chair reading, just like any other night. Normally, he would kiss her on the cheek, tell her to wash up and go to bed, which she would. However, that night, Pa did not kiss her.

As she started to walk away, he barked, "If that phone stops working, you will have to work off the damage you caused to it."

Josie stood with her back to him. She nodded but waited to be dismissed.

"Josie, I've never been so embarrassed in my life. If there was no company...it wouldn't have been your behind."

Josie sucked in a big breath and dared a response. She

burned to tell someone what she heard, but she knew they would not believe a child.

"The voice, Pa, the voice scared me, and it said mean and untrue things." With her back still to him, she absent-mindedly touched the raw skin on her behind.

"It was the operator asking you who you wanted to be connected to. That is how the phone works. You pick it up and tell the dame who you want to talk to, and she connects you. You can ask her the time too. That's who you talked to."

Josie wanted to turn and run to him, to bury her face in his chest and tell him what she really heard, just like Ma would have allowed her to do, but she knew Pa would not tolerate that. So, she nodded and headed to bed. Unfortunately, she had to pass through the kitchen, right by that damn phone.

Josie kept her eyes on it as she passed, as if the thing might leap and strangle her with the thick brown cord. It didn't, and she made it to her room successfully, but the damn thing was only ten steps away from her bed.

Sleeping is not going to be easy, she thought as she put on her nightgown and washed her face in the basin.

Sure enough, every time she closed her eyes, she thought of the creepy black phone. In her mind, it would grow in size, the cord turning slimy and pulsing like a birthing cow's umbilical cord. The thought of that cord whipping out like a lasso, grabbing her tight and pulling her towards it, made her sit up and gasp for air.

It wasn't a half second later that the phone's trill bell rang. It sounded like a metallic kitten purring during an angry nightmare.

Two quick tinny purrs.

Josie felt faint but forced herself to jump up and flip on the light switch. Instead of a flood of light, the bulb popped in a fat electric snap. Josie yelled and pushed her body against the door.

He is coming for me. He wants me.

Puurrrrriiing.

Puurrrrriiing.

Josie had never wanted her mother more.

Puurrrrriiing.

Puurrrrriiing.

The ringing seemed to get louder as she sank to the floor, holding the door shut. Crossing herself, Josie started to pray—fast, hard, and with more conviction than she ever had.

Puurrrrriiing.

Puurrrrriiing.

Yet, it wouldn't stop.

Why isn't Pa waking up? Why doesn't he get the gal darn phone?

Anger started to take over the fear, the ringing making her want to smash the phone into pieces. Over and over, it wouldn't stop. It grew so loud she couldn't hear her own prayers anymore. She had to answer it. She had to tell the voice to leave her alone, or else.

Or else what?

As she stood up, her legs wobbled in a way that made her think of a newborn calf...*and that throbbing umbilical cord.* With a deep breath, she grabbed the handle and pulled the door open, half-expecting to see Satan himself standing in the kitchen, holding the phone out to her.

But it was just her kitchen, the phone on the counter the only outlier in the room.

The ringing was so loud she had to cover her ears. There was no way Pa could sleep through it. It was louder than a dozer stuck in a mud pit, revving its engines full throttle. After a quick look around the room to be certain there were no demons, Josie locked her eyes on the phone. Despite the noise it was making, it was eerily still.

She stood two feet from the phone, the phone that had caused her such embarrassment and the scratches on her buttocks, not to mention the fright of a lifetime. Josie reached out to the receiver, slowly, as if it might bite. The ringing was so deafening she was nervous her ears would start to bleed. The painful cacophony instantly cut to dead silence as she lifted the receiver, the muting so blissful that she silently thanked God.

"Baby J, is that you? Baby J?" It was a voice she had not heard in three years, though she replayed it plenty in her head.

Ma.

She knew it was her, besides the voice being so distinct, because no one else had ever called her Baby J.

"Mama...Mama...how...? Is it really you?" Tears streamed down Josie's face, feelings of joy and relief pouring over her.

"Yes, Baby J. Yes," her Ma's voice whispered so wonderfully in her ear.

A second later, Josie spewed out sentence after sentence

of how much she missed her, how she was so scared, what the voice said. But then, she slowed down and asked the important question.

"Ma, how are...where are you?"

There was a long pause, and Josie thought she could hear wind and other whispers in the background.

"Baby J, I'm...in the place you go when you die an unnatural death. I'm stuck here. I can't go to the good place just yet."

Hearing that made Josie's tears of joy turn to sorrow. Ma was dead, and she *wasn't* in Heaven.

"I...I don't understand. You died by accident. Your dress got caught in the hay baler. Wait, how are you talking to me?"

There was a longer pause. Again, she could hear the whispers through the static.

"The phone, us, the dead, we have found a way to reach through it. It's almost like a door or a window that we can yell through to be heard."

Josie accepted the explanation and waited for her Ma to keep going.

"I-I don't want to tell you this Baby J, but your Pa, he killed me. I can't go to the good place until he pays for what he did with his own life."

Josie felt faint again. Pa was not a loving or kind man, but she never thought he could kill Ma. Then she thought of the anger in the spanking earlier, how he had to be stopped, all the times he did worse to Ma.

"I need you to help me, Baby J. If you don't, I'll be stuck here forever. But worse, when you become a woman, he will do the same things to you that he did to me. We can't let that happen."

Josie felt confused, her stomach twisting and gurgling with fear and a touch of excitement. "Okay." A sudden fear of Pa waking up and walking into the room surged through her.

"See the cord, Baby J? The one attached to the earpiece?"

"Uh huh." Josie didn't want to look at that stinking cord, even if it was bringing her ma's voice to her ear. She might have been just a "mere pup," as Uncle Carl called her, but she was old enough to understand that she was going to have to do something awful with that cord.

You could just hang up, her mind thought briefly, but Ma was the only one who had ever cared about her. And deep down, Josie knew her death hadn't been an accident.

The night before Ma died, she told Josie to pack a bag and keep it under her bed; they were leaving at first light while Pa was in the field. But when Josie woke, it was already bright. Ma hadn't gotten her up. She was already dead, and Pa had blood on him. He showered and changed before going into town to get help, a detail he told Josie to not tell anyone about ever...or else.

By that night, Pa was playing the role of the grieving father, hugging her in front of the neighbors, kept repeating that Ma was in a *better place*. She was younger then, and she believed him.

Now, though, now she believed Ma's voice.

"Go tell your Pa that the phone rang. Say the person said it was important. When he sits to take the call, you need to wrap the cord around his neck. We will do the rest." Her ma's voice was changing slightly. Certain words sounded almost like a reptile, but Josie brushed it off as a bad connection.

"If I do that, you'll go to Heaven, Ma?" Josie asked, picturing her ma floating up to the heavenly gates she'd learned about in Sunday school.

"If you do that, you will open the door for us, for me, Baby J, and I will be free from this place."

She didn't say Heaven, but Josie knew that was what her ma meant. Ma had to nudge her a few more times, but finally, Josie agreed to go get her Pa, only because she couldn't take thinking of Ma in a bad place forever.

<hr>

Josie always hated how the hallway floorboards creaked like they were screaming out in pain when stepped on. As she walked down the hallway to wake her pa, the sound was worse than ever. It was like the boards were shouting to her to stop, to go back to bed, which she desperately wanted, but the image of Ma at the gates of Heaven pushed her past the wailing wood to the open doorway of Pa's bedroom. She licked her lips and took a deep breath as she stared at the large lump under the white comforter that Ma had knitted a few months before she died. Thinking of Ma sitting in her chair, knitting and telling her stories, made Josie angry at Pa for taking her away.

"Pa!" She screamed before even knowing she was going to. The white blanket shot up in the air, her pa following behind. "The phone kept ringing. I answered it. They asked for you, said it was important."

Her father was never a pleasant man, but waking him that way, Josie saw that *he* was really the devil, not the voice she heard earlier. Pa screamed and cussed up a storm, then pushed her aside as he stomped down the hall in his pajama bottoms and no shirt. Being pushed against the wall made her already sore buttocks sting, giving her all the motivation she needed to heed Ma's instructions.

She followed Pa into the kitchen, her eyes squinting as he snapped on the lights. Thankfully, Pa did just as Ma said he would; he sat in the chair next to the phone before answering it. Pa put the receiver to his ear, said "Hello" over and over, growing angrier each time.

Josie slipped up next to him and grabbed the candlestick phone, garnering an inquisitive and confused look from her father.

"Josie, if this is some sort of prank, you won't be able to sit for a month!" he barked, growing more confused and annoyed as she quickly raced the phone around him.

Just before he could swat at her, she threw the stick over his shoulder, leaving the cord wrapped around his neck like a lazy scarf.

"Josie!" he screamed, rage dripping from every syllable.

In that moment, Josie feared that she did it wrong, that it wasn't going to work, that she would get the beating of her life, all while Ma had to suffer in that place forever.

But then it happened.

The cord pulled taut as if invisible hands were tugging

it in opposite ways. Her father dropped the receiver and grabbed at his throat. The cord started to quiver, bubble, and grow. It expanded, grew chunky and ropy, just like an umbilical cord.

I knew it, she thought to herself as she backed away.

The light suddenly burst, and the explosion was followed by a loud noise that sounded like a thousand people yawning at once. It came from the phone, growing louder every second. Josie pushed herself against the wall, scared but also proud. Pa's eyes bulged out of his skull in an unnatural way, his face a deep purple; sweat, spit, and snot dripped everywhere. He reached out for her, but the force wouldn't let him move.

It was then that she saw the cord. It was slimy and getting thicker. Somehow, it looked angry. As she stared at it, she noticed it was cutting her father's neck. Blood began to ooze out.

Pa's head suddenly did a small hop up in the air. It paused as his mouth fell slack, then dropped to the floor, blood spraying from his severed neck, pouring, dripping as his hand grasped at nothing before the body fell after its master.

Josie held her breath. She couldn't think, she couldn't move, and she wanted her ma.

When the whispers turned to voices, she got excited and strained to hear her mother's, but there were so many that she couldn't separate them. She stared at the phone, which was shaking and jumping like popping corn, bouncing in each direction, the umbilical throbbing and growing.

"Ma?" Josie whispered, praying to hear "Baby J" in her ears. Instead, the voices grew to growls and grunts, laughs and cackles, screams and guttural, painful sounds that reminded her of when Pa slaughtered a sow. Then, it all stopped. The phone dropped to the counter and lay still. The umbilical continued to grow bigger and bigger, but the phone still looked normal. Josie took the opportunity to pick up the receiver.

"Ma! Mama!" she yelled into the mouthpiece, the ear-piece crammed tight to her head.

She felt a tiny tickle in her ear. She brushed it off like she would a horse fly, but then it turned from a tickle to an actual...*touch*. She pulled the receiver away to look at it, everything inside of her turning to liquid. Reaching out of the small circle was a brown, rotting finger with a broken, jagged fingernail.

Josie threw the phone down and instantly regretted it.

You have to be careful with expensive things, Josie. Pa's words rang in her head as the receiver shattered, freeing whatever was attached to that awful finger.

Josie backed up in horror, tripped over her pa's legs, and fell on to the floor, feeling the sting of her raw bottom. She looked to her left and saw her pa's purple, severed head.

"I'm sorry," she whispered as the creatures, one by one, crawled out of the ever-growing cord.

She closed her eyes, hugged her knees, and prayed that one of them would be her ma, but she knew better.

Instead, she heard the raspy, awful voice from earlier.

"Thank you for answering, Josie."

Michael Gore
About the Author

Michael Gore is a reclusive, dark and twisted horror author who specializes in gut wrenching, terrifying short stories. His hit short story collections Tales from a Mortician and Skeletons in the Attic are currently being developed into Film and Television properties. A fourth short story collection will be available in 2022 and a Halloween themed collection will be out in 2023. Numerous short stories of Michael's can be read in various anthologies.

https://www.facebook.com/AuthorMikeAloisi/

THE NEXT TIME AROUND
R. L. MEZA

"I think about poisoning the neighborhood dogs a lot, you know?"

I thought maybe she was kidding. Maggie was like that—always dropping unsettling one-liners like questions, like bait, letting them roll off her tongue while watching from the corner of her eye, waiting for you to laugh her off or put up a fight.

But this was different.

Her eyes didn't slide sideways or anything to check my reaction, I mean. She just kept staring out the window with her head cocked to one side, muscles twitching under her thin cotton T-shirt, jumping a little when a fresh volley of barks chopped the silence into frenzied pieces.

Then, so softly that I almost lost it beneath the rumble of a passing garbage truck, she murmured, "Just to see if they'll come."

"The dogs?"

Looking back now, I realize how stupid that question

was. I could have asked a hundred different questions; any one of them would have brought me closer to saving us, to understanding. Maybe I could have stopped it, even. But that's the thing; after somebody's died, you don't really know what to say to them. It changes the rules, the—ah— dynamics of the relationship. You're expecting something like a permanent breakup but worse, gut-wrenching loss, grief, or—if things weren't tops—maybe you're relieved, feeling a bit giddy about it. The door swings one way, and once they're through it, there's nothing left to do in their absence but suffer—or celebrate—and get busy healing. Move on.

But Maggie, she was dead for a week before she came back. And once she was back, her smile never touched her eyes. Her laugh rattled like gravel in a tin can; her words crumbled between her lips like dry dirt. All those unfinished sentences, the incomplete thoughts, they started to add up, and if I'm guilty of anything, it's that I stopped trying to string them together, to make sense of whatever she was trying to tell me. Her death was supposed to be an ending, but with her coming back like that—tracking mud through the front door and into the bedroom, crawling into our bed to rub herself clean on the sheets—it was more like a hiccup. A blip. It was easy to misread the situation, to feel hope, to think it was a second chance and not a whole new beginning. Uncharted territory.

The door's not supposed to swing back in. Some days, I think I should have known; others, I know I couldn't have. There's no precedent for this kind of shit. The door swung back in, and something came with her. Maybe a lot of some-things. I can't sleep at night, not thinking about them.

I didn't expect her to actually poison the dogs. You think you know somebody, and then you're out for your morning jog around the block, and every two or three hous-es, there's a whiff of vomit on the breeze, tearful kids getting packed into the back of a minivan, a blanket-wrapped bun-dle weighing some red-eyed neighbor's arms down. And you think again.

I asked her about it after. I think she expected me to just shrug it off as another Maggie-thing, but it wasn't. You have to understand; the old Maggie only *said* things to read your reaction. New Maggie was something else, a lot of something elses rolled into one. New Maggie did the things she said and more.

Christ, I'm botching this.

I should have started with the skin. The morning after she came back from the dead, I found it in the hamper. Not like she'd been trying to hide it, but right on top—casual—like Maggie'd woken up, stripped it off over her head in a single piece, and tossed it into the hamper without looking. Hollowed-out arms sagging like empty sleeves, grave dirt sifting out onto the tile as I lifted the skin, shook it out, held it up to the light above the bathroom sink.

I hear you telling me that I should have called someone. It's easy to do that, right—to offer advice in hindsight? Lay it down like fact. Well, I did call someone—quite a few of them, if you must know—since she wouldn't get in the car, refused to come with me to the hospital. She was weird about cars after. Most electronic devices seemed to give her the willies, but I digress. I called a doctor to the house. I left her in bed to answer the door.

When I led the doctor back into the bedroom, the door to our attached bathroom was shut. I knocked, opened it just a crack to peek through. Maybe I uttered a vaguely reassuring phrase about the doctor, feeling good about my decision to call for help. I don't remember. Seeing her bent over the hamper with the last few naked inches of that wrinkled skin disappearing between her lips, I guess my thoughts got jumbled. It was gone before I got the door open.

I remember the doctor examining Maggie, pressing his stethoscope here and there, shining lights in her eyes and ears and probing her glands, and I remember thinking that he wasn't looking in the right places. That to find the problem, he needed to probe something intangible, part the incomprehensible with his fingers, try to locate whatever was still human inside her and hold it up to the light like I had the skin as proof. Proof of something worth saving.

He didn't find anything. Neither did her family, her friends. It was a miracle, they said, Maggie coming back like that. A gift. And then they stopped coming, leaving me alone with whatever she really was. New Maggie.

"What happened, Maggie? To the dogs."

A smile ghosted her lips.

I wish to hell and back that I'd been looking anywhere else when I asked. I could have missed it. Instead, I said, "Did they come?"

And she whispered. I swear I heard it, though her lips

were pressed into a thin white seam, her blank eyes rolled up to the sky like polished black stones. Old Maggie's eyes were like warm honey, soft and golden.

"Oh, yes," said New Maggie.

Dog skins. The next morning, I jogged through the neighborhood, shoes drifting from sidewalk to asphalt at the sight of all those limp, deflated skins puddled on front lawns, draped over bushes, hanging from the bare branches of trees like snagged kites, furry tails fluttering in the cold winter breeze. I should have kept running past our two-bedroom house at the end of the cul-de-sac, through the woods behind it and the mountains beyond, clear to the ocean.

Hindsight, right?

The real trouble began when Maggie started going for walks. I know, I know—I've got nothing against dogs, and that shit was bad too—but when she started in with the kids, that was *real* trouble. When the one you love murders a bunch of loveable animals, you think about leaving them; when the *kids* start dropping like flies, leaving just won't cut it. You have to do something. You're worse than a monster if you don't.

It took a while to sink in, though. Because she didn't bring it up the way she had with the dogs. I was too caught up with the whole song and dance of playing pretend—pretending that we could move forward by cuddling together on the couch and watching movies, eating home-cooked meals, making love. If only I could have gotten her stiff limbs to lay flush with mine, if I could have just kept the one-sided conversations going, then it wouldn't matter so much that she never touched her food. That one look at her face during our passionless grinding was enough to shrivel me inside her, padding my soft retreat with mumbled apologies as I tried to hide my relief from Maggie, from myself.

All the warmth had gone out of her, my Maggie, and her hair smelled like raw earth. She never looked right at me, in my eyes; she looked through me, past me. And whatever she saw there, she must have liked it better. Or maybe she just never made it all the way back through, and she was caught in between, holding the door for the next—

This is harder than I expected.

The kids.

This boy, Kenneth, he couldn't have been much older than twelve. Most mornings before school, he rode around the neighborhood on his bike, throwing newspapers at doorsteps like he was really aiming for windows and the lucky people still asleep in their beds. Anyway, it seemed innocent, almost like a sign that Maggie was finally falling back into some semblance of normalcy, her sitting on the front porch and sipping hot coffee, lazy zigzags of cigarette smoke drifting around her nest of auburn curls while she waited for the morning paper. She'd wave to him—this weird, mechanical movement, like how the arm of a parking garage gate lifts after you pay your fee—a passably human gesture. Distant. An ocean of grass between them, a brick walkway, a mailbox done up to look like a birdhouse.

Innocent.

Maggie went for walks, and the kids came home late for dinner, took longer than usual to walk back from school.

They stayed out all night. Got lost in the woods behind the neighborhood. But they always came back. And they were smarter than the dogs, see. The kids didn't leave the skins lying around.

Kenneth wasn't the first, but he's the only one I can be *sure* of. I was mistaken, thinking that Maggie would try to hide her actions, that my suspicions could remain outside our four walls, lurking in the darkness without confirmation. I don't think it occurred to her that I might object. It's not like I came home early, surprised her in the middle of it.

It was the weekend. One minute, I'm asleep in the back yard, slumped in a lawn chair with a beer, and the next, the beer's straining my bladder, needing a way out. Maggie was already in the bathroom, lying face down in our clawfoot bathtub. Certain as I was that she'd slipped, drowned, I didn't realize that the tub was empty until I touched her. She shuddered, so very alive, and then she rose—as if invisible fingers were drawing her up, like a puppet on strings—climbed from the tub, and shouldered past me without making a sound.

I saw who had been lying beneath her.

What was left of him.

I went to my knees on the bathmat, the strength running out of my legs, the bathroom walls closing in. Maggie, pressing in behind me, gripped me by the shoulders. She whispered something in my ear. I don't remember what. If I heard it again, I could tell you, but I don't think I ever will hear it again. I'll tell you this, since I buried Maggie for the second time, I haven't listened to music or watched television, won't read anything longer than a street address, afraid that Maggie's words will find me again.

I wish I could tell you that I killed her then.

Kenneth was standing at the foot of our bed that night, while Maggie lay asleep beside me, coiled like a snake in my armpit. New Kenneth's eyes glittered like onyx in the moonlight, studding his cheeks and forehead and chin like rhinestones. I felt him smile.

You wouldn't think Kenneth could smile with a mouth like that, a shapeless dark hole eating up the middle of his face, bristling fangs clicking together like hollow needles, wind whistling through his gaping throat like a seal had been broken and all the air was leaking out of the bedroom. Or maybe it was the vacuum of space, the cold, breathless void, rushing in. But he did—smile, I mean—and a whole lot more. You wouldn't believe the half of it. I don't, and I was there.

The kids came and went as they pleased, all of them, long walks around the neighborhood, trailing after Maggie. I wondered about their parents, whether they were like me, glimpsing the daily parades of newly made flesh through drawn blinds, quivering inside. Immobilized. I wondered if the ones Maggie had called with the dead dogs were finite, or if the door was still swinging, if they'd keep coming through for as long as she held it open. I never saw the dogs again. Maybe they couldn't survive it, burned out too quickly. The kids marched unsmiling down the sidewalk, around the cul-de-sac, into the neighboring streets beyond.

Cars sat in their driveways. The sun went down, and

the windows stayed dark. If you stared up at the sky long enough, you'd see that even the birds were avoiding us, entire flocks splitting down the middle to circle round, giving a wide berth to our poisoned air. Traffic accelerated past our subdivision, feet pressed to pedals, spurring engines from twenty-five to forty, fifty miles an hour, so many that a police car took to parking along the road, picking off the speeders. I thought a lot about walking out to that police car, leading the officer into our neighborhood by the wrist and telling him to look around, really *look* and please just *do something*. Didn't the guy ever notice, parked there for days at a time, that no one ever came out?

My biggest mistake was thinking that Maggie wouldn't see me coming, that she didn't think I was capable of hurting her. I spend a lot of sleepless nights thinking about that, my last mistake.

She knew.

Maggie had been through that door once and come back. Maybe whatever was riding her shoulders wasn't impressed with us; maybe it got bored. Or perhaps it was never meant to be a permanent situation. Is that all we were to Them—a vacation? Slip into our skins, take them for a spin, and when They were finished—what? All those parents left with no choice but to snuff out their kids, one by one, punching Their tickets to send Them home. I did exactly what she wanted, and now you, in the service of justice, you'll do it too.

You know they're still trying to pass us off as a cult on the news? I'm sure you've read all the conspiracy stories, formed your own theories about what happened. Nothing sets tongues wagging like mass murder. Because it's not supposed to happen *here*, not in this civilized part of the world, and certainly not to the children.

You want to know where Maggie is buried? I'll draw you a map, but I won't lead you there. I'd chew my hands off like a fox caught in a snare before I'd ever lay them on that patch of cursed earth again.

You want to find her.

You're asking me all these questions like I've got something left to hide, like the bars of a prison cell aren't just about the most comforting thing I can think of right now, slammed shut between me and the rest of the world. Put them between me and Maggie, those bars, and maybe I'll be able to sleep again. These fits of random laughter, the seizures, the wads of cotton I keep stuffed in my ears always—I can put them to rest.

But there are questions you haven't asked, questions you should consider before you sink your shovel into the dirt, start whittling away at the distance between you and...

Like what does Maggie want?

Is she waiting for you there, listening for the sound of your footsteps above her? Are you arriving right on schedule?

What will she be like this time around, her second rebirth?

Will she do things differently?

Will They?

One Door Closes
R. L. Meza

"Open it."

Reece hesitates, small fingers curled around the tarnished brass knob. The red imprint of pillow wrinkles spreads across her cheek and forehead like ripples in desert sand, and her tangled blonde hair stands on end, lingering evidence that not long ago—hours, maybe even minutes, before they woke in this featureless, strange room—they were asleep, vying for space in the twin bed of Erin's cramped studio apartment.

The gray walls ascend into the darkness like a massive throat, with mother and daughter trapped at the bottom. Erin thinks of Jonah in the belly of the whale and wonders if this is punishment or a test.

And then, because Reece is a cringing, clingy girl of seven, Erin says it again, sharper this time, irritation sinking its claws in deep. "Open it, Reece. Don't be a baby."

The room is the exact size of their apartment. She sits on the floor, hugging her knees, sensing the room's dimensions, its confines, like plastic wrap shrunk tightly against her skin. It's the same suffocating closeness Erin has felt since the night of Reece's conception, the rough press and push of flesh that left her belly swollen with unwanted seed. Reece looks more and more like *him* every day, with her thin lips and dimpled cheeks, her eyes the bright, burning blue of an autumn sky. Erin meets those eyes, finding only the memory of pain, and looks away.

There's just the one door, smooth and ivory white, the color of bone, of teeth. No windows or ceiling that Erin can see. No bulbs or fixtures. Dim light in muted shades of gray emanates from the walls like sunlight viewed through skin stretched taut. There are no shadows.

Erin frowns. "Dammit, Reece—"

"Okay." Reece draws out the vowels with her insufferable whine.

Erin's hands form fists, nails digging into her palms, as she suppresses the urge to slap her. Reece didn't ask to be the daughter of a monster. Erin didn't ask to be her mother. But here they are, all the same.

Reece turns the knob, and a sliver of black opens in the gray gloom. Reece's head disappears inside, then her shoulders. Her voice is muffled. "There's another room."

Curiosity pulls Erin to her feet while Reece shrinks back from the door to duck behind her mother's legs. She clings to Erin's cotton pajama pants, pulling them slightly down over her narrow hips as Erin moves closer to the open door. Erin pries Reece's hand free and holds it loosely in her own, the way she carries the small animal corpses left behind by their cat, touching the blood-matted fur and stiff limbs as little as possible before dropping them into the garbage bin. Reece resists, and Erin lets her hand fall.

"I don't want to go in there, Mommy. It's dark."

"Then stay here." Erin ventures through the door into the next room.

It *is* dark. But as she pads barefooted to the center of the room, the walls flare with enough cold, gray light to illuminate Reece standing in the open doorway, her legs crossed over at the knees, bouncing like she needs to pee.

The room behind Reece goes black, though not entirely; there's movement, some ill-defined shape churning like smoke, gnawing at the darkness and turning it to void, a starless vacuum of space. Just looking at it steals the breath from Erin's lungs, strains her sanity to the point of breaking. Shadow fingers brush Reece's hair, and Erin feels like she's falling from a great height, wind rushing past her ears, her stomach rising into her throat. Erin crosses the distance between her and Reece in three steps, grabs a fistful of her daughter's shirt, and yanks her over the threshold.

The door slams shut.

Erin recoils, and their legs tangle together, spilling them to the floor. Her teeth clack shut on her tongue, a muffled, meaty crunch that floods her mouth with blood, and she spits. The bright crimson spatter splits the room's muted grays like an open wound.

"Mommy," Reece says, going pale. Her eyes start to roll up, like maybe she's going to faint.

Erin wants to feel concerned, wants to comfort her

daughter, assure Reece that she's okay, that they're both okay.

But they aren't, really.

Have they ever been?

The lying is exhausting.

And there is another door standing in the wall opposite the first. This door is fleshy pink, threaded with red-blue pulsing arterial and venous branches spread wide like trees worshipping the sun's light. Only, there are no leaves, no sun.

When one door closes...

Pa's voice echoes in Erin's head, a grating sound that makes her think of gravel crunching under heavy boots, of glass ground to dust. Whiskey breath mingles with pipe smoke, filling her nostrils. She can hear the thin rustle of her mother's Bible pages turning, feel her father's rough hands clamp down on her arms, the weight of him crushing the air from her lungs, drowning her in the bedsheets...

"Another door opens," Erin mutters under her breath. Her twenty-three years stretch behind her like a hotel hallway. No stranger to closed doors, she peeks through the keyholes, glimpsing possibility, potential futures barricaded beyond her grasp, missed opportunities.

One door forced open was enough to close all the others.

"You want me to open this one too?" Reece's hand drifts to the knob, gleaming gold metal formed into the shape of an anatomical heart.

"Yeah, sure. Or—I don't know. No. Wait a minute."

Erin's skin crawls. Something is off. This room is smaller than the one they just left. She starts in the corner, pacing the length of the wall to be sure, and yes, seven paces are all it takes. Seven, instead of ten. From behind the bone-colored door comes a grinding noise, chewing, like the room they left behind is being slowly fed into a woodchipper. They can't go back that way; they can't stay. This room is just as empty as the first.

"Mommy?" Reece holds the heart-shaped knob, gazing at her reflection in the shining gold meat of the right ventricle.

"I'll open it. Move." The knob is hot and beating against Erin's palm.

Reece hangs onto Erin's pants again, and a forbidden thought skitters through Erin's mind. She could slip out of the pajamas, like a snake shedding its skin, slither quickly through the door, and shut it behind her.

Leave the pants behind.

Leave behind everything—every*one*—weighing her down.

Instead, she wraps an arm around her daughter's shoulders and holds Reece against her leg. It's an awkward position, unnatural. They never fit together well.

"Ready?"

She feels Reece nod. Heat emanates from the door. There's a pulse, a rhythm that's almost soothing, coming from the raised network of veins and arteries. She wants to lay her head against the door, let it lull her to sleep. Erin turns the knob, and the door swings inward.

This time, Erin pushes Reece in ahead of her. As Reece stumbles to the center of the next room and sprawls, scuffing her chin on the gray floor, Erin turns around to watch the room they've left grow dark. The air stirs, not with a breeze—there are no windows or vents—but with change. Transformation. Atoms broken into parts, compressed into nothing. Black and something darker, gobbling up the gray, the walls, and floor. Erin closes her eyes to greet it, the corners of her mouth twitching into a smile.

Maybe nothing would be better.

Then Reece is tugging on her, arms wrapped around Erin's waist, pulling and kicking. Her foot finds the back of Erin's knee and makes it buckle.

As she falls out of the threshold, Erin watches the door slam shut and utters a desperate cry. Fury and loss choke her throat with nails, with fire. Reece retreats into the corner and squats, shaking. Her chin is bleeding, staining the knees of her monkey pajamas. Reece is hurt, and somehow this cuts through Erin's rage, puts her out like a firehose extinguishes a structure fire, leaving her feeling gutted and blackened, wet and heavy and sagging with shame.

"I'm sorry, baby." The apology staggers off her tongue. It's weak, worn from overuse, a flimsy band-aid applied to a festering wound, but it's all Erin has to offer as she slumps to the floor and wraps an arm around her daughter's shoulders.

"I want to go home. Where are we? Why is this happening?"

"I don't," Erin says, thinking of their musty apartment: the way the wall shakes when their neighbor throws his wife against it, the heaps of unwashed laundry, the stack of bills she can't afford to pay—not on the minimum wage she makes at the donut shop. Reece's follow-up questions take a moment to sink in, but she's staring at Erin, her mouth a puzzled punctuation mark in her round face. "Know. I don't know."

She doesn't say that maybe this is purgatory. Maybe it's hell.

"Mommy? I'm thirsty."

Erin's stomach growls in reply. She thinks of that last TV dinner, how their power went out halfway through microwaving the damn thing, and how Reece dragged furrows through the freezer-burnt puddle of creamed corn with her fork, tapping the tines on the brown glacier resting in its lake of congealed gravy. *Homestyle Meatloaf*—or so the box claimed—and was that yesterday? The day before? She hangs her head. Lank brown hair falls in her eyes, but she doesn't move to clear it. There's an illusion of privacy.

Small fingers part the curtain, seeking her face. Erin pictures a mother with a warm, reassuring smile and does her best imitation, feeling her cheek muscles resist like rusted hinges.

"I'm scared," Reece says. "This room is worse."

Erin glances around. Reece's assessment is accurate. This room is worse.

Smaller. Colder.

Reece's mouth-breathing fogs the frigid air with white clouds that hover like ghosts around her runny nose. Her teeth are chattering, the *tack-a-tack-tack* rhythm echoing in the otherwise silent space. Erin wants to curl into a ball, sleep, but she stands and forces herself to pace the length of one wall. She stops at five. A lonely inch separates the tip of her nose from the door set in the wall.

The new door. This door is worse too.

There's no comforting pulse, no warmth. Beneath a taut membrane, slippery-looking folds twist and turn over the door's surface like bloated pink worms squirming through a maze. Erin doesn't want to touch it, but her fingers move of their own accord to dimple the membrane, pressing into the yielding furrows. Electrical impulses race over the door's surface, crackling like static. She curls her fingers, and her nails bite into the membrane. Clear fluid trickles from the tear.

"Stop. Mommy, *stop it*."

Erin looks back to find Reece cowering in the corner. The light has dimmed so that only the whites of her eyes are visible. Erin pulls her hand from the tear in the door, and the membrane knits closed.

The light returns.

And Erin realizes she can see the ceiling in this room. She doesn't know how she missed it before; it's close enough to touch. The ceiling's visible presence makes the absence of windows unbearable. Erin's claustrophobia fastens its hooks into her lungs and throat, tightening her muscles and constricting her chest like iron bands, cranks, and spikes closing in.

This room is a crypt, a grave.

Erin tries to breathe, but Reece is pitching a fit, screaming in the corner about how she wants to go home, and Erin falls to her knees, gasping.

The other door—the one they just came through. Maybe they can go back. Erin crawls to the door on hands and knees, but its surface lies flush with the gray wall. Smooth. There is no knob on this side for her to turn.

Erin screams for help. She pries at the thin seam between the door and its frame, and her fingernails split, peeling back from the quicks like fish scales. Sobbing, she collapses on the floor.

Exhausted by fear, Erin slips into a fitful doze. There is no clock, no sun to track the passage of time. Minutes or hours later, she jolts awake from a nightmare, certain that she can hear someone whispering. Reece is asleep beside her, pinning her arm. Erin tries to extract her numb limb without waking her daughter, but then Reece's head thumps to the floor, and she grimaces, moaning as she sits up.

Erin says, "Do you hear that?"

Reece tilts her head to one side. "Hear what?"

"*Shh*. Listen." Erin doesn't want to touch the new door again, but she can't hear the whisper over the sound of Reece's mouth-breathing. She claps a hand over her daughter's lips, then presses her ear to the membrane, wincing at the wet suction that clings to her cartilage as she pulls away. It's not coming through the new door, the whispering. She tries the door they came through, hears only the rhythmic thumping of a beating heart. Frustrated, Erin pounds the door with her fists.

A fist pounds back.

The heart door leaps in its frame.

No way back, the fist says. *One door closes.*

The whispering is coming from the walls. Erin moves across them, ear pressed flat, listening. She can't make out the words, but she recognizes the voice.

It's Erin's pa.

Reece's father.

You killed me, the walls say. *Killed your own pa, you selfish, silly child.*

Her father's bulging eyes haunt her, the brutish fingers clawing at the corded muscles of his throat, the canned soup she'd heated on the stove bubbling as she shook the poison in, how it frothed orange between his lips and leaked onto the floorboards. Her mother might have screamed, if she had seen. But cancer had whittled Momma down to the marrow, and she hadn't had the strength to get out of bed, couldn't fight off the pillow when Erin put it over her face and pressed down, hard and relentless, the way Pa had pressed Erin down so many times. She had ignored Momma's muffled pleas, same as Momma had ignored hers.

Another door opens.

Reece fiddles with the knob on the new door, an intricate silver brain the size of both her fists held together.

She never seems to stop moving, eager to press forward. Erin envies her daughter and all the possibilities that lie before her, if only Reece can keep moving long enough, fast enough, to outrun the past. Most days, Erin feels like a mosquito trapped in amber.

Locked in place.

Unable to move.

"Would you quit rattling that goddamn door?" she snaps.

Reece's hands retreat from the knob to form a ball of wrestling, nervous fingers. Her lower lip quivers. Reece is going to start crying again, and Erin wonders if her daughter will ever grow a spine. She tries to envision Reece holding a pillow over her face—smothering Erin to free them both—but she can't. She feels disappointment and shame in equal measures.

"I thought—" Reece's chest hitches. A bubble of snot forms at her left nostril, inflates, bursts. "We have to keep going, don't we?"

"Yeah?" Erin's blood is boiling. She's screaming, can feel the burning in her throat, but the gray walls swallow the volume, drinking greedily. "What if the next room is even smaller? You think we're going to open that door and there'll be—what—food and blankets? A way out? You think it can't get worse, Reece?"

Erin is panting, sweating despite the cold. Reece opens her mouth, closes it, opens it again. *She looks like a fish*, Erin thinks, a fish flopping around on the shore, gasping, waiting for someone to bash its head in with a rock. Erin snorts and throws her hands up.

"Fine, go ahead. You know best, right? Go on and open it."

"Are you coming with me?"

I want to be alone. It's all I've ever wanted. "Yeah. What choice do I have?"

Reece turns the knob. Erin can feel the rush of heat from across the room. It contrasts sharply with the frigid breath stroking the small hairs on the back of her neck. Reece turns, and her mouth drops open. Her round blue eyes—*Pa's eyes*—are staring over Erin's left shoulder at the thing that's gathering Erin's hair into its fist. Erin smells pipe smoke and aftershave, tomato soup. Warm bubbles froth over the nape of her neck, staining her nightshirt orange.

Erin lunges forward. She twists like a fish on a line, and in her peripheral, she sees the yawning maw of the heart door behind her, standing open, the blackness seeping into the brain room like spilled ink. She throws a hand behind her, clawing. Stubble rasps against her wrist. A thick tongue pokes between her fingers. Teeth scrape her knuckles. Erin releases a feral shriek, but she doesn't look behind her. She can smell the rot.

She throws herself toward the door that Reece is holding open, shrieking again. Her head snaps back, and her scalp is on fire, but she doesn't stop until she feels the hair rip free. And then she's free, free and pinwheeling her arms for balance, trip-racing across the room and over the threshold with Reece smashed between her breasts.

They land with a *whumph*, the air rushing from their lungs.

And the door behind them stands open.

It's lumbering through the darkness—*Pa* is coming for them—and the brain door isn't swinging shut. Erin kicks at it, but her toes swish through empty air.

"The door," she tries to say. Her voice is hoarse from screaming. "Close it. You have to—"

The door slams closed. Reece leans against it, small hands sunk wrist-deep in the pink flesh of the door. She doesn't look relieved.

Why—why doesn't she look relieved?

Reece is staring at the opposite wall.

The new room has four walls, a ceiling, a floor. Erin's sitting in the center of the room, and if she leans side to side, forward and back, she can touch the walls with ease, the ceiling, too. Heat emanates from the walls, accompanied by a rosy light. The new room is cozy—womb-like.

Suffocating.

But there is no door. Erin's stomach performs a nauseating backflip. The door they came through is gone. She squints and crawls, knees and toes slipping on the moist viscera that coats the floor. Her splayed hands slide over the slick walls, searching for a crack or crevice. An edge. Anything.

There's nothing new.

No way forward.

Her fingers carve trenches in the soft tissue. She grabs it by the fistfuls, tossing chunks behind her, and Erin can hear laughing. She's laughing, sobbing, gibbering in a language she doesn't recognize, though its meaning is clear.

She's lost her mind.

It's the language of the damned.

Behind her, a fist pounds once, twice. The fleshy walls shiver, shrink inward. Touching Erin's forehead, her shoulders, clinging to her feet, the small of her back. Reece's head is digging into her stomach.

"There's nothing here," Erin screams.

Nothing to open; nowhere to run.

"Mommy, please," Reece whimpers. "You're scaring me."

Erin's hands form claws. The ceiling pushes against the back of her head, forcing her to stoop, to bend at the knees.

Reece.

When one door closes, another opens.

Reece's eyes are the bright blue of an autumn sky, the color of flight, of freedom.

Escape.

Erin slides her hands around either side of her daughter's head. She can feel the smooth curves of Reece's ears against her palms. Erin's thumbs are poised, hooked.

There's something else her father used to say.

About eyes and windows.

R.L. Meza
About the Author

R.L. Meza is an author of horror fiction. She lives in a century-old Victorian house on the coast of northern California with her husband and the collection of strange animals they call family.

More from Eerie River

Eerie River Publishing, is a small independant publishing house that is devoted to releasing quality dark fiction books and anthologies.

To stay up to date with all our new releases and upcoming giveaways, follow us on Facebook, Twitter, Instagram and YouTube. Sign up for our monthly newsletter and receive a free ebook Darkness Reclaimed, as our thank you gift.

https://mailchi.mp/71e45b6d5880/welcomebook

Interested in becoming a Patreon member?
Patreon membership gives you exclusive sneak peeks at upcoming books, early chapter releases, covers art as well as free ebooks and discounts on paperbacks.

https://www.patreon.com/EerieRiverPub.

ALSO AVAILABLE FROM
EERIE RIVER PUBLISHING

NOVELS
Storming Area 51: Horror At the Gate
In Solitudes Shadow
Dead Man Walking
Devil Walks in Blood
SENTINEL

ANTHOLOGIES
It Calls From The Forest: Volume I
It Calls From The Forest: Volume II
It Calls From The Sky
Darkness Reclaimed
With Blood and Ash
With Bone and Iron

DRABBLE COLLECTIONS
Forgotten Ones: Drabbles of Myth and Legend
Dark Magic: Drabbles of Magic and Lore

COMING SOON
AFTER: A Post-Apocalyptic Survivor Series
The Void
A Sword Named Sorrow
Last Stop
Blood Vengeance

www.EerieRiverPublishing.com

MORE FROM EERIE RIVER

It Calls From the Sea

Sentinel by Drew Starling

In Solitude's Shadow by David Green

In Solitude's Shadow by David Green

9 781990 245435